Praise for Stieg Larsson's

THE GIRL WITH THE DRAGON TATTOO

"Exceptional. . . . Meticulously plotted, beautifully paced, and features a cast of two indelible sleuths and many juicy suspects."
—*The Boston Globe*

"Compelling. . . . Combine the chilly Swedish backdrop and moody psychodrama of a Bergman movie with the grisly pyrotechnics of a serial-killer thriller, then add an angry punk heroine and a down-on-his-luck investigative journalist, and you have the ingredients of Stieg Larsson's first novel."
—Michiko Kakutani, *The New York Times*

"Larsson's novel could serve as the definition of page-turner."
—*Time Out New York*

"This sexy, addictive thriller is everything you never knew you could get from a crime novel."
—*Glamour*

"A big, intricately plotted, darkly humorous work, rich with ironies, quirky but believable characters and a literary playfulness that only a master of the genre and its history could bring off."
—*Pittsburgh Post-Gazette*

"A compelling, well-woven tale that succeeds in transporting the reader to Sweden for a good crime story."

—*Los Angeles Times*

"A meticulous exploration of both evidence and character, plus finely crafted revenge. . . . With subplots tucked inside subplots like a set of nested Russian dolls. . . . Exemplary."

—*Houston Chronicle*

"Already a blazing literary sensation internationally, Swedish journalist's dark-hearted thriller *The Girl with the Dragon Tattoo* is now poised to burn up bestseller lists in America. . . . To the new breed of Watson and Holmes, *skoal!*" —*Vanity Fair*

"[Larsson] tells his crime story cleverly, but the zing in *Dragon Tattoo* is inked in its two central characters."

—*The Plain Dealer*

"Electrifying. . . . Larsson's debut thriller succeeds on so many levels it's hard to know where to begin. . . . . An absolute page-turner." —*Portsmouth Herald* (New Hampshire)

"A fine, complex and rewarding novel."

—*The Dallas Morning News*

"Engrossing. . . . Lisbeth Salander is the most fascinating female protagonist in mystery fiction since Patricia Cornwell introduced Kay Scarpetta." —*The Advocate* (Baton Rouge)

"The story has a great setting, very human characters and a plot that becomes more intriguing with every turn of the page."

—*Kansas City Star*

Stieg Larsson

THE GIRL WITH THE DRAGON TATTOO

Stieg Larsson, who lived in Sweden, was the editor in chief of the magazine *Expo* and a leading expert on antidemocratic right-wing extremist and Nazi organizations. He died in 2004, shortly after delivering the manuscripts for *The Girl with the Dragon Tattoo*, *The Girl Who Played with Fire*, and the third novel in the series.

ALSO BY STIEG LARSSON

The Girl Who Played with Fire

THE GIRL WITH THE DRAGON TATTOO

Stieg Larsson

Translated from the Swedish by Reg Keeland

VINTAGE CRIME/BLACK LIZARD
Vintage Books
A Division of Random House, Inc.
New York

FIRST VINTAGE CRIME/BLACK LIZARD EDITION, JUNE 2009

Translation copyright © 2008 by Reg Keeland
Excerpt from The Girl Who Played with Fire *translation © 2009 by Reg Keeland*

All rights reserved. Published in the United States by Vintage Books, a division of Random House, Inc., New York. Originally published in Sweden as *Män Som Hatar Kvinnor* by Norstedts, Stockholm, in 2005. Published with agreement of Norstedts Agency. Copyright © 2005 by Norstedts Agency. This translation originally published in Great Britain by MacLehose Press, an imprint of Quercus, London, and subsequently published in hardcover, by arrangement with Quercus Publishing, PLC (UK), in the United States by Alfred A. Knopf, a division of Random House, Inc., New York, in 2008.

Vintage is a registered trademark and Vintage Crime/Black Lizard and colophon are trademarks of Random House, Inc.

This is a work of fiction. Names, characters, places, and incidents either are the product of the author's imagination or are used fictitiously. Any resemblance to actual persons, living or dead, events, or locales is entirely coincidental.

This book contains an excerpt from the forthcoming *The Girl Who Played with Fire* by Stieg Larsson. This excerpt has been set for this edition only and may not reflect the final content of the forthcoming edition.

The Library of Congress has cataloged the Knopf edition as follows:
Larsson, Stieg, 1954–2004.
[Män som hatar kvinnor, English]
The girl with the dragon tattoo / by Stieg Larsson; translated from Swedish by Reg Keeland.—1st American ed.
p. cm.
Originally published: Stockholm: Norstedt, 2005. I. Title.
PT9876.22.A6933M36 2008
839.73'8—dc22
2008017771

Vintage ISBN: 978-0-307-45454-6

Book design by Virginia Tan

www.vintagebooks.com

Printed in the United States of America
10 9

THE GIRL WITH THE DRAGON TATTOO

PROLOGUE

A Friday in November

It happened every year, was almost a ritual. And this was his eighty-second birthday. When, as usual, the flower was delivered, he took off the wrapping paper and then picked up the telephone to call Detective Superintendent Morell who, when he retired, had moved to Lake Siljan in Dalarna. They were not only the same age, they had been born on the same day—which was something of an irony under the circumstances. The old policeman was sitting with his coffee, waiting, expecting the call.

"It arrived."

"What is it this year?"

"I don't know what kind it is. I'll have to get someone to tell me what it is. It's white."

"No letter, I suppose."

"Just the flower. The frame is the same kind as last year. One of those do-it-yourself ones."

"Postmark?"

"Stockholm."

"Handwriting?"

"Same as always, all in capitals. Upright, neat lettering."

With that, the subject was exhausted, and not another word was exchanged for almost a minute. The retired policeman leaned back in his kitchen chair and drew on his pipe. He knew he was no longer expected to come up with a pithy comment or any sharp question which would shed a new light on the case. Those days had long since passed, and the exchange between the two men seemed like a ritual attaching to a mystery which no-one else in the whole world had the least interest in unravelling.

The Latin name was *Leptospermum (Myrtaceae) rubinette.* It was a plant about four inches high with small, heather-like foliage and a white flower with five petals about one inch across.

The plant was native to the Australian bush and uplands, where it was to be found among tussocks of grass. There it was called Desert Snow. Someone at the botanical gardens in Uppsala would later confirm that it was a plant seldom cultivated in Sweden. The botanist wrote in her report that it was related to the tea tree and that it was sometimes confused with its more common cousin *Leptospermum scoparium,* which grew in abundance in New Zealand. What distinguished them, she pointed out, was that *rubinette* had a small number of microscopic pink dots at the tips of the petals, giving the flower a faint pinkish tinge.

Rubinette was altogether an unpretentious flower. It had no known medicinal properties, and it could not induce hallucinatory experiences. It was neither edible, nor had a use in the manufacture of plant dyes. On the other hand, the aboriginal people of Australia regarded as sacred the region and the flora around Ayers Rock.

The botanist said that she herself had never seen one before, but after consulting her colleagues she was to report that attempts had been made to introduce the plant at a nursery in Göteborg, and that it might, of course, be cultivated by amateur botanists. It was difficult to grow in Sweden because it thrived in a dry climate and had to remain indoors half of the year. It would not thrive in calcareous soil and it had to be watered from below. It needed pampering.

The fact of its being so rare a flower ought to have made it easier to trace the source of this particular specimen, but in practice it was an impossible task. There was no registry to look it up in, no licences to explore. Anywhere from a handful to a few hundred enthusiasts could have had access to seeds or plants. And those could have changed hands between friends or been bought by mail order from anywhere in Europe, anywhere in the Antipodes.

But it was only one in the series of mystifying flowers that each year arrived by post on the first day of November. They were always beautiful and for the most part rare flowers, always pressed, mounted on watercolour paper in a simple frame measuring six inches by eleven inches.

The strange story of the flowers had never been reported in the press; only a very few people knew of it. Thirty years ago the regular arrival of the flower was the object of much scrutiny—at the National Forensic Laboratory, among fingerprint experts, graphologists, criminal investigators, and one or two relatives and friends of the recipient. Now the actors in the drama were but three: the elderly birthday boy, the retired police detective, and the person who had posted the flower. The first two at least had reached such an age that the group of interested parties would soon be further diminished.

The policeman was a hardened veteran. He would never forget his first case, in which he had had to take into custody a violent and appallingly drunk worker at an electrical substation before he caused others harm. During his career he had brought in poachers, wife beaters, con men, car thieves, and drunk drivers. He had dealt with burglars, drug dealers, rapists, and one deranged bomber. He had been involved in nine murder or manslaughter cases. In five of these the murderer had called the police himself and, full of remorse, confessed to having killed his wife or brother or some other relative. Two others were solved within a few days. Another required the assistance of the National Criminal Police and took two years.

The ninth case was solved to the police's satisfaction, which is to say that they knew who the murderer was, but because the evidence was so insubstantial the public prosecutor decided not to proceed with the case. To the detective superintendent's dismay, the statute of limitations eventually put an end to the matter. But all in all he could look back on an impressive career.

He was anything but pleased.

For the detective, the "Case of the Pressed Flowers" had been nagging at him for years—his last, unsolved, and frustrating case. The situation was doubly absurd because after spending literally thousands of hours brooding, on duty and off, he could not say beyond doubt that a crime had indeed been committed.

The two men knew that whoever had mounted the flowers would have worn gloves, that there would be no fingerprints on the frame or the glass. The frame could have been bought in camera shops or stationery stores the world over. There was, quite simply, no lead to follow. Most often the parcel was posted in Stockholm, but three times from London, twice from Paris, twice from Copenhagen, once from Madrid, once from Bonn, and once from Pensacola, Florida. The detective superintendent had had to look it up in an atlas.

After putting down the telephone the eighty-two-year-old birthday boy sat for a long time looking at the pretty but meaningless flower whose name he did not yet know. Then he looked up at the wall above his desk. There hung forty-three pressed flowers in their frames. Four rows of ten, and one at the bottom with four. In the top row one was missing from the ninth slot. Desert Snow would be number forty-four.

Without warning he began to weep. He surprised himself with this sudden burst of emotion after almost forty years.

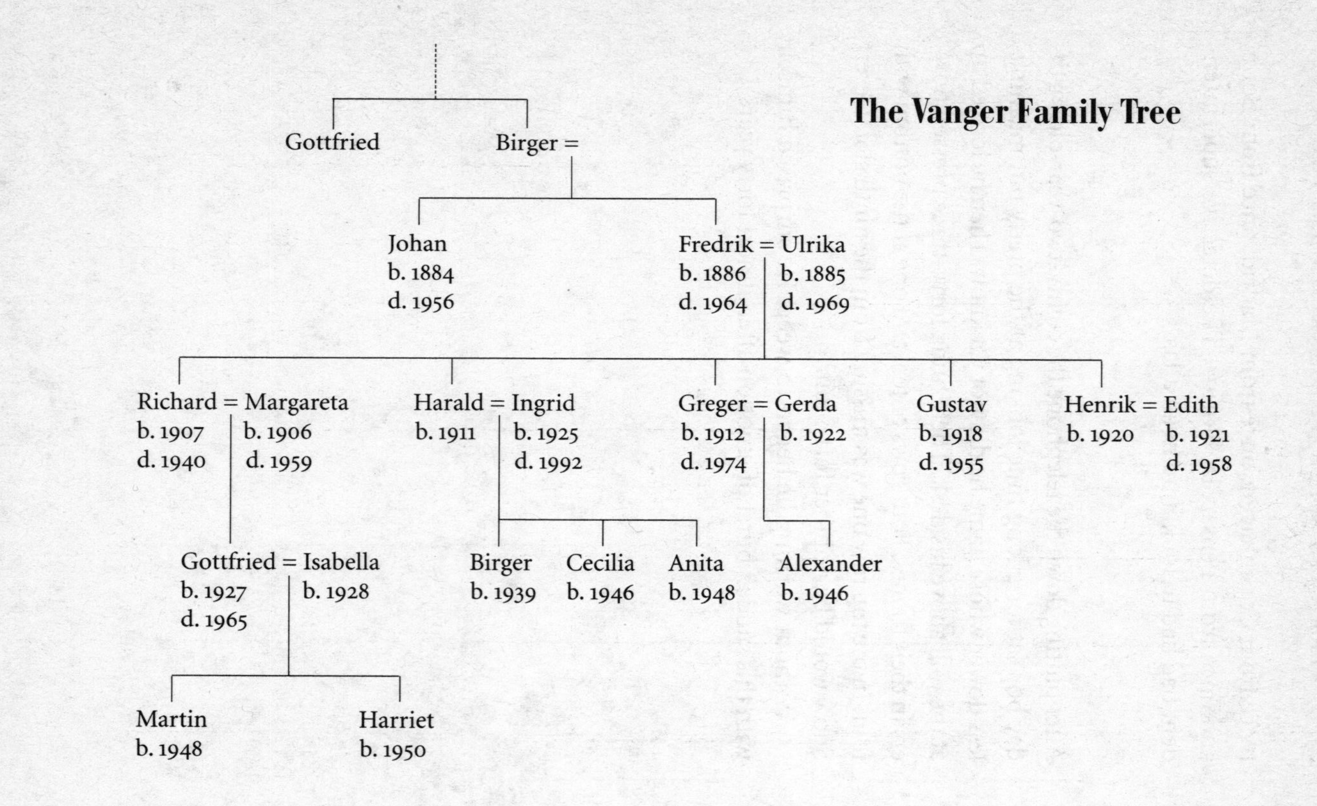
The Vanger Family Tree
Gottfried
Birger =
Johan b. 1884 d. 1956
Fredrik = Ulrika
b. 1886 d. 1964
b. 1885 d. 1969
Richard = Margareta
b. 1907 d. 1940
b. 1906 d. 1959
Harald = Ingrid
b. 1911
b. 1925 d. 1992
Greger = Gerda
b. 1912 d. 1974
b. 1922
Gustav b. 1918 d. 1955
Henrik = Edith
b. 1920
b. 1921 d. 1958
Gottfried = Isabella
b. 1927 d. 1965
b. 1928
Birger b. 1939
Cecilia b. 1946
Anita b. 1948
Alexander b. 1946
Martin b. 1948
Harriet b. 1950

PART 1

Incentive

DECEMBER 20–JANUARY 3

Eighteen percent of the women in Sweden have at one time been threatened by a man.

CHAPTER 1

Friday, December 20

The trial was irretrievably over; everything that could be said had been said, but he had never doubted that he would lose. The written verdict was handed down at 10:00 on Friday morning, and all that remained was a summing up from the reporters waiting in the corridor outside the district court.

"Carl" Mikael Blomkvist saw them through the doorway and slowed his step. He had no wish to discuss the verdict, but questions were unavoidable, and he—of all people—knew that they had to be asked and answered. *This is how it is to be a criminal,* he thought. *On the other side of the microphone.* He straightened up and tried to smile. The reporters gave him friendly, almost embarrassed greetings.

"Let's see . . . *Aftonbladet, Expressen,* TT wire service, TV4, and . . . where are you from? . . . ah yes, *Dagens Nyheter*. I must be a celebrity," Blomkvist said.

"Give us a sound bite, *Kalle Blomkvist.*" It was a reporter from one of the evening papers.

Blomkvist, hearing the nickname, forced himself as always not to roll his eyes. Once, when he was twenty-three and had just started his first summer job as a journalist, Blomkvist had chanced upon a gang which had pulled off five bank robberies over the past two years. There was no doubt that it was the same gang in every instance. Their trademark was to hold up two banks at a time with military precision. They wore masks from Disney World, so inevitably police logic dubbed them the Donald Duck Gang. The newspapers renamed them the Bear Gang, which sounded more sinister, more appropriate to the fact that on two occasions they had recklessly fired warning shots and threatened curious passersby.

Their sixth outing was at a bank in Östergötland at the height of the holiday season. A reporter from the local radio station happened to be in the bank at the time. As soon as the robbers were gone he went to a public telephone and dictated his story for live broadcast.

Blomkvist was spending several days with a girlfriend at her parents' summer cabin near Katrineholm. Exactly why he made the connection he could not explain, even to the police, but as he was listening to the news report he remembered a group of four men in a summer cabin a few hundred feet down the road. He had seen them playing badminton out in the yard: four blond, athletic types in shorts with their shirts off. They were obviously bodybuilders, and there had been something about them that had made him look twice—maybe it was because the game was being played in blazing sunshine with what he recognised as intensely focused energy.

There had been no good reason to suspect them of being the bank robbers, but nevertheless he had gone to a hill overlooking their cabin. It seemed empty. It was about forty minutes before a Volvo drove up and parked in the yard. The young men got out, in a hurry, and were each carrying a sports bag, so they might have been doing nothing more than coming back from a swim. But one of them returned to the car and took out from the boot something which he hurriedly covered with his jacket. Even from Blomkvist's relatively distant observation post he could tell that it was a good old AK4, the rifle that had been his constant companion for the year of his military service.

He called the police and that was the start of a three-day siege of the cabin, blanket coverage by the media, with Blomkvist in a front-row seat and collecting a gratifyingly large fee from an evening paper. The police set up their headquarters in a caravan in the garden of the cabin where Blomkvist was staying.

The fall of the Bear Gang gave him the star billing that launched him as a young journalist. The downside of his celebrity was that the other evening newspaper could not resist using the headline "Kalle Blomkvist solves the case." The tongue-in-cheek story was written by an older female columnist and contained references to the young detective in Astrid Lindgren's books for children. To make matters worse, the paper had run the story with a grainy photograph of Blomkvist with his mouth half open even as he raised an index finger to point.

It made no difference that Blomkvist had never in life used the name Carl. From that moment on, to his dismay, he was nicknamed Kalle Blomkvist by his peers—an epithet employed with taunting provocation, not unfriendly but not really friendly either. In spite of his respect for Astrid Lindgren—whose books he loved—he detested the nickname. It took him several years and far weightier journalistic successes before the nickname began to fade, but he still cringed if ever the name was used in his hearing.

Right now he achieved a placid smile and said to the reporter from the evening paper: "Oh come on, think of something yourself. You usually do."

His tone was not unpleasant. They all knew each other, more or less, and Blomkvist's most vicious critics had not come that morning. One of the journalists there had at one time worked with him. And at a party some years ago he had nearly succeeded in picking up one of the reporters—the woman from *She* on TV4.

"You took a real hit in there today," said the one from *Dagens Nyheter,* clearly a young part-timer. "How does it feel?"

Despite the seriousness of the situation, neither Blomkvist nor the older journalists could help smiling. He exchanged glances with TV4. *How does it feel?* The half-witted sports reporter shoves his microphone in the face of the Breathless Athlete on the finishing line.

"I can only regret that the court did not come to a different conclusion," he said a bit stuffily.

"Three months in gaol and 150,000 kronor damages. That's pretty severe," said *She* from TV4.

"I'll survive."

"Are you going to apologise to Wennerström? Shake his hand?"

"I think not."

"So you still would say that he's a crook?" *Dagens Nyheter.*

The court had just ruled that Blomkvist had libelled and defamed the financier Hans-Erik Wennerström. The trial was over and he had no plans to appeal. So what would happen if he repeated his claim on the courthouse steps? Blomkvist decided that he did not want to find out.

"I thought I had good reason to publish the information that was in my possession. The court has ruled otherwise, and I must accept that the judicial process has taken its course. Those of us on the editorial staff will have to discuss the judgement before we decide what we're going to do. I have no more to add."

"But how did you come to forget that journalists actually have to back up their assertions?" *She* from TV4. Her expression was neutral, but Blomkvist thought he saw a hint of disappointed repudiation in her eyes.

The reporters on site, apart from the boy from *Dagens Nyheter*, were all veterans in the business. For them the answer to that question was beyond the conceivable. "I have nothing to add," he repeated, but when the others had accepted this TV4 stood him against the doors to the courthouse and asked her questions in front of the camera. She was kinder than he deserved, and there were enough clear answers to satisfy all the reporters still standing behind her. The story would be in the headlines but he reminded himself that they were not dealing with the media event of the year here. The reporters had what they needed and headed back to their respective newsrooms.

He considered walking, but it was a blustery December day and he was already cold after the interview. As he walked down the courtroom steps, he saw William Borg getting out of his car. He must have been sitting there during the interview. Their eyes met, and then Borg smiled.

"It was worth coming down here just to see you with that paper in your hand."

Blomkvist said nothing. Borg and Blomkvist had known each other for fifteen years. They had worked together as cub reporters for the financial section of a morning paper. Maybe it was a question of chemistry, but the foundation had been laid there for a lifelong enmity. In Blomkvist's eyes, Borg had been a third-rate reporter and a troublesome person who annoyed everyone around him with crass jokes and made disparaging remarks about the more experienced, older reporters.

He seemed to dislike the older female reporters in particular. They had their first quarrel, then others, and anon the antagonism turned personal.

Over the years, they had run into each other regularly, but it was not until the late nineties that they became serious enemies. Blomkvist had published a book about financial journalism and quoted extensively a number of idiotic articles written by Borg. Borg came across as a pompous ass who got many of his facts upside down and wrote homages to dot-com companies that were on the brink of going under. When thereafter they met by chance in a bar in Söder they had all but come to blows. Borg left journalism, and now he worked in PR—for a considerably higher salary—at a firm that, to make things worse, was part of industrialist Hans-Erik Wennerström's sphere of influence.

They looked at each other for a long moment before Blomkvist turned on his heel and walked away. It was typical of Borg to drive to the courthouse simply to sit there and laugh at him.

The number 40 bus braked to a stop in front of Borg's car and Blomkvist hopped on to make his escape. He got off at Fridhemsplan, undecided what to do. He was still holding the judgement document in his hand. Finally he walked over to Kafé Anna, next to the garage entrance leading underneath the police station.

Half a minute after he had ordered a caffe latte and a sandwich, the lunchtime news came on the radio. The story followed that of a suicide bombing in Jerusalem and the news that the government had appointed a commission to investigate the alleged formation of a new cartel within the construction industry.

> Journalist Mikael Blomkvist of the magazine *Millennium* was sentenced this morning to 90 days in gaol for aggravated libel of industrialist Hans-Erik Wennerström. In

an article earlier this year that drew attention to the so-called Minos affair, Blomkvist claimed that Wennerström had used state funds intended for industrial investment in Poland for arms deals. Blomkvist was also sentenced to pay 150,000 SEK in damages. In a statement, Wennerström's lawyer Bertil Camnermarker said that his client was satisfied with the judgement. It was an exceptionally outrageous case of libel, he said.

The judgement was twenty-six pages long. It set out the reasons for finding Blomkvist guilty on fifteen counts of aggravated libel of the businessman Hans-Erik Wennerström. So each count cost him ten thousand kronor and six days in gaol. And then there were the court costs and his own lawyer's fee. He could not bring himself to think about all the expenses, but he calculated too that it might have been worse; the court had acquitted him on seven other counts.

As he read the judgement, he felt a growing heaviness and discomfort in his stomach. This surprised him. As the trial began he knew that it would take a miracle for him to escape conviction, and he had become reconciled to the outcome. He sat through the two days of the trial surprisingly calm, and for eleven more days he waited, without feeling anything in particular, for the court to finish deliberating and to come up with the document he now held in his hand. It was only now that a physical unease washed over him.

When he took a bite of his sandwich, the bread seemed to swell up in his mouth. He could hardly swallow it and pushed his plate aside.

This was the first time that Blomkvist had faced any charge. The judgement was a trifle, relatively speaking. A lightweight crime. Not armed robbery, murder, or rape after all. From a financial point of view, however, it was serious—*Millennium* was not a flagship of the media world with unlimited resources, the magazine barely broke even—but the judgement did not spell catastrophe. The problem was that Blomkvist was one of *Millennium*'s part owners, and at the same time, idiotically enough, he was both a writer and the magazine's publisher. The damages of 150,000 kronor he would pay himself, although that would just about wipe out his savings. The magazine would take care of the court costs. With prudent budgeting it would work out.

He pondered the wisdom of selling his apartment, though it would break his heart. At the end of the go-go eighties, during a period when he had a steady job and a pretty good salary, he had looked around for a permanent place to live. He ran from one apartment showing to another before he stumbled on an attic flat of 700 square feet right at the end of Bellmansgatan. The previous owner was in the middle of making it liveable but suddenly got a job at a dot-com company abroad, and Blomkvist was able to buy it inexpensively.

He rejected the original interior designer's sketches and finished the work himself. He put money into fixing up the bathroom and the kitchen area, but instead of putting in a parquet floor and interior walls to make it into the planned two-room apartment, he sanded the floorboards, whitewashed the rough walls, and hid the worst patches behind two watercolours by Emanuel Bernstone. The result was an open living space, with the bedroom area behind a bookshelf, and the dining area and the living room next to the small kitchen behind a counter. The apartment had two dormer windows and a gable window with a view of the rooftops towards Gamla Stan, Stockholm's oldest section, and the water of Riddarfjärden. He had a glimpse of water by the Slussen locks and a view of City Hall. Today he would never be able to afford such an apartment, and he badly wanted to hold on to it.

But that he might lose the apartment was nothing beside the fact that professionally he had received a real smack in the nose. It would take a long time to repair the damage—if indeed it could ever be repaired.

It was a matter of trust. For the foreseeable future, editors would hesitate to publish a story under his byline. He still had plenty of friends in the business who would accept that he had fallen victim to bad luck and unusual circumstances, but he was never again going to be able to make the slightest mistake.

What hurt most was the humiliation. He had held all the trumps and yet he had lost to a semi-gangster in an Armani suit. A despicable stock-market speculator. A yuppie with a celebrity lawyer who sneered his way through the whole trial.

How in God's name had things gone so wrong?

The Wennerström affair had started out with such promise in the cockpit of a thirty-seven-foot Mälar-30 on Midsummer Eve a year and a half earlier. It began by chance, all because a former journalist colleague, now a PR flunky at the county council, wanted to impress his new girlfriend. He had rashly hired a Scampi for a few days of romantic sailing in the Stockholm archipelago. The girlfriend, just arrived from Hallstahammar to study in Stockholm, had agreed to the outing after putting up token resistance, but only if her sister and her sister's boyfriend could come too. None of the trio from Hallstahammar had any sailing experience, and unfortunately Blomkvist's old colleague had more enthusiasm than experience. Three days before they set off he had called in desperation and persuaded him to come as a fifth crew member, one who knew navigation.

Blomkvist had not thought much of the proposal, but he came around when promised a few days of relaxation in the archipelago with good food and pleasant company. These promises came to naught, and the expedition turned into more of a disaster than he could have imagined. They had sailed the beautiful but not very dramatic route from Bullandö up through Furusund Strait at barely 9 knots, but the new girlfriend was instantly seasick. Her sister started arguing with her boyfriend, and none of them showed the slightest interest in learning the least little thing about sailing. It quickly became clear that Blomkvist was expected to take charge of the boat while the others gave him well-intentioned but basically meaningless advice. After the first night in a bay on Ängsö he was ready to dock the boat at Furusund and take the bus home. Only their desperate appeals persuaded him to stay.

At noon the next day, early enough that there were still a few spaces available, they tied up at the visitors' wharf on the picturesque island of Arholma. They had thrown some lunch together and had just finished when Blomkvist noticed a yellow fibreglass M-30 gliding into the bay using only its mainsail. The boat made a graceful tack while the helmsman looked for a spot at the wharf. Blomkvist too scanned the space around and saw that the gap between their Scampi and an H-boat on the starboard side was the only slot left. The narrow M-30 would just fit. He stood up in the stern and pointed; the man in the M-30 raised a hand in thanks and steered towards the wharf. A lone sailor who was not going to bother starting up the engine, Blomkvist noticed. He heard the rattle of the anchor chain and seconds later the main came down, while the skipper moved like a scalded cat to guide the rudder straight for the slot and at the same time ready the line from the bow.

Blomkvist climbed up on the railing and held out a hand for the painter. The new arrival made one last course correction and glided perfectly up to the stern of the Scampi, by now moving very slowly. It was only as the man tossed the painter to Blomkvist that they recognised each other and smiled in delight.

"Hi, Robban. Why don't you use your engine so you don't scrape the paint off all the boats in the harbour?"

"Hi, Micke. I thought there was something familiar about you. I'd love to use the engine if I could only get the piece of crap started. It died two days ago out by Rödlöga."

They shook hands across the railings.

An eternity before, at Kungsholmen school in the seventies, Blomkvist and Robert Lindberg had been friends, even very good friends. As so often happens with school buddies, the friendship faded after they had gone their separate ways. They had met maybe half a dozen times in the past twenty years, the last one seven or eight years ago. Now they studied each other with interest. Lindberg had tangled hair, was tanned and had a two-week-old beard.

Blomkvist immediately felt in much better spirits. When the PR guy and his silly girlfriend went off to dance around the Midsummer pole in front of the general store on the other side of the island, he stayed behind with his herring and aquavit in the cockpit of the M-30, shooting the breeze with his old school pal.

Sometime that evening, after they had given up the battle with Arholma's notorious mosquitoes and moved down to the cabin, and after quite a few shots of aquavit, the conversation turned to friendly banter about ethics in the corporate world. Lindberg had gone from school to the Stockholm School of Economics and into the banking business. Blomkvist had graduated from the Stockholm School of Journalism and devoted much of his professional life to exposing corruption in the banking and business world. Their talk began to explore what was ethically satisfactory in certain golden parachute agreements during the nineties. Lindberg eventually conceded there were one or two immoral bastards in the business world. He looked at Blomkvist with an expression that was suddenly serious.

"Why don't you write about Hans-Erik Wennerström?"

"I didn't know there was anything to write about him."

"Dig. Dig, for God's sake. How much do you know about the AIA programme?"

"Well, it was a sort of assistance programme in the nineties to help industry in the former Eastern Bloc countries get back on their feet. It was shut down a couple of years ago. It's nothing I've ever looked into."

"The Agency for Industrial Assistance was a project that was backed by the state and administered by representatives of about a dozen big Swedish firms. The AIA obtained government guarantees for a number of projects initiated in agreement with the governments in Poland and the Baltics. The Swedish Trade Union Confederation, LO, also joined in as a guarantor that the workers' movement in the East would be strengthened as well by following the Swedish model. In theory, it was an assistance project that built on the principle of offering help for self-help, and it was supposed to give the regimes in the East the opportunity to restructure their economies. In practice, however, it meant that Swedish companies would get state subventions for going in and establishing themselves as part owners in companies in Eastern European countries. That goddammed minister in the Christian party was an ardent advocate of the AIA, which was going to set up a paper mill in Krakow and provide new equipment for a metals industry in Riga, a cement factory in Tallinn, and so on. The funds would be distributed by the AIA board, which consisted of a number of heavyweights from the banking and corporate world."

"So it was tax money?"

"About half came from government contributions, and the banks and corporations put up the rest. But it was far from an ideal operation. The banks and industry were counting on making a sweet profit. Otherwise they damn well wouldn't have bothered."

"How much money are we talking about?"

"Hold on, listen to this. The AIA was dealing primarily with big Swedish firms who wanted to get into the Eastern European market. Heavy industries like ASEA Brown Boveri and Skanska Construction and the like. Not speculation firms, in other words."

"Are you telling me that Skanska doesn't do speculation? Wasn't it their managing director who was fired after he let some of his boys speculate away half a billion in quick stock turnovers? And how about their hysterical property deals in London and Oslo?"

"Sure, there are idiots in every company the world over, but you know what I mean. At least those companies actually produce something. The backbone of Swedish industry and all that."

"Where does Wennerström come into the picture?"

"Wennerström is the joker in the pack. Meaning that he's a guy who turns up out of the blue, who has no background whatsoever in heavy industry, and who really has no business getting involved in these projects. But he has amassed a colossal fortune on the stock market and has invested in solid companies. He came in by the back door, so to speak."

As he sat there in the boat, Blomkvist filled his glass with Reimersholms brandy and leaned back, trying to remember what little he knew about Wennerström. Born up in Norrland, where in the seventies he set up an investment company. He made money and moved to Stockholm, and there his career took off in the eighties. He created *Wennerströmgruppen*, the Wennerström Group, when they set up offices in London and New York and the company started to get mentioned in the same articles as Beijer. He traded stock and options and liked to make quick deals, and he emerged in the celebrity press as one of Sweden's numerous billionaires with a city home on Strandvägen, a fabulous summer villa on the island of Värmdö, and an eighty-two-foot motor yacht that he bought from a bankrupt former tennis star. He was a bean counter, naturally, but the eighties was the decade of the bean counters and property speculators, and Wennerström had not made a significantly big splash. On the contrary, he had remained something of a man in the shadows among his peers. He lacked Jan Stenbeck's flamboyance and did not spread himself all over the tabloids like Percy Barnevik. He said goodbye to real estate and instead made massive investments in the former Eastern Bloc. When the bubble burst in the nineties and one managing director after another was forced to cash in his golden parachute, Wennerström's company came out of it in remarkably good shape. "A Swedish success story," as the *Financial Times* called it.

"That was 1992," Lindberg said. "Wennerström contacted AIA and said he wanted funding. He presented a plan, seemingly backed by interests in Poland, which aimed at establishing an industry for the manufacture of packaging for foodstuffs."

"A tin-can industry, you mean."

"Not quite, but something along those lines. I have no idea who he knew at the AIA, but he walked out with sixty million kronor."

"This is starting to get interesting. Let me guess: that was the last anyone saw of the money."

"Wrong." Lindberg gave a sly smile before he fortified himself with a few more sips of brandy.

"What happened after that is a piece of classic bookkeeping. Wennerström really did set up a packaging factory in Poland, in Lódz. The company was called Minos. AIA received a few enthusiastic reports during 1993, then silence. In 1994, Minos, out of the blue, collapsed."

Lindberg put his empty glass down with an emphatic smack.

"The problem with AIA was that there was no real system in place for reporting on the project. You remember those days: everyone was so optimistic when the Berlin Wall came down. Democracy was going to be introduced, the threat of nuclear war was over, and the Bolsheviks would turn into regular little capitalists overnight. The government wanted to nail down democracy in the East. Every capitalist wanted to jump on the bandwagon and help build the new Europe."

"I didn't know that capitalists were so anxious to get involved in charity."

"Believe me, it was a capitalist's wet dream. Russia and Eastern Europe may be the world's biggest untapped markets after China. Industry had no problem joining hands with the government, especially when the companies were required to put up only a token investment. In all, AIA swallowed about thirty billion kronor of the taxpayers' money. It was supposed to come back in future profits. Formally, AIA was the government's initiative, but the influence of industry was so great that in actual fact the AIA board was operating independently."

"So is there a story in all this?"

"Be patient. When the project started there was no problem with financing. Sweden hadn't yet been hit by the interest-rate shock. The government was happy to plug AIA as one of the biggest Swedish efforts to promote democracy in the East."

"And this was all under the Conservative government?"

"Don't get politics mixed up in this. It's all about money and it makes no difference if the Social Democrats or the moderates appoint the ministers. So, full speed ahead. Then came the foreign-exchange problems, and after that some crazy New Democrats—remember them?—started whining that there was a shortage of oversight in what AIA was into. One of their henchmen had confused AIA with the Swedish International Development Authority and thought it was all some damn do-gooder project like the one in Tanzania. In the spring of 1994 a commission was appointed to investigate. At that time there were concerns about several projects, but one of the first to be investigated was Minos."

"And Wennerström couldn't show what the funds had been used for."

"Far from it. He produced an excellent report which showed that around fifty-four million kronor was invested in Minos. But it turned out that there were too many huge administrative problems in what was left of Poland for a modern packaging industry to be able to function. In practice their factory was shut out by the competition from a similar German project. The Germans were doing their best to buy up the entire Eastern Bloc."

"You said that he had been given sixty million kronor."

"Exactly. The money served as an interest-free loan. The idea, of course, was that the companies would pay back part of the money over a number of years. But Minos had gone under and Wennerström could not be blamed for it. Here the state guarantees kicked in, and Wennerström was indemnified. All he needed to do was pay back the money that was lost when Minos went under, and he could also show that he had lost a corresponding amount of his own money."

"Let me see if I understand this correctly. The government supplied billions in tax money, and diplomats to open doors. Industries got the money and used it to invest in joint ventures from which they later reaped vast profits. In other words, business as usual."

"You're a cynic. The loans were supposed to be paid back to the state."

"You said that they were interest-free. So that means the taxpayers got nothing at all for putting up the cash. Wennerström got sixty million, and invested fifty-four million of it. What happened to the other six million?"

"When it became clear that the AIA project was going to be investigated, Wennerström sent a cheque for six million to AIA for the difference. So the matter was settled, legally at least."

"It sounds as though Wennerström frittered away a little money for AIA. But compared with the half billion that disappeared from Skanska or the CEO of ABB's golden parachute of more than a billion kronor—which really upset people—this doesn't seem to be much to write about," Blomkvist said. "Today's readers are pretty tired of stories about incompetent speculators, even if it's with public funds. Is there more to the story?"

"It gets better."

"How do you know all this about Wennerström's deals in Poland?"

"I worked at Handelsbanken in the nineties. Guess who wrote the reports for the bank's representative in AIA?"

"Aha. Tell me more."

"Well, AIA got their report from Wennerström. Documents were drawn up. The balance of the money had been paid back. That six million coming back was very clever."

"Get to the point."

"But, my dear Blomkvist, that *is* the point. AIA was satisfied with Wennerström's report. It was an investment that went to hell, but there was no criticism of the way it had been managed. We looked at invoices and transfers and all the documents. Everything was meticulously accounted for. I believed it. My boss believed it. AIA believed it, and the government had nothing to say."

"Where's the hook?"

"This is where the story gets ticklish," Lindberg said, looking surprisingly sober. "And since you're a journalist, this is off the record."

"Come off it. You can't sit there telling me all this stuff and then say I can't use it."

"I certainly can. What I've told you so far is in the public record. You can look up the report if you want. The rest of the story—what I haven't told you—you can write about, but you'll have to treat me as an anonymous source."

"OK, but 'off the record' in current terminology means that I've been told something in confidence and can't write about it."

"Screw the terminology. Write whatever the hell you want, but I'm your anonymous source. Are we agreed?"

"Of course," Blomkvist said.

In hindsight, this was a mistake.

"All right then. The Minos story took place more than a decade ago, just after the Wall came down and the Bolsheviks starting acting like decent capitalists. I was one of the people who investigated Wennerström, and the whole time I thought there was something damned odd about his story."

"Why didn't you say so when you signed off on his report?"

"I discussed it with my boss. But the problem was that there wasn't anything to pinpoint. The documents were all OK, I had only to sign the report. Every time I've seen Wennerström's name in the press since then I think about Minos, and not least because some years later, in the mid-nineties, my bank was doing some business with Wennerström. Pretty big business, actually, and it didn't turn out so well."

"He cheated you?"

"No, nothing that obvious. We both made money on the deals. It was more that . . . I don't know quite how to explain it, and now I'm talking about my own employer, and I don't want to do that. But what struck me—the lasting and overall impression, as they say—was not positive. Wennerström is presented in the media as a tremendous financial oracle. He thrives on that. It's his 'trust capital.' "

"I know what you mean."

"My impression was that the man was all bluff. He wasn't even particularly bright as a financier. In fact, I thought he was damned ignorant about certain subjects although he had some really sharp young warriors for advisers. Above all, I really didn't care for him personally."

"So?"

"A few years ago I went down to Poland on some other matter. Our group had dinner with some investors in Lódz, and I found myself at the same table as the mayor. We talked about the difficulty of getting Poland's economy on its feet and all that, and somehow or other I mentioned the Minos project. The mayor looked quite astonished for a moment—as if he had never heard of Minos. He told me it was some crummy little business and nothing ever came of it. He laughed and said—I'm quoting word for word—that if that was the best our investors could manage, then Sweden wasn't long for this life. Are you following me?"

"That mayor of Lódz is obviously a sharp fellow, but go on."

"The next day I had a meeting in the morning, but the rest of my day was free. For the hell of it I drove out to look at the shut-down Minos factory in a small town outside of Lódz. The giant Minos factory was a ramshackle structure. A corrugated iron storage building that the Red Army had built in the fifties. I found a watchman on the property who could speak a little German and discovered that one of his cousins had worked at Minos and we went over to his house nearby. The watchman interpreted. Are you interested in hearing what he had to say?"

"I can hardly wait."

"Minos opened in the autumn of 1992. There were at most fifteen employees, the majority of them old women. Their pay was around one hundred fifty kronor a month. At first there were no machines, so the workforce spent their time cleaning up the place. In early October three cardboard box machines arrived from Portugal. They were old and completely obsolete. The scrap value couldn't have been more than a few thousand kronor. The machines did work, but they kept breaking down. Naturally there were no spare parts, so Minos suffered endless stoppages."

"This is starting to sound like a story," Blomkvist said. "What did they make at Minos?"

"Throughout 1992 and half of 1993 they produced simple cardboard boxes for washing powders and egg cartons and the like. Then they started making paper bags. But the factory could never get enough raw materials, so there was never a question of much volume of production."

"This doesn't sound like a gigantic investment."

"I ran the numbers. The total rent must have been around 15,000 kronor for two years. Wages may have amounted to 150,000 SEK at most—and I'm being generous here. Cost of machines and cost of freight . . . a van to deliver the egg cartons . . . I'm guessing 250,000. Add fees for permits, a little travelling back and forth—apparently one person from Sweden did visit the site a few times. It looks as though the whole operation ran for under two million. One day in the summer of 1993 the foreman came down to the factory and said it was shut down, and a while later a Hungarian lorry appeared and carried off the machinery. Bye-bye, Minos."

In the course of the trial Blomkvist had often thought of that Midsummer Eve. For large parts of the evening the tone of the conversation made it feel as if they were back at school, having a friendly argument. As teenagers they had shared the burdens common to that stage in life. As grown-ups they were effectively strangers, by now quite different sorts of people. During their talk Blomkvist had thought that he really could not recall what it was that had made them such friends at school. He remembered Lindberg as a reserved boy, incredibly shy with girls. As an adult he was a successful . . . well, climber in the banking world.

He rarely got drunk, but that chance meeting had transformed a disastrous sailing trip into a pleasant evening. And because the conversation had so much an echo of a schoolboy tone, he did not at first take Lindberg's story about Wennerström seriously. Gradually his professional instincts were aroused. Eventually he was listening attentively, and the logical objections surfaced.

"Wait a second," he said. "Wennerström is a top name among market speculators. He's made himself a billion, has he not?"

"The Wennerström Group is sitting on somewhere close to two hundred billion. You're going to ask why a billionaire should go to the trouble of swindling a trifling fifty million."

"Well, put it this way: why would he risk his own and his company's good name on such a blatant swindle?"

"It wasn't so obviously a swindle given that the AIA board, the bankers, the government, and Parliament's auditors all approved Wennerström's accounting without a single dissenting vote."

"It's still a ridiculously small sum for so vast a risk."

"Certainly. But just think: the Wennerström Group is an investment company that deals with property, securities, options, foreign exchange . . . you name it. Wennerström contacted AIA in 1992 just as the bottom was about to drop out of the market. Do you remember the autumn of 1992?"

"Do I? I had a variable-rate mortgage on my apartment when the interest rate shot up five hundred percent in October. I was stuck with nineteen percent interest for a year."

"Those were indeed the days," Lindberg said. "I lost a bundle that year myself. And Hans-Erik Wennerström—like every other player in the market—was wrestling with the same problem. The company had billions tied up in paper of various types, but not so much cash. All of a sudden they could no longer borrow any amount they liked. The usual thing in such a situation is to unload a few properties and lick your wounds, but in 1992 nobody wanted to buy real estate."

"Cash-flow problems."

"Exactly. And Wennerström wasn't the only one. Every businessman . . ."

"Don't say businessman. Call them what you like, but calling them businessmen is an insult to a serious profession."

"All right, every speculator had cash-flow problems. Look at it this way: Wennerström got sixty million kronor. He paid back six mil, but only after three years. The real cost of Minos didn't come to more than two million. The interest alone on sixty million for three years, that's quite a bit. Depending on how he invested the money, he might have doubled the AIA money, or maybe grown it ten times over. Then we're no longer talking about cat shit. *Skål,* by the way."

CHAPTER 2

Friday, December 20

Dragan Armansky was born in Croatia fifty-six years ago. His father was an Armenian Jew from Belorussia. His mother was a Bosnian Muslim of Greek extraction. She had taken charge of his upbringing and his education, which meant that as an adult he was lumped together with that large, heterogeneous group defined by the media as Muslims. The Swedish immigration authorities had registered him, strangely enough, as a Serb. His passport confirmed that he was a Swedish citizen, and his passport photograph showed a squarish face, a strong jaw, five-o'clock shadow, and greying temples. He was often referred to as "The Arab," although he did not have a drop of Arab blood.

He looked a little like the stereotypical local boss in an American gangster movie, but in fact he was a talented financial director who had begun his career as a junior accountant at Milton Security in the early seventies. Three decades later he had advanced to CEO and COO of the company.

He had become fascinated with the security business. It was

like war games—to identify threats, develop counter-strategies, and all the time stay one step ahead of the industrial spies, blackmailers and thieves. It began for him when he discovered how the swindling of a client had been accomplished through creative bookkeeping. He was able to prove who, from a group of a dozen people, was behind it. He had been promoted and played a key role in the firm's development and was an expert in financial fraud. Fifteen years later he became CEO. He had transformed Milton Security into one of Sweden's most competent and trusted security firms.

The company had 380 full-time employees and another 300 freelancers. It was small compared to Falck or Swedish Guard Service. When Armansky first joined, the company was called Johan Fredrik Milton's General Security AB, and it had a client list consisting of shopping centres that needed floorwalkers and muscular guards. Under his leadership the firm was now the internationally recognised Milton Security and had invested in cutting-edge technology. Night watchmen well past their prime, uniform fetishists, and moonlighting university students had been replaced by people with real professional skills. Armansky hired mature ex-policemen as operations chiefs, political scientists specialising in international terrorism, and experts in personal protection and industrial espionage. Most importantly, he hired the best telecommunications technicians and IT experts. The company moved from Solna to state-of-the-art offices near Slussen, in the heart of Stockholm.

By the start of the nineties, Milton Security was equipped to offer a new level of security to an exclusive group of clients, primarily medium-sized corporations and well-to-do private individuals—nouveau-riche rock stars, stock-market speculators, and dot-com high flyers. A part of the company's activity was providing bodyguard protection and security solutions to Swedish firms abroad, especially in the Middle East. This area of their business now accounted for 70 percent of the company's turnover. Under Armansky, sales had increased from about forty million SEK annually to almost two billion. Providing security was a lucrative business.

Operations were divided among three main areas: *security consultations,* which consisted of identifying conceivable or imagined threats; *counter-measures,* which usually involved the installation of security cameras, burglar and fire alarms, electronic locking mechanisms and IT systems; and *personal protection* for private individuals or companies. This last market had grown forty times over in ten years. Lately a new client group had arisen: affluent women seeking protection from former boyfriends or husbands or from stalkers. In addition, Milton Security had a cooperative arrangement with similar firms of good repute in Europe and the United States. The company also handled security for many international visitors to Sweden, including an American actress who was shooting a film for two months in Trollhättan. Her agent felt that her status warranted having bodyguards accompany her whenever she took her infrequent walks near the hotel.

A fourth, considerably smaller area that occupied only a few employees was what was called PI or P-In, in internal jargon *pinders,* which stood for *personal investigations.*

Armansky was not altogether enamoured of this part of their business. It was troublesome and less lucrative. It put greater demands on the employees' judgement and experience than on their knowledge of telecommunications technology or the installation of surveillance apparatus. Personal investigations were acceptable when it was a matter of credit information, background checks before hiring, or to investigate suspicions that some employee had leaked company information or engaged in criminal activity. In such cases the *pinders* were an integral part of the operational activity. But not infrequently his business clients would drag in private problems that had a tendency to create unwelcome turmoil. *I want to know what sort of creep my daughter is going out with . . . I think my wife is being unfaithful . . . The guy is OK but he's mixed up with bad company . . . I'm being blackmailed . . .* Armansky often gave them a straightforward no. If the daughter was an adult, she had the right to go out with any creep she wanted to, and he thought infidelity was something that husbands and wives ought to work out on their own. Hidden in all such inquiries were traps that could lead to scandal and create legal problems for Milton Security. Which was why Dragan Armansky kept a close watch on these assignments, in spite of how modest the revenue was.

The morning's topic was just such a personal investigation. Armansky straightened the crease in his trousers before he leaned back in his comfortable chair. He glanced suspiciously at his colleague Lisbeth Salander, who was thirty-two years his junior. He thought for the thousandth time that nobody seemed more out of place in a prestigious security firm than she did. His mistrust was both wise and irrational. In Armansky's eyes, Salander was beyond doubt the most able investigator he had met in all his years in the business. During the four years she had worked for him she had never once fumbled a job or turned in a single mediocre report.

On the contrary, her reports were in a class by themselves. Armansky was convinced that she possessed a unique gift. Anybody could find out credit information or run a check with police records. But Salander had imagination, and she always came back with something different from what he expected. How she did it, he had never understood. Sometimes he thought that her ability to gather information was sheer magic. She knew the bureaucratic archives inside out. Above all, she had the ability to get under the skin of the person she was investigating. If there was any dirt to be dug up, she would home in on it like a cruise missile.

Somehow she had always had this gift.

Her reports could be a catastrophe for the individual who landed in her radar. Armansky would never forget the time he assigned her to do a routine check on a researcher in the pharmaceutical industry before a corporate buyout. The job was scheduled to take a week, but it dragged on for a while. After four weeks' silence and several reminders, which she ignored, Salander came back with a report documenting that the subject in question was a paedophile. On two occasions he had bought sex from a thirteen-year-old child prostitute in Tallinn, and there were indications that he had an unhealthy interest in the daughter of the woman with whom he was currently living.

Salander had habits that sometimes drove Armansky to the edge of despair. In the case of the paedophile, she did not pick up the telephone and call Armansky or come into his office wanting to talk to him. No, without indicating by a single word that the report might contain explosive material, she laid it on his desk one evening, just as Armansky was about to leave for the day. He read it only late that evening, as he was relaxing over a bottle of wine in front of the TV with his wife in their villa on Lidingö.

The report was, as always, almost scientifically precise, with footnotes, quotations, and source references. The first few pages gave the subject's background, education, career, and financial situation. Not until page 24 did Salander drop the bombshell about the trips to Tallinn, in the same dry-as-dust tone she used to report that he lived in Sollentuna and drove a dark blue Volvo. She referred to documentation in an exhaustive appendix, including photographs of the thirteen-year-old girl in the company of the subject. The pictures had been taken in a hotel corridor in Tallinn, and the man had his hand under the girl's sweater. Salander had tracked down the girl in question and she had provided her account on tape.

The report had created precisely the chaos that Armansky had wanted to avoid. First he had to swallow a few ulcer tablets prescribed by his doctor. Then he called in the client for a sombre emergency meeting. Finally—over the client's fierce objections—he was forced to refer the material to the police. This meant that Milton Security risked being drawn into a tangled web. If Salander's evidence could not be substantiated or the man was acquitted, the company might risk a libel suit. It was a nightmare.

However, it was not Lisbeth Salander's astonishing lack of emotional involvement that most upset him. Milton's image was one of conservative stability. Salander fitted into this picture about as well as a buffalo at a boat show. Armansky's star researcher was a pale, anorexic young woman who had hair as short as a fuse, and a pierced nose and eyebrows. She had a wasp tattoo about an inch long on her neck, a tattooed loop around the biceps of her left arm and another around her left ankle. On those occasions when she had been wearing a tank top, Armansky also saw that she had a dragon tattoo on her left shoulder blade. She was a natural redhead, but she dyed her hair raven black. She looked as though she had just emerged from a week-long orgy with a gang of hard rockers.

She did not in fact have an eating disorder, Armansky was sure of that. On the contrary, she seemed to consume every kind of junk food. She had simply been born thin, with slender bones that made her look girlish and fine-limbed with small hands, narrow wrists, and childlike breasts. She was twenty-four, but she sometimes looked fourteen.

She had a wide mouth, a small nose, and high cheekbones that gave her an almost Asian look. Her movements were quick and spidery, and when she was working at the computer her fingers flew over the keys. Her extreme slenderness would have made a career in modelling impossible, but with the right make-up her face could have put her on any billboard in the world. Sometimes she wore black lipstick, and in spite of the tattoos and the pierced nose and eyebrows she was . . . well . . . attractive. It was inexplicable.

The fact that Salander worked for Dragan Armansky at all was astonishing. She was not the sort of woman with whom he would normally come into contact.

She had been hired as a jill-of-all-trades. Holger Palmgren, a semi-retired lawyer who looked after old J. F. Milton's personal affairs, had told Armansky that this Lisbeth Salander was a quick-witted girl with "a rather trying attitude." Palmgren had appealed to him to give her a chance, which Armansky had, against his better judgement, promised to do. Palmgren was the type of man who would only take "no" as an encouragement to redouble his efforts, so it was easier to say "yes" right away. Armansky knew that Palmgren devoted himself to troubled kids and other social misfits, but he did have good judgement.

He had regretted his decision to hire the girl the moment he met her. She did not just seem difficult—in his eyes she was the very quintessence of difficult. She had dropped out of school and had no sort of higher education.

The first few months she had worked full time, well, almost full time. She turned up at the office now and then. She made coffee, went to the post office, and took care of the copying, but conventional office hours or work routines were anathema to her. On the other hand, she had a talent for irritating the other employees. She became known as "the girl with two brain cells"—one for breathing and one for standing up. She never talked about herself. Colleagues who tried to talk to her seldom got a response and soon gave up. Her attitude encouraged neither trust nor friendship, and she quickly became an outsider wandering the corridors of Milton like a stray cat. She was generally considered a hopeless case.

After a month of nothing but trouble, Armansky sent for her, fully intending to let her go. She listened to his catalogue of her offences without objection and without even raising an eyebrow. She did not have the "right attitude," he concluded, and was about to tell her that it would probably be a good idea if she looked for employment with another firm that could make better use of her skills. Only then did she interrupt him.

"You know, if you just want an office serf you can get one from the temp agency. I can handle anything and anyone you want, and if you don't have any better use for me than sorting post, then you're an idiot."

Armansky sat there, stunned and angry, and she went on unperturbed.

"You have a man here who spent three weeks writing a completely useless report about that yuppie they're thinking of recruiting for that dot-com company. I copied the piece of crap for him last night, and I see it's lying on your desk now."

Armansky's eyes went to the report, and for a change he raised his voice.

"You're not supposed to read confidential reports."

"Apparently not, but the security routines in your firm have a number of shortcomings. According to your directive he's supposed to copy such things himself, but he chucked the report at me before he left for the bar yesterday. And by the way, I found his previous report in the canteen."

"You did *what?*"

"Calm down. I put it in his in-box."

"Did he give you the combination to his document safe?" Armansky was aghast.

"Not exactly; he wrote it on a piece of paper he kept underneath his blotter along with the password to his computer. But the point is that your joke of a private detective has done a worthless personal investigation. He missed the fact that the guy has old gambling debts and snorts cocaine like a vacuum cleaner. Or that his girlfriend had to seek help from the women's crisis centre after he beat the shit out of her."

Armansky sat for a couple of minutes turning the pages of the report. It was competently set out, written in clear language, and filled with source references as well as statements from the subject's friends and acquaintances. Finally he raised his eyes and said two words: "Prove it."

"How much time have I got?"

"Three days. If you can't prove your allegations by Friday afternoon you're fired."

Three days later she delivered a report which, with equally exhaustive source references, transformed the outwardly pleasant young yuppie into an unreliable bastard. Armansky read her report over the weekend, several times, and spent part of Monday doing a half-hearted double-check of some of her assertions. Even before he began he knew that her information would prove to be accurate.

Armansky was bewildered and also angry with himself for having so obviously misjudged her. He had taken her for stupid, maybe even retarded. He had not expected that a girl who had cut so many classes in school that she did not graduate could write a report so grammatically correct. It also contained detailed observations and information, and he quite simply could not comprehend how she could have acquired such facts.

He could not imagine that anyone else at Milton Security would have lifted excerpts from the confidential journal of a doctor at a women's crisis centre. When he asked her how she had managed that, she told him that she had no intention of burning her sources. It became clear that Salander was not going to discuss her work methods, either with him or with anyone else. This disturbed him—but not enough for him to resist the temptation to test her.

He thought about the matter for several days. He recalled Holger Palmgren's saying when he had sent her to him, "Everyone deserves a chance." He thought about his own Muslim upbringing, which had taught him that it was his duty to God to help the outcasts. Of course he did not believe in God and had not been in a mosque since he was a teenager, but he recognised Lisbeth Salander as a person in need of resolute help. He had not done much along these lines over the past few decades.

Instead of giving Salander the boot, he summoned her for a meeting in which he tried to work out what made the difficult girl tick. His impression was confirmed that she suffered from some serious emotional problem, but he also discovered that behind her sullen facade there was an unusual intelligence. He found her prickly and irksome, but much to his surprise he began to like her.

Over the following months Armansky took Salander under his wing. In truth, he took her on as a small social project. He gave her straightforward research tasks and tried to give her guidelines on how to proceed. She would listen patiently and then set off to carry out the assignment just as she saw fit. He asked Milton's technical director to give her a basic course in IT science. They sat together all afternoon until he reported back that she seemed to have a better understanding of computers than most of the staff.

But despite development discussions, offers of in-house training, and other forms of enticement, it was evident that Salander had no intention of adapting to Milton's office routines. This put Armansky in a difficult spot.

He would not have put up with any other employee coming and going at will, and under normal circumstances he would have demanded that she change or go. But he had a hunch that if he gave Salander an ultimatum or threatened to fire her she would simply shrug her shoulders and be gone.

A more serious problem was that he could not be sure of his own feelings for the young woman. She was like a nagging itch, repellent and at the same time tempting. It was not a sexual attraction, at least he did not think so. The women he was usually attracted to were blonde and curvaceous, with full lips that aroused his fantasies. And besides, he had been married for twenty years to a Finnish woman named Ritva who still more than satisfied these requirements. He had never been unfaithful, well . . . something may have happened just once, and his wife might have misunderstood if she had known about it. But the marriage was happy and he had two daughters of Salander's age. In any case, he was not interested in flat-chested girls who might be mistaken for skinny boys at a distance. That was not his style.

Even so, he had caught himself having inappropriate daydreams about Lisbeth Salander, and he recognised that he was not completely unaffected by her. But the attraction, Armansky thought, was that Salander was a foreign creature to him. He might just as well have fallen in love with a painting of a nymph or a Greek amphora. Salander represented a life that was not real for him, that fascinated him though he could not share it—and in any case she forbade him from sharing it.

On one occasion Armansky was sitting at a café on Stortorget in Gamla Stan when Salander came sauntering up and sat at a table a short distance away. She was with three girls and a boy, all dressed in much the same way. Armansky had watched her with interest. She seemed to be just as reserved as she was at work, but she had actually almost smiled at a story told by one of her companions, a girl with purple hair.

Armansky wondered how she would react if one day he came to work with green hair, worn-out jeans, and a leather jacket covered with graffiti and rivets. She probably would just smirk at him.

She had been sitting with her back to him and did not turn around once, obviously unaware that he was there. He felt strangely disturbed by her presence. When at last he got up to slink away unnoticed, she suddenly turned and stared straight at him, as though she had been aware all the time that he was sitting there and had him on her radar. Her gaze had come so surprisingly that it felt like an attack, and he pretended not to see her and hurriedly left the café. She had not said hello even, but she followed him with her eyes, he was sure of it, and not until he turned the corner did they stop burning into his neck.

She rarely laughed. But over time Armansky thought he noticed a softening of her attitude. She had a dry sense of humour, to put it mildly, which could prompt a crooked, ironic smile.

Armansky felt so provoked by her lack of emotional response that sometimes he wanted to grab hold of her and shake her. To force his way into her shell and win her friendship, or at least her respect.

Only once, after she had been working for him for nine months, had he tried to discuss these feelings with her. It was at Milton Security's Christmas party one evening in December, and for once he was not sober. Nothing inappropriate had happened—he had just tried to tell her that he actually liked her. Most of all he wanted to explain that he felt protective towards her, and if she ever needed help with anything, she should not hesitate to come to him. He had even tried to give her a hug. All in friendliness, of course.

She had wriggled out of his clumsy embrace and left the party. After that she had not appeared at the office or answered her mobile. Her absence had felt like torture—almost a form of personal punishment. He had nobody to discuss his feelings with, and for the first time he realised with appalling clarity what a destructive hold she had over him.

Three weeks later, when Armansky was working late one evening going over the year-end bookkeeping, Salander reappeared. She came into his office as silently as a ghost, and he became aware that she was standing in the shadows inside the doorway, watching him. He had no idea how long she had been there.

"Would you like some coffee?" she asked. She handed him a cup from the espresso machine in the canteen. Mutely he accepted it, feeling both relief and terror when she shoved the door closed with her foot. She sat down opposite his desk and looked him straight in the eye. Then she asked the question in a way that could neither be laughed off nor avoided.

"Dragan, are you attracted to me?"

Armansky sat as if paralysed, while desperately wondering how to answer. His first impulse was to pretend to be insulted. Then he saw her expression and it came to him that this was the first time she had ever uttered any such personal question. It was seriously meant, and if he tried to laugh it off she would take it as an affront. She wanted to talk to him, and he wondered how long it had taken her to get up the courage to ask that question. He slowly put down his pen and leaned back in his chair. Finally he relaxed.

"What makes you think that?" he said.

"The way you look at me, and the way you don't look at me. And the times you were about to reach out your hand and touch me but stopped yourself."

He smiled at her. "I reckon you'd bite off my hand if I laid a finger on you."

She did not smile. She was waiting.

"Lisbeth, I'm your boss, and even if I were attracted to you, I'd never act on it."

She was still waiting.

"Between us—yes, there have been times when I have felt attracted to you. I can't explain it, but that's the way it is. For some reason I don't really understand, I like you a lot. But it's not a physical thing."

"That's good. Because it'll never happen."

Armansky laughed. The first time she had said something personal and it was the most disheartening news a man could imagine receiving. He struggled to find the right words.

"Lisbeth, I understand that you're not interested in an old man of fifty plus."

"I'm not interested in an old man of fifty plus *who's my boss.*" She held up a hand. "Wait, let me speak. You're sometimes stupid and maddeningly bureaucratic, but you're actually an attractive man, and . . . I can also feel . . . But you're my boss and I've met your wife and I want to keep my job with you, and the most idiotic thing I could do is get involved with you."

Armansky said nothing, hardly daring to breathe.

"I'm aware of what you've done for me, and I'm not ungrateful. I appreciate that you actually showed yourself to be greater than your prejudices and have given me a chance here. But I don't want you for my lover, and you're not my father."

After a while Armansky sighed helplessly. "What exactly do you want from me?"

"I want to continue working for you. If that's OK with you."

He nodded and then answered her as honestly as he could. "I really do want you to work for me. But I also want you to feel some sort of friendship and trust in me."

She nodded.

"You're not a person who encourages friendship," he said.

She seemed to withdraw, but he went on. "I understand that you don't want anyone interfering in your life, and I'll try not to do that. But is it all right if I continue to like you?"

Salander thought about it for a long time. Then she replied by getting up, walking around the desk, and giving him a hug. He was totally shocked. Only when she released him did he take her hand.

"We can be friends?"

She nodded once.

That was the only time she ever showed him any tenderness, and the only time she ever touched him. It was a moment that Armansky fondly remembered.

After four years she had still vouchsafed hardly a detail about her private life or her background to Armansky. Once he applied his own knowledge of the *pinder*'s art on her. He also had a long talk with Holger Palmgren—who did not seem surprised to see him—and what he finally found out did not increase his trust in her. He never mentioned a word about this to her or let her know that he had been snooping into her life. Instead he hid his uneasiness and increased his watchfulness.

Before that strange evening was over, Armansky and Salander had come to an agreement. In future she would do research projects for him on a freelance basis. She would receive a small monthly income whether she did any assignments or not. The real money would be made when she was paid per assignment. She could work the way she wanted to; in return she pledged never to do anything that might embarrass him or risk subjecting Milton Security to scandal.

For Armansky this was a solution that was advantageous to him, the company, and Salander herself. He cut the troublesome PI department down to a single full-time employee, an older colleague who handled routine jobs perfectly well and ran credit checks. All complicated or tricky assignments he turned over to Salander and a few other freelancers who—in the last resort—were independent contractors for whom Milton Security had actually no responsibility. Since he regularly engaged her services, she earned a good salary. It could have been much higher, but Salander worked only when she felt like it.

Armansky accepted her as she was, but she was not allowed to meet the clients. Today's assignment was an exception.

Salander was dressed for the day in a black T-shirt with a picture on it of E.T. with fangs, and the words I AM ALSO AN ALIEN. She had on a black skirt that was frayed at the hem, a worn-out black, mid-length leather jacket, rivet belt, heavy Doc Marten boots, and horizontally striped, green-and-red knee socks. She had put on make-up in a colour scheme that indicated she might be colourblind. In other words, she was exceptionally decked out.

Armansky sighed and shifted his gaze to the conservatively dressed guest with the thick glasses. Dirch Frode, a lawyer, had insisted on meeting and being able to ask questions of the employee who prepared the report. Armansky had done all he civilly could to prevent the meeting taking place, saying that Salander had a cold, was away, or was swamped with other work. The lawyer replied calmly that it made no difference—the matter was not urgent and he could easily wait a couple of days. At last there was no way to avoid bringing them together. Now Frode, who seemed to be in his late sixties, was looking at Lisbeth Salander with evident fascination. Salander glowered back with an expression that did not indicate any warm feelings.

Armansky sighed and looked once more at the folder she had placed on his desk labelled CARL MIKAEL BLOMKVIST. The name was followed by a social security number, neatly printed on the cover. He said the name out loud. Herr Frode snapped out of his bewitched state and turned to Armansky.

"So what can you tell me about Mikael Blomkvist?" he said.

"This is Ms. Salander, who prepared the report." Armansky hesitated a second and then went on with a smile that was intended to engender confidence, but which seemed helplessly apologetic. "Don't be fooled by her youth. She is our absolute best researcher."

"I'm persuaded of that," Frode said in a dry tone that hinted at the opposite. "Tell me what she found out."

It was clear that Frode had no idea how to act towards Salander. He resorted to directing the question to Armansky, as if she had not been in the room. Salander blew a big bubble with her gum. Before Armansky could answer, she said, "Could you ask the client whether he would prefer the long or the short version?"

There was a brief, embarrassed silence before Frode finally turned to Salander and tried to repair the damage by assuming a friendly, avuncular tone.

"I would be grateful if the young lady would give me a verbal summary of the results."

For a moment her expression was so surprisingly hostile that it sent a cold shiver down Frode's spine. Then just as quickly her expression softened and Frode wondered whether he had imagined that look. When she began to speak she sounded like a civil servant.

"Allow me to say first that this was not a very complicated assignment, apart from the fact that the description of the task itself was somewhat vague. You wanted to know 'everything that could be dug up' about him, but gave no indication of whether there were anything in particular you were looking for. For this reason it's something of a potpourri of his life. The report is 193 pages long, but 120 pages are copies of articles he wrote or press clippings. Blomkvist is a public person with few secrets and not very much to hide."

"But he does have some secrets?" Frode said.

"Everyone has secrets," she replied neutrally. "It's just a matter of finding out what they are."

"Let's hear."

"Mikael Blomkvist was born on January 18, 1960, which makes him forty-two years old. He was born in Borlänge but has never lived there. His parents, Kurt and Anita Blomkvist, were around thirty-five when the child was born. Both have since died. His father was a machinery installer and moved around a good deal. His mother, as far as I could see, was never anything but a housewife. The family moved house to Stockholm when Mikael started school. He has a sister three years younger named Annika who is a lawyer. He also has some cousins, both male and female. Were you planning to serve coffee?"

This last was directed at Armansky, who hastily pumped three cups of coffee from the thermos he had ordered for the meeting. He motioned for Salander to go on.

"So in 1966 the family lived in Lilla Essingen. Blomkvist went to school first in Blomma and then to prep school on Kungsholmen. He had decent graduating marks—there are copies in the folder. During his prep school days he studied music and played bass in a rock band named Bootstrap, which actually put out a single that was played on the radio in the summer of 1979. After prep school he worked as a ticket collector in the tunnelbana, saved some money, and travelled abroad. He was away for a year, mostly bumming around Asia—India, Thailand—and a swing down to Australia. He began studying to be a journalist in Stockholm when he was twenty-one, but interrupted his studies after the first year to do his military service as a rifleman in Kiruna in

Lapland. It was some sort of macho unit, and he left with good marks. After military service he completed his journalism degree and has worked in the field ever since. How detailed do you want me to be?"

"Just tell what you think is important."

"He comes off a little like Practical Pig in *The Three Little Pigs*. So far he has been an excellent journalist. In the eighties he had a lot of temporary jobs, first in the provincial press and then in Stockholm. There's a list. His breakthrough came with the story about the Bear Gang—the bank robbers he identified."

"Kalle Blomkvist."

"He hates the nickname, which is understandable. Some-body'd get a fat lip if they ever called me Pippi Longstocking on a newspaper placard."

She cast a dark look at Armansky, who swallowed hard. On more than one occasion he had thought of Salander as precisely Pippi Longstocking. He waved for her to get on with it.

"One source declares that up to then he wanted to be a crime reporter—and he interned as one at an evening paper. But he has become known for his work as a political and financial reporter. He has primarily been a freelancer, with one full-time position at an evening paper in the late eighties. He left in 1990 when he helped start the monthly magazine *Millennium*. The magazine began as a real outsider, without any big publishing company to hold its hand. Its circulation has grown and today is 21,000 copies monthly. The editorial office is on Götgatan only a few blocks from here."

"A left-wing magazine."

"That depends on how you define the concept 'left-wing.' *Millennium* is generally viewed as critical of society, but I'm guessing the anarchists think it's a wimpy bourgeois crap magazine along the lines of *Arena* or *Ordfront,* while the Moderate Students Association probably thinks that the editors are all

Bolsheviks. There is nothing to indicate that Blomkvist has ever been active politically, even during the left-wing wave when he was going to prep school. While he was plugging away at the School of Journalism he was living with a girl who at the time was active in the Syndicalists and today sits in Parliament as a representative of the Left party. He seems to have been given the left-wing stamp primarily because as a financial journalist he specialises in investigative reporting about corruption and shady transactions in the corporate world. He has done some devastating individual portraits of captains of industry and politicians—which were most likely well deserved—and caused a number of resignations and legal repercussions. The most well-known was the Arboga affair, which resulted in the forced resignation of a Conservative politician and the sentencing of a former councillor to a year in prison for embezzlement. Calling attention to crimes can hardly be considered an indication that someone is left-wing."

"I understand what you mean. What else?"

"He has written two books. One about the Arboga affair and one about financial journalism entitled *The Knights Templar*, which came out three years ago. I haven't read the book, but judging from the reviews it seems to have been controversial. It prompted a good deal of debate in the media."

"Money?" Frode said.

"He's not rich, but he's not starving. Income tax returns are attached to the report. He has about 250,000 SEK in the bank, in both a retirement fund and a savings account. He has an account of around 100,000 kronor that he uses as cash for working expenses, travel and such. He owns a co-op apartment that's paid off—700 square feet on Bellmansgatan—and he has no loans or debts. He has one other asset—some property in Sandhamn out in the archipelago. It's a cottage of 270 square feet, furnished as a summer cabin and by the water, right in the most attractive part of the village. Apparently an uncle of his bought it in the forties, when such things were still possible for normal mortals, and the cabin ended up in Blomkvist's hands. They divided things up so that his sister got the parents' apartment in Lilla Essingen and Blomkvist got the cabin. I have no idea what it might be worth today—certainly a few million—but on the other hand he doesn't seem to want to sell, and he goes out to Sandhamn fairly often."

"Income?"

"He's part owner of *Millennium,* but he only takes out about 12,000 in salary each month. The rest he earns from his freelance jobs—the total varies. He had a big year three years ago when he took in around 450,000. Last year he only made 120,000 from freelance jobs."

"He has to pay 150,000 in taxes in addition to lawyer's fees, et cetera," Frode said. "Let's assume that the total is rather high. He'll also be losing money while serving his gaol term."

"Which means that he's going to be cleaned out," Salander said.

"Is he honest?"

"That's his trust capital, so to speak. His image is to appear as the guardian of robust morality as opposed to the business world, and he is invited pretty regularly to pontificate on television."

"There probably isn't much left of that capital after his conviction today," Frode said.

"I don't want to claim that I know exactly what demands are made on a journalist, but after this setback it will probably be a long time before Master Detective Blomkvist wins the Grand Prize for Journalism. He's really made a fool of himself this time," Salander said. "If I may make a personal comment . . ."

Armansky opened his eyes wide. In the years Salander had worked for him, she had never made a single personal comment in an investigation of an individual. Bone-dry facts were all that mattered to her.

"It wasn't part of my assignment to look at the question of fact in the Wennerström affair, but I did follow the trial and have to admit that I was actually flabbergasted. The thing felt wrong, and it's totally . . . out of character for Mikael Blomkvist to publish something that seems to be so off the wall."

Salander scratched her neck. Frode looked patient. Armansky wondered whether he might be mistaken or whether Salander really was unsure how to continue. The Salander he knew was never unsure or hesitant. Finally she seemed to make up her mind.

"Quite off the record, so to speak . . . I haven't studied the Wennerström affair properly, but I really think that Mikael Blomkvist was set up. I think there's something totally different in this story than what the court's verdict is indicating."

The lawyer scrutinised Salander with searching eyes, and Armansky noticed that for the first time since she began her report, the client was showing more than a polite interest. He made a mental note that the Wennerström affair held a certain interest for Frode. Correction, Armansky thought at once, Frode was not interested in the Wennerström affair—it was when Salander hinted that Blomkvist was set up that Frode reacted.

"How do you mean, exactly?" Frode said.

"It's speculation on my part, but I'm convinced that someone tricked him."

"And what makes you think so?"

"Everything in Blomkvist's background shows that he's a very careful reporter. Every controversial revelation he published before was always well documented. I went to court one day and listened. He seemed to have given up without a fight. That doesn't accord with his character at all. If we are to believe the court, he made up a story about Wennerström without a shred of evidence and published it like some sort of journalistic suicide bomber. That's simply not Blomkvist's style."

"So what do you think happened?"

"I can only guess. Blomkvist believed in his story, but something happened along the way and the information turned out to be false. This in turn means that the source was someone he trusted or that someone deliberately fed him false information—which sounds improbably complicated. The alternative is that he was subjected to such a serious threat that he threw in the towel and would rather be seen as an incompetent idiot than fight back. But I'm just speculating, as I said."

When Salander made an attempt to continue her account, Frode held up his hand. He sat for a moment, drumming his fingers on the armrest of his chair before he hesitantly turned to her again.

"If we should decide to engage you to unravel the truth in the Wennerström affair . . . how much chance is there that you'd find out anything?"

"I can't answer that. There may not be anything to find."

"But would you be willing to make an attempt?"

She shrugged. "It's not my place to decide. I work for Herr Armansky, and he decides what jobs he wants to assign to me. And then it depends what sort of information you're looking for."

"Let me put it this way . . . and I take it that we're speaking in confidence?" Armansky nodded. "I don't know anything about this particular matter, but I do know beyond any doubt that in other situations Wennerström has acted dishonestly. The Wennerström case has seriously affected Mikael Blomkvist's life, and I have an interest in discerning whether there's anything in your speculations."

The conversation had taken an unexpected turn, and Armansky was instantly on the alert. What Frode was asking was for Milton Security to poke around in a case that had already been concluded. A case in which there may have been some sort of threat to the man Blomkvist, and if they took this on, Milton would risk colliding with Wennerström's regiment of lawyers. Armansky was not in the least comforted by the thought of turning Salander loose in such a situation, like a cruise missile out of control.

It was not merely a matter of concern for the company. Salander had made plain that she did not want Armansky to act as some sort of worried stepfather, and since their agreement he had been careful never to behave like one, but in reality he would never stop worrying about her. He sometimes caught himself comparing Salander to his daughters. He considered himself a good father who did not interfere unnecessarily in their lives. But he knew that he would not tolerate it if his daughters behaved like Salander or lived the life she led.

In the depths of his Croatian—or possibly Bosnian or Armenian—heart he had never been able to shed the conviction that Salander's life was heading for disaster. She seemed the perfect victim for anyone who wished her ill, and he dreaded the morning he would be awakened by the news that someone had done her harm.

"An investigation of this kind could get expensive," Armansky said, issuing a warning so as to gauge the seriousness of Frode's inquiry.

"Then we'll set a ceiling," Frode said. "I don't demand the impossible, but it's obvious that your colleague, just as you assured me, is exceedingly competent."

"Salander?" Armansky said, turning to her with a raised eyebrow.

"I'm not working on anything else right now."

"OK. But I want us to be in agreement about the constraints of the job. Let's hear the rest of your report."

"There isn't much more apart from his private life. In 1986 he married Monica Abrahamsson and the same year they had a daughter, Pernilla. The marriage didn't last; they were divorced in 1991. Abrahamsson has remarried, but they seem to be friends still. The daughter lives with her mother and doesn't see Blomkvist often."

Frode asked for more coffee and then turned to Salander.

"You said that everyone has secrets. Did you find any?"

"I meant that all people have things they consider to be private and that they don't go around airing in public. Blomkvist is obviously a big hit with women. He's had several love affairs and a great many casual flings. But one person has kept turning up in his life over the years, and it's an unusual relationship."

"In what way?"

"Erika Berger, editor in chief of *Millennium*: upper-class girl, Swedish mother, Belgian father resident in Sweden. Berger and Blomkvist met in journalism school and have had an on-and-off relationship ever since."

"That may not be so unusual," Frode said.

"No, possibly not. But Berger happens to be married to the artist Greger Beckman, a minor celebrity who has done a lot of terrible things in public venues."

"So she's unfaithful."

"Beckman knows about their relationship. It's a situation apparently accepted by all parties concerned. Sometimes she sleeps at Blomkvist's and sometimes at home. I don't know exactly how it works, but it was probably a contributing factor to the breakup of Blomkvist's marriage to Abrahamsson."

CHAPTER 3

Friday, December 20– Saturday, December 21

Erika Berger looked up quizzically when an apparently freezing Blomkvist came into the editorial office. *Millennium*'s offices were in the centre of the trendy section of Götgatan, above the offices of Greenpeace. The rent was actually a bit too steep for the magazine, but they had all agreed to keep the space.

She glanced at the clock. It was 5:10, and darkness had fallen over Stockholm long before. She had been expecting him around lunchtime.

"I'm sorry," he said before she managed to say anything. "But I was feeling the weight of the verdict and didn't feel like talking. I went for a long walk to think things over."

"I heard the verdict on the radio. *She* from TV4 called and wanted a comment."

"What'd you say?"

"Something to the effect that we were going to read the judgement carefully before we make any statements. So I said nothing. And my opinion still holds: it's the wrong strategy. We come off looking weak with the media. They will run something on TV this evening."

Blomkvist looked glum.

"How are you doing?"

Blomkvist shrugged and plopped down in his favourite armchair next to the window in Erika's office. The decor was spartan, with a desk and functional bookcases and cheap office furniture. All of it was from IKEA apart from the two comfortable and extravagant armchairs and a small end table—a concession to my upbringing, she liked to say. She would sit reading in one of the armchairs with her feet tucked underneath her when she wanted to get away from the desk. Blomkvist looked down on Götgatan, where people were hurrying by in the dark. Christmas shopping was in full swing.

"I suppose it'll pass," he said. "But right now it feels as if I've got myself a very raw deal."

"Yes, I can imagine. It's the same for all of us. Janne Dahlman went home early today."

"I assume he wasn't over the moon about the verdict."

"He's not the most positive person anyway."

Mikael shook his head. For the past nine months Dahlman had been managing editor. He had started there just as the Wennerström affair got going, and he found himself on an editorial staff in crisis mode. Blomkvist tried to remember what their reasoning had been when he and Berger decided to hire him. He was competent, of course, and had worked at the TT news bureau, the evening papers, and Eko on the radio. But he apparently did not like sailing against the wind. During the past year Blomkvist had often regretted that they had hired Dahlman, who had an enervating habit of looking at everything in as negative a light as possible.

"Have you heard from Christer?" Blomkvist asked without taking his eyes off the street.

Christer Malm was the art director and designer of *Millennium*. He was also part owner of the magazine together with Berger and Blomkvist, but he was on a trip abroad with his boyfriend.

"He called to say hello."

"He'll have to be the one who takes over as publisher."

"Lay off, Micke. As publisher you have to count on being punched in the nose every so often. It's part of the job description."

"You're right about that. But I was the one who wrote the article that was published in a magazine of which I also happen to be the publisher. That makes everything look different all of a sudden. Then it's a matter of bad judgement."

Berger felt that the disquiet she had been carrying with her all day was about to explode. In the weeks before the trial started, Blomkvist had been walking around under a black cloud. But she had never seen him as gloomy and dejected as he seemed to be now in the hour of his defeat. She walked to his side of the desk and sat on his lap, straddling him, and put her arms round his neck.

"Mikael, listen to me. We both know exactly how it happened. I'm as much to blame as you are. We simply have to ride out the storm."

"There isn't any storm to ride out. As far as the media are concerned, the verdict means that I've been shot in the back of the head. I can't stay on as the publisher of *Millennium*. The vital thing is to maintain the magazine's credibility, to stop the bleeding. You know that as well as I do."

"If you think I intend to let you take the rap all by yourself, then you haven't learned a damn thing about me in the years we've worked together."

"I know how you operate, Ricky. You're 100 percent loyal to your colleagues. If you had to choose, you'd keep fighting against Wennerström's lawyers until your credibility was gone too. We have to be smarter than that."

"And you think it's smart to jump ship and make it look as if I sacked you?"

"If *Millennium* is going to survive, it depends on you now. Christer is great, but he's just a nice guy who knows about images and layout and doesn't have a clue about street fighting with billionaires. It's just not his thing. I'm going to have to disappear for a while, as publisher, reporter, and board member. Wennerström knows that I know what he did, and I'm absolutely sure that as long as I'm anywhere near *Millennium* he's going to try to ruin us."

"So why not publish everything we know? Sink or swim?"

"Because we can't prove a damn thing, and right now I have no credibility at all. Let's accept that Wennerström won this round."

"OK, I'll fire you. What are you going to do?"

"I need a break, to be honest. I'm burned right out. I'm going to take some time for myself for a while, some of it in prison. Then we'll see."

Berger put her arms around him and pulled his head down to her breasts. She hugged him hard.

"Want some company tonight?" she said.

Blomkvist nodded.

"Good. I've already told Greger I'm at your place tonight."

The street lights reflecting off the corners of the windows were all that lit the room. When Berger fell asleep sometime after 2:00 in the morning, Blomkvist lay awake studying her profile in the dimness. The covers were down around her waist, and he watched her breasts slowly rising and falling. He was relaxed, and the anxious knot in his stomach had eased. She had that effect on him. She always had had. And he knew that he had the same effect on her.

Twenty years, he thought. That's how long it had been. As far as he was concerned, they could go on sleeping together for another two decades. At least. They had never seriously tried to hide their relationship, even when it led to awkwardness in their dealings with other people.

They had met at a party when they were both in their second year at journalism school. Before they said goodnight they had exchanged telephone numbers. They both knew that they would end up in bed together, and in less than a week they realised this conviction without telling their respective partners.

Blomkvist was sure that it was not the old-fashioned kind of love that leads to a shared home, a shared mortgage, Christmas trees, and children. During the eighties, when they were not bound by other relationships, they had talked of moving in together. He had wanted to, but Erika always backed out at the last minute. It wouldn't work, she said, they would risk what they had if they fell in love too. Blomkvist had often wondered whether it were possible to be more possessed by desire for any other woman. The fact was that they functioned well together, and they had a connection as addictive as heroin.

Sometimes they were together so often that it felt as though they really were a couple; sometimes weeks and months would go by before they saw each other. But even as alcoholics are drawn to the state liquor store after a stint on the wagon, they always came back to each other.

Inevitably it did not work in the long run. That kind of relationship was almost bound to cause pain. They had both left broken promises and unhappy lovers behind—his own marriage had collapsed because he could not stay away from Erika Berger. He had never lied about his feelings for her to his wife, Monica, but she had thought it would end when they married and their daughter was born. And Berger had almost simultaneously married Greger Beckman. Blomkvist too had thought it would end, and for the first years of his marriage he and Berger had only seen each other professionally. Then they started *Millennium* and within a few weeks all their good intentions had dissolved, and one late evening they had furious sex on her desk. That led to a troublesome period in which Blomkvist wanted very much to live with his family and see his daughter grow up, but at the same time he was helplessly drawn to Berger. Just as Salander had guessed, it was his continual infidelity that drove his wife to leave.

Strangely enough, Beckman seemed to accept their relationship. Berger had always been open about her feelings for Mikael, and she told her husband as soon as they started having sex again. Maybe it took the soul of an artist to handle such a situation, someone so wrapped up in his own creativity, or possibly just wrapped up in himself, that he did not rebel when his wife slept with another man. She even divided up her holiday so she could spend two weeks with her lover in his summer cabin at Sandhamn. Blomkvist did not think very highly of Beckman, and he had never understood Berger's love for him. But he was glad that he accepted that she could love two men at the same time.

Blomkvist could not sleep, and at 4:00 he gave up. He went to the kitchen and read the court judgement one more time from beginning to end. Having the document in his hand he had a sense that there had been something almost fateful about the meeting at Arholma. He could never be sure whether Lindberg had told him the details of Wennerström's swindle simply for the sake of a good story between toasts in the privacy of his boat's cabin or whether he had really wanted the story to be made public.

He tended to believe the first. But it may have been that Lindberg, for his own personal or business reasons, had wanted to damage Wennerström, and he had seized the opportunity of having a captive journalist on board. Lindberg had been sober enough to insist on Blomkvist treating him as an anonymous source. From that moment Lindberg could say what he liked, because his friend would never be able to disclose his source.

If the meeting at Arholma had been a set-up, then Lindberg could not have played his role better. But the meeting had to have happened by chance.

Lindberg could have had no notion of the extent of Blomkvist's contempt for people like Wennerström. For all that, after years of study, he was privately convinced that there was not a single bank director or celebrity corporate executive who wasn't also a cretin.

Blomkvist had never heard of Lisbeth Salander and was happily innocent of her report delivered earlier that day, but had he listened to it he would have nodded in agreement when she spoke of his loathing for bean counters, saying that it was not a manifestation of his left-wing political radicalism. Mikael was not uninterested in politics, but he was extremely sceptical of political "isms." He had voted only once in a parliamentary election—in 1982—and then he had hesitantly plumped for the Social Democrats, there being nothing in his imagination worse than three years more with Gösta Bohman as finance minister and Thorbjörn Fälldin (or possibly Ola Ullsten) as prime minister. So he had voted for Olof Palme, and got instead the assassination of his prime minister plus the Bofors scandal and Ebbe Carlsson.

His contempt for his fellow financial journalists was based on something that in his opinion was as plain as morality. The equation was simple. A bank director who blows millions on foolhardy speculations should not keep his job. A managing director who plays shell company games should do time. A slum landlord who forces young people to pay through the nose and under the table for a one-room apartment with shared toilet should be hung out to dry.

The job of the financial journalist was to examine the sharks who created interest crises and speculated away the savings of small investors, to scrutinise company boards with the same merciless zeal with which political reporters pursue the tiniest steps out of line of ministers and members of Parliament. He could not for the life of him understand why so many influential financial reporters treated mediocre financial whelps like rock stars.

These recalcitrant views had time after time brought him into conflict with his peers. Borg, for one, was going to be an enemy for life. His taking on a role of social critic had actually transformed him into a prickly guest on TV sofas—he was always the one invited to comment whenever any CEO was caught with a golden parachute worth billions.

Mikael had no trouble imagining that champagne bottles had been uncorked in some newspapers' back rooms that evening.

Erika had the same attitude to the journalist's role as he did. Even when they were in journalism school they had amused themselves by imagining a magazine with just such a mission statement.

Erika was the best boss Mikael could imagine. She was an organiser who could handle employees with warmth and trust but who at the same time wasn't afraid of confrontation and could be very tough when necessary. Above all, she had an icy gut feeling when it came to making decisions about the contents of the upcoming issue. She and Mikael often had differing views and could have healthy arguments, but they also had unwavering confidence in each other, and together they made an unbeatable team. He did the field work of tracking down the story, while she packaged and marketed it.

Millennium was their mutual creation, but it would never have become reality without her talent for digging up financing. It was the working-class guy and the upper-class girl in a beautiful union. Erika came from old money. She had put up the initial seed money and then talked both her father and various acquaintances into investing considerable sums in the project.

Mikael had often wondered why Erika had set her sights on *Millennium*. True, she was a part owner—the majority partner, in fact—and editor in chief of her own magazine, which gave her prestige and the control over publicity that she could hardly have obtained in any other job. Unlike Mikael, she had concentrated on television after journalism school. She was tough, looked fantastic on camera, and could hold her own with the competition. She also had good contacts in the bureaucracy. If she had stuck to it, she would undoubtedly have had a managerial job at one of the TV channels at a considerably higher salary than she paid herself now.

Berger had also convinced Christer Malm to buy into the magazine. He was an exhibitionist gay celebrity who sometimes appeared with his boyfriend in "at home with" articles. The interest in him began when he moved in with Arnold Magnusson, an actor with a background at the Royal Dramatic Theatre who had made a serious breakthrough when he played himself in a docu-soap. Christer and Arn had then become a media item.

At thirty-six, Malm was a sought-after professional photographer and designer who gave *Millennium* a modern look. He ran his business from an office on the same floor as *Millennium*, and he did graphic design one week in every month.

The *Millennium* staff consisted of three full-time employees, a full-time trainee, and two part-timers. It was not a lucrative affair, but the magazine broke even, and the circulation and advertising revenue had increased gradually but steadily. Until today the magazine was known for its frank and reliable editorial style.

Now the situation would in all probability be changing. Blomkvist read through the press release which he and Berger had drafted and which had quickly been converted to a wire service story from TT that was already up on *Aftonbladet*'s website.

CONVICTED REPORTER LEAVES MILLENNIUM

Stockholm (T.T.). Journalist Mikael Blomkvist is leaving his post as publisher of the magazine *Millennium,* reports editor in chief and majority shareholder Erika Berger.

Blomkvist is leaving *Millennium* of his own choice. "He's exhausted after the drama of recent months and needs time off," says Berger, who will take over the role of publisher.

Blomkvist was one of the founders of *Millennium,* started in 1990. Berger does not think that the magazine will suffer in the wake of the so-called "Wennerström affair."

The magazine will come out as usual next month, says Berger. "Mikael Blomkvist has played a major role in the magazine's development, but now we're turning a new page."

Berger states that she regards the Wennerström affair as the result of a series of unfortunate circumstances. She regrets the nuisance to which Hans-Erik Wennerström was subjected. Blomkvist could not be reached for comment.

"It makes me mad," Berger said when the press release was emailed out. "Most people are going to think that you're an idiot and I'm a bitch who's taking the opportunity to sack you."

"At least our friends will have something new to laugh about." Blomkvist tried to make light of it; she was not the least amused.

"I don't have a plan B, but I think we're making a mistake," she said.

"It's the only way out. If the magazine collapses, all our years of work will have been in vain. We've already taken a beating on the ads revenue. How did it go with the computer company, by the way?"

She sighed. "They told me this morning that they didn't want to take space in the next issue."

"Wennerström has a chunk of stock in that company, so it's no accident."

"We can scare up some new clients. Wennerström may be a big wheel, but he doesn't own everything in Sweden, and we have our contacts."

Blomkvist put an arm around her and pulled her close.

"Some day we're going to nail Herr Wennerström so hard Wall Street is going to jump out of its socks. But today *Millennium* has to get out of the spotlight."

"I know all that, but I don't like coming across as a fucking bitch, and you're being forced into a disgusting situation if we pretend that there's some sort of division between you and me."

"Ricky, as long as you and I trust each other we've got a chance. We have to play it by ear, and right now it's time to retreat."

She reluctantly admitted that there was a depressing logic to what he said.

CHAPTER 4

Monday, December 23–Thursday, December 26

Berger stayed over the weekend. They got up only to go to the bathroom or to get something to eat, but they had not only made love. They had lain head to foot for hours and talked about the future, weighing up the possibilities, and the odds. When dawn came on Monday morning it was the day before Christmas Eve and she kissed him goodbye—until next time—and drove home.

Blomkvist spent Monday washing dishes and cleaning the apartment, then walking down to the office and clearing out his desk. He had no intention of breaking ties with the magazine, but he had eventually convinced Berger that he had to be separated from the magazine for a time. He would work from home.

The office was closed for the Christmas holidays and all his colleagues were gone. He was weeding through trays of papers and packing books in cartons to take away when the telephone rang.

"I'm looking for Mikael Blomkvist," said a hopeful but unfamiliar voice on the line.

"Speaking."

"Forgive me for bothering you like this unannounced, so to speak. My name is Dirch Frode." Blomkvist noted the name and the time. "I'm a lawyer, and I represent a client who would very much like to have a talk with you."

"That's fine, please ask your client to call me."

"I mean that he wants to meet with you in person."

"OK, make an appointment and send him up to the office. But you'd better hurry; I'm clearing out my desk right now."

"My client would like you to visit him in Hedestad—it's only three hours by train."

Blomkvist pushed a filing tray aside. The media have the ability to attract the craziest people to call in perfectly absurd tips. Every newsroom in the world gets updates from UFOlogists, graphologists, scientologists, paranoiacs, every sort of conspiracy theorist.

Blomkvist had once listened to a lecture by the writer Karl Alvar Nilsson at the ABF hall on the anniversary of the murder of Prime Minister Olof Palme. The lecture was serious, and in the audience were Lennart Bodström and other friends of Palme's. But a surprising number of amateur investigators had turned up. One of them was a woman in her forties who during the Q and A had taken the proffered microphone and then lowered her voice to a barely audible whisper. This alone heralded an interesting development, and nobody was surprised when the woman began by claiming, "I know who murdered Olof Palme." From the stage it was suggested somewhat ironically that if the woman had this information then it would be helpful if she shared it with the Palme investigation at once. She hurried to reply: "I can't," she said so softly it was almost impossible to hear. "It's too dangerous!"

Blomkvist wondered whether this Frode was another one of the truth-sayers who could reveal the secret mental hospital where Säpo, the Security Police, ran experiments on thought control.

"I don't make house calls," he said.

"I hope I can convince you to make an exception. My client is over eighty, and for him it would be too exhausting to come down to Stockholm. If you insist, we could certainly arrange something, but to tell you the truth, it would be preferable if you would be so kind . . ."

"Who is your client?"

"A person whose name I suspect you have heard in your work. Henrik Vanger."

Blomkvist leaned back in surprise. Henrik Vanger—of course he had heard of him. An industrialist and former head of the Vanger companies, once renowned in the fields of sawmills, mines, steel, metals, textiles. Vanger had been one of the really big fish in his day, with a reputation for being an honourable, old-fashioned patriarch who would not bend in a strong wind. A cornerstone of Swedish industry, one of the twenty-point stags of the old school, along with Matts Carlgren of MoDo and Hans Werthén at the old Electrolux. The backbone of industry in the welfare state, et cetera.

But the Vanger companies, still family-owned, had been racked in the past twenty-five years by reorganisations, stock-market crises, interest crises, competition from Asia, declining exports, and other nuisances which taken together had consigned the name Vanger to the backwater. The company was run today by Martin Vanger, whose name Blomkvist associated with a short, plump man with thick hair who occasionally flickered past on the TV screen. He did not know much about him. Henrik Vanger had been out of the picture for at least twenty years.

"Why does Henrik Vanger want to meet me?"

"I've been Herr Vanger's lawyer for many years, but he will have to tell you himself what he wants. On the other hand, I *can* say that Herr Vanger would like to discuss a possible job with you."

"Job? I don't have the slightest intention of going to work for the Vanger company. Is it a press secretary you need?"

"Not exactly. I don't know how to put it other than to say that Herr Vanger is exceedingly anxious to meet you and consult with you on a private matter."

"You couldn't get more equivocal, could you?"

"I beg your pardon for that. But is there any possibility of convincing you to pay a visit to Hedestad? Naturally we will pay all your expenses and a reasonable fee."

"Your call comes at rather an inconvenient time. I have quite a lot to take care of and . . . I suppose you've seen the headlines about me in the past few days."

"The Wennerström affair?" Frode chuckled. "Yes, that did have a certain amusement value. But to tell you the truth, it was the publicity surrounding the trial that caused Herr Vanger to take notice of you. He wants to offer you a freelance assignment. I'm only a messenger. What the matter concerns is something only he can explain."

"This is one of the odder calls I've had in a long time. Let me think about it. How can I reach you?"

Blomkvist sat looking at the disorder on his desk. He could not imagine what sort of job Vanger would want to offer him, but the lawyer had succeeded in arousing his curiosity.

He Googled the Vanger company. It might be in the backwaters but it seemed to be in the media almost daily. He saved a dozen company analyses and then searched for Frode, and Henrik and Martin Vanger.

Martin Vanger appeared diligent in his capacity as CEO of the Vanger Corporation. Frode kept a low profile; he was on the board of the Hedestad Country Club and active in the Rotary Club. Henrik Vanger appeared, with one exception, only in articles giving the background of the company. The *Hedestad Courier* had published a tribute to the former magnate on his eightieth birthday two years ago, and it included a short sketch. He put together a folder of fifty pages or so. Then finally he emptied his desk, sealed the cartons, and, having no idea whether he would come back, went home.

Salander spent Christmas Eve at the Äppelviken Nursing Home in Upplands-Väsby. She had brought presents: a bottle of eau de toilette by Dior and an English fruitcake from Åhléns department store. She drank coffee as she watched the forty-six-year-old woman who with clumsy fingers was trying to untie the knot on the ribbon. Salander had tenderness in her eyes, but that this strange woman was her mother never ceased to amaze her. She could recognise not the slightest resemblance in looks or nature.

Her mother gave up the struggle and looked helplessly at the package. It was not one of her better days. Salander pushed across the scissors that had been in plain sight on the table and her mother suddenly seemed to wake up.

"You must think I'm stupid."

"No, Mum. You're not stupid. But life is unfair."

"Have you seen your sister?"

"Not in a long time."

"She never comes."

"I know, Mum. She doesn't see me either."

"Are you working?"

"Yes. I'm doing fine."

"Where do you live? I don't even know where you live."

"I live in your old apartment on Lundagatan. I've lived there for several years. I had to take over the payments."

"In the summertime maybe I can come and see you."

"Of course. In the summertime."

Her mother at last got the Christmas present open and sniffed at the aroma, enchanted. "Thank you, Camilla," she said.

"Lisbeth. I'm Lisbeth."

Her mother looked embarrassed. Salander said that they should go to the TV room.

Blomkvist spent the hour of the Disney special on Christmas Eve with his daughter Pernilla at the home of his ex-wife, Monica, and her new husband in Sollentuna. After discussions with her mother they had agreed to give Pernilla an iPod, an MP3 player hardly bigger than a matchbox which could store her huge CD collection.

Father and daughter spent the time together in her room upstairs. Pernilla's parents were divorced when she was five, and she had had a new father since she was seven. Pernilla came to see him about once a month and had week-long holidays with him in Sandhamn. When they spent time together they usually got along well, but Blomkvist had let his daughter decide how often she wanted to see him, the more so after her mother remarried. There had been a couple of years in her early teens when contact almost stopped, and it was only in the past two years that she seemed to want to see him more often.

She had followed the trial in the firm belief that things were just as her father said: he was innocent, but he could not prove it.

She told him about a sort-of boyfriend who was in another class, and she surprised him by saying that she had joined a church. Blomkvist refrained from comment.

He was invited to stay for dinner but he was expected with his sister and her family out in the yuppie suburb of Stäket.

That morning he had also had an invitation to celebrate Christmas Eve with the Beckmans in Saltsjöbaden. He said no, but thank you, certain that there was a limit to Beckman's indulgence and quite sure that he had no ambition to find out what that limit might be.

Instead he was knocking on the door where Annika Blomkvist, now Annika Giannini, lived with her Italian-born husband and their two children. With a platoon of her husband's relatives, they were about to carve the Christmas ham. During dinner he answered questions about the trial and received much well-meaning and quite useless advice.

The only one who had nothing to say about the verdict was his sister, although she was the only lawyer in the room. She had worked as clerk of a district court and as an assistant prosecutor for several years before she and three colleagues opened a law firm of their own with offices on Kungsholmen. She specialised in family law, and without Blomkvist having taken stock of its happening, his little sister began to appear in newspapers as representing battered or threatened women, and on panel discussions on TV as a feminist and women's rights advocate.

As he was helping her prepare the coffee, she put a hand on his shoulder and asked him how he was doing. He told her he felt as low as he had in life.

"Get yourself a real lawyer next time," she said.

"It probably wouldn't have helped in this case. But we'll talk it all the way through, Sis, some other time when all the dust is settled."

She gave him a hug and kissed him on the cheek before they carried out the Christmas cake and the coffee. Then Blomkvist excused himself and asked to use the telephone in the kitchen.

He called the lawyer in Hedestad and could hear there too the buzz of voices in the background.

"Merry Christmas," Frode said. "Dare I hope you have made up your mind?"

"I really don't have any immediate plans and I am curious to know more. I'll come up the day after Christmas if that suits you."

"Excellent, excellent. I am incredibly pleased. You will forgive me, I've got children and grandchildren visiting and can hardly hear myself think. Can I call you tomorrow to agree on a time? Where can I reach you?"

Blomkvist regretted his decision even before he left for home, but by then it was too awkward to call and cancel. So on the morning of December 26 he was on the train heading north. He had a driver's license, but he had never felt the need to own a car.

Frode was right, it was not a long journey. After Uppsala came the string of small industrial towns along the Norrland coast. Hedestad was one of the smaller ones, a little more than an hour north of Gävle.

On Christmas night there had been a big snowstorm, but the skies had now cleared and the air was ice-cold when Blomkvist alighted at Hedestad. He realised at once that he wasn't wearing enough clothes for winter in Norrland. Frode knew what he looked like and kindly collected him from the platform and led him straight to the warmth of his Mercedes. In the centre of Hedestad, snow clearing was in full swing, and Frode wove his careful way through the narrow streets. High banks of snow presented a picturesque contrast to Stockholm. The town seemed almost like another planet, yet he was only a little more than three hours from Sergels Torg in downtown Stockholm. He stole a glance at the lawyer: an angular face with sparse, bristly white hair and thick glasses perched on an impressive nose.

"First time in Hedestad?" Frode said.

Blomkvist nodded.

"It's an old industrial town with a harbour. Population of only 24,000. But people like living here. Herr Vanger lives in Hedeby—at the southern edge of the town."

"Do you live here too?"

"I do now. I was born in Skåne down south, but I started working for Vanger right after I graduated in 1962. I'm a corporate lawyer, and over the years Herr Vanger and I became friends. Today I'm officially retired, and Herr Vanger is my only client. He's retired too, of course, and doesn't need my services very often."

"Only to scrape up journalists with ruined reputations."

"Don't sell yourself short. You're not the first one to lose a match against Hans-Erik Wennerström."

Blomkvist turned to Frode, unsure how to read that reply.

"Does this invitation have anything to do with Wennerström?" he said.

"No," said Frode. "But Herr Vanger is not remotely in Wennerström's circle of friends, and he followed the trial with interest. He wants to meet you to discuss a wholly different matter."

"Which you don't want to tell me about."

"Which it isn't my place to tell you about. We have arranged it so that you can spend the night at Herr Vanger's house. If you would rather not do that, we can book you a room in the Grand Hotel in town."

"I might be taking the evening train back to Stockholm."

The road into Hedeby was still unploughed, and Frode manoeuvred the car down frozen tyre ruts. The old town centre consisted of houses along the Gulf of Bothnia, and around them larger, more modern homes. The town began on the mainland and spilled across a bridge to a hilly island. On the mainland side of the bridge stood a small, white stone church, and across the street glowed an old-fashioned neon sign that read SUSANNE'S BRIDGE CAFÉ AND BAKERY. Frode drove about a hundred yards farther and turned left on to a newly shovelled courtyard in front of a stone building. The farmhouse was too small to be called a manor, but it was considerably larger than the rest of the houses in the settlement. This was the master's domain.

"This is the Vanger farm," Frode said. "Once it was full of life and hubbub, but today only Henrik and a housekeeper live there. There are plenty of guest rooms."

They got out. Frode pointed north.

"Traditionally the person who leads the Vanger concern lives here, but Martin Vanger wanted something more modern, so he built his house on the point there."

Blomkvist looked around and wondered what insane impulse he had satisfied by accepting Frode's invitation. He decided that if humanly possible he would return to Stockholm that evening. A stone stairway led to the entry, but before they reached it the door was opened. He immediately recognised Henrik Vanger from the photograph posted on the Internet.

In the pictures there he was younger, but he looked surprisingly vigorous for eighty-two: a wiry body with a rugged, weather-beaten face and thick grey hair combed straight back. He wore neatly pressed dark trousers, a white shirt, and a well-worn brown casual jacket. He had a narrow moustache and thin steel-rimmed glasses.

"I'm Henrik Vanger," he said. "Thank you for agreeing to visit me."

"Hello. It was a surprising invitation."

"Come inside where it's warm. I've arranged a guest room

for you. Would you like to freshen up? We'll be having dinner a little later. And this is Anna Nygren, who looks after me."

Blomkvist shook hands with a short, stout woman in her sixties. She took his coat and hung it in a hall cupboard. She offered him a pair of slippers because of the draught.

Mikael thanked her and then turned to Henrik Vanger. "I'm not sure that I shall be staying for dinner. It depends on what this game is all about."

Vanger exchanged a glance with Frode. There was an understanding between the two men that Blomkvist could not interpret.

"I think I'll take this opportunity to leave you two alone," said Frode. "I have to go home and discipline the grandkids before they tear the house down."

He turned to Mikael.

"I live on the right, just across the bridge. You can walk there in five minutes; the third house towards the water down from the bakery. If you need me, just telephone."

Blomkvist reached into his jacket pocket and turned on a tape recorder. He had no idea what Vanger wanted, but after the past twelve months of havoc with Wennerström he needed a precise record of all strange occurrences anywhere near him, and an unlooked-for invitation to Hedestad came into that category.

Vanger patted Frode on the shoulder in farewell and closed the front door before turning his attention to Blomkvist.

"I'll get right to the point in that case. This is no game. I ask you to listen to what I have to say and then make up your mind. You're a journalist, and I want to give you a freelance assignment. Anna has served coffee upstairs in my office."

The office was a rectangle of more than 1,300 square feet. One wall was dominated by a floor-to-ceiling bookshelf thirty feet long containing a remarkable assortment of literature: biographies, history, business and industry, and A4 binders. The books were arranged in no apparent order. It looked like a bookshelf that was used. The opposite wall was dominated by a desk of dark oak. On the wall behind the desk was a large collection of pressed flowers in neat meticulous rows.

Through the window in the gable the desk had a view of the bridge and the church. There was a sofa and coffee table where the housekeeper had set out a thermos, rolls, and pastries.

Vanger gestured towards the tray, but Blomkvist pretended not to see; instead he made a tour of the room, first studying the bookshelf and then the wall of framed flowers. The desk was orderly, only a few papers in one heap. At its edge was a silver-framed photograph of a dark-haired girl, beautiful but with a mischievous look; a young woman on her way to becoming dangerous, he thought. It was apparently a confirmation portrait that had faded over the years it had been there.

"Do you remember her, Mikael?" Vanger said.

"Remember?"

"Yes, you met her. And actually you have been in this room before."

Blomkvist turned and shook his head.

"No, how could you remember? I knew your father. I hired Kurt first as an installer and machinist several times in the fifties and sixties. He was a talented man. I tried to persuade him to keep studying and become an engineer. You were here the whole summer of 1963, when we put new machinery in the paper mill in Hedestad. It was hard to find a place for your family to live, so we solved it by letting you live in the wooden house across the road. You can see it from the window."

Vanger picked up the photograph.

"This is Harriet Vanger, granddaughter of my brother Richard. She took care of you many times that summer. You were two, going on three. Maybe you were already three then—I don't recall. She was thirteen."

"I am sorry, but I don't have the least recollection of what you're telling me." Blomkvist could not even be sure that Vanger was telling the truth.

"I understand. But I remember you. You used to run around everywhere on the farm with Harriet in tow. I could hear your shrieks whenever you fell. I remember I gave you a toy once, a yellow, sheet-metal tractor that I had played with myself as a boy. You were crazy about it. I think that was the colour."

Blomkvist felt a chill inside. The yellow tractor he did remember. When he was older it had stood on a shelf in his bedroom.

"Do you remember that toy?"

"I do. And you will be amused to know that the tractor is still alive and well, at the Toy Museum in Stockholm. They put out a call for old original toys ten years ago."

"Really?" Vanger chuckled with delight. "Let me show you . . ."

The old man went over to the bookshelf and pulled a photograph album from one of the lower shelves. Blomkvist noticed that he had difficulty bending over and had to brace himself on the bookshelf when he straightened up. He laid the album on the coffee table. He knew what he was looking for: a black-and-white snapshot in which the photographer's shadow showed in the bottom left corner. In the foreground was a fair-haired boy in shorts, staring at the camera with a slightly anxious expression.

"This is you. Your parents are sitting on the garden bench in the background. Harriet is partly hidden by your mother, and the boy to the left of your father is Harriet's brother, Martin, who runs the Vanger company today."

Blomkvist's mother was obviously pregnant—his sister was on the way. He looked at the photograph with mixed feelings as Vanger poured coffee and pushed over the plate of rolls.

"Your father is dead, I know. Is your mother still alive?"

"She died three years ago," Blomkvist said.

"She was a nice woman. I remember her very well."

"But I'm sure you didn't ask me to come here to talk about old times you had with my parents."

"You're right. I've been working on what I wanted to say to you for several days, but now that you're actually here I don't quite know where to begin. I suppose you did some research, so you know that I once wielded some influence in Swedish industry and the job market. Today I'm an old man who will probably die fairly soon, and death perhaps is an excellent starting point for our conversation."

Blomkvist took a swallow of black coffee—plainly boiled in a pan in true Norrland style—and wondered where this was going to lead.

"I have pain in my hip and long walks are a thing of the past. One day you'll discover for yourself how strength seeps away, but I'm neither morbid nor senile. I'm not obsessed by death, but I'm at an age when I have to accept that my time is about up. You want to close the accounts and take care of unfinished business. Do you understand what I mean?"

Blomkvist nodded. Vanger spoke in a steady voice, and Blomkvist had already decided that the old man was neither senile nor irrational. "I'm mostly curious about why I'm here," he said again.

"Because I want to ask for your help with this closing of accounts."

"Why me? What makes you think I'd be able to help you?"

"Because as I was thinking about hiring someone, your name cropped up in the news. I knew who you were, of course. And maybe it's because you sat on my knee when you were a little fellow. Don't misunderstand me." He waved the thought away.

"I don't look to you to help me for sentimental reasons. It was just that I had the impulse to contact you specifically."

Mikael gave a friendly laugh. "Well, I don't remember being perched on your knee. But how could you make the connection? That was in the early sixties."

"You misunderstood me. Your family moved to Stockholm when your father got the job as the workshop foreman at Zarinder's Mechanical. I was the one who got him the job. I knew he was a good worker. I used to see him over the years when I had business with Zarinder's. We weren't close friends, but we would chat for a while. The last time I saw him was the year before he died, and he told me then that you had got into journalism school. He was extremely proud. Then you became famous with the story of the bank robber gang. I've followed your career and read many of your articles over the years. As a matter of fact, I read *Millennium* quite often."

"OK, I'm with you, but what is it exactly that you want me to do?"

Vanger looked down at his hands, then sipped his coffee, as if he needed a pause before he could at last begin to broach what he wanted.

"Before I get started, Mikael, I'd like to make an agreement with you. I want you to do two things for me. One is a pretext and the other is my real objective."

"What form of agreement?"

"I'm going to tell you a story in two parts. The first is about the Vanger family. That's the pretext. It's a long, dark story, and I'll try to stick to the unvarnished truth. The second part of the story deals with my actual objective. You'll probably think some of the story is . . . crazy. What I want is for you to hear me out—about what I want you to do and also what I am offering—before you make up your mind whether to take on the job or not."

Blomkvist sighed. Obviously Vanger was not going to let him go in time to catch the afternoon train. He was sure that if he called Frode to ask for a lift to the station, the car would somehow refuse to start in the cold.

The old man must have thought long and hard how he was going to hook him. Blomkvist had the feeling that every last thing that had happened since he arrived was staged: the introductory surprise that as a child he had met his host, the picture of his parents in the album, and the emphasis on the fact that his father and Vanger had been friends, along with the flattery that the old man knew who Mikael Blomkvist was and that he had been following his career for years from a distance. . . . No doubt it had a core of truth, but it was also pretty elementary psychology. Vanger was a practised manipulator—how else had he become one of Sweden's leading industrialists?

Blomkvist decided that Vanger wanted him to do something that he was not going to have the slightest desire to do. He had only to wrest from him what this was and then say no thank you. And just possibly be in time to catch the afternoon train.

"Forgive me, Herr Vanger," he said, "I've been here already for twenty minutes. I'll give you exactly thirty minutes more to tell me what you want. Then I'm calling a taxi and going home."

For a moment the mask of the good-natured patriarch slipped, and Blomkvist could detect the ruthless captain of industry from his days of power confronted by a setback. His mouth curled in a grim smile.

"I understand."

"You don't have to beat around the bush with me. Tell me what you want me to do, so that I can decide whether I want to do it or not."

"So if I can't convince you in half an hour then I wouldn't be able to do it in a month either—that's what you think."

"Something along that line."

"But my story is long and complicated."

"Shorten and simplify it. That's what we do in journalism. Twenty-nine minutes."

Vanger held up a hand. "Enough. I get your point. But it's never good psychology to exaggerate. I need somebody who can do research and think critically, but who also has integrity. I think you have it, and that's not flattery. A good journalist ought to possess these qualities, and I read your book *The Knights Templar* with great interest. It's true that I picked you because I knew your father and because I know who you are. If I understood the matter correctly, you left your magazine as a result of the Wennerström affair. Which means that you have no job at the moment, and probably you're in a tight financial spot."

"So you might be able to exploit my predicament, is that it?"

"Perhaps. But Mikael—if I may call you Mikael?—I won't lie to you. I'm too old for that. If you don't like what I say, you can tell me to jump in the lake. Then I'll have to find someone else to work with me."

"OK, tell me what this job involves."

"How much do you know about the Vanger family?"

"Well, only what I managed to read on the Net since Frode called me on Monday. In your day the Vanger Corporation was one of the most important industrial firms in Sweden; today it's somewhat diminished. Martin Vanger runs it. I know quite a bit more, but what are you getting at?"

"Martin is . . . he's a good man but basically he's a fair-weather sailor. He's unsuited to be the managing director of a company in crisis. He wants to modernise and specialise—which is good thinking—but he can't push through his ideas and his financial management is weak too. Twenty-five years ago the Vanger concern was a serious competitor to the Wallenberg Group. We had forty thousand employees in Sweden. Today many of these jobs are in Korea or Brazil. We are down to about ten thousand employees and in a year or two—if Martin doesn't get some wind into his sails—we'll have five thousand, primarily in small manufacturing industries, and the Vanger companies will be consigned to the scrap heap of history."

Blomkvist nodded. He had come to roughly this conclusion on the basis of the pieces he had downloaded.

"The Vanger companies are still among the few family-held firms in the country. Thirty family members are minority shareholders. This has always been the strength of the corporation, but also our greatest weakness." Vanger paused and then said in a tone of mounting urgency, "Mikael, you can ask questions later, but I want you to take me at my word when I say that I detest most of the members of my family. They are for the most part thieves, misers, bullies, and incompetents. I ran the company for thirty-five years—almost all the time in the midst of relentless bickering. They were my worst enemies, far worse than competing companies or the government.

"I said that I wanted to commission you to do two things. First, I want you to write a history or biography of the Vanger family. For simplicity's sake, we can call it my autobiography. I will put my journals and archives at your disposal. You will have access to my innermost thoughts and you can publish all the dirt you dig up. I think this story will make Shakespeare's tragedies read like light family entertainment."

"Why?"

"Why do I want to publish a scandalous history of the Vanger family? Or why do I ask you to write it?"

"Both, I suppose."

"To tell you the truth, I don't care whether the book is ever published. But I do think that the story should be written, if only in a single copy that you deliver directly to the Royal Library. I want this story to be there for posterity when I die. My motive is the simplest imaginable: revenge."

"What do you want to revenge?"

"I'm proud that my name is a byword for a man who keeps his word and remembers his promises. I've never played political games. I've never had problems negotiating with trade unions. Even Prime Minister Erlander had respect for me in his day. For me it was a matter of ethics; I was responsible for the livelihoods of thousands of people, and I cared about my employees. Oddly enough, Martin has the same attitude, even though he's a very different person. He too has tried to do the right thing. Sadly Martin and I are rare exceptions in our family. There are many reasons why the Vanger Corporation is on the ropes today, but one of the key ones is the short-termism and greed of my relatives. If you accept the assignment, I'll explain how my family went about torpedoing the firm."

"I won't lie to you either," Blomkvist said. "Researching and writing a book like this would take months. I don't have the motivation or the energy to do it."

"I believe I can talk you into it."

"I doubt it. But you said there were two things. The book is the pretext. What is the real objective?"

Vanger stood up, laboriously again, and took the photograph of Harriet Vanger from the desk. He set it down in front of Blomkvist.

"While you write the biography I want you to scrutinise the family with the eyes of a journalist. It will also give you an alibi for poking around in the family history. What I want is for you to solve a mystery. That's your real assignment."

"What mystery?"

"Harriet was the granddaughter of my brother Richard. There were five brothers. Richard was the eldest, born in 1907. I was the youngest, born in 1920. I don't understand how God could create this flock of children who . . ." For several seconds Vanger lost the thread, immersed in his thoughts. Then he went on with new decisiveness. "Let me tell you about my brother Richard. Think of this as a small sample from the family chronicle I want you to write."

He poured more coffee for himself.

"In 1924, now seventeen, Richard was a fanatical nationalist and anti-Semite. He joined the Swedish National Socialist Freedom League, one of the first Nazi groups in Sweden. Isn't it fascinating that Nazis always manage to adopt the word *freedom*?"

Vanger pulled out another album and leafed through it until he found the page he was looking for. "Here's Richard with the veterinarian Birger Furugård, soon to become the leader of the so-called Furugård movement, the big Nazi movement of the early thirties. But Richard did not stay with him. He joined, a few years later, the Swedish Fascist Battle Organisation, the SFBO, and there he got to know Per Engdahl and others who would be the disgrace of the nation."

He turned the page in the album: Richard Vanger in uniform.

"He enlisted—against our father's wishes—and during the thirties he made his way through most of the Nazi groups in the country. Any sick conspiratorial association that existed, you can be sure his name was on their roster. In 1933 the Lindholm movement was formed, that is, the National Socialist Workers' Party. How well do you know the history of Swedish Nazism?"

"I'm no historian, but I've read a few books."

"In 1939 the Second World War began, and in 1940 the Winter War in Finland. A large number of the Lindholm movement joined as Finland volunteers. Richard was one of them and by then a captain in the Swedish army. He was killed in February 1940—just before the peace treaty with the Soviet Union—and thereby became a martyr in the Nazi movement and had a battle group named after him. Even now a handful of idiots gather at a cemetery in Stockholm on the anniversary of his death to honour him."

"I understand."

"In 1926, when he was nineteen, he was going out with a woman called Margareta, the daughter of a teacher in Falun. They met in some political context and had a relationship which resulted in a son, Gottfried, who was born in 1927. The couple married when the boy was born. During the first half of the thirties, my brother sent his wife and child here to Hedestad while he was stationed with his regiment in Gävle. In his free time he travelled around and did proselytising for Nazism. In 1936 he had a huge fight with my father which resulted in my father cutting him off. After that Richard had to make his own living. He moved with his family to Stockholm and lived in relative poverty."

"He had no money of his own?"

"The inheritance he had in the firm was tied up. He couldn't sell outside the family. Worse than their straitened circumstances, Richard was a brutal domestic. He beat his wife and abused his son. Gottfried grew up cowed and bullied. He was thirteen when Richard was killed. I suspect it was the happiest day of his life up to that point. My father took pity on the widow and child and brought them here to Hedestad, where he found an apartment for Margareta and saw to it that she had a decent life.

"If Richard personified the family's dark, fanatical side, Gottfried embodied the indolent one. When he reached the age of eighteen I decided to take him under my wing—he was my dead brother's son, after all—and you have to remember that the age difference between Gottfried and me was not so great. I was only seven years older, but by then I was on the firm's board, and it was clear that I was the one who would take over from my father, while Gottfried was more or less regarded as an outsider."

Vanger thought for a moment.

"My father didn't really know how to deal with his grandson, so I was the one who gave him a job in the company. This was after the war. He did try to do a reasonable job, but he was lazy. He was a charmer and good-time Charlie; he had a way with women, and there were periods when he drank too much. It isn't easy to describe my feelings for him . . . he wasn't a good-for-nothing, but he was not the least bit reliable and he often disappointed me deeply. Over the years he turned into an alcoholic, and in 1965 he died—the victim of an accidental drowning. That happened at the other end of Hedeby Island, where he'd had a cabin built, and where he used to hide away to drink."

"So he's the father of Harriet and Martin?" Blomkvist said, pointing at the portrait on the coffee table. Reluctantly he had to admit that the old man's story was intriguing.

"Correct. In the late forties Gottfried met a German woman by the name of Isabella Koenig, who had come to Sweden after the war. She was quite a beauty—I mean that she had a lovely radiance like Garbo or Ingrid Bergman. Harriet probably got more of her genes from her mother rather than from Gottfried. As you can see from the photograph, she was pretty even at fourteen."

Blomkvist and Vanger contemplated the picture.

"But let me continue. Isabella was born in 1928 and is still alive. She was eleven when the war began, and you can imagine what it was like to be a teenager in Berlin during the aerial bombardments. It must have felt as if she had arrived in paradise on earth when she landed in Sweden. Regrettably she shared many of Gottfried's vices; she was lazy and partied incessantly. She travelled a great deal in Sweden and abroad, and lacked all sense of responsibility. Obviously this affected the children. Martin was born in 1948 and Harriet in 1950. Their childhood was chaotic, with a mother who was forever leaving them and a father who was virtually an alcoholic.

"In 1958 I'd had enough and decided to try to break the vicious cycle. At the time, Gottfried and Isabella were living in Hedestad—I insisted that they move out here. Martin and Harriet were more or less left to fend for themselves."

Vanger glanced at the clock.

"My thirty minutes are almost up, but I'm close to the end of the story. Will you give me a reprieve?"

"Go on," Blomkvist said.

"In short, then. I was childless—in striking contrast to my brothers and other family members, who seemed obsessed with the need to propagate the house of Vanger. Gottfried and Isabella did move here, but their marriage was on the rocks. After only a year Gottfried moved out to his cabin. He lived there alone for long periods and went back to Isabella when it got too cold. I took care of Martin and Harriet, and they became in many ways the children I never had.

"Martin was . . . to tell the truth, there was a time in his youth when I was afraid he was going to follow in his father's footsteps. He was weak and introverted and melancholy, but he could also be delightful and enthusiastic. He had some troubled years in his teens, but he straightened himself out when he started at the university. He is . . . well, in spite of everything he *is* CEO of what's left of the Vanger Corporation, which I suppose is to his credit."

"And Harriet?"

"Harriet was the apple of my eye. I tried to give her a sense of security and develop her self-confidence, and we took a liking to each other. I looked on her as my own daughter, and she ended up being closer to me than to her parents. You see, Harriet was very special. She was introverted—like her brother—and as a teenager she became wrapped up in religion, unlike anyone else in the family. But she had a clear talent and she was tremendously intelligent. She had both morals and backbone.

When she was fourteen or fifteen I was convinced that she was the one—and not her brother or any of the mediocre cousins, nephews, and nieces around me—who was destined to run the Vanger business one day, or at least play a central role in it."

"So what happened?"

"Now we come to the real reason I want to hire you. I want you to find out who in the family murdered Harriet, and who since then has spent almost forty years trying to drive me insane."

CHAPTER 5

Thursday, December 26

For the first time since he began his monologue, the old man had managed to take Blomkvist by surprise. He had to ask him to repeat it to be sure he had heard correctly. Nothing in the cuttings had hinted at a murder.

"It was September 24, 1966. Harriet was sixteen and had just begun her second year at prep school. It was a Saturday, and it turned into the worst day of my life. I've gone over the events so many times that I think I can account for what happened in every minute of that day—except the most important thing."

He made a sweeping gesture. "Here in this house a great number of my family had gathered. It was the loathsome annual dinner. It was a tradition which my father's father introduced and which generally turned into pretty detestable affairs. The tradition came to an end in the eighties, when Martin simply decreed that all discussions about the business would take place at regular board meetings and by voting. That's the best decision he ever made."

"You said that Harriet was murdered . . ."

"Wait. Let me tell you what happened. It was a Saturday, as I said. It was also the day of the party, with the Children's Day parade that was arranged by the sports club in Hedestad. Harriet had gone into the town during the day and watched the parade with some of her schoolfriends. She came back here to Hedeby Island just after 2:00 in the afternoon. Dinner was supposed to begin at 5:00, and she was expected to take part along with the other young people in the family."

Vanger got up and went over to the window. He motioned Blomkvist to join him, and pointed.

"At 2:15, a few minutes after Harriet came home, a dramatic accident occurred out there on the bridge. A man called Gustav Aronsson, brother of a farmer at Östergården—a smallholding on Hedeby Island—turned on to the bridge and crashed head-on with an oil truck. Evidently both were going too fast and what should have been a minor collision proved a catastrophe. The driver of the truck, presumably instinctively, turned his wheel away from the car, hit the railing of the bridge and the tanker flipped over; it ended up across the bridge with its trailer hanging over the edge. One of the railings had been driven into the oil tank and flammable heating oil began spurting out. In the meantime Aronsson sat pinned inside his car, screaming in pain. The tanker driver was also injured but managed to scramble out of his cabin."

The old man went back to his chair.

"The accident actually had nothing to do with Harriet. But it was significant in a crucial way. A shambles ensued: people on both sides of the bridge hurried to try to help; the risk of fire was significant and a major alarm was sounded. Police officers, an ambulance, the rescue squad, the fire brigade, reporters, and sightseers arrived in rapid succession. Naturally all of them assembled on the mainland side; here on the island side we did what we could to get Aronsson out of the wreck, which proved to be damnably difficult. He was pinned in and seriously injured.

"We tried to prise him loose with our bare hands, and that didn't work. He would have to be cut or sawed out, but we couldn't do anything that risked striking a spark; we were standing in the middle of a sea of oil next to a tanker truck lying on its side. If it had exploded we would have all been killed. It took a long time before we could get help from the mainland side; the truck was wedged right across the bridge, and climbing over it would have been the same as climbing over a bomb."

Blomkvist could not resist the feeling that the old man was telling a meticulously rehearsed story, deliberately to capture his interest. The man was an excellent storyteller, no question. On the other hand, where was the story heading?

"What matters about the accident is that the bridge was blocked for twenty-four hours. Not until Sunday evening was the last of the oil pumped out, and then the truck could be lifted up by crane and the bridge opened for traffic. During these twenty-four hours Hedeby Island was to all intents and purposes cut off from the rest of the world. The only way to get across to the mainland was on a fireboat that was brought in to transport people from the small-boat harbour on this side to the old harbour below the church. For several hours the boat was used only by rescue crews—it wasn't until quite late on Saturday night that stranded islanders began to be ferried across. Do you understand the significance of this?"

"I assume that something happened to Harriet here on the island," Blomkvist said, "and that the list of suspects consists of the finite number of people trapped here. A sort of locked-room mystery in island format?"

Vanger smiled ironically. "Mikael, you don't know how right you are. Even I have read my Dorothy Sayers. These are the facts: Harriet arrived here on the island about 2:10. If we also include children and unmarried guests, all in all about forty family members arrived in the course of the day. Along with servants and residents, there were sixty-four people either here or near the farm. Some of them—the ones who were going to spend the night—were busy getting settled in neighbouring farms or in guest rooms.

"Harriet had previously lived in a house across the road, but given that neither Gottfried nor Isabella was consistently stable, and one could clearly see how that upset the girl, undermined her studies and so on, in 1964, when she was fourteen, I arranged for her to move into my house. Isabella probably thought that it was just fine to be spared the responsibility for her daughter. Harriet had been living here for the past two years. So this is where she came that day. We know that she met and exchanged some words with Harald in the courtyard—he's one of my older brothers. Then she came up the stairs, to this room, and said hello to me. She said that she wanted to talk to me about something. Right then I had some other family members with me and I couldn't spare the time for her. But she seemed anxious and I promised I'd come to her room when I was free. She left through that door, and that was the last time I saw her. A minute or so later there was the crash on the bridge and the bedlam that followed upset all our plans for the day."

"How did she die?"

"It's more complicated than that, and I have to tell the story in chronological order. When the accident occurred, people dropped whatever they were doing and ran to the scene. I was . . . I suppose I took charge and was feverishly occupied for the next few hours. Harriet came down to the bridge right away—several people saw her—but the danger of an explosion made me instruct anyone who wasn't involved in getting Aronsson out of his car to stay well back. Five of us remained. There were myself and my brother Harald. There was a man named Magnus Nilsson, one of my workers. There was a sawmill worker named Sixten Nordlander who had a house down by the fishing harbour. And there was a fellow named Jerker Aronsson. He was only sixteen, and I should really have sent him away, but he was the nephew of Gustav in the car.

"At about 2:40 Harriet was in the kitchen here in the house. She drank a glass of milk and talked briefly to Astrid, our cook. They looked out of the window at the commotion down at the bridge.

"At 2:55 Harriet crossed the courtyard. She was seen by Isabella. About a minute later she ran into Otto Falk, the pastor in Hedeby. At that time the parsonage was where Martin Vanger has his villa today, and the pastor lived on this side of the bridge. He had been in bed, nursing a cold, when the accident took place; he had missed the drama, but someone had telephoned and he was on his way to the bridge. Harriet stopped him on the road and apparently wanted to say something to him, but he waved her off and hurried past. Falk was the last person to see her alive."

"How did she die?" Blomkvist said again.

"I don't know," Vanger said with a troubled expression. "We didn't get Aronsson out of his car until around 5:00—he survived, by the way, although he was not in good shape—and sometime after 6:00 the threat of fire was considered past. The island was still cut off, but things began to calm down. It wasn't until we sat down at the table to have our long-delayed dinner around 8:00 that we discovered Harriet was missing. I sent one of the cousins to get Harriet from her room, but she came back to say that she couldn't find her. I didn't think much about it; I probably assumed she had gone for a walk or she hadn't been told that dinner was served. And during the evening I had to deal with various discussions and arguments with the family. So it wasn't until the next morning, when Isabella went to find her, that we realised that nobody knew where Harriet was and that no-one had seen her since the day before." He spread his arms out wide. "And from that day, she has been missing without a trace."

"Missing?" Blomkvist echoed.

"For all these years we haven't been able to find one microscopic scrap of her."

"But if she vanished, as you say, you can't be sure that she was murdered."

"I understand the objection. I've had thoughts along the same lines. When a person vanishes without a trace, one of four things could have happened. She could have gone off of her own free will and be hiding somewhere. She could have had an accident and died. She could have committed suicide. And finally, she could have been the victim of a crime. I've weighed all these possibilities."

"But you believe that someone took Harriet's life. Why?"

"Because it's the only reasonable conclusion." Vanger held up one finger. "From the outset I hoped that she had run away. But as the days passed, we all realised that this wasn't the case. I mean, how would a sixteen-year-old from such a protected world, even a very able girl, be able to manage on her own? How could she stay hidden without being discovered? Where would she get money? And even if she got a job somewhere, she would need a social security card and an address."

He held up two fingers.

"My next thought was that she had had some kind of accident. Can you do me a favour? Go to the desk and open the top drawer. There's a map there."

Blomkvist did as he was asked and unfolded the map on the coffee table. Hedeby Island was an irregularly shaped land mass about two miles long with a maximum width of about one mile.

A large part of the island was covered by forest. There was a built-up area by the bridge and around the little summer-house harbour. On the other side of the island was the smallholding, Östergården, from which the unfortunate Aronsson had started out in his car.

"Remember that she couldn't have left the island," Vanger said. "Here on Hedeby Island you could die in an accident just like anywhere else. You could be struck by lightning—but there was no thunderstorm that day. You could be trampled to death by a horse, fall down a well, or tumble into a rock crevice. There are no doubt hundreds of ways to fall victim to an accident here. I've thought of most of them."

He held up three fingers.

"There's just one catch, and this also applies to the third possibility—that the girl, contrary to every indication, took her own life. *Her body must be somewhere in this limited area.*"

Vanger slammed his fist down on the map.

"In the days after she disappeared, we searched everywhere, criss-crossing the island. The men waded through every ditch, scoured every patch of field, cliff, and uprooted tree. We went through every building, chimney, well, barn, and hidden garret."

The old man looked away from Blomkvist and stared into the darkness outside the window. His voice grew lower and more intimate.

"The whole autumn I looked for her, even after the search parties stopped and people had given up. When I wasn't tending to my work I began going for walks back and forth across the island. Winter came on and we still hadn't found a trace of her. In the spring I kept on looking until I realised how preposterous my search was. When summer came I hired three experienced woodsmen who did the entire search over again with dogs. They combed every square foot of the island. By that time I had begun to think that someone must have killed her. So they also searched for a grave. They worked at it for three months. We found not the slightest vestige of the girl. It was as if she had dissolved into thin air."

"I can think of a number of possibilities," Blomkvist ventured.

"Let's hear them."

"She could have drowned, accidentally or on purpose. This is an island, and water can hide most things."

"True, but the probability isn't great. Consider the following: if Harriet met with an accident and drowned, logically it must have occurred somewhere in the immediate vicinity of the village. Remember that the excitement on the bridge was the most sensational thing that had happened here on Hedeby Island in several decades. It was not a time when a sixteen-year-old girl with a normal sense of curiosity would decide to go for a walk to the other side of the island.

"But more important," he said, "there's not much of a current here, and the winds at that time of year were out of the north or northeast. If anything falls into the water, it comes up somewhere along the beach on the mainland, and over there it's built up almost everywhere. Don't think that we didn't consider this. We dragged almost all the spots where she could conceivably have gone down to the water. I also hired young men from a scuba-diving club here in Hedestad. They spent the rest of the season combing the bottom of the sound and along the beaches . . . I'm convinced she's not in the water; if she had been we would have found her."

"But could she not have met with an accident somewhere else? The bridge was blocked, of course, but it's a short distance over to the mainland. She could have swum or rowed across."

"It was late September and the water was so cold that Harriet would hardly have set off to go swimming in the midst of all the commotion. But if she suddenly got the idea to swim to the mainland, she would have been seen and drawn a lot of attention. There were dozens of eyes on the bridge, and on the mainland side there were two or three hundred people along the water watching the scene."

"A rowing boat?"

"No. That day there were precisely thirteen boats on Hedeby Island. Most of the pleasure boats were already in storage on land. Down in the small-boat harbour by the summer cabins there were two Pettersson boats in the water. There were seven *eka* rowing boats, of which five were pulled up on shore. Below the parsonage one rowing boat was on shore and one in the water. By Östergården there was a rowing boat and a motorboat. All these boats were checked and were exactly where they were supposed to be. If she had rowed across and run away, she would have had to leave the boat on the other side."

Vanger held up four fingers.

"So there's only one reasonable possibility left, namely that Harriet disappeared against her will. Someone killed her and got rid of the body."

Lisbeth Salander spent Christmas morning reading Mikael Blomkvist's controversial book about financial journalism, *The Knights Templar: A Cautionary Tale for Financial Reporters.* The cover had a trendy design by Christer Malm featuring a photograph of the Stockholm Stock Exchange. Malm had worked in PhotoShop, and it took a moment to notice that the building was floating in air. It was a dramatic cover with which to set the tone for what was to come.

Salander could see that Blomkvist was a fine writer. The book was set out in a straightforward and engaging way, and even people with no insight into the labyrinth of financial journalism could learn something from reading it. The tone was sharp and sarcastic, but above all it was persuasive.

The first chapter was a sort of declaration of war in which Blomkvist did not mince words. In the last twenty years, Swedish financial journalists had developed into a group of incompetent lackeys who were puffed up with self-importance and who had no record of thinking critically. He drew this conclusion because time after time, without the least objection, so many financial reporters seemed content to regurgitate the statements issued by CEOs and stock-market speculators—even when this information was plainly misleading or wrong. These reporters were thus either so naive and gullible that they ought to be packed off to other assignments, or they were people who quite consciously betrayed their journalistic function. Blomkvist claimed that he had often been ashamed to be called a financial reporter, since then he would risk being lumped together with people whom he did not rate as reporters at all.

He compared the efforts of financial journalists with the way crime reporters or foreign correspondents worked. He painted a picture of the outcry that would result if a legal correspondent began uncritically reproducing the prosecutor's case as gospel in a murder trial, without consulting the defence arguments or interviewing the victim's family before forming an opinion of what was likely or unlikely. According to Blomkvist the same rules had to apply to financial journalists.

The rest of the book consisted of a chain of evidence to support his case. One long chapter examined the reporting of a famous dot-com in six daily papers, as well as in the *Financial Journal, Dagens Industri,* and "A-ekonomi," the business report on Swedish TV. He first quoted and summarised what the reporters had said and written. Then he made a comparison with the actual situation. In describing the development of the company he listed time after time the simple questions that a serious reporter would have asked but which the whole corps of financial reporters had neglected to ask. It was a neat move.

Another chapter dealt with the IPO of Telia stock—it was the book's most jocular and ironic section, in which some financial writers were castigated by name, including one William Borg, to whom Blomkvist seemed to be particularly hostile. A chapter near the end of the book compared the level of competence of Swedish and foreign financial reporters. He described how serious reporters at London's *Financial Times*, the *Economist*, and some German financial newspapers had reported similar subjects in their own countries. The comparison was not favourable to the Swedish journalists. The final chapter contained a sketch with suggestions as to how this deplorable situation could be remedied. The conclusion of the book echoed the introduction:

> If a parliamentary reporter handled his assignment by uncritically taking up a lance in support of every decision that was pushed through, no matter how preposterous, or if a political reporter were to show a similar lack of judgement—that reporter would be fired or at the least reassigned to a department where he or she could not do so much damage. In the world of financial reporting, however, the normal journalistic mandate to undertake critical investigations and objectively report findings to the readers appears not to apply. Instead the most successful rogue is applauded. In this way the future of Sweden is also being created, and all remaining trust in journalists as a corps of professionals is being compromised.

Salander had no difficulty understanding the agitated debate that had followed in the trade publication *The Journalist*, certain financial newspapers, and on the front pages and in the business sections of the daily papers. Even though only a few reporters were mentioned by name in the book, Salander guessed that the field was small enough that everyone would know exactly which individuals were being referred to when various newspapers were quoted. Blomkvist had made himself some bitter enemies, which was also reflected in the malicious comments to the court in the Wennerström affair.

She closed the book and looked at the photograph on the back. Blomkvist's dark blond shock of hair fell a bit carelessly across his forehead, as if caught in a gust of wind. Or (and this was more plausible) as if Christer Malm had posed him. He was looking into the camera with an ironic smile and an expression perhaps aiming to be charming and boyish. *A very good-looking man. On his way to do three months in the slammer.*

"Hello, Kalle Blomkvist," she said to herself. "You're pretty pleased with yourself, aren't you?"

At lunchtime Salander booted up her iBook and opened Eudora to write an email. She typed: "Have you got time?" She signed it *Wasp* and sent it to the address <Plague_xyz_666@hotmail.com>. To be on the safe side, she ran the message through her PGP encryption programme.

Then she put on black jeans, heavy winter boots, a warm polo shirt, a dark pea jacket, and matching knitted gloves, cap, and scarf. She took the rings out of her eyebrows and nostril, put on a pale pink lipstick, and examined herself in the bathroom mirror. She looked like any other woman out for a weekend stroll, and she regarded her outfit as appropriate camouflage for an expedition behind enemy lines. She took the tunnelbana from Zinkensdamm to Östermalmstorg and walked down towards Strandvägen. She sauntered along the central reserve reading the numbers on the buildings. She had almost got to Djurgårds Bridge when she stopped and looked at the door she had been searching for. She crossed the street and waited a few feet from the street door.

She noticed that most people who were out walking in the cold weather on the day after Christmas were walking along the quay; only a few were on the pavement side.

She had to wait for almost half an hour before an old woman with a cane approached from the direction of Djurgården. The woman stopped and studied Salander with suspicion. Salander gave her a friendly smile in return. The lady with the cane returned her greeting and looked as though she were trying to remember when she had last seen the young woman. Salander turned her back and took a few steps away from the door, as though she were impatiently waiting for someone, pacing back and forth. When she turned, the lady had reached the door and was slowly putting in a number on the code lock. Salander had no difficulty seeing that the combination was 1260.

She waited five minutes more before she went to the door. She punched in the code and the lock clicked. She peered into the stairwell. There was a security camera which she glanced at and ignored; it was a model that Milton Security carried and was activated only if an alarm for a break-in or an attack was sounded on the property. Farther in, to the left of an antique lift cage, there was a door with another code lock; she tried 1260 and it worked for the entrance to the cellar level and rubbish room. *Sloppy, very sloppy*. She spent three minutes investigating the cellar level, where she located an unlocked laundry room and a recycling room. Then she used a set of picklocks that she had "borrowed" from Milton's locksmith to open a locked door to what seemed to be a meeting room for the condominium association. At the back of the cellar was a hobby room. Finally she found what she was looking for: the building's small electrical room. She examined the meters, fuse boxes, and junction boxes and then took out a Canon digital camera the size of a cigarette packet. She took three pictures.

On the way out she cast her eye down the list of residents by the lift and read the name for the apartment on the top floor. *Wennerström.*

Then she left the building and walked rapidly to the National Museum, where she went into the cafeteria to have some coffee and warm up. After about half an hour she made her way back to Söder and went up to her apartment.

There was an answer from <Plague_xyz_666@hotmail.com>. When she decoded it in PGP it read: 20.

CHAPTER 6

Thursday, December 26

The time limit set by Blomkvist had been exceeded by a good margin. It was 4:30, and there was no hope of catching the afternoon train, but he still had a chance of making the evening train at 9:30. He stood by the window rubbing his neck as he stared out at the illuminated facade of the church on the other side of the bridge. Vanger had shown him a scrapbook with articles from both the local newspaper and the national media. There had been quite a bit of media interest for a while—girl from noted industrialist's family disappears. But when no body was found and there was no breakthrough in the investigation, interest gradually waned. Despite the fact that a prominent family was involved, thirty-six years later the case of Harriet Vanger was all but forgotten. The prevailing theory in articles from the late sixties seemed to be that she drowned and was swept out to sea—a tragedy, but something that could happen to any family.

Blomkvist had been fascinated by the old man's account, but when Vanger excused himself to go to the bathroom, his scepticism returned. The old man had still not got to the end, and Blomkvist had finally promised to listen to the whole story.

"What do you think happened to her?" he said when Vanger came back into the room.

"Normally there were some twenty-five people living here year-round, but because of the family gathering there were more than sixty on Hedeby Island that day. Of these, between twenty and twenty-five can be ruled out, pretty much so. I believe that of those remaining, someone—and in all likelihood it was someone from the family—killed Harriet and hid the body."

"I have a dozen objections to that."

"Let's hear them."

"Well, the first one is that even if someone hid her body, it should have been found if the search was as thorough as the one you described."

"To tell you the truth, the search was even more extensive than I've described. It wasn't until I began to think of Harriet as a murder victim that I realised several ways in which her body could have disappeared. I can't prove this, but it's at least within the realm of possibility."

"Tell me."

"Harriet went missing sometime around 3:00 that afternoon. At about 2:55 she was seen by Pastor Falk, who was hurrying to the bridge. At almost exactly the same time a photographer arrived from the local paper, and for the next hour he took a great number of pictures of the drama. We—the police, I mean—examined the photographs and confirmed that Harriet was not in any one of them; but every other person in town was seen in at least one, apart from very small children."

Vanger took out another album and placed it on the table.

"These are pictures from that day. The first one was taken in

Hedestad during the Children's Day parade. The same photographer took it around 1:15 p.m., and Harriet is there in it."

The photograph was taken from the second floor of a building and showed a street along which the parade—clowns on trucks and girls in bathing suits—had just passed. Spectators thronged the pavements. Vanger pointed at a figure in the crowd.

"That's Harriet. It's about two hours before she will disappear; she's with some of her schoolfriends in town. This is the last picture taken of her. But there's one more interesting shot."

Vanger leafed through the pages. The album contained about 180 pictures—five rolls—from the crash on the bridge. After having heard the account, it was almost too much to suddenly see it in the form of sharp black-and-white images. The photographer was a professional who had managed to capture the turmoil surrounding the accident. A large number of the pictures focused on the activities around the overturned tanker truck. Blomkvist had no problem identifying a gesticulating, much younger Henrik Vanger soaked with heating oil.

"This is my brother Harald." The old man pointed to a man in shirtsleeves bending forward and pointing at something inside the wreck of Aronsson's car. "My brother Harald may be an unpleasant person, but I think he can be eliminated from the list of suspects. Except for a very short while, when he had to run back here to the farm to change his shoes, he spent the afternoon on the bridge."

Vanger turned some more pages. One image followed another. Focus on the tanker truck. Focus on spectators on the foreshore. Focus on Aronsson's car. General views. Close-ups with a telephoto lens.

"This is the interesting picture," Vanger said. "As far as we could determine it was taken between 3:40 and 3:45, or about 45 minutes after Harriet ran into Falk. Take a look at the house, the middle second floor window. That's Harriet's room. In the preceding picture the window was closed. Here it's open."

"Someone must have been in Harriet's room."

"I asked everyone; nobody would admit to opening the window."

"Which means that either Harriet did it herself, and she was still alive at that point, or else that someone was lying to you. But why would a murderer go into her room and open the window? And why should anyone lie about it?"

Vanger shook his head. No explanation presented itself.

"Harriet disappeared sometime around 3:00 or shortly thereafter. These pictures give an impression of where certain people were at that time. That's why I can eliminate a number of people from the list of suspects. For the same reason I can conclude that some people who were not in the photographs at that time must be added to the list of suspects."

"You didn't answer my question about how you think the body was removed. I realise, of course, that there must be some plausible explanation. Some sort of common old illusionist's trick."

"There are actually several very practical ways it could have been done. Sometime around 3:00 the killer struck. He or she presumably didn't use any sort of weapon—or we would have found traces of blood. I'm guessing that Harriet was strangled and I'm guessing that it happened here—behind the wall in the courtyard, somewhere out of the photographer's line of sight and in a blind spot from the house. There's a path, if you want to take a shortcut, to the parsonage—the last place she was seen—and back to the house. Today there's a small flower bed and lawn there, but in the sixties it was a gravelled area used for parking. All the killer had to do was open the boot of a car and put Harriet inside. When we began searching the island the next day, nobody was thinking that a crime had been committed. We focused on the shorelines, the buildings, and the woods closest to the village."

"So nobody was checking the boots of cars."

"And by the following evening the killer would have been free to get in his car and drive across the bridge to hide the body somewhere else."

"Right under the noses of everyone involved in the search. If that's the way it happened, we're talking about a cold-blooded bastard."

Vanger gave a bitter laugh. "You just gave an apt description of quite a few members of the Vanger family."

They continued their discussion over supper at 6:00. Anna served roast hare with currant jelly and potatoes. Vanger poured a robust red wine. Blomkvist still had plenty of time to make the last train. He thought it was about time to sum things up.

"It's a fascinating story you've been telling me, I admit it. But I still don't know why you wanted me to hear it."

"I told you. I want to nail the swine who murdered Harriet. And I want to hire you to find out who it was."

"Why?"

Vanger put down his knife and fork. "Mikael, for thirty-six years I've driven myself crazy wondering what happened to Harriet. I've devoted more and more of my time to it."

He fell silent and took off his glasses, scrutinising some invisible speck of dirt on the lens. Then he raised his eyes and looked at Blomkvist.

"To be completely honest with you, Harriet's disappearance was the reason why gradually I withdrew from the firm's management. I lost all motivation. I knew that there was a killer somewhere nearby and the worrying and searching for the truth began to affect my work. The worst thing is that the burden didn't get any lighter over time—on the contrary. Around 1970 I had a period when I just wanted to be left alone. Then Martin joined the board of directors, and he had to take on more and more of my work. In 1976 I retired and Martin took over as CEO. I still have a seat on the board, but I haven't sailed many knots since I turned fifty. For the last thirty-six years not a day has passed that I have not pondered Harriet's disappearance. You may think I'm obsessed with it—at least most of my relatives think so."

"It was a horrific event."

"More than that. It ruined my life. That's something I've become more aware of as time has passed. Do you have a good sense of yourself?"

"I think so, yes."

"I do too. I can't forget what happened. But my motives have changed over the years. At first it was probably grief. I wanted to find her and at least have a chance to bury her. It was about getting justice for Harriet."

"In what way has that changed?"

"Now it's more about finding the bastard who did it. But the funny thing is, the older I get, the more of an all-absorbing hobby it has become."

"Hobby?"

"Yes, I would use that word. When the police investigation petered out I kept going. I've tried to proceed systematically and scientifically. I've gathered all the information that could possibly be found—the photographs, the police report, I've written down everything people told me about what they were doing that day. So in effect I've spent almost half my life collecting information about a single day."

"You realise, I suppose, that after thirty-six years the killer himself might be dead and buried?"

"I don't believe that."

Blomkvist raised his eyebrows at the conviction in his voice.

"Let's finish dinner and go back upstairs. There's one more detail before my story is done. And it's the most perplexing of all."

Salander parked the Corolla with the automatic transmission by the commuter railway station in Sundbyberg. She had borrowed the Toyota from Milton Security's motor pool. She had not exactly asked permission, but Armansky had never expressly forbidden her from using Milton's cars. Sooner or later, she thought, I have to get a vehicle of my own. She did own a second-hand Kawasaki 125, which she used in the summertime. During the winter the bike was locked in her cellar.

She walked to Högklintavägen and rang the bell at 6:00 on the dot. Seconds later the lock on the street door clicked and she went up two flights and rang the doorbell next to the name of Svensson. She had no idea who Svensson might be or if any such person even lived in that apartment.

"Hi, Plague," she said.

"Wasp. You only pop in when you need something."

As usual, it was dark in the apartment; the light from a single lamp seeped out into the hall from the bedroom he used as an office. The man, who was three years older than Salander, was six foot two and weighed 330 pounds. She herself was four feet eleven and weighed 90 pounds and had always felt like a midget next to Plague. The place smelled stuffy and stale.

"It's because you never take a bath, Plague. It smells like a monkey house in here. If you ever went out I could give you some tips on soap. They have it at the Konsum."

He gave her a wan smile, but said nothing. He motioned her to follow him into the kitchen. He plopped down on a chair by the kitchen table without turning on a light. The only illumination came from the street light beyond the window.

"I mean, I may not hold the record in cleaning house either, but if I've got old milk cartons that smell like maggots I bundle them up and put them out."

"I'm on a disability pension," he said. "I'm socially incompetent."

"So that's why the government gave you a place to live and forgot about you. Aren't you ever afraid that your neighbours are going to complain to the inspectors? Then you might fetch up in the funny farm."

"Have you something for me?"

Salander unzipped her jacket pocket and handed him five thousand kronor.

"It's all I can spare. It's my own money, and I can't really deduct you as a dependant."

"What do you want?"

"The electronic cuff you talked about two months ago. Did you get it?"

He smiled and laid a box on the table.

"Show me how it works."

For the next few minutes she listened intently. Then she tested the cuff. Plague might be a social incompetent, but he was unquestionably a genius.

Vanger waited until he once more had Blomkvist's attention. Blomkvist looked at his watch and said, "One perplexing detail."

Vanger said: "I was born on November 1. When Harriet was eight she gave me a birthday present, a pressed flower, framed."

Vanger walked around the desk and pointed to the first flower. Bluebell. It had an amateurish mounting.

"That was the first. I got it in 1958." He pointed to the next one. "1959." Buttercup. "1960." Daisy. "It became a tradition. She would make the frame sometime during the summer and save it until my birthday. I always hung them on the wall in this room. In 1966 she disappeared and the tradition was broken."

Vanger pointed to a gap in the row of frames. Blomkvist felt the hairs rise on the back of his neck. The wall was filled with pressed flowers.

"1967, a year after she disappeared, I received this flower on my birthday. It's a violet."

"How did the flower come to you?"

"Wrapped in what they call gift paper and posted in a padded envelope from Stockholm. No return address. No message."

"You mean that . . ." Blomkvist made a sweeping gesture.

"Precisely. On my birthday every damn year. Do you know how that feels? It's directed at me, precisely as if the murderer wants to torture me. I've worried myself sick over whether Harriet might have been taken away because someone wanted to get at me. It was no secret that she and I had a special relationship and that I thought of her as my own daughter."

"So what is it you want me to do?" Blomkvist said.

When Salander returned the Corolla to the garage under Milton Security, she made sure to go to the toilet upstairs in the office. She used her card key in the door and took the lift straight up to the third floor to avoid going in through the main entrance on the second floor, where the duty officer worked. She used the toilet and got a cup of coffee from the espresso machine that Armansky had bought when at long last he recognised that Salander would never make coffee just because it was expected of her. Then she went to her office and hung her leather jacket over the back of her chair.

The office was a 6½-by-10-foot glass cubicle. There was a desk with an old model Dell desktop PC, a telephone, one office chair, a metal waste paper basket, and a bookshelf. The bookshelf contained an assortment of directories and three blank notebooks. The two desk drawers housed some ballpoints, paper clips, and a notebook. On the window sill stood a potted plant with brown, withered leaves. Salander looked thoughtfully at the plant, as if it were the first time she had seen it, then she deposited it firmly in the waste paper basket.

She seldom had anything to do in her office and visited it no more than half a dozen times a year, mainly when she needed to sit by herself and prepare a report just before handing it in. Armansky had insisted that she have her own space. His reasoning was that she would then feel like part of the company although she worked as a freelancer. She suspected that Armansky hoped that this way he would have a chance to keep an eye on her and meddle in her affairs. At first she had been given space farther down the corridor, in a larger room that she was expected to share with a colleague. But since she was never there Armansky finally moved her into the cubbyhole at the end of the corridor.

Salander took out the cuff. She looked at it, meditatively biting her lower lip.

It was past 11:00 and she was alone on the floor. She suddenly felt excruciatingly bored.

After a while she got up and walked to the end of the hall and tried the door to Armansky's office. Locked. She looked around. The chances of anyone turning up in the corridor around midnight on December 26 were almost nonexistent. She opened the door with a pirate copy of the company's card key, which she had taken the trouble to make several years before.

Armansky's office was spacious: in front of his desk were guest chairs, and a conference table with room for eight people was in the corner. It was impeccably neat. She had not snooped in his office for quite some time, but now that she was here . . . She spent a while at his desk to bring herself up to date regarding the search for a suspected mole in the company, which of her colleagues had been planted undercover in a firm where a theft ring was operating, and what measures had been taken in all secrecy to protect a client who was afraid her child was in danger of being kidnapped by the father.

At last she put the papers back precisely the way they were, locked Armansky's door, and walked home. She felt satisfied with her day.

"I don't know whether we'll find out the truth, but I refuse to go to my grave without giving it one last try," the old man said. "I simply want to commission you to go through all the evidence one last time."

"This is crazy," Blomkvist said.

"Why is it crazy?"

"I've heard enough. Henrik, I understand your grief, but I have to be honest with you. What you're asking me to do is a waste of my time and your money. You are asking me to conjure up a solution to a mystery that the police and experienced investigators with considerably greater resources have failed to solve all these years. You're asking me to solve a crime getting on for forty years after it was committed. How could I possibly do that?"

"We haven't discussed your fee," Vanger said.

"That won't be necessary."

"I can't force you, but listen to what I'm offering. Frode has already drawn up a contract. We can negotiate the details, but the contract is simple, and all it needs is your signature."

"Henrik, this is absurd. I really don't believe I can solve the mystery of Harriet's disappearance."

"According to the contract, you don't have to. All it asks is that you do your best. If you fail, then it's God's will, or—if you don't believe in Him—it's fate."

Blomkvist sighed. He was feeling more and more uncomfortable and wanted to end this visit to Hedeby, but he relented.

"All right, let's hear it."

"I want you to live and work here in Hedeby for a year. I want you to go through the investigative report on Harriet's disappearance one page at a time. I want you to examine everything with new eyes. I want you to question all the old conclusions exactly the way an investigative reporter would. I want you to look for something that I and the police and other investigators may have missed."

"You're asking me to set aside my life and career to devote myself for a whole year to something that's a complete waste of time."

Vanger smiled. "As to your career, we might agree that for the moment it's somewhat on hold."

Blomkvist had no answer to that.

"I want to buy a year of your life. Give you a job. The salary is better than any offer you'll ever get in your life. I will pay you 200,000 kronor a month—that's 2.4 million kronor if you accept and stay the whole year."

Blomkvist was astonished.

"I have no illusions. The possibility you will succeed is minimal, but if against all odds you should crack the mystery then I'm offering a bonus of double payment, or 4.8 million kronor. Let's be generous and round it off to five million."

Vanger leaned back and cocked his head.

"I can pay the money into any bank account you wish, anywhere in the world. You can also take the money in cash in a suitcase, so it's up to you whether you want to report the income to the tax authorities."

"This is . . . not healthy," Blomkvist stammered.

"Why so?" Vanger said calmly. "I'm eighty-two and still in full possession of my faculties. I have a large personal fortune; I can spend it any way I want. I have no children and absolutely no desire to leave any money to relatives I despise. I've made my last will and testament; I'll be giving the bulk of my fortune to the World Wildlife Fund. A few people who are close to me will receive significant amounts—including Anna."

Blomkvist shook his head.

"Try to understand me," Vanger said. "I'm a man who's going to die soon. There's one thing in the world I want to have—and that's an answer to this question that has plagued me for half my life. I don't expect to find the answer, but I do have resources to make one last attempt. Is that unreasonable? I owe it to Harriet. And I owe it to myself."

"You'll be paying me several million kronor for nothing. All I need to do is sign the contract and then twiddle my thumbs for a year."

"You wouldn't do that. On the contrary—you'll work harder than you've ever worked in your life."

"How can you be so sure?"

"Because I can offer you something that you can't buy for any price, but which you want more than anything in the world."

"And what would that be?"

Vanger's eyes narrowed.

"I can give you Hans-Erik Wennerström. I can prove that he's a swindler. He happened, thirty-five years ago, to begin his career with me, and I can give you his head on a platter. Solve the mystery and you can turn your defeat in court into the story of the year."

CHAPTER 7

Friday, January 3

Erika set her coffee cup on the table and stood by the window looking out at the view of Gamla Stan. It was 9:00 in the morning. All the snow had been washed away by the rain over New Year's.

"I've always loved this view," she said. "An apartment like this would make me give up living in Saltsjöbaden."

"You've got the keys. You can move over from your upper-class reserve any time you want," Blomkvist said. He closed the suitcase and put it by the front door.

Berger turned and gave him a disbelieving look. "You can't be serious, Mikael," she said. "We're in our worst crisis and you're packing to go and live in Tjottahejti."

"Hedestad. A couple of hours by train. And it's not for ever."

"It might as well be Ulan Bator. Don't you see that it will look as if you're slinking off with your tail between your legs?"

"That's precisely what I am doing. Besides, I have to do some gaol time too."

Christer Malm was sitting on the sofa. He was uncomfortable. It was the first time since they founded *Millennium* that he had seen Berger and Blomkvist in such disagreement. Over all the years they had been inseparable. Sometimes they had furious clashes, but their arguments were always about business matters, and they would invariably resolve all those issues before they hugged each other and went back to their corners. Or to bed. Last autumn had not been fun, and now it was as if a great gulf had opened up between them. Malm wondered if he was watching the beginning of the end of *Millennium*.

"I don't have a choice," Blomkvist said. "*We* don't have a choice."

He poured himself a coffee and sat at the kitchen table. Berger shook her head and sat down facing him.

"What do you think, Christer?" she said.

He had been expecting the question and dreading the moment when he would have to take a stand. He was the third partner, but they all knew that it was Blomkvist and Berger who were *Millennium*. The only time they asked his advice was when they could not agree.

"Honestly," Malm said, "you both know perfectly well it doesn't matter what I think."

He shut up. He loved making pictures. He loved working with graphics. He had never considered himself an artist, but he knew he was a damned good designer. On the other hand, he was helpless at intrigue and policy decisions.

Berger and Blomkvist looked at each other across the table. She was cool and furious. He was thinking hard.

This isn't an argument, Malm thought. It's a divorce.

"OK, let me present my case one last time," Blomkvist said. "This does *not* mean I've given up on *Millennium*. We've spent too much time working our hearts out for that."

"But now you won't be at the office—Christer and I will have to carry the load. Can't you see that? You're the one marching into self-imposed exile."

"That's the second thing. I need a break, Erika. I'm not functioning anymore. I'm burned out. A paid sabbatical in Hedestad might be exactly what I need."

"The whole thing is idiotic, Mikael. You might as well take a job in a circus."

"I know. But I'm going to get 2.4 million for sitting on my backside for a year, and I won't be wasting my time. That's the third thing. Round One with Wennerström is over, and he knocked me out. Round Two has already started—he's going to try to sink *Millennium* for good because he knows that the staff here will always know what he's been up to, for as long as the magazine exists."

"I know what he's doing. I've seen it in the monthly ad sales figures for the last six months."

"That's exactly why I *have* to get out of the office. I'm like a red rag waving at him. He's paranoid as far as I'm concerned. As long as I'm here, he'll just keep on coming. Now we have to prepare ourselves for Round Three. If we're going to have the slightest chance against Wennerström, we have to retreat and work out a whole new strategy. We have to find something to hammer him with. That'll be my job this year."

"I understand all that," Berger said. "So go ahead and take a holiday. Go abroad, lie on a beach for a month. Check out the love life on the Costa Brava. Relax. Go out to Sandhamn and look at the waves."

"And when I come back nothing will be different. Wennerström is going to crush *Millennium* unless he is appeased by my having stood down. You know that. The only thing which might otherwise stop him is if we get something on him that we can use."

"And you think that's what you will find in Hedestad?"

"I checked the cuttings. Wennerström did work at the Vanger company from 1969 to 1972. He was in management and was responsible for strategic placements. He left in a hurry. Why should we rule out the possibility that Henrik Vanger does have something on him?"

"But if what he did happened thirty years ago, it's going to be hard to prove it today."

"Vanger promised to set out in detail what he knows. He's obsessed with this missing girl—it seems to be the only thing he's interested in, and if this means he has to burn Wennerström then I think there's a good chance he'll do it. We certainly can't ignore the opportunity—he's the first person who's said he's willing to go on record with evidence against Wennerström."

"We couldn't use it even if you came back with incontrovertible proof that it was Wennerström who strangled the girl. Not after so many years. He'd massacre us in court."

"The thought had crossed my mind, but it's no good: he was plugging away at the Stockholm School of Economics and had no connection with the Vanger companies at the time she disappeared." Blomkvist paused. "Erika, I'm not going to leave *Millennium,* but it's important for it to look as if I have. You and Christer have to go on running the magazine. If you can . . . if you have a chance to . . . arrange a cease-fire with Wennerström, then do it. You can't do that if I'm still on the editorial board."

"OK, but it's a rotten situation, and I think you're grasping at straws going to Hedestad."

"Have you a better idea?"

Berger shrugged. "We ought to start chasing down sources right now. Build up the story from the beginning. And do it right this time."

"Ricky—that story is dead as a doornail."

Dejected, Berger rested her head on her hands. When she spoke, at first she did not want to meet Blomkvist's eyes.

"I'm so fucking angry with you. Not because the story you wrote was baseless—I was in on it as much as you were. And not because you're leaving your job as publisher—that's a smart decision in this situation. I can go along with making it look like a schism or a power struggle between you and me—I understand the logic when it's a matter of making Wennerström believe I'm a harmless bimbo and you're the real threat." She paused and now looked him resolutely in the eye. "But I think you're making a mistake. Wennerström isn't going to fall for it. He's going to keep on destroying *Millennium*. The only difference is that starting from today, I have to fight him alone, and you know that you're needed more than ever on the editorial board. OK, I'd love to wage war against Wennerström, but what makes me so cross is that you're abandoning ship all of a sudden. You're leaving me in the lurch when things are absolutely at their worst ever."

Blomkvist reached across and stroked her hair.

"You're not alone. You've got Christer and the rest of the staff behind you."

"Not Janne Dahlman. By the way, I think you made a mistake hiring him. He's competent, but he does more harm than good. I don't trust him. He went around looking gleeful about your troubles all autumn. I don't know if he hopes he can take over your role or whether it's just personal chemistry between him and the rest of the staff."

"I'm afraid you're right," Blomkvist said.

"So what should I do? Fire him?"

"Erika, you're editor in chief and the senior shareholder of *Millennium*. If you have to, fire him."

"We've never fired anyone, Micke. And now you're dumping this decision on me too. It's no fun any more going to the office in the morning."

At that point Malm surprised them by standing up.

"If you're going to catch that train we've got to get moving." Berger began to protest, but he held up a hand. "Wait, Erika, you asked me what I thought. Well, I think the situation is shitty. But if things are the way Mikael says—that he's about to hit the wall—then he really does have to leave for his own sake. We owe him that much."

They stared at Malm in astonishment and he gave Blomkvist an embarrassed look.

"You both know that it's you two who are *Millennium*. I'm a partner and you've always been fair with me and I love the magazine and all that, but you could easily replace me with some other art director. But since you asked for my opinion, there you have it. As far as Dahlman is concerned, I agree with you. And if you want to fire him, Erika, then I'll do it for you. As long as we have a credible reason. Obviously it's extremely unfortunate that Mikael's leaving right now, but I don't think we have a choice. Mikael, I'll drive you to the station. Erika and I will hold the fort until you get back."

"What I'm afraid of is that Mikael won't ever come back," Berger said quietly.

Armansky woke up Salander when he called her at 1:30 in the afternoon.

"What's this about?" she said, drunk with sleep. Her mouth tasted like tar.

"Mikael Blomkvist. I just talked to our client, the lawyer, Frode."

"So?"

"He called to say that we can drop the investigation of Wennerström."

"Drop it? But I've just started working on it."

"Frode isn't interested any more."

"Just like that?"

"He's the one who decides."

"We agreed on a fee."

"How much time have you put in?"

Salander thought about it. "Three full days."

"We agreed on a ceiling of forty thousand kronor. I'll write an invoice for ten thousand; you'll get half, which is acceptable for three days of time wasted. He'll have to pay because he's the one who initiated the whole thing."

"What should I do with the material I've gathered?"

"Is there anything dramatic?"

"No."

"Frode didn't ask for a report. Put it on the shelf in case he comes back. Otherwise you can shred it. I'll have a new job for you next week."

Salander sat for a while holding the telephone after Armansky hung up. She went to her work corner in the living room and looked at the notes she had pinned up on the wall and the papers she had stacked on the desk. What she had managed to collect was mostly press cuttings and articles downloaded from the Internet. She took the papers and dropped them in a desk drawer.

She frowned. Blomkvist's strange behaviour in the courtroom had presented an interesting challenge, and Salander did not like aborting an assignment once she had started. *People always have secrets. It's just a matter of finding out what they are.*

PART 2

Consequence Analyses

JANUARY 3–MARCH 17

Forty-six percent of the women in Sweden have been subjected to violence by a man.

CHAPTER 8

Friday, January 3–
Sunday, January 5

When Blomkvist alighted from his train in Hedestad for the second time, the sky was a pastel blue and the air icy cold. The thermometer on the wall of the station said 0°F. He was wearing unsuitable walking shoes. Unlike on his previous visit, there was no Herr Frode waiting with a warm car. Blomkvist had told them which day he would arrive, but not on which train. He assumed there was a bus to Hedeby, but he did not feel like struggling with two heavy suitcases and a shoulder bag, so he crossed the square to the taxi stand.

It had snowed massively all along the Norrland coast between Christmas and New Year's, and judging by the ridges and piles of snow thrown up by the ploughs, the road teams had been out in full force in Hedestad. The taxi driver, whose name, according to his ID posted on the window, was Hussein, nodded when Blomkvist asked whether they had been having rough weather. In the broadest Norrland accent, he reported that it had been the worst snowstorm in decades, and he bitterly regretted not taking his holiday in Greece over the Christmas period.

Blomkvist directed him to Henrik Vanger's newly shovelled courtyard, where he lifted his suitcases on to the cobblestones and watched the taxi head back towards Hedestad. He suddenly felt lonely and uncertain.

He heard the door open behind him. Vanger was wrapped up in a heavy fur coat, thick boots, and a cap with earflaps. Blomkvist was in jeans and a thin leather jacket.

"If you're going to live up here, you need to learn to dress more warmly for this time of year." They shook hands. "Are you sure you don't want to stay in the main house? No? Then I think we'd better start getting you settled into your new lodgings."

One of the conditions in his negotiations with Vanger and Dirch Frode had been that he have living quarters where he could do his own housekeeping and come and go as he pleased. Vanger led Blomkvist back along the road towards the bridge and then turned to open the gate to another newly shovelled courtyard in front of a small timbered house close to the end of the bridge. The house was not locked. They stepped into a modest hallway where Blomkvist, with a sigh of relief, put down his suitcases.

"This is what we call our guest house. It's where we usually put people up who are going to stay for a longer period of time. This was where you and your parents lived in 1963. It's one of the oldest buildings in the village, but it's been modernised. I asked Nilsson, my caretaker, to light the fire this morning."

The house consisted of a large kitchen and two smaller rooms, totalling about 500 square feet. The kitchen took up half the space and was quite modern, with an electric stove and a small refrigerator. Against the wall facing the front door stood an old cast-iron stove in which a fire had indeed been lit earlier in the day.

"You don't need to use the woodstove unless it gets bitterly cold. The firewood bin is there in the hallway, and you'll find a woodshed at the back. The house has been unlived-in this autumn. The electric heaters are usually sufficient. Just make sure you don't hang any clothes on them, or it may start a fire."

Blomkvist looked around. Windows faced three different directions, and from the kitchen table he had a view of the bridge, about a hundred feet away. The furnishings in the kitchen included three big cupboards, some kitchen chairs, an old bench, and a shelf for newspapers. On top was an issue of *See* from 1967. In one corner was a smaller table that could be used as a desk.

Two narrow doors led to smaller rooms. The one on the right, closest to the outside wall, was hardly more than a cubbyhole with a desk, a chair, and some shelves along the wall. The other room, between the hallway and the little office, was a very small bedroom with a narrow double bed, a bedside table, and a wardrobe. On the walls hung landscape paintings. The furniture and wallpaper in the house were all old and faded, but the place smelled nice and clean. Someone had worked over the floor with a dose of soap. The bedroom had another door to the hallway, where a storeroom had been converted into a bathroom with a shower.

"You may have a problem with the water," Vanger said. "We checked it this morning, but the pipes aren't buried very deep, and if this cold hangs on for long they may freeze. There's a bucket in the hallway so come up and get water from us if you need to."

"I'll need a telephone," Blomkvist said.

"I've already ordered one. They'll be here to install it the day after tomorrow. So, what do you think? If you change your mind, you would be welcome in the main house at any time."

"This will be just fine," Blomkvist said.

"Excellent. We have another hour or so of daylight left. Shall we take a walk so you can familiarise yourself with the village? Might I suggest that you put on some heavy socks and a pair of boots? You'll find them by the front door." Blomkvist did as he suggested and decided that the very next day he would go shopping for long underwear and a pair of good winter shoes.

The old man started the tour by explaining that Blomkvist's neighbour across the road was Gunnar Nilsson, the assistant whom Vanger insisted on calling "the caretaker." But Blomkvist soon realised that he was more of a superintendent for all the buildings on Hedeby Island, and he also had responsibility for several buildings in Hedestad.

"His father was Magnus Nilsson, who was my caretaker in the sixties, one of the men who helped out at the accident on the bridge. Magnus is retired and lives in Hedestad. Gunnar lives here with his wife, whose name is Helena. Their children have moved out."

Vanger paused for a moment to shape what he would say next, which was: "Mikael, the official explanation for your presence here is that you're going to help me write my autobiography. That will give you an excuse for poking around in all the dark corners and asking questions. The real assignment is strictly between you and me and Dirch Frode."

"I understand. And I'll repeat what I said before: I don't think I'm going to be able to solve the mystery."

"All I ask is that you do your best. But we must be careful what we say in front of anyone else. Gunnar is fifty-six, which means that he was nineteen when Harriet disappeared. There's one question that I never got answered—Harriet and Gunnar were good friends, and I think some sort of childish romance went on between them. He was pretty interested in her, at any rate. But on the day she disappeared, he was in Hedestad; he was one of those stranded on the mainland. Because of their relationship, he came under close scrutiny. It was quite unpleasant for him. He was with some friends all day, and he didn't get back here until evening. The police checked his alibi and it was airtight."

"I assume that you have a list of everyone who was on the island and what everybody was doing that day."

"That's correct. Shall we go on?"

They stopped at the crossroads on the hill, and Vanger pointed down towards the old fishing harbour, now used for small boats.

"All the land on Hedeby Island is owned by the Vanger family—or by me, to be more precise. The one exception is the farmland at Östergården and a few houses here in the village. The cabins down there at the fishing harbour are privately owned, but they're summer cottages and are mostly vacant during the winter. Except for that house farthest away—you can see smoke coming from the chimney."

Blomkvist saw the smoke rising. He was frozen to the bone.

"It's a miserably draughty hovel that functions as living quarters year-round. That's where Eugen Norman lives. He's in his late seventies and is a painter of sorts. I think his work is kitsch, but he's rather well known as a landscape painter. You might call him the obligatory eccentric in the village."

Vanger guided Blomkvist out towards the point, identifying one house after the other. The village consisted of six buildings on the west side of the road and four on the east. The first house, closest to Blomkvist's guest house and the Vanger estate, belonged to Henrik Vanger's brother Harald. It was a rectangular, two-storey stone building which at first glance seemed unoccupied. The curtains were drawn and the path to the front door had not been cleared; it was covered with a foot and a half of snow. On second glance, they could see the footprints of someone who had trudged through the snow from the road up to the door.

"Harald is a recluse. He and I have never seen eye to eye. Apart from our disagreements over the firm—he's a shareholder—we've barely spoken to each other in nearly 60 years. He's ninety-two now, and the only one of my four brothers still alive. I'll tell you the details later, but he trained to be a doctor and spent most of his professional life in Uppsala. He moved back to Hedeby when he turned seventy."

"You don't care much for each other, and yet you're neighbours."

"I find him detestable, and I would have rather he'd stayed in Uppsala, but he owns this house. Do I sound like a scoundrel?"

"You sound like someone who doesn't much like his brother."

"I spent the first twenty-five years of my life apologising for people like Harald because we're family. Then I discovered that being related is no guarantee of love and I had few reasons to defend Harald."

The next house belonged to Isabella, Harriet Vanger's mother.

"She'll be seventy-five this year, and she's still as stylish and vain as ever. She's also the only one in the village who talks to Harald, and occasionally visits him, but they don't have much in common."

"How was her relationship with Harriet?"

"Good question. The women have to be included among the suspects. I told you that she mostly left the children to their own devices. I can't be sure, but I think her heart was in the right place; she just wasn't capable of taking responsibility. She and Harriet were never close, but they weren't enemies either. Isabella can be tough, but sometimes she's not all there. You'll see what I mean when you meet her."

Isabella's neighbour was Cecilia Vanger, the daughter of Harald.

"She was married once and lived in Hedestad, but she and her husband separated some twenty years ago. I own the house and offered to let her move in. She is a teacher, and in many ways she's the direct opposite of her father. I might add that she and her father speak to each other only when necessary."

"How old is she?"

"Born in 1946. So she was twenty when Harriet disappeared. And yes, she was one of the guests on the island that day. Cecilia may seem flighty, but in fact she's shrewder than most. Don't underestimate her. If anyone's going to ferret out what you're up to, she's the one. I might add that she's one of my relatives for whom I have the highest regard."

"Does that mean that you don't suspect her?"

"I wouldn't say that. I want you to ponder the matter without any constraints, regardless of what I think or believe."

The house closest to Cecilia's was also owned by Henrik Vanger, but it was leased to an elderly couple formerly part of the management team of the Vanger companies. They had moved to Hedeby Island in the eighties, so they had nothing to do with Harriet's disappearance. The next house was owned by Birger Vanger, Cecilia's brother. The house had been empty for many years since Birger moved to a modern house in Hedestad.

Most of the buildings lining the road were solid stone structures from the early twentieth century. The last house was of a different type, a modern, architect-designed home built of white brick with black window frames. It was in a beautiful situation, and Blomkvist could see that the view from the top floor must be magnificent, facing the sea to the east and Hedestad to the north.

"This is where Martin lives—Harriet's brother and the Vanger Corporation CEO. The parsonage used to be here, but that building was destroyed by a fire in the seventies, and Martin built this house in 1978 when he took over as CEO."

In the last building on the east side of the road lived Gerda Vanger, widow of Henrik's brother Greger, and her son, Alexander.

"Gerda is sickly. She suffers from rheumatism. Alexander owns a small share of the Vanger Corporation, but he runs a number of his own businesses, including restaurants. He usually spends a few months each year in Barbados, where he has invested a considerable sum in the tourist trade."

Between Gerda's and Henrik's houses was a plot of land with two smaller, empty buildings. They were used as guest houses for family members. On the other side of Henrik's house stood a private dwelling where another retired employee lived with his wife, but it was empty in the winter when the couple repaired to Spain.

They returned to the crossroads, and with that the tour was over. Dusk was beginning to fall. Blomkvist took the initiative.

"Henrik, I'll do what I've been hired to do. I'll write your autobiography, and I'll humour you by reading all the material about Harriet as carefully and critically as I can. I just want you to realise that I'm not a private detective."

"I expect nothing."

"Fine."

"I'm a night owl," Vanger said. "So I'm at your disposal any time after lunch. I'll arrange for you to have an office up here, and you can make use of it whenever you like."

"No, thank you. I have an office in the guest house, and that's where I'll do my work."

"As you wish."

"If I need to talk to you, we'll do it in your office, but I'm not going to start throwing questions at you tonight."

"I understand." The old man seemed improbably timid.

"It's going to take a couple of weeks to read through the

papers. We'll work on two fronts. We'll meet for a few hours each day so that I can interview you and gather material for your biography. When I start having questions about Harriet which I need to discuss with you, I'll let you know."

"That sounds sensible."

"I'm going to require a free hand to do my work, and I won't have any set work hours."

"You decide for yourself how the work should be done."

"I suppose you're aware that I have to spend a couple of months in prison. I don't know exactly when, but I'm not going to appeal. It'll probably be sometime this year."

Vanger frowned. "That's unfortunate. We'll have to solve that problem when it comes up. You can always request a postponement."

"If it's permitted and I have enough material, I might be able to work on your book in prison. One more thing: I'm still part owner of *Millennium* and as of now it's a magazine in crisis. If something happens that requires my presence in Stockholm, I would have to drop what I'm doing and go there."

"I didn't take you on as a serf. I want you to do a thorough job on the assignment I've given you, but, of course, you can set your own schedule and do the work as you see fit. If you need to take some time off, feel free to do it, but if I find out that you're not doing the work, I'll consider that a breach of contract."

Vanger looked over towards the bridge. He was a gaunt man, and Blomkvist thought that he looked at that moment like a melancholy scarecrow.

"As far as *Millennium* is concerned, we ought to have a discussion about what kind of crisis it's in and whether I can help in some way."

"The best assistance you can offer is to give me Wennerström's head on a platter right here and now."

"Oh no, I'm not thinking of doing that." The old man gave

Blomkvist a hard look. "The only reason you took this job was because I promised to expose Wennerström. If I give you the information now, you could stop work on the job whenever you felt like it. I'll give you the information a year from now."

"Henrik, forgive me for saying this, but I can't be sure that a year from now you'll be alive."

Vanger sighed and cast a thoughtful gaze over the fishing harbour.

"Fair enough. I'll talk to Frode and see if we can work something out. But as far as *Millennium* is concerned, I might be able to help in another way. As I understand it, the advertisers have begun to pull out."

"The advertisers are the immediate problem, but the crisis goes deeper than that. It's a matter of trust. It doesn't matter how many advertisers we have if no-one wants to buy the magazine."

"I realise that. I'm still on the board of directors of quite a large corporation, albeit in a passive role. We have to place advertisements somewhere. Let's discuss the matter at some stage. Would you like to have dinner . . ."

"No. I want to get settled, buy some groceries, and take a look around. Tomorrow I'll go to Hedestad and shop for winter clothes."

"Good idea."

"I'd like the files about Harriet to be moved over to my place."

"They need to be handled . . ."

"With great care—I understand."

Blomkvist returned to the guest house. His teeth were chattering by the time he got indoors. The thermometer outside the window said 5°F, and he couldn't remember ever feeling so cold as after that walk, which had lasted barely twenty minutes.

He spent an hour settling himself into what was to be his

home for the coming year. He put his clothes in the wardrobe in the bedroom, his toiletries went in the bathroom cabinet. His second suitcase was actually a trunk on wheels. From it he took books, CDs and a CD player, notebooks, a Sanyo tape recorder, a Microtek scanner, a portable ink-jet printer, a Minolta digital camera, and a number of other items he regarded as essential kit for a year in exile.

He arranged the books and the CDs on the bookshelf in the office alongside two binders containing research material on Hans-Erik Wennerström. The material was useless, but he could not let it go. Somehow he had to turn those two folders into building blocks for his continuing career.

Finally he opened his shoulder bag and put his iBook on the desk in the office. Then he stopped and looked about him with a sheepish expression. The benefits of living in the countryside, forsooth. There was nowhere to plug in the broadband cable. He did not even have a telephone jack to connect an old dial-up modem.

Blomkvist called the Telia telephone company from his mobile. After a slight hassle, he managed to get someone to find the order that Vanger had placed for the guest house. He wanted to know whether the connection could handle ADSL and was told that it would be possible by way of a relay in Hedeby, and that it would take several days.

It was after 4:00 by the time Blomkvist was done. He put on a pair of thick socks and the borrowed boots and pulled on an extra sweater. At the front door he stopped short; he had been given no keys to the house, and his big-city instincts rebelled at the idea of leaving the front door unlocked. He went back to the kitchen and began opening drawers. Finally he found a key hanging from a nail in the pantry.

The temperature had dropped to –1°F. He walked briskly across the bridge and up the hill past the church. The Konsum store was conveniently located about three hundred yards away. He filled two paper bags to overflowing with supplies and then carried them home before returning across the bridge. This time he stopped at Susanne's Bridge Café. The woman behind the counter was in her fifties. He asked whether she was Susanne and then introduced himself by saying that he was undoubtedly going to be a regular customer. He was for the time being the only customer, and Susanne offered him coffee when he ordered sandwiches and bought a loaf of bread. He picked up a copy of the *Hedestad Courier* from the newspaper rack and sat at a table with a view of the bridge and the church, its facade now lit up. It looked like a Christmas card. It took him about four minutes to read the newspaper. The only news of interest was a brief item explaining that a local politician by the name of Birger Vanger (Liberal) was going to invest in "IT TechCent"—a technology development centre in Hedestad. Mikael sat there until the café closed at 6:00.

At 7:30 he called Berger, but was advised that the party at that number was not available. He sat on the kitchen bench and tried to read a novel which, according to the back cover text, was the sensational debut of a teenage feminist. The novel was about the author's attempt to get a handle on her sex life during a trip to Paris, and Blomkvist wondered whether he could be called a feminist if he wrote a novel about his own sex life in the voice of a high-school student. Probably not. He had bought the book because the publisher had hailed the first-time novelist as "a new Carina Rydberg." He quickly ascertained that this was not the case in either style or content. He put the book aside for a while and instead read a Hopalong Cassidy story in an issue of *Rekordmagasinet* from the mid-fifties.

Every half hour he heard the curt, muted clang of the church bell. Lights were visible in the windows at the home of the caretaker across the road, but Blomkvist could not see anyone inside the house. Harald Vanger's house was dark. Around 9:00 a car drove across the bridge and disappeared towards the point. At midnight the lights on the facade of the church were turned off. That was apparently the full extent of the entertainment in Hedeby on a Friday night in early January. It was eerily quiet.

He tried again to call Berger and got her voicemail, asking him to leave his name and a message. He did so and then turned off the light and went to bed. The last thing he thought about before he fell asleep was that he was going to run a high risk of going stir-crazy in Hedeby.

It was strange to awake to utter silence. Blomkvist passed from deep sleep to total alertness in a fraction of a second, and then lay still, listening. It was cold in the room. He turned his head and looked at his wristwatch on a stool next to the bed. It was 7:08—he had never been much of a morning person, and it used to be hard for him to wake up without having at least two alarm clocks. Today he had woken all by himself, and he even felt rested.

He put some water on for coffee before getting into the shower. He was suddenly amused at his situation. *Kalle Blomkvist—on a research trip in the back of beyond.*

The shower head changed from scalding to ice-cold at the slightest touch. There was no morning paper on the kitchen table. The butter was frozen. There was no cheese slicer in the drawer of kitchen utensils. It was still pitch dark outside. The thermometer showed 6 below zero. It was Saturday.

The bus stop for Hedestad was over the road from Konsum, and Blomkvist started off his exile by carrying out his plan to go shopping in town. He got off the bus by the railway station and made a tour of the centre of town. Along the way he bought heavy winter boots, two pairs of long underwear, several flannel shirts, a proper thigh-length winter jacket, a warm cap, and lined gloves. At the electronics store he found a small portable TV with rabbit ears. The sales clerk assured him that he would at least be able to get SVT, the state TV channel, out at Hedeby, and Blomkvist promised to ask for his money back if that turned out not to be the case.

He stopped at the library to get himself a card and borrowed two mysteries by Elizabeth George. He bought pens and notebooks. He also bought a rucksack for carrying his new possessions.

Finally he bought a pack of cigarettes. He had stopped smoking ten years ago, but occasionally he would have a relapse. He stuck the pack in his jacket pocket without opening it. His last stop was the optician's, and there he bought contact lens solution and ordered new lenses.

By 2:00 he was back in Hedeby, and he was just removing the price tags from his new clothes when he heard the front door open. A blonde woman—perhaps in her fifties—knocked on the open kitchen door as she stepped across the threshold. She was carrying a sponge cake on a platter.

"Hello. I just wanted to come over to introduce myself. My name is Helena Nilsson, and I live across the road. I hear we're going to be neighbours."

They shook hands and he introduced himself.

"Oh yes, I've seen you on TV. It's going to be nice to see lights over here in the evening."

Blomkvist put on some coffee. She began to object but then sat at the kitchen table, casting a furtive glance out the window.

"Here comes Henrik with my husband. It looks like some boxes for you."

Vanger and Gunnar Nilsson drew up outside with a dolly, and Blomkvist rushed out to greet them and to help carry the four packing crates inside. They set the boxes on the floor next to the stove. Blomkvist got out the coffee cups and cut into Fröken Nilsson's sponge cake.

The Nilssons were pleasant people. They did not seem curious about why Blomkvist was in Hedestad—the fact that he was working for Henrik Vanger was evidently enough of an explanation. Blomkvist observed the interaction between the Nilssons and Vanger, concluding that it was relaxed and lacking in any sort of gulf between master and servants. They talked about the village and the man who had built the guest house where Blomkvist was living. The Nilssons would prompt Vanger when his memory failed him. He, on the other hand, told a funny story about how Nilsson had come home one night to discover the village idiot from across the bridge trying to break a window at the guest house. Nilsson went over to ask the half-witted delinquent why he didn't go in through the unlocked front door. Nilsson inspected Blomkvist's little TV with misgiving and invited him to come across to their house if there was ever a programme he wanted to see.

Vanger stayed on briefly after the Nilssons left. He thought it best that Blomkvist sort through the files himself, and he could come to the house if he had any problems.

When he was alone once more, Blomkvist carried the boxes into his office and made an inventory of the contents.

Vanger's investigation into the disappearance of his brother's granddaughter had been going on for thirty-six years. Blomkvist wondered whether this was an unhealthy obsession or whether, over the years, it had developed into an intellectual game. What was clear was that the old patriarch had tackled the job with the systematic approach of an amateur archaeologist—the material was going to fill twenty feet of shelving.

The largest section of it consisted of twenty-six binders, which were the copies of the police investigation. Hard to believe an ordinary missing-person case would have produced such comprehensive material. Vanger no doubt had enough clout to keep the Hedestad police following up both plausible and implausible leads.

Then there were scrapbooks, photograph albums, maps, texts about Hedestad and the Vanger firm, Harriet's diary (though it did not contain many pages), her schoolbooks, medical certificates. There were sixteen bound A4 volumes of one hundred or so pages each, which were Vanger's logbook of the investigations. In these notebooks he had recorded in an impeccable hand his own speculations, theories, digressions. Blomkvist leafed through them. The text had a literary quality, and he had the feeling that these texts were fair copies of perhaps many more notebooks. There were ten binders containing material on members of the Vanger family; these pages were typed and had been compiled over the intervening years, Vanger's investigations of his own family.

Around 7:00 he heard a loud meowing at the front door. A reddish-brown cat slipped swiftly past him into the warmth.

"Wise cat," he said.

The cat sniffed around the guest house for a while. Mikael poured some milk into a dish, and his guest lapped it up. Then the cat hopped on to the kitchen bench and curled up. And there she stayed.

It was after 10:00 before Blomkvist had the scope of the material clear in his mind and had arranged it on the shelves. He put on a pot of coffee and made himself two sandwiches. He had not eaten a proper meal all day, but he was strangely uninterested in food. He offered the cat a piece of sausage and some liverwurst. After drinking his coffee, he took the cigarettes out of his jacket pocket and opened the pack.

He checked his mobile. Berger had not called. He tried her once more. Again only her voicemail.

One of the first steps Blomkvist had taken was to scan in the map of Hedeby Island that he had borrowed from Vanger. While all the names were still fresh in his mind, he wrote down who lived in each house. The Vanger clan consisted of such an extensive cast that it would take time to learn who was who.

Just before midnight he put on warm clothes and his new shoes and walked across the bridge. He turned off the road and along the sound below the church. Ice had formed on the sound and inside the old harbour, but farther out he could see a darker belt of open water. As he stood there, the lights on the facade of the church went out, and it was dark all around him. It was icy cold and stars filled the sky.

All of a sudden Blomkvist felt depressed. He could not for the life of him understand how he had allowed Vanger to talk him into taking on this assignment. Berger was right: he should be in Stockholm—in bed with her, for instance—and planning his campaigns against Wennerström. But he felt apathetic about that too, and he didn't even have the faintest idea how to begin planning a counter-strategy.

Had it been daylight, he would have walked straight to Vanger's house, cancelled his contract, and gone home. But from the rise beside the church he could make out all the houses on the island side. Harald Vanger's house was dark, but there were lights on in Cecilia's home, as well as in Martin's villa out by the point and in the house that was leased. In the small-boat harbour there were lights on in the draughty cabin of the artist and little clouds of sparks were rising from his chimney. There were also lights on in the top floor of the café, and Blomkvist wondered whether Susanne lived there, and if so, whether she was alone.

On Sunday morning he awoke in panic at the incredible din that filled the guest house. It took him a second to get his bearings and realise that it was the church bells summoning parishioners to morning service. It was nearly 11:00. He stayed in bed until he heard an urgent meowing in the doorway and got up to let out the cat.

By noon he had showered and eaten breakfast. He went resolutely into his office and took down the first binder from the police investigation. Then he hesitated. From the gable window he could see Susanne's Bridge Café. He stuffed the binder into his shoulder bag and put on his outdoor clothes. When he reached the café, he found it brimming with customers, and there he had the answer to a question that had been in the back of his mind: how could a café survive in a backwater like Hedeby? Susanne specialised in churchgoers and presumably did coffee and cakes for funerals and other functions.

He took a walk instead. Konsum was closed on Sundays, and he continued a few hundred yards towards Hedestad, where he bought newspapers at a petrol station. He spent an hour walking around Hedeby, familiarising himself with the town before the bridge. The area closest to the church and past Konsum was the centre, with older buildings—two-storey stone structures which Blomkvist guessed had been built in the 1910s or '20s and which formed a short main street. North of the road into town were well-kept apartment buildings for families with children.

Along the water and to the south of the church were mostly single-family homes. Hedeby looked to be a relatively well-to-do area for Hedestad's decision-makers and civil servants.

When he returned to the bridge, the assault on the café had ebbed, but Susanne was still clearing dishes from the tables.

"The Sunday rush?" he said in greeting.

She nodded as she tucked a lock of hair behind one ear. "Hi, Mikael."

"So you remember my name."

"Hard to forget," she said. "I followed your trial on TV."

"They have to fill up the news with something," he muttered, and drifted over to the corner table with a view of the bridge. When he met Susanne's eyes, she smiled.

At 3:00 Susanne announced that she was closing the café for the day. After the church rush, only a few customers had come and gone. Blomkvist had read more than a fifth of the first binder of the police investigation. He stuck his notebook into his bag and walked briskly home across the bridge.

The cat was waiting on the steps. He looked around, wondering whose cat it was. He let it inside all the same, since the cat was at least some sort of company.

He made one more vain attempt to reach Berger. Obviously she was furious with him still. He could have tried calling her direct line at the office or her home number, but he had already left enough messages. Instead, he made himself coffee, moved the cat farther along the kitchen bench, and opened the binder on the table.

He read carefully and slowly, not wanting to miss any detail. By late evening, when he closed the binder, he had filled several pages of his own notebook—with reminders and questions to which he hoped to find answers in subsequent binders. The material was all arranged in chronological order. He could not tell whether Vanger had reorganised it that way or whether that was the system used by the police at the time.

The first page was a photocopy of a handwritten report form headed Hedestad Police Emergency Centre. The officer who had taken the call had signed his name D.O. Ryttinger, and Blomkvist assumed the "D.O." stood for "duty officer." The caller was Henrik Vanger. His address and telephone number had been noted. The report was dated Sunday, September 25, 1966, at 11:14 a.m. The text was laconic:

Call from Hrk. Vanger, stating that his brother's daughter (?) Harriet Ulrika VANGER, born 15 Jan. 1950 (age 16) has been missing from her home on Hedeby Island since Saturday afternoon. The caller expressed great concern.

A note sent at 11:20 a.m. stated that P-014 (police car? patrol? pilot of a boat?) had been sent to the site.

Another at 11:35 a.m., in a less legible hand than Ryttinger's, inserted that *Off. Magnusson reports that bridge to Hedeby Island still blocked. Transp. by boat.* In the margin an illegible signature.

At 12:14 p.m. Ryttinger is back: *Telephone conversation Off. Magnusson in H-by confirms that 16-year-old Harriet Vanger missing since early Saturday afternoon. Family expressed great concern. Not believed to have slept in her bed last night. Could not have left island due to blocked bridge. None of family members has any knowledge as to HV's whereabouts.*

At 12:19 p.m.: *G.M. informed by telephone about the situation.*

The last note was recorded at 1:42 p.m.: *G.M. on site at H-by; will take over the matter.*

The next page revealed that the initials "G.M." referred to Detective Inspector Gustaf Morell, who arrived at Hedeby Island by boat and there took over command, preparing a formal report on the disappearance of Harriet Vanger. Unlike the initial notations with their needless abbreviations, Morell's reports were written on a typewriter and in very readable prose. The following pages recounted what measures had been taken, with an objectivity and wealth of detail that surprised Blomkvist.

Morell had first interviewed Henrik Vanger along with Isabella Vanger, Harriet's mother. Then he talked in turn with Ulrika Vanger, Harald Vanger, Greger Vanger, Harriet's brother Martin Vanger, and Anita Vanger. Blomkvist came to the conclusion that these interviews had been conducted according to a scale of decreasing importance.

Ulrika Vanger was Henrik Vanger's mother, and evidently she held a status comparable to that of a dowager queen. Ulrika lived at the Vanger estate and was able to provide no information. She had gone to bed early on the previous night and had not seen Harriet for several days. She appeared to have insisted on meeting Detective Inspector Morell solely to give air to her opinion that the police had to act at once, immediately.

Harald Vanger ranked as number two on the list. He had seen Harriet only briefly when she returned from the festivities in Hedestad, but he *had not seen her since the accident on the bridge occurred and he had no knowledge of where she might be at present.*

Greger Vanger, brother of Henrik and Harald, stated that he had seen the missing sixteen-year-old in Henrik Vanger's study, asking to speak with Henrik after her visit to Hedestad earlier in the day. Greger Vanger stated that he had not spoken with her himself, merely given her a greeting. He had no idea where she might be found, but he expressed the view that she had probably, thoughtlessly, gone to visit some friend without telling anyone and would reappear soon. When asked how she might in that case have left the island, he offered no answer.

Martin Vanger was interviewed in a cursory fashion. He was

in his final year at the preparatory school in Uppsala, where he lived in the home of Harald Vanger. There was no room for him in Harald's car, so he had taken the train home to Hedeby, arriving so late that he was stranded on the wrong side of the bridge accident and could not cross until late in the evening by boat. He was interviewed in the hope that his sister might have confided in him and perhaps given him some clue if she was thinking of running away. The question was met with protests from Harriet Vanger's mother, but at that moment Inspector Morell was perhaps thinking that Harriet's having run away would be the best they could hope for. But Martin had not spoken with his sister since the summer holiday and had no information of value.

Anita Vanger, daughter of Harald Vanger, was erroneously listed as Harriet's "first cousin." She was in her first year at the university in Stockholm and had spent the summer in Hedeby. She was almost the same age as Harriet and they had become close friends. She stated that she had arrived at the island with her father on Saturday and was looking forward to seeing Harriet, but she had not had the opportunity to find her. Anita stated that she felt uneasy, and that it was not like Harriet to go off without telling the family. Henrik and Isabella Vanger confirmed that this was the case.

While Inspector Morell was interviewing family members, he had told Magnusson and Bergman—patrol 014—to organise the first search party while there was still daylight. The bridge was still closed to traffic, so it was difficult to call in reinforcements. The group consisted of about thirty available individuals, men and women of varying ages. The areas they searched that afternoon included the unoccupied houses at the fishing harbour, the shoreline at the point and along the sound, the section of woods closest to the village, and the hill called Söderberget behind the fishing harbour. The latter was searched because someone had put forward the theory that Harriet might have gone up there to get a good view of the scene on the bridge. Patrols were also sent out to Östergården and to Gottfried's cabin on the other side of the island, which Harriet occasionally visited.

But the search was fruitless; it was not called off until long after dark fell, at 10:00 at night. The temperature overnight dropped to freezing.

During the afternoon Inspector Morell set up his headquarters in a drawing room that Henrik Vanger had put at his disposal on the ground floor of the Vanger estate office. He had undertaken a number of measures.

In the company of Isabella Vanger, he had examined Harriet's room and tried to ascertain whether anything was missing: clothes, a suitcase, or the like, which would indicate that Harriet had run away from home. Isabella, a note implied, had not been helpful and did not seem to be familiar with her daughter's wardrobe. *She often wore jeans, but they all look the same, don't they?* Harriet's purse was on her desk. It contained ID, a wallet holding nine kronor and fifty öre, a comb, a mirror, and a handkerchief. After the inspection, Harriet's room was locked.

Morell had summoned more people to be interviewed, family members and employees. All the interviews were meticulously reported.

When the participants in the first search party began returning with disheartening reports, the inspector decided that a more systematic search had to be made. That evening and night, reinforcements were called in. Morell contacted, among others, the chairman of Hedestad's Orienteering Club and appealed for help in summoning volunteers for the search party. By midnight he was told that fifty-three members, mostly from the junior division, would be at the Vanger estate at 7:00 the next morning. Henrik Vanger called in part of the morning shift, numbering fifty men, from the paper mill. He also arranged for food and drink for them all.

Blomkvist could vividly imagine the scenes played out at the Vanger estate during those days. The accident on the bridge had certainly contributed to the confusion during the first hours—by making it difficult to bring in reinforcements, and also because people somehow thought that these two dramatic events happening at the same place and close to the same time must in some way have been connected. When the tanker truck was hoisted away, Inspector Morell went down to the bridge to be sure that Harriet Vanger had not, by some unlikely turn of events, ended up under the wreck. That was the only irrational action that Mikael could detect in the inspector's conduct, since the missing girl had unquestionably been seen on the island after the accident had occurred.

During those first confused twenty-four hours, their hopes that the situation would come to a swift and happy resolution sank. Instead, they were gradually replaced by two theories. In spite of the obvious difficulties in leaving the island unnoticed, Morell refused to discount the possibility that she had run away. He decided that an all-points bulletin should be sent out for Harriet Vanger, and he gave instructions for the patrol officers in Hedestad to keep their eyes open for the missing girl. He also sent a colleague in the criminal division to interview bus drivers and staff at the railway station, to find out whether anyone might have seen her.

As the negative reports came in, it became increasingly likely that Harriet Vanger had fallen victim to some sort of misfortune. This theory ended up dominating the investigative work of the following days.

The big search party two days after her disappearance was

apparently, as far as Blomkvist could tell, carried out effectively. Police and firefighters who had experience with similar operations had organised the search. Hedeby Island did have some parts that were almost inaccessible, but it was nevertheless a small area, and the island was searched with a fine-tooth comb in one day. A police boat and two volunteer Pettersson boats did what they could to search the waters around the island.

On the following day the search was continued with decreased manpower. Patrols were sent out to make a second sweep of the particularly rugged terrain, as well as an area known as "the fortress"—a now-abandoned bunker system that was built during the Second World War. That day they also searched cubbyholes, wells, vegetable cellars, outhouses, and attics in the village.

A certain frustration could be read in the official notes when the search was called off on the third day after the girl's disappearance. Morell was, of course, not yet aware of it, but at that moment he had actually reached as far in the investigation as he would ever get. He was puzzled and struggled to identify the natural next step or any place where the search ought to be pursued. Harriet Vanger seemed to have dissolved into thin air, and Henrik Vanger's years of torment had begun.

CHAPTER 9

Monday, January 6–Wednesday, January 8

Blomkvist kept reading until the small hours and did not get up until late on Epiphany Day. A navy blue, late-model Volvo was parked outside Vanger's house. Even as he reached for the door handle, the door was opened by a man on his way out. They almost collided. The man seemed to be in a hurry.

"Yes? Can I help you?"

"I'm here to see Henrik Vanger," Blomkvist said.

The man's eyes brightened. He smiled and stuck out his hand. "You must be Mikael Blomkvist, the one who's going to help Henrik with the family chronicle, right?"

They shook hands. Vanger had apparently begun spreading Blomkvist's cover story. The man was overweight—the result, no doubt, of too many years of negotiating in offices and conference rooms—but Blomkvist noticed at once the likeness, the similarity between his face and Harriet Vanger's.

"I'm Martin Vanger," the man said. "Welcome to Hedestad."

"Thank you."

"I saw you on TV a while ago."

"Everybody seems to have seen me on TV."

"Wennerström is . . . not very popular in this house."

"Henrik mentioned that. I'm waiting to hear the rest of the story."

"He told me a few days ago that he'd hired you." Martin Vanger laughed. "He said it was probably because of Wennerström that you took the job up here."

Blomkvist hesitated before deciding to tell the truth. "That was one important reason. But to be honest, I needed to get away from Stockholm, and Hedestad cropped up at the right moment. At least I think so. I can't pretend that the court case never happened. And anyway, I'm going to have to go to prison."

Martin Vanger nodded, suddenly serious. "Can you appeal?"

"It won't do any good."

Vanger glanced at his watch.

"I have to be in Stockholm tonight, so I must hurry away. I'll be back in a few days. Come over and have dinner. I'd really like to hear what actually went on during that trial. Henrik is upstairs. Go right in."

Vanger was sitting on a sofa in his office where he had the *Hedestad Courier, Dagens Industri, Svenska Dagbladet,* and both national evening papers on the coffee table.

"I ran into Martin outside."

"Rushing off to save the empire," Vanger said. "Coffee?"

"Yes, please." Blomkvist sat down, wondering why Vanger looked so amused.

"You're mentioned in the paper."

Vanger shoved across one of the evening papers, open at a page with the headline "Media Short Circuit." The article was written by a columnist who had previously worked for *Monopoly*

Financial Magazine, making a name for himself as one who cheerfully ridiculed everyone who felt passionate about any issue or who stuck their neck out. Feminists, anti-racists, and environmental activists could all reckon on receiving their share. The writer was not known for espousing a single conviction of his own. Now, several weeks after the trial in the Wennerström affair, he was bringing his fire to bear on Mikael Blomkvist, whom he described as a complete idiot. Erika Berger was portrayed as an incompetent media bimbo:

> A rumour is circulating that *Millennium* is on the verge of collapse in spite of the fact that the editor in chief is a feminist who wears mini-skirts and pouts her lips on TV. For several years the magazine has survived on the image that has been successfully marketed by the editors—young reporters who undertake investigative journalism and expose the scoundrels of the business world. This advertising trick may work with young anarchists who want to hear just such a message, but it doesn't wash in the district court. As Kalle Blomkvist recently found out.

Blomkvist switched on his mobile and checked to see if he had any calls from Berger. There were no messages. Vanger waited without saying anything. Blomkvist realised that the old man was allowing him to break the silence.

"He's a moron," Blomkvist said.

Vanger laughed, but he said: "That may be. But he's not the one who was sentenced by the court."

"That's true. And he never will be. He never says anything original; he always just jumps on the bandwagon and casts the final stone in the most damaging terms he can get away with."

"I've had many enemies over the years. If there's one thing I've learned, it's never engage in a fight you're sure to lose. On the other hand, never let anyone who has insulted you get away with it. Bide your time and strike back when you're in a position of strength—even if you no longer need to strike back."

"Thank you for your wisdom, Henrik. Now I'd like you to tell me about your family." He set the tape recorder between them on the table and pressed the record button.

"What do you want to know?"

"I've read through the first binder, about the disappearance and the searches, but there are so many Vangers mentioned that I need your help identifying them all."

For nearly ten minutes Salander stood in the empty hall with her eyes fixed on the brass plaque that said "Advokat N. E. Bjurman" before she rang the bell. The lock on the entry door clicked.

It was Tuesday. It was their second meeting, and she had a bad feeling about it.

She was not afraid of Bjurman—Salander was rarely afraid of anyone or anything. On the other hand, she felt uncomfortable with this new guardian. His predecessor, Advokat Holger Palmgren, had been of an entirely different ilk: courteous and kind. But three months ago Palmgren had had a stroke, and Nils Erik Bjurman had inherited her in accordance with some bureaucratic pecking order.

In the twelve years that Salander had been under social and psychiatric guardianship, two of those years in a children's clinic, she had never once given the same answer to the simple question: "So, how are you today?"

When she turned thirteen, the court had decided, under laws governing the guardianship of minors, that she should be entrusted to the locked ward at St. Stefan's Psychiatric Clinic for Children in Uppsala. The decision was primarily based on the fact that she was deemed to be emotionally disturbed and dangerously violent towards her classmates and possibly towards herself.

All attempts by a teacher or any authority figure to initiate a conversation with the girl about her feelings, emotional life, or the state of her health were met, to their great frustration, with a sullen silence and a great deal of intense staring at the floor, ceiling, and walls. She would fold her arms and refuse to participate in any psychological tests. Her resistance to all attempts to measure, weigh, chart, analyse, or educate her applied also to her school work—the authorities could have her carried to a classroom and could chain her to the bench, but they could not stop her from closing her ears and refusing to lift a pen to write anything. She completed the nine years of compulsory schooling without a certificate.

This had consequently become associated with the great difficulty of even diagnosing her mental deficiencies. In short, Lisbeth Salander was anything but easy to handle.

By the time she was thirteen, it was also decided that a trustee should be assigned to take care of her interests and assets until she came of age. This trustee was Advokat Palmgren who, in spite of a rather difficult start, had succeeded where psychiatrists and doctors had failed. Gradually he won not only a certain amount of trust but also a modest amount of warmth from the girl.

When she turned fifteen, the doctors had more or less agreed that she was not, after all, dangerously violent, nor did she represent any immediate danger to herself. Her family had been categorised as dysfunctional, and she had no relatives who could look after her welfare, so it was decided that Lisbeth Salander should be released from the psychiatric clinic for children in Uppsala and eased back into society by way of a foster family.

That had not been an easy journey. She ran away from the

first foster family after only two weeks. The second and third foster families fell by the wayside in quick succession. At that point Palmgren had a serious discussion with her, explaining bluntly that if she persisted on this path she would be institutionalised again. This threat had the effect that she accepted foster family number four—an elderly couple who lived in Midsommarkransen.

But it did not mean, however, that she behaved herself. At the age of seventeen, Salander was arrested by the police on four occasions; twice she was so intoxicated that she ended up in the emergency room, and once she was plainly under the influence of narcotics. On one of these occasions she was found dead drunk, with her clothes in disarray, in the back seat of a car parked at Söder Mälarstrand. She was with an equally drunk and much older man.

The last arrest occurred three weeks before her eighteenth birthday, when she, perfectly sober, kicked a male passenger in the head inside the gates of the Gamla Stan tunnelbana station. She was charged with assault and battery. Salander claimed that the man had groped her, and her testimony was supported by witnesses. The prosecutor dismissed the case. But her background was such that the district court ordered a psychiatric evaluation. Since she refused, as was her custom, to answer any questions or to participate in the examinations, the doctors consulted by the National Board of Health and Welfare handed down an opinion based on "observations of the patient." It was unclear precisely what could be observed when it was a matter of a silent young woman sitting on a chair with her arms folded and her lower lip stuck out. The only determination made was that she must suffer from some kind of emotional disturbance, whose nature was of the sort that could not be left untreated. The medical/legal report recommended care in a closed psychiatric institution. An assistant head of the social welfare board wrote an opinion in support of the conclusions of the psychiatric experts.

With regard to her personal record, the opinion concluded that there was *grave risk of alcohol and drug abuse*, and that she *lacked self-awareness*. By then her casebook was filled with terms such as *introverted, socially inhibited, lacking in empathy, ego-fixated, psychopathic and asocial behaviour, difficulty in cooperating*, and *incapable of assimilating learning*. Anyone who read her casebook might be tempted to conclude that Salander was seriously retarded. Another mark against her was that the social services street patrol had on several occasions observed her "with various men" in the area around Mariatorget. She was once stopped and frisked in Tantolunden, again with a much older man. It was feared that Salander was possibly operating as, or ran the risk of becoming, a prostitute.

When the district court—the institution that would determine her future—met to decide on the matter, the outcome seemed a foregone conclusion. She was obviously a problem child, and it was unlikely that the court would come to any decision other than to accept the recommendations of both the psychiatric and the social inquiries.

On the morning the court hearing was to take place, Salander was brought from the psychiatric clinic for children where she had been confined since the incident in Gamla Stan. She felt like a prisoner from a concentration camp: she had no hope of surviving the day. The first person she saw in the courtroom was Palmgren, and it took a while for her to realise that he was not there in the role of a trustee but rather as her legal representative.

To her surprise, he was firmly in her corner, and he made a powerful appeal against institutionalisation. She did not betray with so much as a raised eyebrow that she was surprised, but she listened intently to every word that was said. Palmgren was brilliant during the two hours in which he cross-examined the physician, a Dr. Jesper H. Löderman, who had signed his name to the recommendation that Salander be locked away in an institution. Every detail of the opinion was scrutinised, and the doctor was required to explain the scientific basis for each statement. Eventually it became clear that since the patient had refused to complete a single test, the basis for the doctor's conclusions was in fact nothing more than guesswork.

At the end of the hearing, Palmgren intimated that compulsory institutionalisation was in all probability not only contrary to Parliament's decisions in similar situations, but in this particular case it might in addition be the subject of political and media reprisals. So it was in everyone's interest to find an appropriate alternative solution. Such language was unusual for negotiations in this type of situation, and the members of the court had squirmed nervously.

The solution was also a compromise. The court concluded that Lisbeth Salander was indeed emotionally disturbed, but that her condition did not necessarily warrant internment. On the other hand, the social welfare director's recommendation of guardianship was taken under consideration. The chairman of the court turned, with a venomous smile, to Holger Palmgren, who up until then had been her trustee, and inquired whether he might be willing to take on the guardianship. The chairman obviously thought that Palmgren would back away and try to push the responsibility on to someone else. On the contrary, Palmgren declared that he would be happy to take on the job of serving as Fröken Salander's guardian—but on one condition: "that Fröken Salander must be willing to trust me and accept me as her guardian."

He turned to face her. Lisbeth Salander was somewhat bewildered by the exchange that had gone back and forth over her head all day. Until now no-one had asked for her opinion. She looked at Holger Palmgren for a long time and then nodded once.

Palmgren was a peculiar mixture of jurist and social worker, of the old school. At first he had been a politically appointed member of the social welfare board, and he had spent nearly all his life dealing with problem youths. A reluctant sense of respect, almost bordering on friendship, had in time formed between Palmgren and his ward, who was unquestionably the most difficult he had ever had to deal with.

Their relationship had lasted eleven years, from her thirteenth birthday until the previous year, when a few weeks before Christmas she had gone to see Palmgren at home after he missed one of their scheduled monthly meetings.

When he did not open the door even though she could hear sounds coming from his apartment, she broke in by climbing up a drainpipe to the balcony on the fourth floor. She found him lying on the floor in the hall, conscious but unable to speak or move. She called for an ambulance and accompanied him to Söder Hospital with a growing feeling of panic in her stomach. For three days she hardly left the corridor outside the intensive care unit. Like a faithful watchdog, she kept an eye on every doctor and nurse who went in or out of the door. She wandered up and down the corridor like a lost soul, fixing her eyes on every doctor who came near. Finally a doctor whose name she never discovered took her into a room to explain the gravity of the situation. Herr Palmgren was in critical condition following a severe cerebral haemorrhage. He was not expected to regain consciousness. He was only sixty-four years old. She neither wept nor changed her expression. She stood up, left the hospital, and did not return.

Five weeks later the Guardianship Agency summoned Salander to the first meeting with her new guardian. Her initial impulse was to ignore the summons, but Palmgren had imprinted in her consciousness that every action has its consequences. She had learned to analyse the consequences and so she had come to the conclusion that the easiest way out of this present dilemma was to satisfy the Guardianship Agency by behaving as if she cared about what they had to say.

Thus, in December—taking a break from her research on Mikael Blomkvist—she arrived at Bjurman's office on St. Eriksplan, where an elderly woman representing the board had handed over Salander's extensive file to Advokat Bjurman. The woman had kindly asked Salander how things were going, and she seemed satisfied with the stifled silence she received in reply. After about half an hour she left Salander in the care of Advokat Bjurman.

Salander decided that she did not like Advokat Bjurman. She studied him furtively as he read through her casebook. Age: over fifty. Trim body. Tennis on Tuesdays and Fridays. Blond. Thinning hair. A slight cleft in his chin. Hugo Boss aftershave. Blue suit. Red tie with a gold tiepin and ostentatious cufflinks with the initials NEB. Steel-rimmed glasses. Grey eyes. To judge by the magazines on the side table, his interests were hunting and shooting.

During the years she had known Palmgren, he had always offered her coffee and chatted with her. Not even her worst escapes from foster homes or her regular truancy from school had ever ruffled his composure. The only time Palmgren had been really upset was when she had been charged with assault and battery after that scumbag had groped her in Gamla Stan. *Do you understand what you've done? You have harmed another human being, Lisbeth.* He had sounded like an old teacher, and she had patiently ignored every word of his scolding.

Bjurman did not have time for small talk. He had

immediately concluded that there was a discrepancy between Palmgren's obligations, according to the regulations of guardianship, and the fact that he had apparently allowed the Salander girl to take charge of her own household and finances. Bjurman started in on a sort of interrogation: *How much do you earn? I want a copy of your financial records. Who do you spend time with? Do you pay your rent on time? Do you drink? Did Palmgren approve of those rings you have on your face? Are you careful about hygiene?*

Fuck you.

Palmgren had become her trustee right after All The Evil had happened. He had insisted on meetings with her at least once a month, sometimes more often. After she moved back to Lundagatan, they were also practically neighbours. He lived on Hornsgatan, a couple of blocks away, and they would run into each other and go for coffee at Giffy's or some other café nearby. Palmgren had never tried to impose, but a few times he had visited her, bringing some little gift for her birthday. She had a standing invitation to visit him whenever she liked, a privilege that she seldom took advantage of. But when she moved to Söder, she had started spending Christmas Eve with him after she went to see her mother. They would eat Christmas ham and play chess. She had no real interest in the game, but after she learned the rules, she never lost a match. He was a widower, and Salander had seen it as her duty to take pity on him on those lonely holidays.

She considered herself in his debt, and she always paid her debts.

It was Palmgren who had sublet her mother's apartment on Lundagatan for her until Salander needed her own place to live. The apartment was about 500 square feet, shabby and unrenovated, but at least it was a roof over her head.

Now Palmgren was gone, and another tie to established society had been severed. Nils Bjurman was a wholly different sort of person. No way she would be spending Christmas Eve at his house. His first move had been to put in place new rules on the management of her account at Handelsbanken. Palmgren had never had any problems about bending the conditions of his guardianship so as to allow her to take care of her own finances. She paid her bills and could use her savings as she saw fit.

Prior to the meeting with Bjurman the week before Christmas she had prepared herself; once there, she had tried to explain that his predecessor had trusted her and had never been given occasion to do otherwise. Palmgren had let her take care of her own affairs and not interfered in her life.

"That's one of the problems," Bjurman said, tapping her casebook. He then made a long speech about the rules and government regulations on guardianship.

"He let you run free, is that it? I wonder how he got away with it."

Because he was a crazy social democrat who had worked with troubled kids all his life.

"I'm not a child any more," Salander said, as if that were explanation enough.

"No, you're not a child. But I've been appointed your guardian, and as long as I have that role, I am legally and financially responsible for you."

He opened a new account in her name, and she was supposed to report it to Milton's personnel office and use it from now on. The good old days were over. In future Bjurman would pay her bills, and she would be given an allowance each month. He told her that he expected her to provide receipts for all her expenses. She would receive 1,400 kronor a week—"for food, clothing, film tickets, and such like."

Salander earned more than 160,000 kronor a year. She could double that by working full-time and accepting all the assignments Armansky offered her. But she had few expenses and did not need much money. The cost of her apartment was about 2,000 kronor a month, and in spite of her modest income, she had 90,000 kronor in her savings account. But she no longer had access to it.

"This has to do with the fact that I'm responsible for your money," he said. "You have to put money aside for the future. But don't worry; I'll take care of all that."

I've taken care of myself since I was ten, you creep!

"You function well enough in social terms that you don't need to be institutionalised, but this society is responsible for you."

He questioned her closely about what kind of work assignments she was given at Milton Security. She had instinctively lied about her duties. The answer she gave him was a description of her very first weeks at Milton. Bjurman got the impression that she made coffee and sorted the post—suitable enough tasks for someone who was a little slow—and seemed satisfied.

She did not know why she had lied, but she was sure it was a wise decision.

Blomkvist had spent five hours with Vanger, and it took much of the night and all of Tuesday to type up his notes and piece together the genealogy into a comprehensible whole. The family history that emerged was a dramatically different version from the one presented as the official image of the family. Every family had a few skeletons in their cupboards, but the Vanger family had an entire gallimaufry of them.

Blomkvist had had to remind himself several times that his real assignment was not to write a biography of the Vanger family but to find out what had happened to Harriet Vanger. The Vanger biography would be no more than playing to the gallery.

After a year he would receive his preposterous salary—the contract drawn up by Frode had been signed. His true reward, he hoped, would be the information about Wennerström that Vanger claimed to possess. But after listening to Vanger, he began to see that the year did not have to be a waste of time. A book about the Vanger family had significant value. It was, quite simply, a terrific story.

The idea that he might light upon Harriet Vanger's killer never crossed his mind—assuming she had been murdered, that is, and did not just die in some freak accident. Blomkvist agreed with Vanger that the chances of a sixteen-year-old girl going off of her own accord and then staying hidden for thirty-six years, despite the oversight of all the government bureaucracy, were nonexistent. On the other hand, he did not exclude the possibility that Harriet Vanger had run away, maybe heading for Stockholm, and that something had befallen her subsequently—drugs, prostitution, an assault, or an accident pure and simple.

Vanger was convinced, for his part, that Harriet had been murdered and that a family member was responsible—possibly in collaboration with someone else. His argument was based on the fact that Harriet had disappeared during the confusion in the hours when the island was cut off and all eyes were directed at the accident.

Berger had been right to say that his taking the assignment was beyond all common sense if the goal was to solve a murder mystery. But Blomkvist was beginning to see that Harriet's fate had played a central role in the family, and especially for Henrik Vanger. No matter whether he was right or wrong, Vanger's accusation against his relatives was of great significance in the family's history. The accusation had been aired openly for more than thirty years, and it had coloured the family gatherings and given rise to poisonous animosities that had contributed to destabilising the corporation. A study of Harriet's disappearance would consequently function as a chapter all on its own, as well as provide a red thread through the family history—and there was an abundance of source material. One starting point, whether Harriet Vanger was his primary assignment or whether he made do with writing a family chronicle, would be to map out the gallery of characters. That was the gist of his first long conversation that day with Vanger.

The family consisted of about a hundred individuals, counting all the children of cousins and second cousins. The family was so extensive that he was forced to create a database in his iBook. He used the NotePad programme (www.ibrium.se), one of those full-value products that two men at the Royal Technical College had created and distributed as shareware for a pittance on the Internet. Few programmes were as useful for an investigative journalist. Each family member was given his or her own document in the database.

The family tree could be traced back to the early sixteenth century, when the name was Vangeersad. According to Vanger the name may have originated from the Dutch van Geerstat; if that was the case, the lineage could be traced as far back as the twelfth century.

In modern times, the family came from northern France, arriving in Sweden with King Jean Baptiste Bernadotte in the early nineteenth century. Alexandre Vangeersad was a soldier and not personally acquainted with the king, but he had distinguished himself as the capable head of a garrison. In 1818 he was given the Hedeby estate as a reward for his service. Alexandre Vangeersad also had his own fortune, which he used to purchase considerable sections of forested land in Norrland. His son, Adrian, was born in France, but at his father's request he moved to Hedeby in that remote area of Norrland, far from the salons of Paris, to take over the administration of the estate. He took up farming and forestry, using new methods imported from

Europe, and he founded the pulp and paper mill around which Hedestad was built.

Alexandre's grandson was named Henrik, and he shortened his surname to Vanger. He developed trade with Russia and created a small merchant fleet of schooners that served the Baltics and Germany, as well as England with its steel industry during the mid-1800s. The elder Henrik Vanger diversified the family enterprises and founded a modest mining business, as well as several of Norrland's first metal industries. He left two sons, Birger and Gottfried, and they were the ones who laid the basis for the high-finance Vanger clan.

"Do you know anything about the old inheritance laws?" Vanger had asked.

"No."

"I'm confused about it too. According to family tradition, Birger and Gottfried fought like cats—they were legendary competitors for power and influence over the family business. In many respects the power struggle threatened the very survival of the company. For that reason their father decided—shortly before he died—to create a system whereby all members of the family would receive a portion of the inheritance—a share—in the business. It was no doubt well-intentioned, but it led to a situation in which instead of being able to bring in skilled people and possible partners from the outside, we had a board of directors consisting only of family members."

"And that applies today?"

"Precisely. If a family member wishes to sell his shares, they have to stay within the family. Today the annual shareholders' meeting consists of 50 percent family members. Martin holds more than 10 percent of the shares; I have 5 percent after selling some of my shares, to Martin among others. My brother Harald owns 7 percent, but most of the people who come to the shareholders' meeting have only one or half a percent."

"It sounds medieval in some ways."

"It's ludicrous. It means that today, if Martin wants to implement some policy, he has to waste time on a lobbying operation to ensure support from at least 20 percent to 25 percent of the shareholders. It's a patchwork quilt of alliances, factions, and intrigues."

Vanger resumed the history:

"Gottfried Vanger died childless in 1901. Or rather, may I be forgiven, he was the father of four daughters, but in those days women didn't really count. They owned shares, but it was the men in the family who constituted the ownership interest. It wasn't until women won the right to vote, well into the twentieth century, that they were even allowed to attend the shareholders' meetings."

"Very liberal."

"No need to be sarcastic. Those were different times. At any rate—Gottfried's brother, Birger Vanger, had three sons: Johan, Fredrik, and Gideon Vanger. They were all born towards the end of the nineteenth century. We can ignore Gideon; he sold his shares and emigrated to America. There is still a branch of the family over there. But Johan and Fredrik Vanger made the company the modern Vanger Corporation."

Vanger took out a photograph album and showed Blomkvist pictures from the gallery of characters as he talked. The photographs from the early 1900s showed two men with sturdy chins and plastered-down hair who stared into the camera lens without a hint of a smile.

"Johan Vanger was the genius of the family. He trained as an engineer, and he developed the manufacturing industry with several new inventions, which he patented. Steel and iron became the basis of the firm, but the business also expanded into other areas, including textiles. Johan Vanger died in 1956 and had three daughters: Sofia, Märit, and Ingrid, who were the first women automatically to win admittance to the company's shareholders' meetings.

"The other brother, Fredrik Vanger, was my father. He was a businessman and industry leader who transformed Johan's inventions into income. My father lived until 1964. He was active in company management right up until his death, although he had turned over daily operations to me in the fifties.

"It was exactly like the preceding generation—but in reverse. Johan had only daughters." Vanger showed Blomkvist pictures of big-busted women with wide-brimmed hats and carrying parasols. "And Fredrik—my father—had only sons. We were five brothers: Richard, Harald, Greger, Gustav, and myself."

Blomkvist had drawn up a family tree on several sheets of A4 paper taped together. He underlined the names of all those on Hedeby Island for the family meeting in 1966 and thus, at least theoretically, who could have had something to do with Harriet Vanger's disappearance.

He left out children under the age of twelve—he had to draw the line somewhere. After some pondering, he also left out Henrik Vanger. If the patriarch had had anything to do with the disappearance of his brother's granddaughter, his actions over the past thirty-six years would fall into the psychopathic arena. Vanger's mother, who in 1966 was already eighty-one, could reasonably also be eliminated. Remaining were twenty-three family members who, according to Vanger, had to be included in the group of "suspects." Seven of these were now dead, and several had now reached a respectable old age.

Blomkvist was not willing to share Vanger's conviction that a family member was behind Harriet's disappearance. A number of others had to be added to the list of suspects.

Dirch Frode began working for Vanger as his lawyer in the

spring of 1962. And aside from the family, who were the servants when Harriet vanished? Gunnar Nilsson—alibi or not—was nineteen years old, and his father, Magnus, was in all likelihood present on Hedeby Island, as were the artist Norman and the pastor Falk. Was Falk married? The Östergården farmer Aronsson, as well as his son Jerker Aronsson, lived on the island, close enough to Harriet Vanger while she was growing up—what sort of relationship did they have? Was Aronsson still married? Did other people live at that time on the farm?

FREDRIK VANGER	JOHAN VANGER
(1884–1956)	(1886–1964)
married to Ulrika	married to Gerda
(1885–1969)	(1888–1960)
Richard (1907–1940)	Sofia (1909–1977)
married to Margareta	married to Åke Sjögren
(1906–1959)	(1906–1967)
Gottfried (1927–1965)	Magnus Sjögren (1929–1994)
married to Isabella (1928–)	Sara Sjögren (1931–)
Martin (1948–)	Erik Sjögren (1951–)
Harriet (1950–?)	Håkan Sjögren (1955–)
Harald (1911–)	Märit (1911–1988)
married to Ingrid	married to Algot Günther
(1925–1992)	(1904–1987)
Birger (1939–)	Ossian Günther (1930–)
Cecilia (1946–)	married to Agnes (1933–)
Anita (1948–)	Jakob Günther (1952–)

<u>Greger</u> (1912–1974) married to <u>Gerda</u> (1922–) <u>Alexander</u> (1946–)	<u>Ingrid</u> (1916–1990) married to <u>Harry Karlman</u> (1912–1984) <u>Maria Karlman</u> (1944–) <u>Gunnar Karlman</u> (1948–)
Gustav (1918–1955) unmarried, childless	
Henrik (1920–) married to Edith (1921–1958) childless	

As Blomkvist wrote down all the names, the list had grown to forty people. It was 3:30 in the morning and the thermometer read −6°F. He longed for his own bed on Bellmansgatan.

He was awoken by the workman from Telia. By 11:00 he was hooked up and no longer felt quite as professionally handicapped. On the other hand, his own telephone remained stubbornly silent. He was starting to feel quite pig-headed and would not call the office.

He switched on his email programme and looked rapidly through the nearly 350 messages sent to him over the past week. He saved a dozen; the rest were spam or mailing lists that he subscribed to. The first email was from <demokrat88@yahoo.com>: I HOPE YOU SUCK COCK IN THE SLAMMER YOU FUCKING COMMIE PIG. He filed it in the "INTELLIGENT CRITICISM" folder.

He wrote to <erika.berger@millennium.se>: "Hi Ricky. Just to tell you that I've got the Net working and can be reached when you can forgive me. Hedeby is a rustic place, well worth a visit. M." When it felt like lunchtime he put his iBook in his bag and walked to Susanne's Bridge Café. He parked himself at his usual corner table. Susanne brought him coffee and sandwiches, casting an inquisitive glance at his computer. She asked him what he was working on. For the first time Blomkvist used his cover story. They exchanged pleasantries. Susanne urged him to check with her when he was ready for the real revelations.

"I've been serving Vangers for thirty-five years, and I know most of the gossip about that family," she said, and sashayed off to the kitchen.

With children, grandchildren, and great-grandchildren—whom he had not bothered to include—the brothers Fredrik and Johan Vanger had approximately fifty living offspring today. The family had a tendency to live to a ripe old age. Fredrik Vanger lived to be seventy-eight, and his brother Johan to seventy-two. Of Fredrik's sons who were yet alive, Harald was ninety-two and Henrik was eighty-two.

The only exception was Gustav, who died of lung disease at the age of thirty-seven. Vanger had explained that Gustav had always been sickly and had gone his own way, never really fitting in with the rest of the family. He never married and had no children.

The others who had died young had succumbed to other factors than illness. Richard Vanger was killed in the Winter War, only thirty-three years old. Gottfried Vanger, Harriet's father, had drowned the year before she disappeared. And Harriet herself was only sixteen. Mikael made note of the strange symmetry in that particular branch of the family—grandfather, father, and daughter had all been struck by misfortune. Richard's only remaining descendant was Martin Vanger who, at fifty-four, was still unmarried. But Vanger had explained that his nephew was a veritable hermit with a woman who lived in Hedestad.

Blomkvist noted two factors in the family tree. The first was that no Vanger had ever divorced or remarried, even if their spouse had died young. He wondered how common that was, in terms of statistics. Cecilia Vanger had been separated from her husband for years, but apparently, they were still married.

The other peculiarity was that whereas Fredrik Vanger's descendants, including Henrik, had played leading roles in the business and lived primarily in or near Hedestad, Johan Vanger's branch of the family, which produced only daughters, had married and dispersed to Stockholm, Malmö, and Göteborg or abroad. And they only came to Hedestad for summer holidays or the more important meetings. The single exception was Ingrid Vanger, whose son, Gunnar Karlman, lived in Hedestad. He was the editor in chief of the *Hedestad Courier.*

Thinking as a private detective might, Vanger thought that the underlying motive for Harriet's murder might be found in the structure of the company—the fact that early on he had made it known that Harriet was special to him; the motive might have been to harm Vanger himself, or perhaps Harriet had discovered some sensitive information concerning the company and thereby became a threat to someone. These were mere speculations; nevertheless, in this manner he had identified a circle consisting of thirteen individuals whom he considered to be of potential interest.

Blomkvist's conversation with Vanger the day before had been illuminating on one other point. From the start the old man had talked to Blomkvist about so many members of his family in a contemptuous and denigrating manner. It struck him as odd. Blomkvist wondered whether the patriarch's suspicions about his family had warped his judgement in the matter of Harriet's disappearance, but now he was starting to realise that Vanger had made an amazingly sober assessment.

The image that was emerging revealed a family that was socially and financially successful, but in all the more ordinary aspects was quite clearly dysfunctional.

Henrik Vanger's father had been a cold, insensitive man who sired his children and then let his wife look after their upbringing and welfare. Until the children reached the age of sixteen they barely saw their father except at special family gatherings when they were expected to be present but also invisible. Henrik could not remember his father ever expressing any form of love, even in the smallest way. On the contrary, the son was often told that he was incompetent and was the target of devastating criticism. Corporal punishment was seldom used; it wasn't necessary. The only times he had won his father's respect came later in life, through his accomplishments within the Vanger Corporation.

The oldest brother, Richard, had rebelled. After an argument—the reason for which was never discussed in the family—the boy had moved to Uppsala to study. There had been sown the seeds of the the Nazi career which Vanger had already mentioned, and which would eventually lead to the Finnish trenches. What the old man had not mentioned previously was that two other brothers had had similar careers.

In 1930 Harald and Greger had followed in Richard's footsteps to Uppsala. The two had been close, but Vanger was not sure to what extent they had spent time with Richard. It was quite clear that the brothers all joined Per Engdahl's fascist movement, The New Sweden. Harald had loyally followed Per Engdahl over the years, first to Sweden's National Union, then to the Swedish Opposition group, and finally The New Swedish

Movement after the war. Harald continued to be a member until Engdahl died in the nineties, and for certain periods he was one of the key contributors to the hibernating Swedish fascist movement.

Harald Vanger studied medicine in Uppsala and landed almost immediately in circles that were obsessed with race hygiene and race biology. For a time he worked at the Swedish Race Biology Institute, and as a physician he became a prominent campaigner for the sterilisation of undesirable elements in the population.

> Quote, Henrik Vanger, tape 2, 02950:
> *Harald went even further. In 1937 he co-authored—under a pseudonym, thank God—a book entitled* The People's New Europe. *I didn't find this out until the seventies. I have a copy that you can read. It must be one of the most disgusting books ever published in the Swedish language. Harald argued not only for sterilisation but also for euthanasia—actively putting to death people who offended his aesthetic tastes and didn't fit his image of the perfect Swedish race. In other words, he was appealing for wholesale murder in a text that was written in impeccable academic prose and contained all the required medical arguments. Get rid of those who are handicapped. Don't allow the Saami people to spread; they have a Mongolian influence. People who are mentally ill would regard death as a form of liberation, wouldn't they? Loose women, vagrants, gypsies, and Jews—you can imagine. In my brother's fantasies, Auschwitz could have been located in Dalarna.*

After the war Greger Vanger became a secondary-school teacher and eventually the headmaster of the Hedestad preparatory school. Vanger thought that he no longer belonged to any party after the war and had given up Nazism. He died in 1974, and it wasn't until he went through his brother's correspondence that he learned that in the fifties Greger had joined the politically ineffectual but totally crackpot sect called the Nordic National Party. He had remained a member until his death.

Quote, Henrik Vanger, tape 2, 04167:
Consequently, three of my brothers were politically insane. How sick were they in other respects?

The only brother worthy of a measure of empathy in Vanger's eyes was the sickly Gustav, who died of lung disease in 1955. Gustav had never been interested in politics, and he seemed to be some sort of misanthropic artistic soul, with absolutely no interest in business or working in the Vanger Corporation.

Blomkvist asked Vanger: "Now you and Harald are the only ones left. Why did he move back to Hedeby?"

"He moved home in 1979. He owns that house."

"It must feel strange living so close to a brother that you hate."

"I don't hate my brother. If anything, I may pity him. He's a complete idiot, and he's the one who hates me."

"He hates you?"

"Precisely. I think that's why he came back here. So that he could spend his last years hating me at close quarters."

"Why does he hate you?"

"Because I got married."

"I think you're going to have to explain that."

Vanger had lost contact with his older brothers early on. He was the only brother to show an aptitude for business—he was his father's last hope. He had no interest in politics and steered clear of Uppsala. Instead he studied economics in Stockholm. After he turned eighteen he spent every break and summer holiday working at one of the offices within the Vanger Corporation or working with the management of one of its companies. He became familiar with all the labyrinths of the family business.

On 10 June, 1941—in the midst of an all-out war—Vanger was sent to Germany for a six-week visit at the Vanger Corporation business offices in Hamburg. He was only twenty-one and the Vanger's German agent, a company veteran by the name of Hermann Lobach, was his chaperone and mentor.

"I won't tire you with all the details, but when I went there, Hitler and Stalin were still good friends and there wasn't yet an Eastern Front. Everyone still believed that Hitler was invincible. There was a feeling of . . . both optimism and desperation. I think those are the right words. More than half a century later, it's still difficult to put words to the mood. Don't get me wrong—I was not a Nazi, and in my eyes Hitler seemed like some absurd character in an operetta. But it would have been almost impossible not to be infected by the optimism about the future, which was rife among ordinary people in Hamburg. Despite the fact that the war was getting closer, and several bombing raids were carried out against Hamburg during the time I was there, the people seemed to think it was mostly a temporary annoyance—that soon there would be peace and Hitler would establish his *Neuropa*. People wanted to believe that Hitler was God. That's what it sounded like in the propaganda."

Vanger opened one of his many photograph albums.

"This is Lobach. He disappeared in 1944, presumably lost in some bombing raid. We never knew what his fate was. During my weeks in Hamburg I became close to him. I was staying with him and his family in an elegant apartment in a well-to-do neighbourhood of Hamburg. We spent time together every day.

He was no more a Nazi than I was, but for convenience he was a member of the party. His membership card opened doors and facilitated opportunities for the Vanger Corporation—and business was precisely what we did. We built freight wagons for their trains—I've always wondered whether any of our wagons were destined for Poland. We sold fabric for their uniforms and tubes for their radio sets—although officially we didn't know what they were using the goods for. And Lobach knew how to land a contract; he was entertaining and good-natured. The perfect Nazi. Gradually I began to see that he was also a man who was desperately trying to hide a secret.

"In the early hours of June 22 in 1941, Lobach knocked on the door of my bedroom. My room was next to his wife's bedroom, and he signalled me to be quiet, get dressed, and come with him. We went downstairs and sat in the smoking salon. Lobach had been up all night. He had the radio on, and I realised that something serious had happened. Operation Barbarossa had begun. Germany had invaded the Soviet Union on Midsummer Eve." Vanger gestured in resignation. "Lobach took out two glasses and poured a generous aquavit for each of us. He was obviously shaken. When I asked him what it all meant, he replied with foresight that it meant the end for Germany and Nazism. I only half believed him—Hitler seemed undefeatable, after all—but Lobach and I drank a toast to the fall of Germany. Then he turned his attention to practical matters."

Blomkvist nodded to signal that he was still following the story.

"First, he had no possibility of contacting my father for instructions, but on his own initiative he had decided to cut short my visit to Germany and send me home. Second, he asked me to do something for him."

Vanger pointed to a yellowed portrait of a dark-haired woman, in three-quarter view.

"Lobach had been married for forty years, but in 1919 he met a wildly beautiful woman half his age, and he fell hopelessly in love with her. She was a poor, simple seamstress. Lobach courted her, and like so many other wealthy men, he could afford to install her in an apartment a convenient distance from his office. She became his mistress. In 1921 she had a daughter, who was christened Edith."

"Rich older man, poor young woman, and a love child—that can't have caused much of a scandal in the forties," Blomkvist said.

"Absolutely right. If it hadn't been for one thing. The woman was Jewish, and consequently Lobach was the father of a Jew in the midst of Nazi Germany. He was what they called a 'traitor to his race.' "

"Ah . . . That does change the situation. What happened?"

"Edith's mother had been picked up in 1939. She disappeared, and we can only guess what her fate was. It was known, of course, that she had a daughter who was not yet included on any transport list, and who was now being sought by the department of the Gestapo whose job it was to track down fugitive Jews. In the summer of 1941, the week that I arrived in Hamburg, Edith's mother was somehow linked to Lobach, and he was summoned for an interview. He acknowledged the relationship and his paternity, but he stated that he had no idea where his daughter might be, and he had not had any contact with her in ten years."

"So where was the daughter?"

"I had seen her every day in the Lobachs' home. A sweet and quiet twenty-year-old girl who cleaned my room and helped serve dinner. By 1937 the persecution of the Jews had been going on for several years, and Edith's mother had begged Lobach for help. And he did help—Lobach loved his illegitimate child just as much as his legitimate children. He hid her in the most unlikely place he could think of—right in front of everyone's nose. He had arranged for counterfeit documents, and he had taken her in as their housekeeper."

"Did his wife know who she was?"

"No, it seemed she had no idea. It had worked for four years, but now Lobach felt the noose tightening. It was only a matter of time before the Gestapo would come knocking on the door. Then he went to get his daughter and introduced her to me as such. She was very shy and didn't even dare look me in the eye. She must have been up half the night waiting to be called. Lobach begged me to save her life."

"How?"

"He had arranged the whole thing. I was supposed to be staying another three weeks and then to take the night train to Copenhagen and continue by ferry across the sound—a relatively safe trip, even in wartime. But two days after our conversation a freighter owned by the Vanger Corporation was to leave Hamburg headed for Sweden. Lobach wanted to send me with the freighter instead, to leave Germany without delay. The change in my travel plans had to be approved by the security service; it was a formality, but not a problem. But Lobach wanted me on board that freighter."

"Together with Edith, I presume."

"Edith was smuggled on board, hidden inside one of three hundred crates containing machinery. My job was to protect her if she should be discovered while we were still in German territorial waters, and to prevent the captain of the ship from doing anything stupid. Otherwise I was supposed to wait until we were a good distance from Germany before I let her out."

"It sounds terrifying."

"It sounded simple to me, but it turned into a nightmare journey. The captain was called Oskar Granath, and he was far from pleased to be made responsible for his employer's snotty little heir. We left Hamburg around 9:00 in the evening in late June. We were just making our way out of the inner harbour when the air-raid sirens went off. A British bombing raid—the heaviest I had then experienced, and the harbour was, of course, the main target. But somehow we got through, and after an engine breakdown and a miserably stormy night in mine-filled waters we arrived the following afternoon at Karlskrona. You're probably going to ask me what happened to the girl."

"I think I know."

"My father was understandably furious. I had put everything at risk with my idiotic venture. And the girl could have been deported from Sweden at any time. But I was already just as hopelessly in love with her as Lobach had been with her mother. I proposed to her and gave my father an ultimatum—either he accepted our marriage or he'd have to look for another fatted calf for the family business. He gave in."

"But she died?"

"Yes, far too young, in 1958. She had a congenital heart defect. And it turned out that I couldn't have children. And that's why my brother hates me."

"Because you married her."

"Because—to use his own words—I married a filthy Jewish whore."

"But he's insane."

"I couldn't have put it better myself."

CHAPTER 10

Thursday, January 9– Friday, January 31

According to the *Hedestad Courier,* Blomkvist's first month out in the country was the coldest in recorded memory, or (as Vanger informed him) at least since the wartime winter of 1942. After only a week in Hedeby he had learned all about long underwear, woolly socks, and double undershirts.

He had several miserable days in the middle of the month when the temperature dropped to –35°F. He had experienced nothing like it, not even during the year he spent in Kiruna in Lapland doing his military service.

One morning the water pipes froze. Nilsson gave him two big plastic containers of water for cooking and washing, but the cold was paralysing. Ice flowers formed on the insides of the windows, and no matter how much wood he put in the stove, he was still cold. He spent a long time each day splitting wood in the shed next to the house.

At times he was on the brink of tears and toyed with taking

the first train heading south. Instead he would put on one more sweater and wrap up in a blanket as he sat at the kitchen table, drinking coffee and reading old police reports.

Then the weather changed and the temperature rose steadily to a balmy 14°F.

Mikael was beginning to get to know people in Hedeby. Martin Vanger kept his promise and invited him for a meal of moose steak. His lady friend joined them for dinner. Eva was a warm, sociable, and entertaining woman. Blomkvist found her extraordinarily attractive. She was a dentist and lived in Hedestad, but she spent the weekends at Martin's home. Blomkvist gradually learned that they had known each other for many years but that they had not started going out together until they were middle-aged. Evidently they saw no reason to marry.

"She's actually my dentist," said Martin with a laugh.

"And marrying into this crazy family isn't really my thing," Eva said, patting Martin affectionately on the knee.

Martin Vanger's villa was furnished in black, white, and chrome. There were expensive designer pieces that would have delighted the connoisseur Christer Malm. The kitchen was equipped to a professional chef's standard. In the living room there was a high-end stereo with an impressive collection of jazz records from Tommy Dorsey to John Coltrane. Martin Vanger had money, and his home was both luxurious and functional. It was also impersonal. The artwork on the walls was reproductions and posters, of the sort found in IKEA. The bookshelves, at least in the part of the house that Blomkvist saw, housed a Swedish encyclopedia and some coffee table books that people might have given him as Christmas presents, for want of a better idea. All in all, he could discern only two personal aspects of

Martin Vanger's life: music and cooking. His 3,000 or so LPs spoke for the one and the other could be deduced from the fact of Martin's stomach bulging over his belt.

The man himself was a mixture of simplicity, shrewdness, and amiability. It took no great analytical skill to conclude that the corporate CEO was a man with problems. As they listened to "Night in Tunisia," the conversation was devoted to the Vanger Corporation, and Martin made no secret of the fact that the company was fighting for survival. He was certainly aware that his guest was a financial reporter whom he hardly knew, yet he discussed the internal problems of his company so openly that it seemed reckless. Perhaps he assumed that Blomkvist was one of the family since he was working for his great-uncle; and like the former CEO, Martin took the view that the family members only had themselves to blame for the situation in which the company found itself. On the other hand, he seemed almost amused by his family's incorrigible folly. Eva nodded but passed no judgement of her own. They had obviously been over the same ground before.

Martin accepted the story that Blomkvist had been hired to write a family chronicle, and he inquired how the work was going. Blomkvist said with a smile that he was having the most trouble remembering the names of all the relatives. He asked if he might come back to do an interview in due course. Twice he considered turning the conversation to the old man's obsession with Harriet's disappearance. Vanger must have pestered her brother with his theories, and Martin must realise that if Blomkvist was going to write about the Vangers, he could not ignore the fact that one family member had vanished in dramatic circumstances. But Martin showed no sign of wanting to discuss the subject.

The evening ended, after several rounds of vodka, at 2:00 in the morning. Blomkvist was fairly drunk as he skidded the three hundred yards to the guest house. It had been a pleasant evening.

One afternoon during Blomkvist's second week in Hedeby there was a knock on the door. He put aside the binder from the police report that he had just opened—the sixth in the series—and closed the door to his office before he opened the front door to a blonde woman well wrapped up against the cold.

"Hi. I just thought I'd come and say hello. I'm Cecilia Vanger."

They shook hands and he got out the coffee cups. Cecilia, daughter of Harald Vanger, appeared to be an open and engaging woman. Blomkvist remembered that Vanger had spoken of her appreciatively; he had also said that she was not on speaking terms with her father, her next-door neighbour. They chatted for a while before she brought up the reason for her visit.

"I understand that you're writing a book about the family," she said. "I'm not sure that I care for the idea. I wanted to see what sort of person you are."

"Well, Henrik Vanger hired me. It's his story, so to speak."

"And our good Henrik isn't exactly neutral in his attitude towards the family."

Blomkvist studied her, unsure what she was getting at. "You're opposed to having a book written about the Vanger family?"

"I didn't say that. And it doesn't really matter what I think. But by now you must have realised that it hasn't always been plain sailing to be part of this family."

Blomkvist had no idea what Vanger had said or how much Cecilia knew about his assignment. He threw out his hands.

"I'm contracted by your uncle to write a family chronicle. He has some very colourful views about members of the family, but I'll be sticking strictly to what can be documented."

Cecilia Vanger smiled but without warmth. "What I want to know is: will I have to go into exile or emigrate when the book comes out?"

"I don't expect so," Blomkvist said. "People will be able to tell the sheep from the goats."

"Like my father, for instance?"

"Your father the famous Nazi?" Blomkvist said.

Cecilia Vanger rolled her eyes. "My father is crazy. I only see him a few times a year."

"Why don't you want to see him?"

"Wait a minute—before you start in asking a lot of questions . . . Are you planning to quote anything I say? Or can I carry on a normal conversation with you?"

"My job is to write a book starting with Alexandre Vangeersad's arrival in Sweden with Bernadotte and going up to the present. It's to cover the business empire over many decades, but it will also discuss why the empire is in difficulty and it will touch on the animosity that exists within the family. In such a survey it's impossible to avoid having some dirty linen float to the surface. But that doesn't mean that I'm going to set out to present a malicious portrait of anyone. For example, I've met Martin Vanger; he seems to me a very sympathetic person, and that's how I'm going to describe him."

Cecilia Vanger did not reply.

"What I know about you is that you're a teacher . . ."

"It's actually worse than that—I'm the headmistress of Hedestad preparatory school."

"I'm sorry. I know that your uncle is fond of you, that you're married but separated . . . and that's about all so far. So do please go ahead and talk to me without fear of being quoted. I'm sure I'll come knocking on your door some day soon. Then it will be an official interview, and you can choose whether you want to answer my questions or not."

"So I can talk to you then or now . . . off the record, as they say?"

"Of course."

"And this is off the record?"

"Of course. This is a social visit after all."

"OK. Then can I ask you something?"

"Please."

"How much of this book is going to deal with Harriet?"

Blomkvist bit his lip and then said as casually as he could: "To be honest, I have no idea. It might fill a chapter. It was a dramatic event that has cast a shadow over your uncle, at the very least."

"But you're not here to look into her disappearance?"

"What makes you think that?"

"Well, the fact that Nilsson lugged four massive boxes over here. That could be Henrik's private investigations over the years. I looked in Harriet's old room, where Henrik keeps it, and it was gone."

Cecilia Vanger was no fool.

"You'll have to take the matter up with Henrik, not with me," Blomkvist said. "But it won't surprise you to know that Henrik has talked a lot about the girl's disappearance, and I thought it would be interesting to read through what had been collected."

Cecilia gave him another of her joyless smiles. "I wonder sometimes who's crazier, my father or my uncle. I must have listened to him on Harriet's disappearance a thousand times."

"What do you think happened to her?"

"Is this an interview question?"

"No," he said with a laugh. "I'm just curious."

"What I'm curious about is whether you're a nut case too. Whether you've swallowed Henrik's conviction or whether in fact you're the one who's egging him on."

"You think that Henrik's a nut case?"

"Don't get me wrong. He's one of the warmest and most thoughtful people I know. I'm very fond of him. But on this particular topic, he's obsessive."

"But Harriet really did disappear."

"I'm just so damn sick of the whole story. It's poisoned our lives for decades, and it doesn't stop doing so." She got up abruptly and put on her fur coat. "I have to go. You seem like a pleasant sort. Martin thinks so too, but his judgement isn't always reliable. You're welcome to come for coffee at my house whenever you like. I'm almost always home in the evening."

"Thank you," Blomkvist said. "You didn't answer the question that wasn't an interview question."

She paused at the door and replied without looking at him.

"I have no idea. I think it was an accident that has such a simple explanation that it will astonish us if we ever find out."

She turned to smile at him—for the first time with warmth. Then she was gone.

If it had been an agreeable first meeting with Cecilia Vanger, the same could not be said of his first encounter with Isabella. Harriet's mother was exactly as Henrik Vanger had warned: she proved to be an elegant woman who reminded him vaguely of Lauren Bacall. She was thin, dressed in a black Persian lamb coat with matching cap, and she was leaning on a black cane when Blomkvist ran into her one morning on his way to Susanne's. She looked like an ageing vampire—still strikingly beautiful but as venomous as a snake. Isabella Vanger was apparently on her way home after taking a walk. She called to him from the crossroad.

"Hello there, young man. Come here."

The commanding tone was hard to mistake. Blomkvist

looked around and concluded that he was the one summoned. He did as instructed.

"I am Isabella Vanger," the woman said.

"Hello. My name is Mikael Blomkvist." He stuck out his hand, which she ignored.

"Are you that person who's been snooping around in our family affairs?"

"Well, if you mean am I the person that Henrik Vanger has put under contract to help him with his book about the Vanger family, then yes."

"That's none of your business."

"Which? The fact that Henrik Vanger offered me a contract or the fact that I accepted?"

"You know perfectly well what I mean. I don't care for people poking around in my life."

"I won't poke around in your life. The rest you'll have to discuss with Henrik."

Isabella raised her cane and pressed the handle against Mikael's chest. She did not use much force, but he took a step back in surprise.

"Just you keep away from me," she said, and turned on her heel and walked unsteadily towards her house. Blomkvist went on standing where he was, looking like a man who has just met a real live comic-book character. When he looked up he saw Vanger in the window of his office. In his hand he was holding a cup, which he raised in an ironic salute.

The only travelling that Blomkvist did during that first month was a drive to a bay on Lake Siljan. He borrowed Frode's Mercedes and drove through a snowy landscape to spend the afternoon with Detective Superintendent Morell. Blomkvist had tried to form an impression of Morell based on the way he came across in the police report. What he found was a wiry old man who moved softly and spoke even more slowly.

Blomkvist brought with him a notebook with ten questions, mainly ideas that had cropped up while he was reading the police report. Morell answered each question put to him in a schoolmasterly way. Finally Blomkvist put away his notes and explained that the questions were simply an excuse for a meeting. What he really wanted was to have a chat with him and ask one crucial question: was there any single thing in the investigation that had not been included in the written report? Any hunches, even, that the inspector might be willing to share with him?

Because Morell, like Vanger, had spent thirty-six years pondering the mystery, Blomkvist had expected a certain resistance—he was the new man who had come in and started tramping around in the thicket where Morell had gone astray. But there was not a hint of hostility. Morell methodically filled his pipe and lit it before he replied.

"Well yes, obviously I had my own ideas. But they're so vague and fleeting that I can hardly put them into words."

"What do you think happened?"

"I think Harriet was murdered. Henrik and I agree on that. It's the only reasonable explanation. But we never discovered what the motive might have been. I think she was murdered for a very specific reason—it wasn't some act of madness or a rape or anything like that. If we had known the motive, we'd have known who killed her." Morell stopped to think for a moment. "The murder may have been committed spontaneously. By that I mean that someone seized an opportunity when it presented itself in the coming and going in the wake of the accident. The murderer hid the body and then at some later time removed it while we were searching for her."

"We're talking about someone who has nerves of ice."

"There's one detail . . . Harriet went to Henrik's room wanting to speak to him. In hindsight, it seems to me a strange way to behave—she knew he had his hands full with all the relatives who were hanging around. I think Harriet alive represented a grave threat to someone, that she was going to tell Henrik something, and that the murderer knew she was about to . . . well, spill the beans."

"And Henrik was busy with several family members?"

"There were four people in the room, besides Henrik. His brother Greger, a cousin named Magnus Sjögren, and two of Harald's children, Birger and Cecilia. But that doesn't tell us anything. Let's suppose that Harriet had discovered that someone had embezzled money from the company—hypothetically, of course. She may have known about it for months, and at some point she may even have discussed it with the person in question. She may have tried to blackmail him, or she may have felt sorry for him and felt uneasy about exposing him. She may have decided all of a sudden and told the murderer so, and he in desperation killed her."

"You've said 'he' and 'him.' "

"The book says that most killers are men. But it's also true that in the Vanger family are several women who are real firebrands."

"I've met Isabella."

"She's one of them. But there are others. Cecilia Vanger can be extremely caustic. Have you met Sara Sjögren?"

Blomkvist shook his head.

"She's the daughter of Sofia Vanger, one of Henrik's cousins. In her case we're talking about a truly unpleasant and inconsiderate lady. But she was living in Malmö, and as far as I could ascertain, she had no motive for killing the girl."

"So she's off the list."

"The problem is that no matter how we twisted and turned things, we never came up with a motive. That's the important thing."

"You put a vast amount of work into this case. Was there any lead you remember not having followed up?"

Morell chuckled. "No. I've devoted an endless amount of time to this case, and I can't think of anything that I didn't follow up to the bitter, fruitless end. Even after I was promoted and moved away from Hedestad."

"Moved away?"

"Yes, I'm not from Hedestad originally. I served there from 1963 until 1968. After that I was promoted to superintendent and moved to the Gävle police department for the rest of my career. But even in Gävle I went on digging into the case."

"I don't suppose that Henrik would ever let up."

"That's true, but that's not the reason. The puzzle about Harriet still fascinates me to this day. I mean . . . it's like this: every police officer has his own unsolved mystery. I remember from my days in Hedestad how older colleagues would talk in the canteen about the case of Rebecka. There was one officer in particular, a man named Torstensson—he's been dead for years—who year after year kept returning to that case. In his free time and when he was on holiday. Whenever there was a period of calm among the local hooligans he would take out those folders and study them."

"Was that also a case about a missing girl?"

Morell looked surprised. Then he smiled when he realised that Blomkvist was looking for some sort of connection.

"No, that's not why I mentioned it. I'm talking about the *soul* of a policeman. The Rebecka case was something that happened before Harriet Vanger was even born, and the statute of limitations has long since run out. Sometime in the forties a woman was assaulted in Hedestad, raped, and murdered. That's not altogether uncommon. Every officer, at some point in his career, has to investigate that kind of crime, but what I'm talking about are those cases that stay with you and get under your skin during the investigation. This girl was killed in the most brutal way. The killer tied her up and stuck her head into the smouldering embers of a fireplace. One can only guess how long it took for the poor girl to die, or what torment she must have endured."

"Christ Almighty."

"Exactly. It was so sadistic. Poor Torstensson was the first detective on the scene after she was found. And the murder remained unsolved, even though experts were called in from Stockholm. He could never let go of that case."

"I can understand that."

"My Rebecka case was Harriet. In this instance we don't even know how she died. We can't even prove that a murder was committed. But I have never been able to let it go." He paused to think for a moment. "Being a homicide detective can be the loneliest job in the world. The friends of the victim are upset and in despair, but sooner or later—after weeks or months—they go back to their everyday lives. For the closest family it takes longer, but for the most part, to some degree, they too get over their grieving and despair. Life has to go on; it does go on. But the unsolved murders keep gnawing away and in the end there's only one person left who thinks night and day about the victim: it's the officer who's left with the investigation."

Three other people in the Vanger family lived on Hedeby Island. Alexander Vanger, son of Greger, born in 1946, lived in a renovated wooden house. Vanger told Blomkvist that Alexander was presently in the West Indies, where he gave himself over to his favourite pastimes: sailing and whiling away the time, not doing a scrap of work. Alexander had been twenty and he had been there on that day.

Alexander shared the house with his mother, Gerda, eighty years old and widow of Greger Vanger. Blomkvist had never seen her; she was mostly bedridden.

The third family member was Harald Vanger. During his first month Blomkvist had not managed even a glimpse of him. Harald's house, the one closest to Blomkvist's cabin, looked gloomy and ominous with its blackout curtains drawn across all the windows. Blomkvist sometimes thought he saw a ripple in the curtains as he passed, and once when he was about to go to bed late, he noticed a glimmer of light coming from a room upstairs. There was a gap in the curtains. For more than twenty minutes he stood in the dark at his own kitchen window and watched the light before he got fed up and, shivering, went to bed. In the morning the curtains were back in place.

Harald seemed to be an invisible but ever-present spirit who affected life in the village by his absence. In Blomkvist's imagination, Harald increasingly took on the form of an evil Gollum who spied on his surroundings from behind the curtains and devoted himself to no-one-knew-what matters in his barricaded cavern.

Harald was visited once a day by the home-help service (usually an elderly woman) from the other side of the bridge. She would bring bags of groceries, trudging through the snowdrifts up to his door. Nilsson shook his head when Blomkvist asked about Harald. He had offered to do the shovelling, he said, but Harald did not want anyone to set foot on his property. Only once, during the first winter after Harald had returned to Hedeby Island, did Nilsson drive the tractor up there to clear the snow from the courtyard, just as he did for all the other driveways. Harald had come out of his house at a startling pace, yelling and gesticulating until Nilsson went away.

Unfortunately, Nilsson was unable to clear Blomkvist's yard

because the gate was too narrow for the tractor. A snow shovel and manual labour were still the only way to do it.

In the middle of January Blomkvist asked his lawyer to find out when he was going to be expected to serve his three months in prison. He was anxious to take care of the matter as quickly as possible. Getting into prison turned out to be easier than he had expected. After a very few weeks of discussion, it was decreed that Blomkvist present himself on March 17 at the Rullåker Prison outside Östersund, a minimum-security prison. The lawyer advised him that the sentence would very likely be shortened.

"Fine," Blomkvist said, without much enthusiasm.

He sat at the kitchen table and petted the cat, who now arrived every few days to spend the night with Blomkvist. From the Nilssons he had learned that the cat's name was Tjorven. It did not belong to anyone in particular, it just made the rounds of all the houses.

Blomkvist met his employer almost every afternoon. Sometimes they would have a brief conversation; sometimes they would sit together for hours.

The conversation often consisted of Blomkvist putting up a theory that Vanger would then shoot down. Blomkvist tried to maintain a certain distance from his assignment, but there were moments when he found himself hopelessly fascinated by the enigma of the girl's disappearance.

Blomkvist had assured Berger that he would also formulate a strategy for taking up the battle with Wennerström, but after a month in Hedestad he had not yet opened the files which had brought him to the dock in the district court. On the contrary, he had deliberately pushed the matter aside because every time he thought about Wennerström and his own situation, he would sink into depression and listlessness. He wondered whether he was going crazy like the old man. His professional reputation had imploded, and his means of recovering was to hide himself away in a tiny town in the deep country, chasing ghosts.

Vanger could tell that Blomkvist was on some days a bit off balance. By the end of January, the old man made a decision that surprised even himself. He picked up the telephone and called Stockholm. The conversation lasted twenty minutes and dealt largely with Mikael Blomkvist.

It had taken almost that whole month for Berger's fury to subside. At 9:30 in the evening, on one of the last days in January, she called him.

"Are you really intending to stay up there?" she began. The call was such a surprise that Blomkvist could not at first reply. Then he smiled and wrapped the blanket tighter around him.

"Hi, Ricky. You should try it yourself."

"Why would I? What is so charming about living in the back of beyond?"

"I just brushed my teeth with ice water. It makes my fillings hurt."

"You have only yourself to blame. But it's cold as hell down here in Stockholm too."

"Let's hear the worst."

"We've lost two-thirds of our regular advertisers. No-one wants to come right out and say it, but . . ."

"I know. Make a list of the ones that jump ship. Someday we'll do a good story on them."

"Micke . . . I've run the numbers, and if we don't rope in

some new advertisers, we'll be bust by the autumn. It's as simple as that."

"Things will turn around."

She laughed wearily on the other end of the line.

"That's not something you can say, nestling up there in Laplander hell."

"Erika, I'm . . ."

"I know. A man's gotta do what a man's gotta do, and all that crap. You don't have to say anything. I'm sorry I was such a bitch and didn't answer your messages. Can we start again? Do I dare come up there to see you?"

"Whenever you like."

"Do I need to bring along a rifle with wolf-shot?"

"Not at all. We'll have our own Lapps, dog teams, and all the gear. When are you coming?"

"Friday evening, OK?"

Apart from the narrow shovelled path to the door, there was about three feet of snow covering the property. Blomkvist gave the shovel a long, critical look and then went over to Nilsson's house to ask whether Berger could park her BMW there. That was no problem; they had room in the double garage, and they even had engine heaters.

Berger drove through the afternoon and arrived around 6:00. They stared at each other warily for several seconds and then hugged each other for much longer.

There was not much to see in the darkness except for the illuminated church, and both Konsum and Susanne's Bridge Café were closing up. So they hurried home. Blomkvist cooked dinner while Berger poked around in his house, making remarks about the issues of *Rekordmagasinet* from the fifties that were still there, and getting engrossed in his files in the office.

They had lamb cutlets with potatoes in cream sauce and drank red wine. Blomkvist tried to take up the thread of their earlier conversation, but Berger was in no mood to discuss *Millennium*. Instead they talked for two hours about what Blomkvist was doing up there and how he and Vanger were getting on. Later they went to see if the bed was big enough to hold both of them.

Her third meeting with Advokat Nils Bjurman was rescheduled, and finally set for 5:00 on that same Friday afternoon. At the previous meetings, Salander was greeted by a middle-aged woman who smelled of musk and worked as his secretary. This time she had left for the day, and Bjurman smelled faintly of drink. He waved Salander to a visitor's chair and leafed distractedly through the documents on his desk until he seemed suddenly to become aware of her presence.

It turned out to be another interrogation. This time he asked Salander about her sex life—which she had no intention of discussing with anyone.

After the meeting she knew that she had handled it badly. At first she refused to answer his questions. His interpretation of this was that she was shy, retarded, or had something to hide, and he pressed her for answers. Salander realised that he was not going to give up, so she started giving him brief, colourless answers of the sort she assumed would fit with her psychological profile. She mentioned "Magnus"—who, according to her description, was a nerdy computer programmer her own age who treated her like a gentleman should, took her to the cinema, and sometimes shared her bed. "Magnus" was fiction; she made him up as she went along, but Bjurman took her account as a pretext for meticulously mapping out her sex life. *How often do you have sex?* Occasionally. *Who takes the initiative—you or him?*

I do. *Do you use condoms?* Of course—she knew about HIV. *What's your favourite position?* Hmm, usually on my back. *Do you enjoy oral sex?* Er, wait a second . . . *Have you ever had anal sex?*

"No, it's not particularly nice to be fucked in the arse—but what the hell business is it of yours?"

That was the only time she lost her temper. She had kept her eyes on the floor so they would not betray her exasperation. When she looked at him again, he was grinning at her from across the desk. She left his office with a feeling of disgust. Palmgren would never have dreamed of asking such questions. On the other hand, he had always been there if she had wanted to discuss anything. Not that she did.

Bjurman was on his way to being a *Major Problem.*

CHAPTER 11

Saturday, February 1– Tuesday, February 18

During the brief hours of daylight on Saturday, Blomkvist and Berger took a walk past the small-boat harbour along the road to Östergården. He had been living on Hedeby Island for a month, but he had never taken a walk inland; the freezing temperatures and regular snowstorms had deterred him. But Saturday was sunny and pleasant. It was as if Berger had brought with her a hint of spring. The road was lined with snow, ploughed three feet high. As soon as they left the summer-cabin area they were walking in dense fir forest. Blomkvist was surprised by how much higher and more inaccessible Söderberget, the hill across from the cabins, was than it appeared from the village. He thought about how many times Harriet Vanger must have played here as a child, but then he pushed all thoughts of her out of his mind. After about a mile the woods ended at a fence where the Östergården farmland began. They could see a white wooden structure and red farm buildings arranged in a square. They turned to head back the same way.

As they passed the driveway to the estate house, Vanger knocked on the upstairs window and gestured firmly for them to come up. Blomkvist and Berger looked at each other.

"Would you like to meet a corporate legend?" Blomkvist said.

"Does he bite?"

"Not on Saturdays."

Vanger received them at the door to his office.

"You must be Fröken Berger, I recognise you." he said. "Mikael didn't say a word about your coming to Hedeby."

One of Berger's outstanding talents was her ability to instantly get on friendly terms with the most unlikely individuals. Blomkvist had seen her turn on the charm for five-year-old boys, who within ten minutes were fully prepared to abandon their mothers. Men over eighty seemed not to be an exception. After two minutes Berger and Henrik Vanger were ignoring Blomkvist as they chattered on. It was as if they had known each other since childhood—well, since Erika's childhood, at any rate.

Berger started off quite boldly by scolding Vanger for luring her publisher away into the sticks. The old man replied that as far as he could tell—from assorted press reports—she had in fact fired him. And had she not done so, then now might be high time to get rid of excess ballast in the editorial offices. And in that case, Vanger said, a period of rustic life would do young Blomkvist some good.

For five minutes they discussed Blomkvist's shortcomings in the most irritating terms. Blomkvist leaned back and pretended to be insulted, but he frowned when Berger made some cryptic remarks that might allude to his failings as a journalist but might also have applied to sexual prowess. Vanger tilted his head back and roared with laughter.

Blomkvist was astonished. He had never seen Vanger so natural and relaxed. He could suddenly see that Vanger, fifty years younger—or even thirty years—must have been quite a charming, attractive ladies' man. He had never remarried. There must have been women who crossed his path, yet for nearly half a century he had remained a bachelor.

Blomkvist took a sip of coffee and pricked up his ears again when he realised that the conversation had suddenly turned serious and had to do with *Millennium*.

"Mikael has told me that you're having problems at the magazine." Berger glanced at Blomkvist. "No, he hasn't discussed your internal operations, but a person would have to be deaf and blind not to see that your magazine, just like the Vanger Corporation, is in difficulties."

"I'm confident that we can repair the situation," Berger said.

"I doubt it," Vanger said.

"Why is that?"

"Let's see—how many employees do you have? Six? A monthly magazine with a print run of 21,000, manufacturing costs, salaries, distribution, offices . . . You need revenues of about 10 million. I think we know what percentage of that amount has to come from advertising revenue."

"So?"

"So friend Wennerström is a vengeful and narrow-minded bastard who isn't going to forget his recent contretemps in a hurry. How many advertisers have you lost in the past six months?"

Berger regarded Vanger with a wary expression. Blomkvist caught himself holding his breath. On those occasions when he and the old man had touched on the future of *Millennium*, it had always concerned annoying remarks or the magazine's situation in relation to Blomkvist's ability to finish his work in Hedestad. But Vanger was now addressing Erika alone, one boss to another. Signals passed between them that Blomkvist could not interpret, which might have had to do with the fact that he was basically a poor working-class boy from Norrland and she was an upper-class girl with a distinguished, international family tree.

"Could I have a little more coffee?" Berger asked. Vanger poured her a cup at once. "OK, you've done your homework. We're bleeding."

"How long?"

"We've got six months to turn ourselves around. Eight months, max. We don't have enough capital to keep ourselves afloat longer than that."

The old man's expression was inscrutable as he stared out of the window. The church was still standing there.

"Did you know that I was once in the newspaper business?" he said, once more addressing them both.

Blomkvist and Berger both shook their heads. Vanger laughed again, ruefully.

"We owned six daily newspapers in Norrland. That was back in the fifties and sixties. It was my father's idea—he thought it might be politically advantageous to have a section of the media behind us. We're actually still one of the owners of the *Hedestad Courier*. Birger is the chairman of the board for the group of owners. Harald's son," he added, for Blomkvist's benefit.

"And also a local politician," Blomkvist said.

"Martin is on the board too. He keeps Birger in line."

"Why did you let go of the newspapers you owned?" Blomkvist asked.

"Corporate restructuring in the sixties. Publishing newspapers was in some ways more a hobby than an interest. When we needed to tighten the budget, it was one of the first assets that we sold. But I know what it takes to run a publication . . . May I ask you a personal question?"

This was directed at Erika.

"I haven't asked Mikael about this, and if you don't want to answer, you don't have to. I'd like to know how you ended up in this quagmire. Did you have a story or didn't you?"

Now it was Blomkvist's turn to look inscrutable. Berger hesitated only a second before she said: "We had a story. But it was a very different story."

Vanger nodded, as if he understood precisely what Berger was saying. Blomkvist did not.

"I don't want to discuss the matter." Blomkvist cut the discussion short. "I did the research and wrote the article. I had all the sources I needed. But then it all went to hell."

"You had sources for every last thing you wrote?"

"I did."

Vanger's voice was suddenly sharp. "I won't pretend to understand how the hell you could walk into such a minefield. I can't recall a similar story except perhaps the Lundahl affair in *Expressen* in the sixties, if you youngsters have ever heard of it. Was your source also a mythomaniac?" He shook his head and turned to Berger and said quietly, "I've been a newspaper publisher in the past, and I can be one again. What would you say to taking on another partner?"

The question came like a bolt out of the blue, but Berger did not seem the least bit surprised.

"Tell me more," she said.

Vanger said: "How long are you staying in Hedestad?"

"I'm going home tomorrow."

"Would you consider—you and Mikael, of course—humouring an old man by joining me for dinner tonight? Would 7:00 suit?"

"That would suit us fine. We'd love it. But you're not answering the question I asked. Why would you want to be a partner in *Millennium*?"

"I'm not avoiding the question. I just thought we could discuss it over dinner. I have to talk with my lawyer before I can put together a concrete offer. But in all simplicity I can say that I have money to invest. If the magazine survives and starts making a profit again, then I'll come out ahead. If not—well, I've had significantly bigger losses in my day."

Blomkvist was about to open his mouth when Berger put her hand on his knee.

"Mikael and I have fought hard so that we could be completely independent."

"Nonsense. No-one is completely independent. But I'm not out to take over the magazine, and I don't give a damn about the contents. That bastard Stenbeck got all sorts of points for publishing *Modern Times,* so why can't I back *Millennium*? Which happens to be an excellent magazine, by the way."

"Does this have anything to do with Wennerström?" Blomkvist said.

Vanger smiled. "Mikael, I'm eighty years plus. There are things I regret not doing and people I regret not fighting more. But, apropos this topic—" He turned to Berger again. "This type of investment would have at least one condition."

"Let's hear it," Berger said.

"Mikael Blomkvist must resume his position as publisher."

"No," Blomkvist snapped.

"But yes," Vanger said, equally curt. "Wennerström will have a stroke if we send out a press release saying that the Vanger Corporation is backing *Millennium,* and at the same time you're returning as publisher. That's absolutely the clearest signal we could send—everyone will understand that it's not a takeover and that the editorial policies won't change. And that alone will give the advertisers who are thinking of pulling out reason to reconsider. Wennerström isn't omnipotent. He has enemies too, and there are companies new to you that will consider taking space."

. . .

"What the hell was that all about?" Blomkvist said as soon as Berger pulled the front door shut.

"I think it's what you call advance probes for a business deal," she said. "You didn't tell me that Henrik Vanger is such a sweetie."

Blomkvist planted himself in front of her. "Ricky, you knew exactly what this conversation was going to be about."

"Hey, toy boy. It's only 3:00, and I want to be properly entertained before dinner."

Blomkvist was enraged. But he had never managed to be enraged at Erika Berger for very long.

She wore a black dress, a waist-length jacket, and pumps, which she just happened to have brought along in her little suitcase. She insisted that Blomkvist wear a jacket and tie. He put on his black trousers, a grey shirt, dark tie, and grey sports coat. When they knocked punctually on the door of Vanger's home, it turned out that Dirch Frode and Martin Vanger were also among the guests. Everyone was wearing a jacket and tie except for Vanger.

"The advantage of being over eighty is that no-one can criticise what you wear," he declared. He wore a bow tie and a brown cardigan.

Berger was in high spirits throughout the dinner.

It was not until they moved to the drawing room with the fireplace and cognac was poured that the discussion took on a serious tone. They talked for almost two hours before they had the outline for a deal on the table.

Frode would set up a company to be wholly owned by Henrik Vanger; the board would consist of Henrik and Martin Vanger and Frode. Over a four-year period, this company would invest a sum of money that would cover the gap between income and expenses for *Millennium*. The money would come from Vanger's personal assets. In return, Vanger would have a conspicuous position on the magazine's board. The agreement would be valid for four years, but it could be terminated by *Millennium* after two years. But this type of premature termination would be costly, since Vanger could only be bought out by repayment of the sum he had invested.

In the event of Vanger's death, Martin Vanger would replace him on the *Millennium* board for the remainder of the period during which the agreement was valid. If Martin wished to continue his involvement beyond this period, he could make that decision himself when the time came. He seemed amused by the prospect of getting even with Wennerström, and Blomkvist wondered again what the origin was of the animosity between those two.

Martin refilled their glasses. Vanger made a point of leaning towards Blomkvist, and in a low voice told him that this new arrangement had no effect whatsoever on the agreement that existed between them. Blomkvist could resume his duties as publisher full-time at the end of the year.

It was also decided that the reorganisation, in order to have the greatest impact in the media, should be presented on the same day that Blomkvist began his prison sentence in mid-March. Combining a strongly negative event with a reorganisation was, in PR terms, such a clumsy error that it could not but astonish Blomkvist's detractors and garner optimum attention for Henrik Vanger's new role. But everyone also saw the logic in it—it was a way of indicating that the yellow plague flag fluttering over *Millennium*'s editorial offices was about to be hauled down; the magazine had backers who were willing to be ruthless. The Vanger Corporation might be in a crisis, but it was still a prominent industrial firm which could go on the offence if the need arose.

The whole conversation was a discussion between Berger, on one side, and Henrik and Martin Vanger on the other. No-one asked Blomkvist what he thought.

Late that night Blomkvist lay with his head resting on Erika's breasts, looking into her eyes.

"How long have you and Henrik Vanger been discussing this arrangement?"

"About a week," she said, smiling.

"Is Christer in agreement?"

"Of course."

"Why didn't you tell me?"

"Why in the world should I discuss it with you? You resigned as publisher, you left the editorial staff and the board, and you went to live in the woods."

"So I deserve to be treated like an idiot."

"Oh yes," she said. "Decidedly you do."

"You really have been mad at me."

"Mikael, I've never felt so furious, so abandoned, and so betrayed as when you left. I've never been this upset with you before." She took a firm grip on his hair and then shoved him farther down in the bed.

By the time Berger left Hedeby on Sunday, Blomkvist was still so annoyed with Vanger that he did not want to risk running into either him or any other member of his clan. Instead, on Monday he took the bus into Hedestad and spent the afternoon walking in the town, visiting the library, and drinking coffee in a bakery. In the evening he went to the cinema to see *The Lord of the Rings,* which he had never before had time to see. He thought that orcs, unlike human beings, were simple and uncomplicated creatures.

He ended his outing at McDonald's in Hedestad and caught the last bus to Hedeby. He made coffee, took out a binder, and sat at the kitchen table. He read until 4:00 in the morning.

There were a number of questions regarding the investigation that seemed increasingly odd the further Blomkvist went through the documents. They were not revolutionary discoveries that he made all on his own; they were problems that had preoccupied Inspector Morell for long periods, especially in his free time.

During the last year of her life, Harriet had changed. In some ways this change could be explained as the change that everyone goes through in one form or another during their teenage years. Harriet was growing up. Classmates, teachers, and several members of the family, however, all testified that she had turned in on herself and become uncommunicative.

The girl who, two years earlier, was a lively teenager had begun to distance herself from everyone around her. In school she still spent time with her friends, but now she behaved in an "impersonal" manner, as one of her friends described it. This word was unusual enough for Morell to have made a note of it and then ask more questions. The explanation he got was that Harriet had stopped talking about herself, stopped gossiping, and stopped confiding in her friends.

Harriet Vanger had been a Christian, in a child's sense of the word—attending Sunday school, saying evening prayers, and becoming confirmed. In her last year she seemed to have become yet more religious. She read the Bible and went regularly to church. But she had not turned to Hedeby Island's pastor,

Otto Falk, who was a friend of the Vanger family. Instead, during the spring she had sought out a Pentecostal congregation in Hedestad. Yet her involvement in the Pentecostal church did not last long. After only two months she left the congregation and instead began reading books about the Catholic faith.

The religious infatuation of a teenager? Perhaps, but no-one else in the Vanger family had ever been noticeably religious, and it was difficult to discern what impulses may have guided her. One explanation for her interest in God could, of course, have been that her father had drowned the previous year. Morell came to the conclusion that something had happened in Harriet's life that was troubling her or affecting her. Morell, like Vanger, had devoted a great deal of time to talking to Harriet's friends, trying to find someone in whom she might have confided.

Some measure of hope was pinned on Anita Vanger, two years older than Harriet and the daughter of Harald. She had spent the summer of 1966 on Hedeby Island and they were thought to be close friends. But Anita had no solid information to offer. They had hung out together that summer, swimming, taking walks, talking about movies, pop bands, and books. Harriet had sometimes gone with Anita when she took driving lessons. Once they had got happily drunk on a bottle of wine they stole from the house. For several weeks the two of them had also stayed at Gottfried's cabin on the very tip of the island.

The questions about Harriet's private thoughts and feelings remained unanswered. But Blomkvist did make a note of a discrepancy in the report: the information about her uncommunicative frame of mind came chiefly from her classmates, and to a certain extent from the family. Anita Vanger had not thought of her as being introverted at all. He made a note to discuss this matter with Vanger at some point.

A more concrete question, to which Morell had devoted much more attention, was a surprising page in Harriet's date book, a beautiful bound book she had been given as a Christmas present the year before she disappeared. The first half of the date book was a day-by-day calendar in which Harriet had listed meetings, the dates of exams at school, her homework, and so on. The date book also had a large section for a diary, but Harriet used the diary only sporadically. She began ambitiously enough in January with many brief entries about people she had met over the Christmas holidays and several about films she had seen. After that she wrote nothing personal until the end of the school year when she apparently—depending on how the entries were interpreted—became interested from a distance in some never-named boy.

The pages that listed telephone numbers were the ones that held the real mystery. Neatly, in alphabetical order, were the names and numbers of family members, classmates, certain teachers, several members of the Pentecostal congregation, and other easily identifiable individuals in her circle of acquaintances. On the very last page of the address book, which was blank and not really part of the alphabetical section, there were five names and telephone numbers. Three female names and two sets of initials:

Magda—32016
Sara—32109
R.J.—30112
R.L.—32027
Mari—32018

The telephone numbers that began with 32 were Hedestad numbers in the sixties. The one beginning with 30 was a Norrbyn number, not far from Hedestad. The problem was that when Morell contacted every one of Harriet's friends and acquaintances, no-one had any idea whose numbers they were.

The first number belonging to "Magda" initially seemed promising. It led to a haberdashery at Parkgatan 12. The telephone was in the name of one Margot Lundmark, whose mother's name was actually Magda; she sometimes helped out in the store. But Magda was sixty-nine years old and had no idea who Harriet Vanger was. Nor was there any evidence that Harriet had ever visited the shop or bought anything there. She wasn't interested in sewing.

The second number for "Sara" belonged to a family by the name of Toresson, who lived in Väststan, on the other side of the tracks. The family included Anders and Monica and their children, Jonas and Peter, who at the time were pre-school age. There was no Sara in the family, nor did they know of Harriet Vanger, other than that she had been reported in the media as missing. The only vague connection between Harriet and the Toresson family was that Anders, who was a roofer, had several weeks earlier put a tiled roof on the school which Harriet attended. So theoretically there was a chance that they had met, although it might be considered extremely unlikely.

The remaining three numbers led to similar dead ends. The number 32027 for "R.L." had actually belonged to one Rosmarie Larsson. Unfortunately, she had died several years earlier.

Inspector Morell concentrated a great deal of his attention during the winter of 1966–67 on trying to explain why Harriet had written down these names and numbers.

One possibility was that the telephone numbers were written in some personal code—so Morell tried to guess how a teenage girl would think. Since the thirty-two series obviously pointed to Hedestad, he set about rearranging the remaining three digits. Neither 32601 or 32160 led to a Magda. As Morell continued his numerology, he realised that if he played around with enough of the numbers, sooner or later he would find some link to Harriet. For example, if he added one to each of the three remaining digits in 32016, he got 32127—which was the number to Frode's office in Hedestad. But one link like that meant nothing. Besides, he never discovered a code that made sense of all five of the numbers.

Morell broadened his inquiry. Could the digits mean, for example, car number plates, which in the sixties contained the two-letter county registration code and five digits? Another dead end.

The inspector then concentrated on the names. He obtained a list of everyone in Hedestad named Mari, Magda, or Sara or who had the initials R.L. or R.J. He had a list of 307 people. Among these, 29 actually had some connection to Harriet. For instance, a boy from her class was named Roland Jacobsson—R.J. They scarcely knew each other and had had no contact since Harriet started preparatory school. And there was no link to the telephone number.

The mystery of the numbers in the date book remained unsolved.

Her fourth encounter with Advokat Bjurman was not one of their scheduled meetings. She was forced to make contact with him.

In the second week of February Salander's laptop fell victim to an accident that was so uncalled for that she felt an urgent desire to kill someone. She had ridden her bike to a meeting at Milton Security and parked it behind a pillar in the garage. As she set her rucksack on the ground to put on the bike lock, a dark red Saab began reversing out. She had her back turned but heard the cracking sound from her rucksack. The driver didn't notice a thing and, unwitting, drove off up the exit ramp.

The rucksack contained her white Apple iBook 600 with a 25-gig hard drive and 420 megs of RAM, manufactured in

January 2002 and equipped with a 14-inch screen. At the time she bought it, it was Apple's state-of-the-art laptop. Salander's computers were upgraded with the very latest and sometimes most expensive configurations—computer equipment was the only extravagant entry on her list of expenses.

When she opened the rucksack, she could see that the lid of her computer was cracked. She plugged in the power adapter and tried to boot up the computer; not even a death rattle. She took it over to Timmy's MacJesus Shop on Brännkyrkagatan, hoping that at least something on the hard drive could be saved. After fiddling with it for a short time, Timmy shook his head.

"Sorry. No hope," he said. "You'll have to arrange a nice funeral."

The loss of her computer was depressing but not disastrous. Salander had had an excellent relationship with it during the year she had owned it. She had backed up all her documents, and she had an older desktop Mac G3 at home, as well as a five-year-old Toshiba PC laptop that she could use. But she needed a fast, modern machine.

Unsurprisingly she set her sights on the best available alternative: the new Apple PowerBook G4/1.0 GHz in an aluminium case with a PowerPC 7451 processor with an AltiVec Velocity Engine, 960 MB RAM and a 60 GB hard drive. It had BlueTooth and built-in CD and DVD burners.

Best of all, it had the first 17-inch screen in the laptop world with NVIDIA graphics and a resolution of 1440 x 900 pixels, which shook the PC advocates and outranked everything else on the market.

In terms of hardware, it was the Rolls-Royce of portable computers, but what really triggered Salander's need to have it was the simple feature that the keyboard was equipped with backlighting, so that she could see the letters even if it was pitch dark. So simple. Why had no-one thought of that before?

It was love at first sight.

It cost 38,000 kronor, plus tax.

That was the problem.

Come what may, she put in her order at MacJesus. She bought all her computer accessories there, so they gave her a reasonable discount. She tallied up her expenses. The insurance on her ruined computer would cover a good part of the price, but with the warranty and the higher price of her new acquisition, she was still 18,000 kronor short. She had 10,000 kronor hidden in a coffee tin at home but that was all. She sent evil thoughts to Herr Bjurman, but then she bit the bullet and called her guardian to explain that she needed money for an unexpected expense. Bjurman's secretary said that he had no time to see her that day. Salander replied that it would take the man twenty seconds to write out a cheque for 10,000 kronor. She was told to be at his office at 7:30 that evening.

Blomkvist might have no experience of evaluating criminal investigations, but he reckoned that Inspector Morell had been exceptionally conscientious. When Blomkvist had finished with the police investigation, Morell still kept turning up as a player in Vanger's own notes. They had become friends, and Blomkvist wondered whether Morell had been as obsessed as the captain of industry became.

It was unlikely, in his view, that Morell had missed anything. The solution to the mystery was not going to be found in the police records. Every imaginable question had been asked, and all leads followed up, even some that seemed absurdly far-fetched. He had not read every word of the report, but the further into the investigation he got, the more obscure the subsequent leads and tips became. He was not going to find anything that his professional predecessor and his experienced team had missed, and he was undecided what approach he should adopt to the problem. Eventually it came to him that the only reasonably practical route for him to take was to try to find out the psychological motives of the individuals involved.

The first question had to do with Harriet herself. Who was she?

From his kitchen window Blomkvist had noticed a light go on upstairs in Cecilia Vanger's house at a little after 5:00 in the afternoon. He knocked on her door at 7:30, just as the news broadcast was starting on TV. She opened the door dressed in her bathrobe, her hair wet under a yellow towel. Blomkvist apologised at once for disturbing her and made to retreat, but she waved him into the living room. She turned on the coffeemaker and vanished upstairs for a few minutes. When she came back down, she had put on jeans and a check flannel shirt.

"I was starting to think you were never going to call."

"I should have rung first, but I saw your light was on and came over on impulse."

"I've seen the lights on all night at your place. And you're often out walking after midnight. You're a night owl?"

Blomkvist shrugged. "It's turned out that way." He looked at several textbooks stacked on the edge of the kitchen table. "Do you still teach?"

"No, as headmistress I don't have time. But I used to teach history, religion, and social studies. And I have a few years left."

"Left?"

She smiled. "I'm fifty-six. I'll be retiring soon."

"You don't look a day over fifty, more like in your forties."

"Very flattering. How old are you?"

"Well, over forty," Blomkvist said with a smile.

"And you were just twenty the other day. How fast it all goes. Life, that is."

Cecilia Vanger served the coffee and asked if he was hungry.

He said that he had already eaten, which was partly true. He did not bother with cooking and ate only sandwiches. But he was not hungry.

"Then why did you come over? Is it time to ask me those questions?"

"To be honest . . . I didn't come over to ask questions. I think I just wanted to say hello."

She smiled. "You're sentenced to prison, you move to Hedeby, clamber through all the material of Henrik's favourite hobby, you don't sleep at night and take long nighttime walks when it's freezing cold . . . Have I left anything out?"

"My life is going to the dogs."

"Who was that woman visiting you over the weekend?"

"Erika . . . She's the editor in chief of *Millennium*."

"Your girlfriend?"

"Not exactly. She's married. I'm more a friend and occasional lover."

Cecilia Vanger hooted with laughter.

"What's so funny?"

"The way you said that. Occasional lover. I like the expression."

Blomkvist took a liking to Cecilia Vanger.

"I could use an occasional lover myself," she said.

She kicked off her slippers and propped one foot on his knee. Blomkvist automatically put his hand on her foot and stroked the ankle. He hesitated for a second—he could sense he was getting into unexpected waters. But tentatively he started massaging the sole of her foot with his thumb.

"I'm married too," she said.

"I know. No-one gets divorced in the Vanger clan."

"I haven't seen my husband in getting on for twenty years."

"What happened?"

"That's none of your business. I haven't had sex in . . . hmmm, it must be three years now."

"That surprises me."

"Why? It's a matter of supply and demand. I have no interest in a boyfriend or a married man or someone living with me. I do best on my own. Who should I have sex with? One of the teachers at school? I don't think so. One of the students? A delicious story for the gossiping old ladies. And they keep a close watch on people called Vanger. And here on Hedeby Island there are only relatives and people already married."

She leaned forward and kissed him on the neck.

"Do I shock you?"

"No. But I don't know whether this is a good idea. I work for your uncle."

"And I'm the last one who's going to tell. But to be honest, Henrik probably wouldn't have anything against it."

She sat astride him and kissed him on the mouth. Her hair was still wet and fragrant with shampoo. He fumbled with the buttons on her flannel shirt and pulled it down around her shoulders. She had no bra. She pressed against him when he kissed her breasts.

Bjurman came round the desk to show her the statement of her bank account—which she knew down to the last öre, although it was no longer at her disposal. He stood behind her. Suddenly he was massaging the back of her neck, and he let one hand slide from her left shoulder across her breasts. He put his hand over her right breast and left it there. When she did not seem to object, he squeezed her breast. Salander did not move. She could feel his breath on her neck as she studied the letter opener on his desk; she could reach it with her free hand.

But she did nothing. If there was one lesson Holger Palmgren had taught her over the years, it was that impulsive actions led to trouble, and trouble could have unpleasant consequences. She never did anything without first weighing the consequences.

The initial sexual assault—which in legal terms would be defined as sexual molestation and the exploitation of an individual in a position of dependence, and could in theory get Bjurman up to two years in prison—lasted only a few seconds. But it was enough to irrevocably cross a boundary. For Salander it was a display of strength by an enemy force—an indication that aside from their carefully defined legal relationship, she was at the mercy of his discretion and defenceless. When their eyes met a few seconds later, his lips were slightly parted and she could read the lust on his face. Salander's own face betrayed no emotions at all.

Bjurman moved back to his side of the desk and sat on his comfortable leather chair.

"I can't hand out money to you whenever you like," he said. "Why do you need such an expensive computer? There are plenty of cheaper models that you can use for playing computer games."

"I want to have control of my own money like before."

Bjurman gave her a pitying look.

"We'll have to see how things go. First you need to learn to be more sociable and get along with people."

Bjurman's smile might have been more subdued if he could have read her thoughts behind the expressionless eyes.

"I think you and I are going to be good friends," he said. "We have to be able to trust each other."

When she did not reply he said: "You're a grown woman now, Lisbeth."

She nodded.

"Come here," he said and held out his hand.

Salander fixed her gaze on the letter opener for several

seconds before she stood up and went over to him. *Consequences.* He took her hand and pressed it to his crotch. She could feel his genitals through the dark gabardine trousers.

"If you're nice to me, I'll be nice to you."

He put his other hand around her neck and pulled her down to her knees with her face in front of his crotch.

"You've done this before, haven't you?" he said as he lowered his zip. He smelled as if he had just washed himself with soap and water.

Salander turned her face away and tried to get up, but he held her in a tight grip. In terms of physical strength, she was no match for him; she weighed 90 pounds to his 210. He held her head with both hands and turned her face so their eyes met.

"If you're nice to me, I'll be nice to you," he repeated. "If you make trouble, I can put you away in an institution for the rest of your life. Would you like that?"

She said nothing.

"Would you like that?" he said again.

She shook her head.

He waited until she lowered her eyes, in what he regarded as submission. Then he pulled her closer. Salander opened her lips and took him in her mouth. He kept his grip on her neck and pulled her fiercely towards him. She felt like gagging the whole ten minutes he took to bump and grind; when finally he came, he was holding her so tight she could hardly breathe.

He showed her the bathroom in his office. Salander was shaking all over as she wiped her face and tried to rub off the spots on her sweater. She chewed some of his toothpaste to get rid of the taste. When she went back to his office, he was sitting impassively behind his desk, studying some papers.

"Sit down, Lisbeth," he told her without looking up. She sat down. Finally he looked at her and smiled.

"You're grown-up now, aren't you, Lisbeth?"

She nodded.

"Then you also need to be able to play grown-up games," he said. He used a tone of voice as if he were speaking to a child. She did not reply. A small frown appeared on his brow.

"I don't think it would be a good idea for you to tell anyone about our games. Think about it—who would believe you? There are documents stating that you're non compos mentis. It would be your word against mine. Whose word do you think would carry more weight?"

He sighed when still she did not speak. He was annoyed at the way she just sat there in silence, looking at him—but he controlled himself.

"We're going to be good friends, you and I," he said. "I think you were smart to come and see me today. You can always come to me."

"I need 10,000 kronor for my computer," she said, precisely, as if she were continuing the conversation they were having before the interruption.

Bjurman raised his eyebrows. *Hard-nosed bitch. She really is fucking retarded.* He handed her the cheque he had written when she was in the bathroom. *This is better than a whore. She gets paid with her own money.* He gave her an arrogant smile. Salander took the cheque and left.

CHAPTER 12

Wednesday, February 19

If Salander had been an ordinary citizen, she would most likely have called the police and reported the rape as soon as she left Advokat Bjurman's office. The bruises on her neck, as well as the DNA signature of his semen staining her body and clothing, would have nailed him. Even if the lawyer had claimed that *she wanted to do it* or *she seduced me* or any other excuse that rapists routinely used, he would have been guilty of so many breaches of the guardianship regulations that he would instantly have been stripped of his control over her. A report would have presumably resulted in Salander being given a proper lawyer, someone well-versed in assaults on women, which in turn might have led to a discussion of the very heart of the problem—meaning the reason she had been declared legally incompetent.

Since 1989, the term "legally incompetent" has no longer been applied to adults.

There are two levels of social welfare protection—trusteeship and guardianship.

A *trustee* steps in to offer voluntary help for individuals who, for various reasons, have problems managing their daily lives, paying their bills, or taking proper care of their hygiene. The person who is appointed as a trustee is often a relative or close friend. If there is no-one close to the person in question, the welfare authorities can appoint a trustee. Trusteeship is a mild form of guardianship, in which the *client*—the person declared incompetent—still has control over his or her assets and decisions are made in consultation with the trustee.

Guardianship is a stricter form of control, in which the client is relieved of the authority to handle his or her own money or to make decisions regarding various matters. The exact wording states that the guardian shall take over all of the client's *legal powers*. In Sweden approximately 4,000 people are under guardianship. The most common reason for a guardianship is mental illness or mental illness in conjunction with heavy abuse of alcohol or drugs. A smaller group includes those suffering from dementia. Many of the individuals under guardianship are relatively young—thirty-five or less. One of them was Lisbeth Salander.

Taking away a person's control of her own life—meaning her bank account—is one of the greatest infringements a democracy can impose, especially when it applies to young people. It is an infringement even if the intent may be perceived as benign and socially valid. Questions of guardianship are therefore potentially sensitive political issues, and are protected by rigorous regulations and controlled by the Guardianship Agency. This agency comes under the county administrative board and is controlled, in turn, by the Parliamentary Ombudsman.

For the most part the Guardianship Agency carries out its

activities under difficult conditions. But considering the sensitive issues handled by the authorities, remarkably few complaints or scandals are ever reported in the media.

Occasionally there are reports that charges have been brought against some trustee or guardian who has misappropriated funds or sold his client's co-op apartment and stuffed the proceeds into his own pockets. That those cases are relatively rare may be the result of two things: the authorities are carrying out their jobs in a satisfactory manner, or the clients have no opportunity to complain and in a credible way make themselves heard by the media or by the authorities.

The Guardianship Agency is bound to conduct an annual review to see whether any cause exists for revoking a guardianship. Since Salander persisted in her refusal to submit to psychiatric examination—she would not even exchange a polite "good morning" with her teachers—the authorities had never found any reason to alter their decision. Consequently, a situation of status quo had resulted, and so year after year she was retained under guardianship.

The wording of the law states, however, that the conditions of a guardianship "shall be adapted to each individual case." Palmgren had interpreted this to mean that Salander could take charge of her own money and her own life. He had meticulously fulfilled the requirements of the authorities and submitted a monthly report as well as an annual review. In all other respects he had treated Salander like any other normal being, and he had not interfered with her choice of lifestyle or friends. He did not think it was either his business or that of society to decide whether the young lady should have a ring in her nose or a tattoo on her neck. This rather stubborn attitude vis-à-vis the district court was one of the reasons why they had got along so well.

As long as Palmgren was her guardian, Salander had not paid much attention to her legal status.

. . .

Salander was not like any normal person. She had a rudimentary knowledge of the law—it was a subject she had never had occasion to explore—and her faith in the police was generally exiguous. For her the police were a hostile force who over the years had put her under arrest or humiliated her. The last dealing she had had with the police was in May of the previous year when she was walking past Götgatan on her way to Milton Security. She suddenly found herself facing a visor-clad riot police officer. Without the slightest provocation on her part, he had struck her on the shoulders with his baton. Her spontaneous reaction was to launch a fierce counterattack, using a Coca-Cola bottle that she had in her hand. The officer turned on his heel and ran off before she could injure him. Only later did she find out that "Reclaim the Streets" was holding a demonstration farther down the road.

Visiting the offices of those visor-clad brutes to file a report against Nils Bjurman for sexual assault did not even cross her mind. And besides—what was she supposed to report? Bjurman had touched her breasts. Any officer would take one look at her and conclude that with her miniature boobs, that was highly unlikely. And if it had actually happened, she should be proud that someone had even bothered. And the part about sucking his dick—it was, as he had warned her, her word against his, and generally in her experience the words of other people weighed more heavily than hers. The police were not an option.

She left Bjurman's office and went home, took a shower, ate two sandwiches with cheese and pickles, and then sat on the worn-out sofa in the living room to think.

An ordinary person might have felt that her lack of reaction had shifted the blame to her—it might have been another sign that she was so abnormal that even rape could evoke no adequate emotional response.

Her circle of acquaintances was not large, nor did it contain any members of the sheltered middle class from the suburbs. By the time she was eighteen, Salander did not know a single girl who at some point had not been forced to perform some sort of sexual act against her will. Most of these assaults involved slightly older boyfriends who, using a certain amount of force, made sure that they had their way. As far as Salander knew, these incidents had led to crying and angry outbursts, but never to a police report.

In her world, this was the natural order of things. As a girl she was legal prey, especially if she was dressed in a worn black leather jacket and had pierced eyebrows, tattoos, and zero social status.

There was no point whimpering about it.

On the other hand, there was no question of Advokat Bjurman going unpunished. Salander never forgot an injustice, and by nature she was anything but forgiving.

But her legal status was difficult. For as long as she could remember, she was regarded as cunning and unjustifiably violent. The first reports in her casebook came from the files of the school nurse from elementary school. Salander had been sent home because she hit a classmate and shoved him against a coat peg and drew blood. She still remembered her victim with annoyance—an overweight boy by the name of David Gustavsson who used to tease her and throw things at her; he would grow up to be an arch bully. In those days she did not know what the word "harassment" meant, but when she came to school the next day, the boy had threatened revenge. So she had decked him with a right jab fortified with a golf ball—which led to more bloodshed and a new entry in her casebook.

The rules for social interaction in school had always baffled her. She minded her own business and did not interfere with what anyone around her did. Yet there was always someone who absolutely would not leave her in peace.

In middle school she had several times been sent home after getting into violent fights with classmates. Much stronger boys in her class soon learned that it could be quite unpleasant to fight with that skinny girl. Unlike the other girls in the class, she never backed down, and she would not for a second hesitate to use her fists or any weapon at hand to protect herself. She went around with the attitude that she would rather be beaten to death than take any shit.

And she always got revenge.

Salander once found herself in a fight with a much bigger and stronger boy. She was no match for him physically. At first he amused himself shoving her to the ground several times, then he slapped her when she tried to fight back. But nothing did any good; no matter how much stronger he was, the stupid girl kept attacking him, and after a while even his classmates began to realise that things had gone too far. She was so obviously defenceless it was painful to watch. Finally the boy punched her in the face; it split open her lip and made her see stars. They left her on the ground behind the gym. She stayed at home for two days. On the morning of the third day she waited for her tormentor with a baseball bat, and she whacked him over the ear with it. For that prank she was sent to see the head teacher, who decided to report her to the police for assault, which resulted in a special welfare investigation.

Her classmates thought she was crazy and treated her accordingly. She also aroused very little sympathy among the teachers. She had never been particularly talkative, and she became known as the pupil who never raised her hand and often did not answer when a teacher asked her a direct question. No-one was sure whether this was because she did not know the answer or if there was some other reason, which was reflected in her grades. No doubt that she had problems, but no-one wanted to take responsibility for the difficult girl, even though she was frequently discussed at various teachers' meetings. That was why she ended up in the situation where the teachers ignored her and allowed her to sit in sullen silence.

She left middle school and moved to another, without having a single friend to say goodbye to. An unloved girl with odd behaviour.

Then, as she was on the threshold of her teenage years, All The Evil happened, which she did not want to think about. The last outburst set the pattern and prompted a review of the casebook entries from elementary school. After that she was considered to be legally . . . well, crazy. A freak. Salander had never needed any documents to know that she was different. But it was not something that bothered her for as long as her guardian was Holger Palmgren; if the need arose, she could wrap him around her little finger.

With the appearance of Nils Bjurman, the declaration of incompetence threatened to become a troublesome burden in her life. No matter who she turned to, pitfalls would open up; and what would happen if she lost the battle? Would she be institutionalised? Locked up? There was really no option.

Later that night, when Cecilia Vanger and Blomkvist were lying peacefully with their legs intertwined and Cecilia's breasts resting against his side, she looked up at him.

"Thank you. It's been a long time. And you're not bad."

He smiled. That sort of flattery was always childishly satisfying.

"It was unexpected, but I had fun."

"I'd be happy to do it again," Cecilia said. "If you feel like it."

He looked at her.

"You don't mean that you'd like to have a lover, do you?"

"An occasional lover," Cecilia said. "But I'd like you to go home before you fall asleep. I don't want to wake up tomorrow morning and find you here before I manage to do my exercises and fix my face. And it would be good if you didn't tell the whole village what we've been up to."

"Wouldn't think of it," Blomkvist said.

"Most of all I don't want Isabella to know. She's such a bitch."

"And your closest neighbour . . . I've met her."

"Yes, but luckily she can't see my front door from her house. Mikael, please be discreet."

"I'll be discreet."

"Thank you. Do you drink?"

"Sometimes."

"I've got a craving for something fruity with gin in it. Want some?"

"Sure."

She wrapped a sheet around herself and went downstairs. Blomkvist was standing naked, looking at her bookshelves when she returned with a carafe of iced water and two glasses of gin and lime. They drank a toast.

"Why did you come over here?" she asked.

"No special reason. I just . . ."

"You were sitting at home, reading through Henrik's investigation. And then you came over here. A person doesn't need to be super intelligent to know what you're brooding about."

"Have you read the investigation?"

"Parts of it. I've lived my entire adult life with it. You can't spend time with Henrik without being affected by the mystery of Harriet."

"It's actually a fascinating case. What I believe is known in the trade as a locked-room mystery, on an island. And nothing in the investigation seems to follow normal logic. Every question remains unanswered, every clue leads to a dead end."

"It's the kind of thing people can get obsessed about."

"You were on the island that day."

"Yes. I was here, and I witnessed the whole commotion. I was living in Stockholm at the time, studying. I wish I had stayed at home that weekend."

"What was she really like? People seem to have completely different views of her."

"Is this off the record or . . . ?"

"It's off the record."

"I haven't the least idea what was going on inside Harriet's head. You're thinking of her last year, of course. One day she was a religious crackpot. The next day she put on make-up like a whore and went to school wearing the tightest sweater she possessed. Obviously she was seriously unhappy. But, as I said, I wasn't here and just picked up the gossip."

"What triggered the problems?"

"Gottfried and Isabella, obviously. Their marriage was totally haywire. They either partied or they fought. Nothing physical—Gottfried wasn't the type to hit anyone, and he was almost afraid of Isabella. She had a horrendous temper. Sometime in the early sixties he moved more or less permanently to his cabin, where Isabella never set foot. There were periods when he would turn up in the village, looking like a vagrant. And then he'd sober up and dress neatly again and try to tend to his job."

"Wasn't there anyone who wanted to help Harriet?"

"Henrik, of course. In the end she moved into his house. But don't forget that he was preoccupied playing the role of the big industrialist. He was usually off travelling somewhere and didn't have a lot of time to spend with Harriet and Martin. I missed a lot of this because I was in Uppsala and then in Stockholm—and let me tell you, I didn't have an easy childhood myself with

Harald as my father. In hindsight I've realised that the problem was that Harriet never confided in anyone. She tried hard to keep up appearances and pretend that they were one big happy family."

"Denial."

"Yes. But she changed when her father drowned. She could no longer pretend that everything was OK. Up until then she was . . . I don't know how to explain it: extremely gifted and precocious, but on the whole a rather ordinary teenager. During the last year she was still brilliant, getting top marks in every exam and so on, but it seemed as if she didn't have any soul."

"How did her father drown?"

"In the most prosaic way possible. He fell out of a rowing boat right below his cabin. He had his trousers open and an extremely high alcohol content in his blood, so you can just imagine how it happened. Martin was the one who found him."

"I didn't know that."

"It's funny. Martin has turned out to be a really fine person. If you had asked me thirty-five years ago, I would have said that he was the one in the family who needed psychiatric care."

"Why so?"

"Harriet wasn't the only one who suffered ill effects from the situation. For many years Martin was so quiet and introverted that he was effectively antisocial. Both children had a rough time of it. I mean, we all did. I had my own problems with my father—I assume you realise that he's stark raving mad. My sister, Anita, had the same problem, as did Alexander, my cousin. It was tough being young in the Vanger family."

"What happened to your sister?"

"She lives in London. She went there in the seventies to work in a Swedish travel agency, and she stayed. She married someone, never even introduced him to the family, and anon they separated. Today she's a senior manager of British Airways. She and I get along fine, but we are not much in contact and only see each other every other year or so. She never comes to Hedestad."

"Why not?"

"An insane father. Isn't that explanation enough?"

"But you stayed."

"I did. Along with Birger, my brother."

"The politician."

"Are you making fun of me? Birger is older than Anita and me. We've never been very close. In his own eyes he's a fantastically important politician with a future in Parliament and maybe ministerial rank, if the conservatives should win. In point of fact he's a moderately talented local councillor in a remote corner of Sweden, which will probably be both the high point and the whole extent of his career."

"One thing that tickles me about the Vanger family is that you all have such low opinions of each other."

"That's not really true. I'm very fond of Martin and Henrik. And I always got on well with my sister, for all that we seldom see each other. I detest Isabella and can't abide Alexander. And I never speak to my father. So that's about fifty-fifty in the family. Birger is . . . well, more of a pompous fathead than a bad person. But I see what you mean. Look at it this way: if you're a member of the Vanger family, you learn early on to speak your mind. We do say what we think."

"Oh yes, I've noticed that you all get straight to the point." Blomkvist stretched out his hand to touch her breast. "I wasn't here fifteen minutes before you attacked me."

"To be honest, I've been wondering how you would be in bed ever since I first saw you. And it felt right to try it out."

For the first time in her life Salander felt a strong need to ask someone for advice. The problem was that asking for advice meant that she would have to confide in someone, which in turn would mean revealing her secrets. Who should she tell? She was simply not very good at establishing contact with other people.

After going through her address book in her mind, she had, strictly speaking, ten people who might be considered her circle of acquaintances.

She could talk to Plague, who was more or less a steady presence in her life. But he was definitely not a friend, and he was the last person on earth who would be able to help solve her problem. Not an option.

Salander's sex life wasn't quite as modest as she had led Advokat Bjurman to believe. On the other hand, sex had always (or at least most often) occurred on her conditions and at her initiative. She had had over fifty partners since the age of fifteen. That translated into approximately five partners per year, which was OK for a single girl who had come to regard sex as an enjoyable pastime. But she had had most of these casual partners during a two-year period. Those were the tumultuous years in her late teens when she should have come of age.

There was a time when Salander had stood at a crossroads and did not really have control over her own life—when her future could have taken the form of another series of casebook entries about drugs, alcohol, and custody in various institutions. After she turned twenty and started working at Milton Security, she had calmed down appreciably and—she thought—had got a grip on her life.

She no longer felt the need to please anyone who bought her three beers in a pub, and she did not experience the slightest degree of self-fulfilment by going home with some drunk whose name she could not remember. During the past year she had had only one regular sex partner—hardly promiscuous, as her casebook entries during her late teens had designated her.

For her, sex had most often been with one of a loose group

of friends; she was not really a member, but she was accepted because she knew Cilla Norén. She met Cilla in her late teens when, at Palmgren's insistence, she was trying to get the school certificate she had failed to complete at Komvux. Cilla had plum-red hair streaked with black, black leather trousers, a ring in her nose, and as many rivets on her belt as Salander. They had glared suspiciously at each other during the first class.

For some reason Salander did not understand, they had started hanging out together. Salander was not the easiest person to be friends with, and especially not during those years, but Cilla ignored her silences and took her along to the bar. Through Cilla, she had become a member of "Evil Fingers," which had started as a suburban band consisting of four teenage girls in Enskede who were into hard rock. Ten years later, they were a group of friends who met at Kvarnen on Tuesday nights to talk trash about boys and discuss feminism, the pentagram, music, and politics while they drank large quantities of beer. They also lived up to their name.

Salander found herself on the fringe of the group and rarely contributed to the talk, but she was accepted for who she was. She could come and go as she pleased and was allowed to sit in silence over her beer all evening. She was also invited to birthday parties and Christmas glögg celebrations, though she usually didn't go.

During the five years she hung out with "Evil Fingers," the girls began to change. Their hair colour became less extreme, and the clothing came more often from the H&M boutiques rather than from funky Myrorna. They studied or worked, and one of the girls became a mother. Salander felt as if she were the only one who had not changed a bit, which could also be interpreted as that she was simply marking time and going nowhere.

But they still had fun. If there was one place where she felt any sort of group solidarity, it was in the company of the "Evil

Fingers" and, by extension, with the guys who were friends with the girls.

"Evil Fingers" would listen. They would also stand up for her. But they had no clue that Salander had a district court order declaring her non compos mentis. She didn't want them to be eyeing her the wrong way, too. *Not an option.*

Apart from that, she did not have a single ex-classmate in her address book. She had no network or support group or political contacts of any kind. So who could she turn to and tell about her problems?

There might be one person. She deliberated for a long time about whether she should confide in Dragan Armansky. He had told her that if she needed help with anything, she should not hesitate to come to him. And she was sure that he meant it.

Armansky had groped her one time too, but it had been a friendly groping, no ill intentions, and not a demonstration of power. But to ask him for help went against the grain. He was her boss, and it would put her in his debt. Salander toyed with the idea of how her life would take shape if Armansky were her guardian instead of Bjurman. She smiled. The idea was not unpleasant, but Armansky might take the assignment so seriously that he would smother her with attention. *That was . . . well, possibly an option.*

Even though she was well aware of what a women's crisis centre was for, it never occurred to her to turn to one herself. Crisis centres existed, in her eyes, for *victims,* and she had never regarded herself as a victim. Consequently, her only remaining option was to do what she had always done—take matters in her own hands and solve her problems on her own. That was definitely an option.

And it did not bode well for Herr Advokat Nils Bjurman.

CHAPTER 13

Thursday, February 20–Friday, March 7

During the last week of February Salander acted as her own client, with Bjurman, N., born 1950, as a high-priority special project. She worked almost sixteen hours every day doing a more thorough personal investigation than she had ever done before. She made use of all the archives and public documents she could lay her hands on. She investigated his circle of relatives and friends. She looked at his finances and mapped out every detail of his upbringing and career.

The results were discouraging.

He was a lawyer, member of the Bar Association, and author of a respectably long-winded but exceptionally tedious dissertation on finance law. His reputation was spotless. Advokat Bjurman had never been censured. On only one occasion was he reported to the Bar Association—he was accused nearly ten years ago of being the middleman in an under-the-table property deal, but he had been able to prove his innocence. His finances were in good order; Bjurman was well-to-do, with at least 10 million kronor in assets. He paid more taxes than he owed, was a member of Greenpeace and Amnesty International, and he donated money to the Heart and Lung Association. He had rarely appeared in the mass media, although on several occasions he had signed his name to public appeals for political prisoners in the third world. He lived in a five-room apartment on Upplandsgatan near Odenplan, and he was the secretary of his co-op apartment association. He was divorced and had no children.

Salander focused on his ex-wife, whose name was Elena. She was born in Poland but had lived all her life in Sweden. She worked at a rehabilitation centre and was apparently happily remarried to one of Bjurman's former colleagues. Nothing useful there. The Bjurman marriage had lasted fourteen years, and the divorce went through without disputes.

Advokat Bjurman regularly acted as a supervisor for youths who got into trouble with the law. He had been trustee for four youths before he became Salander's guardian. All of these cases involved minors, and the assignments came to an end with a court decision when they came of age. One of these clients still consulted Bjurman in his role as advokat, so there did not seem to be any animosity there either. If Bjurman had been systematically exploiting his wards, there was no sign of it, and no matter how deeply Salander probed, she could find no trace of wrongdoing. All four had established lives for themselves with a boyfriend or girlfriend; they all had jobs, places to live, and Co-op debit cards.

She called each of the four clients, introducing herself as a social welfare secretary working on a study about how children hitherto under the care of a trustee fared later in life compared to other children. *Yes, naturally, everyone will be anonymous.* She had put together a questionnaire with ten questions, which she asked on the telephone. Several of the questions were designed to get the respondents to give their views on how well the trusteeship had functioned—if they had any opinions about their own trustee, Advokat Bjurman wasn't it? No-one had anything bad to say about him.

When Salander completed her ferreting, she gathered up the documents in a bag from Ica and put it out with the twenty bags of old newspapers out in the hall. Bjurman was apparently beyond reproach. There was nothing in his past that she could use. She knew beyond a doubt that he was a creep and a pig, but she could find nothing to prove it.

It was time to consider another option. After all the analyses were done, one possibility remained that started to look more and more attractive—or at least seemed to be a truly realistic alternative. The easiest thing would be for Bjurman simply to disappear from her life. A quick heart attack. End of problem. The catch was that not even disgusting fifty-three-year-old men had heart attacks at her beck and call.

But that sort of thing could be arranged.

Blomkvist carried on his affair with Headmistress Cecilia Vanger with the greatest discretion. She had three rules: she didn't want anyone to know they were meeting; she wanted him to come over only when she called and was in the mood; and she didn't want him to stay all night.

Her passion surprised and astonished him. When he ran into her at Susanne's, she was friendly but cool and distant. When they met in her bedroom, she was wildly passionate.

Blomkvist did not want to pry into her personal life, but he had been hired to pry into the personal lives of everyone in the Vanger family. He felt torn and at the same time curious. One day he asked Vanger whom she had been married to and what had happened. He asked the question while they were discussing the background of Alexander and Birger.

"Cecilia? I don't think she had anything to do with Harriet."

"Tell me about her background."

"She moved back here after graduating and started working as a teacher. She met a man by the name of Jerry Karlsson, who unfortunately worked for the Vanger Corporation. They married. I thought the marriage was a happy one—anyway in the beginning. But after a couple of years I began to see that things were not as they should be. He mistreated her. It was the usual story—he beat her and she loyally defended him. Finally he hit her one time too many. She was seriously hurt and ended up in the hospital. I offered my help. She moved out here to Hedeby Island and has refused to see her husband since. I made sure he was fired."

"But they are still married?"

"It's a question of how you define it. I don't know why she hasn't filed for divorce. But she has never wanted to remarry, so I suppose it hasn't made any difference."

"This Karlsson, did he have anything to do with . . ."

". . . with Harriet? No, he wasn't in Hedestad in 1966, and he wasn't yet working for the firm."

"OK."

"Mikael, I'm fond of Cecilia. She can be tricky to deal with, but she's one of the good people in my family."

Salander devoted a week to planning Nils Bjurman's demise. She considered—and rejected—various methods until she had narrowed it down to a few realistic scenarios from which to choose. *No acting on impulse.*

Only one condition had to be fulfilled. Bjurman had to die in such a way that she herself could never be linked to the crime. The fact that she would be included in any eventual police investigation she took for granted; sooner or later her name would show up when Bjurman's responsibilities were examined. But she was only one person in a whole universe of present and former clients, she had met him only four times, and there would not be any indication that his death even had a connection with any of his clients. There were former girlfriends, relatives, casual acquaintances, colleagues, and others. There was also what was usually defined as "random violence," when the perpetrator and victim did not know each other.

If her name came up, she would be a helpless, incompetent girl with documents showing her to be mentally deficient. So it would be an advantage if Bjurman's death occurred in such a complicated manner that it would be highly unlikely that a mentally handicapped girl could be the perpetrator.

She rejected the option of using a gun. Acquiring a gun would be no great problem, but the police were awfully good at tracking down firearms.

She considered a knife, which could be purchased at any hardware store, but decided against that too. Even if she turned up without warning and drove the knife into his back, there was no guarantee that he would die instantly and without making a sound, or that he would die at all. Worse, it might provoke a struggle, which could attract attention, and blood could stain her clothes, be evidence against her.

She thought about using a bomb of some sort, but it would be much too complicated. Building the bomb itself would not be a problem—the Internet was full of manuals on how to make the deadliest devices. It would be difficult, on the other hand, to find a place to put the bomb so that innocent passersby would not be hurt. Besides, there was again no guarantee that he would actually die.

The telephone rang.

"Hi, Lisbeth. Dragan. I've got a job for you."

"I don't have time."

"This is important."

"I'm busy."

She put down the receiver.

Finally she settled on poison. The choice surprised her, but on closer consideration it was perfect.

Salander spent several days combing the Internet. There were plenty to choose from. One of them was among the most deadly poisons known to science—hydrocyanic acid, commonly known as prussic acid.

Prussic acid was used as a component in certain chemical industries, including the manufacture of dyes. A few milligrams were enough to kill a person; one litre in a reservoir could wipe out a medium-sized city.

Obviously such a lethal substance was kept under strict control. But it could be produced in almost unlimited quantities in an ordinary kitchen. All that was needed was a modest amount of laboratory equipment, and that could be found in a chemistry set for children for a few hundred kronor, along with several ingredients that could be extracted from ordinary household products. The manual for the process was on the Internet.

Another option was nicotine. From a carton of cigarettes she could extract enough milligrams of the substance and heat it to make a viscous syrup. An even better substance, although slightly more complex to produce, was nicotine sulphate, which had the property that it could be absorbed through the skin. All she would have to do was put on rubber gloves, fill a water pistol, and spray Bjurman in the face. Within twenty seconds he should be unconscious, and within a few minutes he would be dead as a door-nail.

Salander had had no idea that so many household products could be transformed into deadly weapons. After studying the subject for several days, she was persuaded that there were no technical impediments to making short work of her guardian.

There were two problems: Bjurman's death would not of itself give her back control of her own life, and there was no guarantee that Bjurman's successor would be an improvement. *Analysis of the consequences.*

What she needed was a way to *control* her guardian and thus her own situation. She sat on the worn sofa in her living room for one whole evening running through the situation in her mind. By the end of the night, she had scrapped the idea of murder by poison and put together a new plan.

It was not an appealing option, and it required her to allow Bjurman to attack her again. But if she carried it off, she would have won.

At least, so she thought.

By the end of February Blomkvist fell into a daily routine that transformed his stay in Hedeby. He got up at 9:00 every morning, ate breakfast, and worked until noon. During this time he would cram new material into his head. Then he would take an hour-long walk, no matter what the weather was like. In the afternoon he would go on working, either at home or at Susanne's Bridge Café, processing what he had read in the morning or writing sections of what would be Vanger's autobiography. Between 3:00 and 6:00 he was always free. He would shop for groceries, do his laundry, go into Hedestad. Around 7:00 he would go over to see Vanger to ask him questions that had arisen during the day. By 10:00 he was home, and he would read until 1:00 or 2:00 in the morning. He was working systematically through Vanger's documents.

The work of shaping the autobiography was moving smoothly. He had written 120 pages of the family chronicle in rough draft. He had reached the 1920s. Beyond this point he would have to move more slowly and start weighing his words.

Through the library in Hedestad he had ordered books dealing with Nazism during that time, including Helene Lööw's doctoral dissertation, *The Swastika and the Wasa Sheaf*, which dealt with the symbols adopted by the German and Swedish Nazis. He had drafted another forty pages about Vanger and his brothers, focusing on Vanger as the person holding the story together. He had a list of subjects he needed to research on the way the company operated during that time. And he had discovered that the Vanger family was also heavily involved in Ivar Kreuger's empire—another side story he had to explore. He estimated that he had about 300 pages left to write. According to the schedule he had devised, he wanted to have a final draft for Henrik Vanger to look at by the first of September, so that he could spend the autumn revising the text.

For all his reading and listening, Blomkvist had made not an inch of progress in the Harriet Vanger case. No matter how much he brooded over the details in the files, he could find not a single piece of information that contradicted the investigative report.

One Saturday evening in late February he had a conversation with Vanger in which he reported on his lack of progress. The old man listened patiently as Blomkvist listed all the dead ends he had run into.

"No crime is perfect," Vanger said. "I'm sure we must have missed something."

"We still can't say whether a crime was committed."

"Keep at it," Vanger said. "Finish the job."

"It's pointless."

"Maybe so. But don't give up."

Blomkvist sighed.

"The telephone numbers," he said at last.

"Yes."

"They have to mean something."

"I agree."

"They were written down for some purpose."

"Yes."

"But we can't interpret them."

"No."

"Or else we're interpreting them wrong."

"Precisely."

"They're not telephone numbers. They mean *something*."

"Maybe so."

Mikael sighed again and went home to continue reading.

Advokat Bjurman was relieved when Salander called again and explained that she needed more money. She had postponed their most recent scheduled meeting with the excuse that she had to work, and a vague sense of uneasiness gnawed at him. Was she going to turn into an unmanageable problem child? But since she had missed the meeting, she had no allowance, and sooner or later she would be bound to come and see him. He could not help but be concerned that she might have discussed what had happened with some outsider.

She was going to have to be kept in check. She had to understand who was in charge. So he told her that this time the meeting would be at his home near Odenplan, not at the office. Upon hearing this news, Salander was silent for a long time on the other end of the telephone before she finally agreed.

She had planned to meet him at his office, exactly like last time. Now she was forced to see him in unfamiliar territory. The meeting was set for Friday evening. She had been given the building code, and she rang his doorbell at 8:30, half an hour later than agreed. That was how much time she had needed in the darkness of the building's stairwell to run through her plan one last time, consider alternatives, steel herself, and mobilise the courage she would need.

At 8:00 Blomkvist switched off his computer and put on his outdoor clothing. He left the lights on in his office. Outside the sky was bright with stars and the night was freezing. He walked briskly up the hill, past Vanger's house, taking the road to Östergården. Beyond Vanger's house he turned off to the left, following an uglier path along the shore. The lighted buoys flickered out on the water, and the lights from Hedestad gleamed prettily in the dark. He needed fresh air, but above all he wanted to avoid the spying eyes of Isabella Vanger. Not far from Martin Vanger's house he rejoined the road and arrived at Cecilia Vanger's door just after 8:30. They went straight to her bedroom.

They met once or twice a week. Cecilia had not only become his lover out here in his place of exile, she had also become the person he had begun to confide in. It was significantly more rewarding discussing Harriet Vanger with her than with her uncle.

The plan began to go wrong almost from the start.

Bjurman was wearing a bathrobe when he opened the door to his apartment. He was cross at her arriving late and motioned her brusquely inside. She was wearing black jeans, a black T-shirt, and the obligatory leather jacket. She wore black boots and a small rucksack with a strap across her chest.

"Haven't you even learned to tell the time?" Bjurman said. Salander did not reply. She looked around. The apartment looked much as she had expected after studying the building plans in the archives of the City Zoning Office. The light-coloured furniture was birch and beechwood.

"Come on," Bjurman said in a friendlier tone. He put his arm around her shoulders and led her down a hall into the apartment's interior. *No small talk.* He opened the door to the bedroom. There was no doubt as to what services Salander was expected to perform.

She took a quick look around. Bachelor furnishings. A double bed with a high bedstead of stainless steel. A low chest of drawers that also functioned as a bedside table. Bedside lamps with muted lighting. A wardrobe with a mirror along one side. A cane chair and a small desk in the corner next to the door. He took her by the hand and led her to the bed.

"Tell me what you need money for this time. More computer accessories?"

"Food," she said.

"Of course. How stupid of me. You missed our last meeting." He placed his hand under her chin and lifted her face so their eyes met. "How are you?"

She shrugged.

"Have you thought about what I said last time?"

"About what?"

"Lisbeth, don't act any more stupid than you are. I want us to be good friends and to help each other out."

She said nothing. Advokat Bjurman resisted an impulse to give her a slap—to put some life into her.

"Did you like our grown-up game from last time?"

"No."

He raised his eyebrows.

"Lisbeth, don't be foolish."

"I need money to buy food."

"But that's what we talked about last time. If you're nice to me, I'll be nice to you. But if you're just going to cause trouble . . ." His grip on her chin tightened and she twisted away.

"I want my money. What do you want me to do?"

"You know what I want." He grabbed her shoulder and pulled her towards the bed.

"Wait," Salander said hastily. She gave him a resigned look and then nodded curtly. She took off her rucksack and leather jacket with the rivets and looked around. She put her jacket on the chair, set her rucksack on the round table, and took several hesitant steps to the bed. Then she stopped, as if she had cold feet. Bjurman came closer.

"Wait," she said once more, in a tone as if to say that she was trying to talk sense into him. "I don't want to have to suck your dick every time I need money."

The expression on Bjurman's face suddenly changed. He slapped her hard. Salander opened her eyes wide, but before she could react, he grabbed her by the shoulder and threw her on to the bed. The violence caught her by surprise. When she tried to turn over, he pressed her down on the bed and straddled her.

Like the time before, she was no match for him in terms of physical strength. Her only chance of fighting back was if she could hurt him by scratching his eyes or using some sort of weapon. But her planned scenario had already gone to hell. *Shit*, she thought when he ripped off her T-shirt. She realised with terrifying clarity that she was out of her depth.

She heard him open the dresser drawer next to the bed and caught the clanking sound of metal. At first she did not understand what was happening; then she saw the handcuffs close around her wrist. He pulled up her arm, placed the handcuffs around one of the bedposts, and locked her other hand. It did not take him long to pull off her boots and jeans. Then he took off her knickers and held them in his hand.

"You have to learn to trust me, Lisbeth," he said. "I'm going to teach you how this grown-up game is played. If you don't treat me well, you have to be punished. When you're nice to me, we'll be friends."

He sat astride her again.

"So you don't like anal sex," he said.

Salander opened her mouth to scream. He grabbed her hair and stuffed the knickers in her mouth. She felt him putting something around her ankles, spread her legs apart and tie them so that she was lying there completely vulnerable. She heard him moving around the room but she could not see through the T-shirt around her face. It took him several minutes. She could hardly breathe. Then she felt an excruciating pain as he forced something up her anus.

Cecilia Vanger still had a rule that Blomkvist was not to stay all night. Some time after 2:00 in the morning he began to dress while she lay naked on the bed, smiling at him.

"I like you, Mikael. I like your company."

"I like you too."

She pulled him back to the bed and took off the shirt he had just put on. He stayed for one more hour.

When later he passed by Vanger's house, he was sure he saw one of the curtains shift upstairs.

Salander was allowed to put on her clothes. It was 4:00 on Saturday morning. She picked up her leather jacket and rucksack and hobbled to the front door, where he was waiting for her, showered and neatly dressed. He gave her a cheque for 2,500 kronor.

"I'll drive you home," he said, and opened the door.

She crossed the threshold, out of the apartment, and turned to face him. Her body looked fragile and her face was swollen from crying, and he almost recoiled when he met her eyes. Never in his life had he seen such naked, smouldering hatred. Salander looked just as deranged as her casebook indicated.

"No," she said, so quietly that he barely heard the word. "I can get home on my own."

He put a hand on her shoulder.

"Are you sure?"

She nodded. His grip on her shoulder tightened.

"Remember what we agreed. You'll come back here next Saturday."

She nodded again. Cowed. He let her go.

CHAPTER 14

Saturday, March 8–Monday, March 17

Salander spent the week in bed with pain in her abdomen, bleeding from her rectum, and less visible wounds that would take longer to heal. What she had gone through was very different from the first rape in his office; it was no longer a matter of coercion and degradation. This was systematic brutality.

She realised much too late that she had utterly misjudged Bjurman.

She had assumed he was on a power trip and liked to dominate, not that he was an all-out sadist. He had kept her in handcuffs half the night. Several times she believed he meant to kill her, and at one point he had pressed a pillow over her face until she thought she was going to pass out.

She did not cry.

Apart from the tears of pure physical pain she shed not a single tear. When she left the apartment she made her way with difficulty to the taxi stand at Odenplan. With difficulty she climbed the stairs to her own apartment. She showered and wiped the blood from her genitals. Then she drank a pint of water with two Rohypnol and stumbled to her bed and pulled the duvet over her head.

She woke up at midday on Sunday, empty of thoughts and with constant pain in her head, muscles, and abdomen. She got up, drank two glasses of kefir, and ate an apple. Then she took two more sleeping pills and went back to bed.

She did not feel like getting up until Tuesday. She went out and bought a big box of Billy's Pan Pizza, stuck two of them in the microwave, and filled a thermos with coffee. She spent that night on the Internet, reading articles and theses on the psychopathology of sadism.

She found one article published by a women's group in the United States in which the author claimed that the sadist chose his "relationships" with almost intuitive precision; the sadist's best victim was the one who voluntarily went to him because she did not think she had any choice. The sadist specialised in people who were in a position of dependence.

Advokat Bjurman had chosen her as a victim.

That told her something about the way she was viewed by other people.

On Friday, a week after the second rape, she walked from her apartment to a tattoo parlour in the Hornstull district. She had made an appointment, and there were no other customers in the shop. The owner nodded, recognising her.

She chose a simple little tattoo depicting a narrow band and asked to have it put on her ankle. She pointed.

"The skin is very thin there. It's going to hurt a lot," said the tattoo artist.

"That's OK," Salander said, taking off her jeans and putting her leg up.

"OK, a band. You already have loads of tattoos. Are you sure you want another one?"

"It's a reminder."

Blomkvist left the café when Susanne closed at 2:00 on Saturday afternoon. He had spent the morning typing up his notes in his iBook. He walked to Konsum and bought some food and cigarettes before he went home. He had discovered fried sausage with potatoes and beets—a dish he had never been fond of but for some reason it seemed perfectly suited to a cabin in the country.

At around 7:00 in the evening he stood by the kitchen window, thinking. Cecilia Vanger had not called. He had run into her that afternoon when she was buying bread at the café, but she had been lost in her own thoughts. It did not seem likely that she would call this evening. He glanced at the little TV that he almost never used. Instead he sat at the kitchen bench and opened a mystery by Sue Grafton.

Salander returned at the agreed-upon time to Bjurman's apartment near Odenplan. He let her in with a polite, welcoming smile.

"And how are you doing today, dear Lisbeth?"

She did not reply. He put an arm around her shoulder.

"I suppose it was a bit rough last time," he said. "You looked a little subdued."

She gave him a crooked smile and he felt a sudden pang of uncertainty. *This girl is not all there. I have to remember that.* He wondered if she would come around.

"Shall we go into the bedroom?" Salander said.

On the other hand, she may be with it. . . . Today I'll take it easy on her. Build up her trust. He had already put out the handcuffs on the chest of drawers. It was not until they reached the bed that Bjurman realised that something was amiss.

She was the one leading him to the bed, not the other way around. He stopped and gave her a puzzled look when she pulled something out of her jacket pocket which he thought was a mobile telephone. Then he saw her eyes.

"Say goodnight," she said.

She shoved the taser into his left armpit and fired off 75,000 volts. When his legs began to give way she put her shoulder against him and used all her strength to push him down on to the bed.

Cecilia Vanger felt a little tipsy. She had decided not to telephone Blomkvist. Their relationship had developed into a ridiculous bedroom farce, in which Blomkvist had to tiptoe around trying to get to her house unnoticed. She in turn played a lovesick teenage girl who could not control herself. Her behaviour the past few weeks had been reckless.

The problem is that I like him too much, she thought. He's going to end up hurting me. She sat for a long time wishing that Mikael Blomkvist had never come to Hedeby.

She had opened a bottle of wine and drunk two glasses in her loneliness. She turned on the TV to watch *Rapport* and tried to follow the world situation but very soon tired of the reasoned commentary on why President Bush had to bomb Iraq to smithereens. Instead she sat on the living-room sofa and picked up Gellert Tamas' book *The Laser Man*. She read only a few pages before she had to put the book down. That made her instantly think of her father. What kind of fantasies did he have?

The last time they really saw each other was in 1984, when she went with him and Birger, hare-hunting north of Hedestad.

Birger was trying out a new hunting dog—a Swedish foxhound which he had just acquired. Harald Vanger was seventy-three at the time, and she had done her very best to accept his lunacy, which had made her childhood a nightmare and affected her entire adult life.

Cecilia had never before been as fragile as she was then. Her marriage had ended three months earlier. Domestic violence . . . the term was so banal. For her it had taken the form of unceasing abuse. Blows to the head, violent shoving, moody threats, and being knocked to the kitchen floor. Her husband's outbursts were inexplicable and the attacks were not often so severe that she was actually injured. She had become used to it.

Until the day when she struck back and he completely lost control. It ended with him flinging some scissors at her which lodged in her shoulder blade.

He had been remorseful and panicky and drove her to the hospital, making up a story about a bizarre accident which all the staff in the emergency room saw through at once. She had felt ashamed. They gave her twelve stitches and kept her in the hospital for two days. Then her uncle picked her up and drove her to his house. She never spoke to her husband again.

On that sunny autumn day Harald Vanger had been in a good mood, almost friendly. But without warning, a long way into the woods, he began to berate her with humiliating invective and revolting remarks about her morals and sexual predilections. He snarled that no wonder such a whore could never keep a man.

Her brother apparently did not notice that every word from their father struck her like a whiplash. Instead, Birger suddenly laughed and put his arm around his father and in his own way made light of the situation by making some comment to the effect that *you know full well what women are like*. He gave

Cecilia a cheerful wink and suggested that Harald Vanger take up a position on a little ridge.

For a second, a frozen instant, Cecilia Vanger looked at her father and brother and realised that she was holding a loaded shotgun in her hand. She closed her eyes. Her only option at that moment seemed to be to raise the gun and fire both barrels. She wanted to kill them both. Instead she laid down the weapon at her feet, turned on her heel, and went back to where they had parked the car. She left them high and dry, driving home alone. Since that day she refused to let her father into her house and had never been in his.

You ruined my life, Cecilia Vanger thought. *You ruined my life when I was just a child.*

At 8:30 she called Blomkvist.

Bjurman was in pain. His muscles were no use to him. His body seemed to be paralysed. He could not remember if he had lost consciousness, but he was disoriented. When he slowly regained control over his body he discovered that he was lying naked on his bed, his wrists in handcuffs and his legs spread painfully apart. He had stinging burn marks where electrodes had touched his body.

Salander had pulled the cane chair over and was patiently waiting, her boots resting on the bed as she smoked a cigarette. When Bjurman began to speak to her he found that his mouth was sealed. He turned his head. She had pulled out all his drawers and dumped them and the contents on the floor.

"I found your toys," Salander said. She held up a riding whip and poked around in the heap of dildos, harness bits, and rubber masks on the floor. "What's this one for?" She held up a huge anal plug. "No, don't try to speak—I won't hear what you say.

Was this what you used on me last week? All you have to do is nod." She leaned towards him expectantly.

Bjurman felt cold terror piercing his chest and lost his composure. He tugged at his handcuffs. *She had taken control. Impossible.* He could do nothing to resist when Salander bent over and placed the anal plug between his buttocks. "So you're a sadist," she said matter-of-factly. "You enjoy shoving things inside people, is that it?" She looked him in the eyes. Her face was expressionless. "Without a lubricant, right?"

Bjurman howled into the adhesive tape when Salander roughly spread his cheeks and rammed the plug into its proper place.

"Stop whimpering," Salander said, imitating his voice. "If you complain, I'll have to punish you."

She stood up and went to the other side of the bed. He followed her helplessly with his eyes . . . *What the hell was this?* Salander had rolled in his thirty-two-inch TV from the living room. She had placed his DVD player on the floor. She looked at him, still holding the whip in her hand.

"Do I have your undivided attention? Don't try to talk—just nod. Did you hear what I said?" He nodded.

"Good." She bent down and picked up her rucksack. "Do you recognise this?" He nodded. "It's the rucksack I had when I visited you last week. A practical item. I borrowed it from Milton Security." She unzipped the bottom pocket. "This is a digital video camera. Do you ever watch *Insider* on TV3? This is the gear that those nasty reporters use when they have to record something with a hidden camera." She zipped the pocket back up.

"Where's the lens, you're wondering. That's the great thing about it. Wide angle fibre optics. The lens looks like a button and sits hidden in the buckle on a shoulder strap. Maybe you remember that I put the rucksack here on the table before you started to grope me. I made sure that the lens was directed straight at the bed."

She held up a DVD and slipped it into the player. Then she turned the cane chair so that she could sit and watch the screen. She lit another cigarette and pressed the remote. Advokat Bjurman saw himself open the door for Salander.

Haven't you even learned to tell the time?

She played the whole disc for him. The video ended after ninety minutes, in the middle of a scene where a naked Advokat Bjurman sat leaning against the bedstead drinking a glass of wine as he looked at Salander, curled up with her hands fettered behind her.

She turned off the TV and sat in the chair for a good ten minutes without looking at him. Bjurman did not dare move a muscle. Then she got up and went into the bathroom. When she came back she sat again in the chair. Her voice was like sandpaper.

"I made a mistake last week," she said. "I thought you were going to make me give you a blow job again, which is disgusting enough in your case, but not so disgusting that I couldn't do it. I thought I could easily acquire good documentation to prove you're a filthy old prick. I misjudged you. I didn't understand how fucking sick you were.

"I'm going to speak plainly," she said. "This video shows you raping a mentally handicapped twenty-four-year-old girl for whom you were appointed guardian. And you have no idea how mentally handicapped I can be if push comes to shove. Anyone who sees this video will discover that you're not merely a pervert but an insane sadist. This is the second and I hope the last time I'll ever have to watch this video. It's quite instructive, don't you think? My guess is that you're the one who's going to be institutionalised, not me. Are you following me so far?"

She waited. He did not react, but she could see him quivering. She grabbed the whip and flicked it right over his genitals.

"Are you following me?" she said more loudly. He nodded.

"Good. So we're singing from the same song sheet."

She pulled the chair up close so she could look into his eyes. "What do you think we should do about this problem?" He could not give her an answer. "Have you any good ideas?" When he did not react she reached out and grabbed his scrotum and pulled until his face contorted in pain. "Have you got any good ideas?" she repeated. He shook his head.

"Good. I'm going to be pretty fucking mad at you if you ever have any ideas in the future."

She leaned back and stubbed her cigarette out on the carpet. "This is what's going to happen. Next week, as soon as you manage to shit out that oversized rubber plug in your arse, you're going to inform my bank that I—*and I alone*—have access to my account. Do you understand what I'm saying?" Bjurman nodded.

"Good boy. You will never ever contact me again. In the future we will meet only if I decide it's necessary. You're under a restraining order to stay away from me." He nodded repeatedly. *She doesn't intend to kill me.*

"If you ever try to contact me again, copies of this DVD will wind up in every newsroom in Stockholm. Do you understand?"

He nodded. *I have to get hold of that video.*

"Once a year you will turn in your report on my welfare to the Guardianship Agency. You will report that my life is completely normal, that I have a steady job, that I'm supporting myself, and that you don't think there is anything abnormal about my behaviour. OK?"

He nodded.

"Each month you will prepare a report about your non-existent meetings with me. You will describe in detail how positive I am and how well things are going for me. You will post a copy to me. Do you understand?" He nodded again. Salander noticed absent-mindedly the beads of sweat forming on his forehead.

"In a year or so, let's say two, you will initiate negotiations in the district court to have my declaration of incompetence rescinded. You will use your faked reports from our meetings as the basis for your proposal. You will find a shrink who will swear under oath that I am completely normal. You're going to have to make an effort. You will do precisely everything in your power to ensure that I am declared competent."

He nodded.

"Do you know why you're going to do your very best? Because you have a fucking good reason. If you fail I'm going to make this video extremely public."

He listened to every syllable Salander was saying. His eyes were burning with hatred. He decided she had made a mistake by letting him live. *You're going to wind up eating this, you fucking cunt. Sooner or later I'm going to crush you.* But he continued nodding as vigorously as he could in reply to every question.

"The same applies if you try to contact me." She mimed a throat-slitting motion. "Goodbye to this elegant lifestyle and your fine reputation and your millions in that offshore account."

His eyes widened involuntarily when she mentioned the money. *How the fucking hell did she know that . . .*

She smiled and took out another cigarette.

"I want your spare set of keys to this apartment and your office." He frowned. She leaned forward and smiled sweetly.

"In the future I'm going to have control over *your* life. When you least expect it, when you're in bed asleep probably, I'm going to appear in the bedroom with this in my hand." She held up the taser. "I'll be checking up on you. If I ever find out you have been with a girl again—and it doesn't matter if she's here of her own free will—if I ever find you with any woman at all . . . " Salander made the throat-slitting motion again.

"If I should die . . . if I should fall victim to an accident and be run over by a car or something . . . then copies of the video will automatically be posted to the newspapers. Plus a report in which I describe what it's like to have you as a guardian.

"One more thing." She leaned forward again so that her face was only a couple of inches from his. "If you ever touch me again I will kill you. And that's a promise."

Bjurman absolutely believed her. There was not a vestige of bluff in her eyes.

"Keep it in mind that I'm crazy, won't you?"

He nodded.

She gave him a thoughtful look. "I don't think you and I are going to be good friends," Salander said. "Right now you're lying there congratulating yourself that I'm dim enough to let you live. You think you have control even though you're my prisoner, since you think the only thing I can do if I don't kill you is to let you go. So you're full of hope that you can somehow recover your power over me right away. Am I right?"

He shook his head. He was beginning to feel very ill indeed.

"You're going to get a present from me so you'll always remember our agreement."

She gave him a crooked smile and climbed on to the bed and knelt between his legs. Bjurman had no idea what she intended to do, but he felt a sudden terror.

Then he saw the needle in her hand.

He flopped his head back and forth and tried to twist his body away until she put a knee on his crotch and pressed down in warning.

"Lie rather still because this is the first time I've used this equipment."

She worked steadily for two hours. When she was finished he had stopped whimpering. He seemed to be almost in a state of apathy.

She got down from the bed, cocked her head to one side, and regarded her handiwork with a critical eye. Her artistic talents were limited. The letters looked at best impressionistic. She had used red and blue ink. The message was written in caps over five lines that covered his belly, from his nipples to just above his genitals: I AM A SADISTIC PIG, A PERVERT, AND A RAPIST.

She gathered up the needles and placed the ink cartridges in her rucksack. Then she went to the bathroom and washed. She felt a lot better when she came back in the bedroom.

"Goodnight," she said.

She unlocked one of the handcuffs and put the key on his stomach before she left. She took her DVD and his bundle of keys with her.

It was as they shared a cigarette some time after midnight that he told her they could not see each other for a while. Cecilia turned her face to him in surprise.

"What do you mean?"

He looked ashamed. "On Monday I have to go to prison for up to three months."

No other explanation was necessary. Cecilia lay in silence for a long time. She felt like crying.

Dragan Armansky was suspicious when Salander knocked at his door on Monday afternoon. He had seen no sign of her since he called off the investigation of the Wennerström affair in early January, and every time he tried to reach her she either did not answer or hung up saying she was busy.

"Have you got a job for me?" she asked without any greeting.

"Hi. Great to see you. I thought you died or something."

"There were things I had to straighten out."

"You often seem to have things to straighten out."

"This time it was urgent. I'm back now. Have you got a job for me?"

Armansky shook his head. "Sorry. Not at the moment."

Salander looked at him calmly. After a while he started talking.

"Lisbeth, you know I like you and I like to give you jobs. But you've been gone for two months and I've had tons of jobs. You're simply not reliable. I've had to pay other people to cover for you, and right now I actually don't have a thing."

"Could you turn up the volume?"

"What?"

"On the radio."

> . . . the magazine *Millennium*. The news that veteran industrialist Henrik Vanger will be part owner and will have a seat on the board of directors of *Millennium* comes the same day that the former CEO and publisher Mikael Blomkvist begins serving his three-month sentence for the libel of businessman Hans-Erik Wennerström. *Millennium*'s editor in chief Erika Berger announced at a press conference that Blomkvist will resume his role as publisher when his sentence is completed.

"Well, isn't that something," Salander said so quietly that Armansky only saw her lips move. She stood up and headed for the door.

"Wait. Where are you going?"

"Home. I want to check some stuff. Call me when you've got something."

. . .

The news that *Millennium* had acquired reinforcements in the form of Henrik Vanger was a considerably bigger event than Lisbeth Salander had expected. *Aftonbladet*'s evening edition was already out, with a story from the TT wire service summing up Vanger's career and stating that it was the first time in almost twenty years that the old industrial magnate had made a public appearance. The news that he was becoming part owner of *Millennium* was viewed as just as improbable as Peter Wallenberg or Erik Penser popping up as part owners of *ETC* or sponsors of *Ordfront* magazine.

The story was so big that the 7:30 edition of *Rapport* ran it as its third lead and gave it a three-minute slot. Erika Berger was interviewed at a conference table in *Millennium*'s office. All of a sudden the Wennerström affair was news again.

"We made a serious mistake last year which resulted in the magazine being prosecuted for libel. This is something we regret . . . and we will be following up this story at a suitable occasion."

"What do you mean by 'following up the story'?" the reporter said.

"I mean that we will eventually be telling our version of events, which we have not done thus far."

"You could have done that at the trial."

"We chose not to do so. But our investigative journalism will continue as before."

"Does that mean you're holding to the story that prompted the indictment?"

"I have nothing more to say on that subject."

"You sacked Mikael Blomkvist after the verdict was delivered."

"That is inaccurate. Read our press release. He needed a break. He'll be back as CEO and publisher later this year."

The camera panned through the newsroom while the

reporter quickly recounted background information on *Millennium*'s stormy history as an original and outspoken magazine. Blomkvist was not available for comment. He had just been shut up in Rullåker Prison, about an hour from Östersund in Jämtland.

Salander noticed Dirch Frode at the edge of the TV screen passing a doorway in the editorial offices. She frowned and bit her lower lip in thought.

That Monday had been a slow news day, and Vanger got a whole four minutes on the 9:00 news. He was interviewed in a TV studio in Hedestad. The reporter began by stating that after two decades of having stood back from the spotlight the industrialist Henrik Vanger was back. The segment began with a snappy biography in black-and-white TV images, showing him with Prime Minister Erlander and opening factories in the sixties. The camera then focused on a studio sofa where Vanger was sitting perfectly relaxed. He wore a yellow shirt, narrow green tie, and comfortable dark-brown suit. He was gaunt, but he spoke in a clear, firm voice. And he was also quite candid. The reporter asked Vanger what had prompted him to become a part owner of *Millennium*.

"It's an excellent magazine which I have followed with great interest for several years. Today the publication is under attack. It has enemies who are organising an advertising boycott, trying to run it into the ground."

The reporter was not prepared for this, but guessed at once that the already unusual story had yet more unexpected aspects.

"What's behind this boycott?"

"That's one of the things that *Millennium* will be examining closely. But I'll make it clear now that *Millennium* will not be sunk with the first salvo."

"Is this why you bought into the magazine?"

"It would be deplorable if the special interests had the power to silence those voices in the media that they find uncomfortable."

Vanger acted as though he had been a cultural radical espousing freedom of speech all his life. Blomkvist burst out laughing as he spent his first evening in the TV room at Rullåker Prison. His fellow inmates glanced at him uneasily.

Later that evening, when he was lying on the bunk in his cell—which reminded him of a cramped motel room with its tiny table, its one chair, and one shelf on the wall, he admitted that Vanger and Berger had been right about how the news would be marketed. He just knew that something had changed in people's attitude towards *Millennium.*

Vanger's support was no more or less than a declaration of war against Wennerström. The message was clear: in the future you will not be fighting with a magazine with a staff of six and an annual budget corresponding to the cost of a luncheon meeting of the Wennerström Group. You will now be up against the Vanger Corporation, which may be a shadow of its former greatness but still presents a considerably tougher challenge.

The message that Vanger had delivered on TV was that he was prepared to fight, and for Wennerström, that war would be costly.

Berger had chosen her words with care. She had not said much, but her saying that the magazine had not told its version created the impression that there was something to tell. Despite the fact that Blomkvist had been indicted, convicted, and was now imprisoned, she had come out and said—if not in so many words—that he was innocent of libel and that another truth existed. Precisely because she had not used the word "innocent," his innocence seemed more apparent than ever. The fact that he was going to be reinstated as publisher emphasised that *Millennium* felt it had nothing to be ashamed of. In the eyes of the public, credibility was no problem—everyone loves a conspiracy theory, and in the choice between a filthy rich businessman and an outspoken and charming editor in chief, it was not hard to guess where the public's sympathies would lie. The media, however, were not going to buy the story so easily—but Berger may have disarmed a number of critics.

None of the day's events had changed the situation fundamentally, but they had bought time and they had shifted the balance of power a little. Blomkvist imagined that Wennerström had probably had an unpleasant evening. Wennerström could not know how much, or how little, they knew, and before he made his next move he was going to have to find out.

With a grim expression, Berger turned off the TV and the VCR after having watched first her own and then Vanger's interview. It was 2:45 in the morning, and she had to stifle the impulse to call Blomkvist. He was locked up, and it was unlikely that he was allowed to keep his mobile. She had arrived home so late that her husband was already asleep. She went over to the bar and poured herself a healthy measure of Aberlour single malt—she drank alcohol about once a year—and sat at the window, looking out across Saltsjön to the lighthouse at the entrance to Skuru Sound.

She and Blomkvist had argued heatedly when they were alone after she concluded the agreement with Vanger. They had weathered many full-blooded arguments about what angle to use for a specific article, the design of the magazine, the evaluation of their sources' credibility, and a thousand other things involved in putting out a magazine. But the argument in Vanger's guest house had touched on principles that made her aware she was on shaky ground.

"I don't know what to do now," Blomkvist had said. "This

man has hired me to ghostwrite his autobiography. Up until now I've been free to get up and leave the moment he tries to force me to write something that isn't true, or tries to persuade me to slant the story in a way I don't hold with. Now he's a part owner of our magazine—and the only one with the resources to save *Millennium*. All of a sudden I'm sitting on the fence, in a position that a board of professional ethics would never approve."

"Have you got a better idea?" Berger asked him. "Because if you have, spit it out, before we type up the contract and sign it."

"Ricky, Vanger is exploiting us in some sort of private vendetta against Wennerström."

"So what? We have a vendetta against Wennerström ourselves."

Blomkvist turned away from her and lit a cigarette.

Their conversation had gone on for quite a while, until Berger went into the bedroom, undressed, and climbed into bed. She pretended to be asleep when he got in beside her two hours later.

This evening a reporter from *Dagens Nyheter* had asked her the same question: "How is *Millennium* going to be able credibly to assert its independence?"

"What do you mean?"

The reporter thought the question had been clear enough, but he spelled it out anyway.

"One of *Millennium*'s objectives is to investigate corporations. How will the magazine be able to claim in a credible way that it's investigating the Vanger Corporation?"

Berger gave him a surprised look, as if the question were completely unexpected.

"Are you insinuating that *Millennium*'s credibility is diminished because a well-known financier with significant resources has entered the picture?"

"You could not now credibly investigate the Vanger Corporation."

"Is that a rule that applies specifically to *Millennium*?"

"Excuse me?"

"I mean, you work for a publication that is for the most part owned by major corporate entities. Does that mean that none of the newspapers published by the Bonnier Group is credible? *Aftonbladet* is owned by a huge Norwegian corporation, which in turn is a major player in IT and communications—does that mean that anything *Aftonbladet* publishes about the electronics industry is not credible? *Metro* is owned by the Stenbeck Group. Are you saying that no publication in Sweden that has significant economic interests behind it is credible?"

"No, of course not."

"Then why are you insinuating that *Millennium*'s credibility would be diminished because we also have backers?"

The reporter held up his hand.

"OK, I'll retract that question."

"No. Don't do that. I want you to print exactly what I said. And you can add that if *DN* promises to focus a little extra on the Vanger Corporation, then we'll focus a little more on the Bonnier Group."

But it *was* an ethical dilemma.

Blomkvist was working for Henrik Vanger, who was in a position to sink *Millennium* with the stroke of a pen. What would happen if Blomkvist and Vanger became enemies?

And above all—what price did she put on her own credibility, and when had she been transformed from an independent editor into a corrupted one?

Salander closed her browser and shut down her PowerBook. She was out of work and hungry. The first condition did not worry her so much, since she had regained control over her bank account and Bjurman had already taken on the status of a vague unpleasantness in her past. The hunger she dealt with by switching on the coffeemaker. She made three big open rye-bread sandwiches with cheese, caviar, and a hard-boiled egg. She ate her nighttime snacks on the sofa in the living room while she worked on the information she had gathered.

The lawyer Frode from Hedestad had hired her to do an investigation of Mikael Blomkvist, the journalist who was given a prison sentence for libelling financier Hans-Erik Wennerström. A few months later Henrik Vanger, also from Hedestad, joins Blomkvist's magazine's board of directors and claims that there is a conspiracy to crush the magazine. All this on the same day that the former goes to prison. Most fascinating of all: a two-year-old background article—"With two empty hands"—about Hans-Erik Wennerström, which she found in the online edition of *Monopoly Financial Magazine.* It seemed that he began his career in the very same Vanger Corporation in the late sixties.

You didn't have to be a rocket scientist to see that these events were somehow related. There had to be a skeleton in one of their cupboards, and Salander loved hunting skeletons. Besides, she had nothing else on at the moment.

for so much, since she had regained [illegible] backup and [illegible] had already taken on the task of [illegible] unpleasant [illegible] her past. [illegible] with [illegible] coffee [illegible] made [illegible] sandwiches with cheese [illegible] and [illegible] her [illegible] snacks on the [illegible] while [illegible] worked on the [illegible] had.

[illegible] however [illegible] had [illegible] investigation [illegible] the [illegible] was [illegible] prison sentence for [illegible] Hans-Erik Wennerström. A few months later Henrik Vanger [illegible] magazine's board of directors and [illegible] that there [illegible] the same day [illegible]. Most fascinating of all [illegible] background article [illegible] Hans-Erik Wennerström [illegible] found in the online [illegible] it seemed that he began his career in the Vanger Corporation in the late sixties.

[illegible] didn't have to [illegible] to [illegible] that these events were somehow related. [illegible] of their [illegible] and [illegible] besides, she had nothing [illegible] at the moment.

PART 3

Mergers

MAY 16 TO JULY 11

Thirteen percent of the women in Sweden have been subjected to aggravated sexual assault outside of a sexual relationship.

CHAPTER 15

Friday, May 16–Saturday, May 31

Mikael Blomkvist was released from Rullåker Prison on Friday, May 16, two months after he was admitted. The same day he entered the facility, he had submitted an application for parole, with no great optimism. He never did quite understand the technical reasons behind his release, but it may have had something to do with the fact that he did not use any holiday leave and that the prison population was forty-two while the number of beds was thirty-one. In any case, the warden—Peter Sarowsky, a forty-year-old Polish exile—with whom Blomkvist got along well, wrote a recommendation that his sentence be reduced.

His time at Rullåker had been unstressful and pleasant enough. The prison had been designed, as Sarowsky expressed it, for hooligans and drunk drivers, not for hardened criminals. The daily routines reminded him of living in a youth hostel. His fellow prisoners, half of whom were second-generation immigrants, regarded Blomkvist as something of a rare bird in the group. He was the only inmate to appear on the TV news, which lent him a certain status.

On his first day, he was called in for a talk and offered therapy, training from Komvux, or the opportunity for other adult education, and occupational counselling. He did not feel any need at all for social rehabilitation, he had completed his studies, he thought, and he already had a job. On the other hand, he asked for permission to keep his iBook in his cell so that he could continue to work on the book he was commissioned to write. His request was granted without further ado, and Sarowsky arranged to bring him a lockable cabinet so that he could leave the computer in his cell. Not that any of the inmates would have stolen or vandalised it or anything like that. They rather kept a protective eye on him.

In this way Blomkvist spent two months working about six hours a day on the Vanger family chronicle, work that was interrupted only by a few hours of cleaning or recreation each day. Blomkvist and two others, one of whom came from Skövde and had his roots in Chile, were assigned to clean the prison gym each day. Recreation consisted of watching TV, playing cards, or weight training. Blomkvist discovered that he was a passable poker player, but he still lost a few fifty-öre coins every day. Regulations permitted playing for money if the total pot did not exceed five kronor.

He was told of his release only one day before. Sarowsky summoned him to his office and they shared a toast with aquavit.

Blomkvist went straight back to the cabin in Hedeby. When he walked up the front steps he heard a meow and found himself escorted by the reddish-brown cat.

"OK, you can come in," he said. "But I have no milk yet."

He unpacked his bags. It was as if he had been on holiday,

and he realised that he actually missed the company of Sarowsky and his fellow prisoners. Absurd as it seemed, he had enjoyed his time at Rullåker, but his release had come so unexpectedly that he had had no time to let anyone know.

It was just after 6:00 in the evening. He hurried over to Konsum to buy groceries before they closed. When he got home he called Berger. A message said she was unavailable. He asked for her to call him the next day.

Then he walked up to his employer's house. He found Vanger on the ground floor. The old man raised his eyebrows in surprise when he saw Mikael.

"Did you escape?"

"Released early."

"That's a surprise."

"For me too. I found out last night."

They looked at each other for a few seconds. Then the old man surprised Blomkvist by throwing his arms around him and giving him a bear hug.

"I was just about to eat. Join me."

Anna produced a great quantity of bacon pancakes with lingonberries. They sat there in the dining room and talked for almost two hours. Blomkvist told him about how far he had got with the family chronicle, and where there were holes and gaps. They did not talk at all about Harriet, but Vanger told him all about *Millennium*.

"We had a board meeting. Fröken Berger and your partner Malm were kind enough to move two of the meetings up here, while Dirch stood in for me at a meeting in Stockholm. I really wish I were a few years younger, but the truth is that it's too tiring for me to travel so far. I'll try to get down there during the summer."

"No reason not to hold the meetings up here," Blomkvist said. "So how does it feel to be a part owner of the magazine?"

Vanger gave him a wry smile.

"It's actually the most fun I've had in years. I've taken a look at the finances, and they look pretty fair. I won't have to put up as much money as I thought—the gap between income and expenses is dwindling."

"I talked with Erika this week. She says that advertising revenue has perked up."

"It's starting to turn around, yes, but it'll take time. At first the companies in the Vanger Corporation went in and bought up a bunch of full-page ads. But two former advertisers—mobile telephones and a travel bureau—have come back." He smiled broadly. "We're also doing a little more one-to-one hustling among Wennerström's enemies. And, believe me, there's a long list."

"Have you heard directly from Wennerström?"

"Well, not really. But we leaked a story that Wennerström is organising the boycott of *Millennium*. That must have made him look petty. A reporter at *DN* is said to have reached him and got a surly reply."

"You are enjoying this, aren't you?"

"Enjoy isn't the word. I should have devoted myself to this years ago."

"What is it between you and Wennerström, anyway?"

"Don't even try. You'll find out at the end of your year."

When Blomkvist left Vanger around 9:00 there was a distinct feeling of spring in the air. It was dark outside and he hesitated for a moment. Then he made his familiar circuit and knocked on the door of Cecilia Vanger's house.

He wasn't sure what he expected. Cecilia opened her eyes wide and instantly looked uncomfortable as she let him into the hall. They stood there, suddenly unsure of each other. She too asked if he had escaped, and he explained the situation.

"I just wanted to say hello. Am I interrupting something?"

She avoided his eyes. Mikael could sense at once that she wasn't particularly glad to see him.

"No . . . no, come in. Would you like some coffee?"

"I would."

He followed her into the kitchen. She stood with her back to him as she filled the coffeemaker with water. He put a hand on her shoulder, and she stiffened.

"Cecilia, you don't look as if you want to give me coffee."

"I wasn't expecting you for another month," she said. "You surprised me."

He turned her around so that he could see her face. They stood in silence for a moment. She still would not look him in the eye.

"Cecilia. Forget about the coffee. What's going on?"

She shook her head and took a deep breath.

"Mikael, I'd like you to leave. Don't ask. Just leave."

Mikael first walked back to the cottage, but paused at the gate, undecided. Instead of going in he went down to the water by the bridge and sat on a rock. He smoked a cigarette while he sorted out his thoughts and wondered what could have so dramatically changed Cecilia Vanger's attitude towards him.

He suddenly heard the sound of an engine and saw a big white boat slip into the sound beneath the bridge. When it passed, Mikael saw that it was Martin Vanger standing at the wheel, with his gaze focused on avoiding sunken rocks in the water. The boat was a forty-foot motor cruiser—an impressive bundle of power. He stood up and took the beach path. He discovered that several boats were already in the water at various docks, a mixture of motorboats and sailing boats. There were several Pettersson boats, and at one dock an IF-class yacht was rocking in the wake. Other boats were larger and more expensive vessels. He noticed a Hallberg-Rassy. The boats also indicated the class distribution of Hedeby's marina—Martin Vanger had without a doubt the largest and the plushest boat in view.

He stopped below Cecilia Vanger's house and stole a glance at the lighted windows on the top floor. Then he went home and put on some coffee of his own. He went into his office while he waited for it to brew.

Before he presented himself at the prison he had returned the majority of Vanger's documentation on Harriet. It had seemed wise not to leave it in an empty house. Now the shelves looked bare. He had, of the reports, only five of Vanger's own notebooks, and these he had taken with him to Rullåker and now knew by heart. He noticed an album on the top shelf of the bookcase that he had forgotten.

He carried it to the kitchen table. He poured himself coffee and began going through it.

They were photographs that had been taken on the day Harriet disappeared. The first of them was the last photograph of Harriet, at the Children's Day parade in Hedestad. Then there were some 180 crystal-clear pictures of the scene of the accident on the bridge. He had examined the images one by one with a magnifying glass on several occasions previously. Now he turned the pages almost absent-mindedly; he knew he was not going to find anything he had not seen before. In fact he felt all of a sudden fed up with the unexplainable disappearance of Harriet Vanger and slammed the album shut.

Restlessly he went to the kitchen window and peered out into the darkness.

Then he turned his gaze back to the album. He could not have explained the feeling, but a thought flitted through his head, as though he were reacting to something he had just seen. It was as though an invisible creature had whispered in his ear, making the hairs on the back of his neck stand on end.

He opened the album again. He went through it page by page, looking at all the pictures of the bridge. He looked at the younger version of an oil-soaked Henrik Vanger and a younger Harald, a man whom he had still not met. The broken railing, the buildings, the windows, and the vehicles visible in the pictures. He could not fail to identify a twenty-year-old Cecilia in the midst of the onlookers. She had on a light-coloured dress and a dark jacket and was in at least twenty of the photographs.

He felt a fresh excitement, and over the years Blomkvist had learned to trust his instincts. These instincts were reacting to something in the album, but he could not yet say what it was.

He was still at the kitchen table at 11:00, staring one by one again at the photographs when he heard the door open.

"May I come in?" It was Cecilia Vanger. Without waiting for an answer she sat down across from him at the table. Blomkvist had a strange feeling of déjà vu. She was dressed in a thin, loose, light-coloured dress and a greyish-blue jacket, clothes almost identical to those she was wearing in the photographs from 1966.

"You're the one who's the problem," she said.

Blomkvist raised his eyebrows.

"Forgive me, but you took me by surprise when you knocked on the door tonight. Now I'm so unhappy I can't sleep."

"Why are you unhappy?"

"Don't you know?"

He shook his head.

"If I tell you, promise you won't laugh."

"Promise."

"When I seduced you last winter it was an idiotic, impulsive act. I wanted to enjoy myself, that's all. That first night I was quite drunk, and I had no intention of starting anything long-term with you. Then it turned into something else. I want you to know that those weeks with you as my occasional lover were some of the happiest in my life."

"I thought it was lovely too."

"Mikael, I've been lying to you and to myself the whole time. I've never been particularly relaxed about sex. I've had five sex partners in my entire life. Once when I was twenty-one and a debutante. Then with my husband, whom I met when I was twenty-five and who turned out to be a bastard. And then a few times with three guys I met several years apart. But you provoked something in me. I simply couldn't get enough. It had something to do with the fact that you're so undemanding."

"Cecilia, you don't have to . . ."

"Shh—don't interrupt, or I'll never be able to tell you this."

Blomkvist sat in silence.

"The day you left for prison I was absolutely miserable. You were gone, as though you had never existed. It was dark here in the guest house. It was cold and empty in my bed. And there I was, an old maid of fifty-six again."

She said nothing for a while and looked Blomkvist in the eyes.

"I fell in love with you last winter. I didn't mean to, but it happened. And then I took stock and realised that you were only here temporarily; one day you'll be gone for good, and I'll stay here for the rest of my life. It hurt so damn much that I decided I wasn't going to let you in again when you came back from prison."

"I'm sorry."

"It's not your fault. When you left tonight I sat and cried. I wish I had the chance to live my life over again. Then I would decide on one thing."

"What's that?"

She looked down at the table.

"That I would have to be totally insane to stop seeing you just because you're going to leave one day. Mikael, can we start again? Can you forget what happened earlier this evening?"

"It's forgotten," he said. "But thank you for telling me."

She was still looking down at the table.

"If you still want me, let's do it."

She looked at him again. Then she got up and went over to the bedroom door. She dropped her jacket on the floor and pulled her dress over her head as she went.

Blomkvist and Cecilia Vanger woke up when the front door opened and someone was walking through the kitchen. They heard the thud of something heavy being put down near the woodstove. Then Berger was standing in the bedroom doorway with a smile that rapidly changed to shock.

"Oh, good Lord." She took a step back.

"Hi, Erika," Blomkvist said.

"Hi. I'm so sorry. I apologise a thousand times for barging in like this. I should have knocked."

"We should have locked the front door. Erika—this is Cecilia Vanger. Cecilia—Erika Berger is the editor in chief of *Millennium*."

"Hi," Cecilia said.

"Hi," Berger said. She looked as though she could not decide whether to step forward and politely shake hands or just leave. "Uh, I . . . I can go for a walk . . ."

"What do you say to putting on some coffee instead?"

Blomkvist looked at the alarm clock on the bedside table. Just past noon.

Berger nodded and pulled the bedroom door shut. Blomkvist and Cecilia looked at each other. Cecilia appeared embarrassed. They had made love and talked until 4:00 in the morning. Then Cecilia said she thought she'd sleep over and that in the future she wouldn't give a tinker's cuss who knew she was sleeping with Mikael Blomkvist. She had slept with her back to him and with his arm tucked around her breasts.

"Listen, it's OK," he said. "Erika's married and she isn't my girlfriend. We see each other now and then, but she doesn't care at all if you and I have something . . . She's probably pretty embarrassed herself right now."

When they went into the kitchen a while later, Erika had set out coffee, juice, lemon marmalade, cheese, and toast. It smelled good. Cecilia went straight up to her and held out her hand.

"I was a little abrupt in there. Hi."

"Dear Cecilia, I'm so sorry for stomping in like an elephant," said a very embarrassed Erika Berger.

"Forget it, for God's sake. And let's have breakfast."

After breakfast Berger excused herself and left them alone, saying that she had to go and say hello to Vanger. Cecilia cleared the table with her back to Mikael. He went up and put his arms around her.

"What's going to happen now?" Cecilia said.

"Nothing. This is the way it is—Erika is my best friend. She and I have been together off and on for twenty years and will probably be, on and off, together for another twenty. I hope so. But we've never been a couple and we never get in the way of each other's romances."

"Is that what we have? A romance?"

"I don't know what we have, but apparently we get along."

"Where's she going to sleep tonight?"

"We'll find her a room somewhere. One of Henrik's spare rooms. She won't be sleeping in my bed, anyway."

Cecilia thought about this for a moment.

"I don't know if I can handle this. You and she might function that way, but I don't know . . . I've never . . ." She shook her head. "I'm going back to my place. I have to think about this for a while."

"Cecilia, you asked me earlier and I told you about my relationship with Erika. Her existence can't be any great surprise to you."

"That's true. But as long as she was at a comfortable distance down in Stockholm I could ignore her."

Cecilia put on her jacket.

"This situation is ludicrous," she said with a smile. "Come over for dinner tonight. Bring Erika. I think I'm going to like her."

Erika had already solved the problem of where to sleep. On previous occasions when she had been up to Hedeby to visit Vanger she had stayed in one of his spare rooms, and she asked him straight out if she could borrow the room again. Henrik could scarcely conceal his delight, and he assured her that she was welcome at any time.

With these formalities out of the way, Blomkvist and Berger went for a walk across the bridge and sat on the terrace of Susanne's Bridge Café just before closing time.

"I'm really pissed off," Berger said. "I drive all the way up here to welcome you back to freedom and find you in bed with the town femme fatale."

"I'm sorry about that."

"How long have you and Miss Big Tits . . ." Berger waved her index finger.

"From about the time Vanger became part owner."

"Aha."

"What do you mean, aha?"

"Just curious."

"Cecilia's a good woman. I like her."

"I'm not criticising. I'm just pissed off. Candy within reach and then I have to go on a diet. How was prison?"

"Like an uneventful holiday. How are things at the magazine?"

"Better. For the first time in a year the advertising revenue is on the rise. We're way below this time last year, but we've turned the corner. Thanks to Henrik. But the weird thing is that subscriptions are going up too."

"They tend to fluctuate."

"By a couple of hundred one way or the other. But we've picked up three thousand in the past quarter. At first I thought it was just luck, but new subscribers keep coming in. It's our biggest subscription jump ever. At the same time, our existing subscribers are renewing pretty consistently across the board. None of us can understand it. We haven't run any ad campaigns. Christer spent a week doing spot checks on what sort of demographic is showing up. First, they're all brand-new subscribers. Second, 70 percent of them are women. Normally it's the other way around. Third, the subscribers can be described as middle-income white-collar workers from the suburbs: teachers, middle management, civil service workers."

"Think it's the middle-class revolt against big capital?"

"I don't know. But if this keeps up, it'll mean a significant shift in our subscriber profile. We had an editorial conference two weeks ago and decided to start running new types of material in the magazine. I want more articles on professional matters associated with TCO, the Swedish Confederation of Professional Employees, and also more investigative reporting on women's issues, for instance."

"Don't change too much," Blomkvist said. "If we're getting new subscribers then it means that they like what we're running already."

Cecilia had also invited Vanger to dinner, possibly to reduce the risk of troublesome topics of conversation. She had made a venison stew. Berger and Vanger spent a good deal of the time discussing *Millennium*'s development and the new subscribers, but gradually the conversation moved on to other matters. Berger suddenly turned to Blomkvist at one point and asked him how his work was coming along.

"I'm counting on having a draft of the family chronicle complete in a month for Henrik to look at."

"A chronicle in the spirit of the Addams family," Cecilia said.

"It does have certain historical aspects," Blomkvist conceded.

Cecilia glanced at Vanger.

"Mikael, Henrik isn't really interested in a family chronicle. He wants you to solve the mystery of Harriet's disappearance."

Blomkvist did not say a word. Ever since he had begun his relationship with Cecilia he had talked fairly openly about Harriet with her. Cecilia had already deduced that this was his real assignment, even though he never formally admitted it. He had certainly never told Henrik that he and Cecilia had discussed the subject. Vanger's bushy eyebrows drew together a bit. Erika was silent.

"My dear Henrik," Cecilia said. "I'm not stupid. I don't know what sort of agreement you and Mikael have, but his stay here in Hedeby is about Harriet. It is, isn't it?"

Vanger nodded and glanced at Blomkvist.

"I told you she was sharp." He turned to Berger. "I presume that Mikael has explained to you what he's working on here in Hedeby."

She nodded.

"And I presume you think it's a senseless undertaking. No, you don't have to answer that. It *is* an absurd and senseless task. But I have to find out."

"I have no opinion on the matter," Berger said diplomatically.

"Of course you do." He turned to Blomkvist. "Tell me. Have you found anything at all that might take us forward?"

Blomkvist avoided meeting Vanger's gaze. He thought instantly of the cold, unplaceable certainty he had had the night before. The feeling had been with him all day, but he had had no time to work his way through the album again. At last he looked up at Vanger and shook his head.

"I haven't found a single thing."

The old man scrutinised him with a penetrating look. He refrained from commenting.

"I don't know about you young people," he said, "but for me it's time to go to bed. Thank you for dinner, Cecilia. Good night, Erika. Do see me before you leave tomorrow."

When Vanger had closed the front door, silence settled over them. It was Cecilia who spoke first.

"Mikael, what was all that about?"

"It means that Henrik is as sensitive to people's reactions as a seismograph. Last night when you came to the cottage I was looking through an album."

"Yes?"

"I saw *something*. I don't know what it was yet. It was something that almost became an idea, but I missed it."

"So what were you thinking about?"

"I just can't tell you. And then you arrived."

Cecilia blushed. She avoided Berger's gaze and went out to put on some coffee.

It was a warm and sunny day. New green shoots were appearing, and Blomkvist caught himself humming the old song of spring, "Blossom Time Is Coming." It was Monday and Berger had left early.

When he had gone to prison in mid-March, snow still covered the land. Now the birches were turning green and the lawn around his cabin was lush. For the first time he had a chance to look around all of Hedeby Island. At 8:00 he went over and asked to borrow a thermos from Anna. He spoke briefly with Vanger, who was just up, and was given his map of the island. He wanted to get a closer look at Gottfried's cabin. Vanger told him that the cabin was owned by Martin Vanger now but that it had stood mostly vacant over the years. Occasionally some relative would borrow it.

Blomkvist just managed to catch Martin before he left for work. He asked if he might borrow the key. Martin gave him an amused smile.

"I presume the family chronicle has now reached the chapter about Harriet."

"I just want to take a look . . ."

Martin came back with the key in a minute.

"Is it OK then?"

"As far as I'm concerned, you can move in there if you want. Except for the fact that it's stuck right at the other end of the island, it's actually a nicer spot than the cottage you're in."

Blomkvist made coffee and sandwiches. He filled a bottle with water before he set off, stuffing his picnic lunch in a rucksack he slung over one shoulder. He followed a narrow, partially overgrown path that ran along the bay on the north side of Hedeby Island. Gottfried's cabin was on a point about one and a half miles from the village, and it took him only half an hour to cover the distance at a leisurely pace.

Martin Vanger had been right. When Blomkvist came around the bend of the narrow path, a shaded area by the water opened up. There was a marvellous view of the inlet to the Hede River, Hedestad marina to the left, and the industrial harbour to the right.

He was surprised that no-one had wanted to move into Gottfried's cabin. It was a rustic structure made of horizontal dark-stained timber with a tile roof and green frames, and with a small porch at the front door. The maintenance of the cabin had been neglected. The paint around the doors and windows was flaking off, and what should have been a lawn was scrub a yard high. Clearing it would take one whole day's hard work with scythe and saw.

Blomkvist unlocked the door and unscrewed the shutters over the windows from the inside. The framework seemed to be an old barn of less than 1,300 square feet. The inside was finished with planks and consisted of one room with big windows facing the water on either side of the front door. A staircase led to an open sleeping loft at the rear of the cabin that covered half the space. Beneath the stairs was a niche with a propane gas stove, a counter, and a sink. The furnishings were basic; built into the wall to the left of the door there was bench, a rickety desk, and above it a bookcase with teak shelves. Farther down on the same side was a broad wardrobe. To the right of the door was a round table with five wooden chairs; a fireplace stood in the middle of the side wall.

The cabin had no electricity; instead there were several

kerosene lamps. In one window was an old Grundig transistor radio. The antenna was broken off. Blomkvist pressed the power button but the batteries were dead.

He went up the narrow stairs and looked around the sleeping loft. There was a double bed with a bare mattress, a bedside table, and a chest of drawers.

Blomkvist spent a while searching through the cabin. The bureau was empty except for some hand towels and linen smelling faintly of mould. In the wardrobe there were some work clothes, a pair of overalls, rubber boots, a pair of worn tennis shoes, and a kerosene stove. In the desk drawers were writing paper, pencils, a blank sketchpad, a deck of cards, and some bookmarks. The kitchen cupboard contained plates, mugs, glasses, candles, and some packages of salt, tea bags, and the like. In a drawer in the table there were eating utensils.

He found the only traces of any intellectual interests on the bookcase above the desk. Mikael brought over a chair and got up on it to see what was on the shelves. On the lowest shelf lay issues of *Se, Rekordmagasinet, Tidsfördriv,* and *Lektyr* from the late fifties and early sixties. There were several *Bildjournalen* from 1965 and 1966, *Matt Livs Novell,* and a few comic books: *The 91, Phantomen,* and *Romans.* He opened a copy of *Lektyr* from 1964 and smiled to see how chaste the pin-up was.

Of the books, about half were mystery paperbacks from Wahlström's Manhattan series: Mickey Spillane with titles like *Kiss Me, Deadly* with the classic covers by Bertil Hegland. He found half a dozen Kitty books, some Famous Five novels by Enid Blyton, and a Twin Mystery by Sivar Ahlrud—*The Metro Mystery.* He smiled in recognition. Three books by Astrid Lindgren: *The Children of Noisy Village, Kalle Blomkvist and Rasmus,* and *Pippi Longstocking.* The top shelf had a book about shortwave radio, two books on astronomy, a bird guidebook, a book called *The Evil Empire* on the Soviet Union, a book on the Finnish Winter War, Luther's catechism, the *Book of Hymns,* and the Bible.

He opened the Bible and read on the inside cover: *Harriet Vanger, May 12, 1963*. It was her Confirmation Bible. He sadly put it back on the shelf.

Behind the cabin there were a wood and tool shed with a scythe, rake, hammer, and a big box with saws, planes, and other tools. He took a chair on to the porch and poured coffee from his thermos. He lit a cigarette and looked across Hedestad Bay through the veil of undergrowth.

Gottfried's cabin was much more modest than he had expected. Here was the place to which Harriet and Martin's father had retreated when his marriage to Isabella was going to the dogs in the late fifties. He had made this cabin his home and here he got drunk. And down there, near the wharf, he had drowned. Life at the cabin had probably been pleasant in the summer, but when the temperature dropped to freezing it must have been raw and wretched. According to what Vanger told him, Gottfried continued to work in the Vanger Corporation—interrupted by periods when he was on wild binges—until 1964. The fact that he was able to live in the cabin more or less permanently and still appear for work shaven, washed, and in a jacket and tie spoke of a surviving personal discipline.

And here was also the place that Harriet had been to so often that it was one of the first in which they looked for her. Vanger had told him that during her last year, Harriet had gone often to the cabin, apparently to be in peace on weekends or holidays. In her last summer she had lived here for three months, though she came into the village every day. Anita Vanger, Cecilia's sister, spent six weeks with her here.

What had she done out here all alone? The magazines *Mitt Livs Novell* and *Romans,* as well as a number of books about

Kitty, must have been hers. Perhaps the sketchpad had been hers. And her Bible was here.

She had wanted to be close to her lost father—was it a period of mourning she needed to get through? Or did it have to do with her religious brooding? The cabin was spartan—was she pretending to live in a convent?

Blomkvist followed the shoreline to the southeast, but the way was so interrupted by ravines and so grown over with juniper shrubs that it was all but impassable. He went back to the cabin and started back on the road to Hedeby. According to the map there was a path through the woods to something called the Fortress. It took him twenty minutes to find it in the overgrown scrub. The Fortress was what remained of the shoreline defence from the Second World War; concrete bunkers with trenches spread out around a command building. Everything was overrun with long grass and scrub.

He walked down a path to a boathouse. Next to the boathouse he found the wreck of a Pettersson boat. He returned to the Fortress and took a path up to a fence—he had come to Östergården from the other side.

He followed the meandering path through the woods, roughly parallel to the fields of Östergården. The path was difficult to negotiate—there were patches of marsh that he had to skirt. Finally he came to a swamp and beyond it a barn. As far as he could see the path ended there, a hundred yards from the road to Östergården.

Beyond the road lay the hill, Söderberget. Blomkvist walked up a steep slope and had to climb the last bit. Söderberget's summit was an almost vertical cliff facing the water. He followed the ridge back towards Hedeby. He stopped above the summer cottages to enjoy the view of the old fishing harbour and the church and his own cottage. He sat on a flat rock and poured himself the last of the lukewarm coffee.

Cecilia Vanger kept her distance. Blomkvist did not want to be importunate, so he waited a week before he went to her house. She let him in.

"You must think I'm quite foolish, a fifty-six-year-old, respectable headmistress acting like a teenage girl."

"Cecilia, you're a grown woman. You have the right to do whatever you want."

"I know and that's why I've decided not to see you any more. I can't stand . . ."

"Please, you don't owe me an explanation. I hope we're still friends."

"I would like for us to remain friends. But I can't deal with a relationship with you. I haven't ever been good at relationships. I'd like it if you would leave me in peace for a while."

CHAPTER 16

Sunday, June 1– Tuesday, June 10

After six months of fruitless cogitation, the case of Harriet Vanger cracked open. In the first week of June, Blomkvist uncovered three totally new pieces of the puzzle. Two of them he found himself. The third he had help with.

After Berger's visit in May, he had studied the album again, sitting for three hours, looking at one photograph after another, as he tried to rediscover what it was that he had reacted to. He failed again, so he put the album aside and went back to work on the family chronicle instead.

One day in June he was in Hedestad, thinking about something altogether different, when his bus turned on to Järnvägsgatan and it suddenly came to him what had been germinating in the back of his mind. The insight struck him like a thunderbolt out of a clear sky. He felt so confused that he stayed on the bus all the way to the last stop by the railway station. There he took the first bus back to Hedeby to check whether he had remembered correctly.

It was the first photograph in the album, the last picture taken of Harriet Vanger on that fateful day on Järnvägsgatan in Hedestad, while she had been watching the Children's Day parade.

The photograph was an odd one to have included in the album. It was put there because it was taken the same day, but it was the only one of the photographs not of the accident on the bridge. Each time Blomkvist and (he supposed) everyone else had looked at the album, it was the people and the details in the pictures of the bridge that had captured their attention. There was no drama in the picture of a crowd at the Children's Day parade, several hours earlier.

Vanger must have looked at the photograph a thousand times, a sorrowful reminder that he would never see her again.

But that was not what Blomkvist had reacted to.

It was taken from across the street, probably from a first-floor window. The wide-angle lens had caught the front of one of the floats. On the flatbed were women wearing glittering bathing suits and harem trousers, throwing sweets to the crowd. Some of them were dancing. Three clowns were jumping about in front of the float.

Harriet was in the front row of the crowd standing on the pavement. Next to her were three girls, clearly her classmates, and around and behind them were at least a hundred other spectators.

This is what Blomkvist had noticed subconsciously and which suddenly rose to the surface when the bus passed the exact same spot.

The crowd behaved as an audience should. Their eyes always follow the ball in a tennis match or the puck in an ice hockey rink. The ones standing at the far left of the photograph were looking at the clowns right in front of them. The ones closer to the float were all looking at the scantily clad girls. The expressions on their faces were calm. Children pointed. Some were laughing. Everyone looked happy.

All except one.

Harriet Vanger was looking off to the side. Her three friends and everyone else in her vicinity were looking at the clowns. Harriet's face was turned almost 30° to 35° to her right. Her gaze seemed fixed on something across the street, but beyond the left-hand edge of the photograph.

Mikael took the magnifying glass and tried to make out the details. The photograph was taken from too great a distance for him to be entirely sure, but unlike all those around her, Harriet's face lacked excitement. Her mouth was a thin line. Her eyes were wide open. Her hands hung limply at her sides. She looked frightened. Frightened or furious.

Mikael took the print out of the album, put it in a stiff plastic binder, and went to wait for the next bus back into Hedestad. He got off at Järnvägsgatan and stood under the window from which the picture must have been taken. It was at the edge of what constituted Hedestad's town centre. It was a two-storey wooden building that housed a video store and Sundström's Haberdashery, established in 1932 according to a plaque on the front door. He went in and saw that the shop was on two levels; a spiral staircase led to the upper floor.

At the top of the spiral staircase two windows faced the street.

"May I help you?" said an elderly salesman when Blomkvist took out the binder with the photograph. There were only a few people in the shop.

"Well, I just wanted to see where this picture was taken from. Would it be OK if I opened the window for a second?"

The man said yes. Blomkvist could see exactly the spot where

Harriet had stood. One of the wooden buildings behind her in the photograph was gone, replaced by an angular brick building. The other wooden building had been a stationery store in 1966; now it was a health food store and tanning salon. Blomkvist closed the window, thanked the man, and apologised for taking up his time.

He crossed the street and stood where Harriet had stood. He had good landmarks between the window of the upper floor of the haberdashery and the door of the tanning salon. He turned his head and looked along Harriet's line of sight. As far as he could tell, she had been looking towards the corner of the building that housed Sundström's Haberdashery. It was a perfectly normal corner of a building, where a cross street vanished behind it. *What did you see there, Harriet?*

Blomkvist put the photograph in his shoulder bag and walked to the park by the station. There he sat in a pavement café and ordered a latte. He suddenly felt shaken.

In English they call it "new evidence," which has a very different sound from the Swedish term, "new proof material." He had seen something entirely new, something no-one else had noticed in an investigation that had been marking time for thirty-seven years.

The problem was that he wasn't sure what value his new information had, if indeed it could have any at all. And yet he felt it was going to prove significant.

The September day when Harriet disappeared had been dramatic in a number of ways. It had been a day of celebration in Hedestad with crowds of several thousand in the streets, young and old. It had been the family's annual assembly on Hedeby Island. These two events alone represented departures from the daily routine of the area. The crash on the bridge had overshadowed everything else.

Inspector Morell, Henrik Vanger, and everyone else who had brooded about Harriet's disappearance had focused on the events at Hedeby Island. Morell had even written that he could not rid himself of the suspicion that the accident and Harriet's disappearance were related. Blomkvist was now convinced that this notion was wrong.

The chain of events had started not on Hedeby Island but in Hedestad several hours earlier. Harriet Vanger had seen something or someone to frighten her and prompt her to go home, go straight to her uncle, who unhappily did not have time to listen to her. Then the accident on the bridge happened. Then the murderer struck.

Blomkvist paused. It was the first time he had consciously formulated the assumption that Harriet had been murdered. He accepted Vanger's belief. Harriet was dead and he was hunting for a killer.

He went back to the police report. Among all the thousands of pages only a fraction dealt with the events in Hedestad. Harriet had been with three of her classmates, all of whom had been interviewed. They had met at the park by the station at 9:00. One of the girls was going to buy some jeans, and her friends went with her. They had coffee in the EPA department store cafeteria and then went up to the sports field and strolled around among the carnival booths and fishing ponds, where they ran into some other friends from school. At noon they wandered back into town to watch the parade. Just before 2:00 in the afternoon Harriet suddenly told them that she had to go home. They said goodbye at a bus stop near Järnvägsgatan.

None of her friends had noticed anything unusual. One of them was Inger Stenberg, the one who had described Harriet's transformation over the past year by saying that she had become "impersonal." She said that Harriet had been taciturn that day, which was usual, and mostly she just followed the others.

Inspector Morell had talked to all of the people who had encountered Harriet that day, even if they had only said hello in the grounds of the family party. A photograph of her was published in the local newspapers while the search was going on. After she went missing, several residents of Hedestad had contacted the police to say that they thought they had seen her during the day of the parade, but no-one had reported anything out of the ordinary.

The next morning Blomkvist found Vanger at his breakfast table.

"You said that the Vanger family still has an interest in the *Hedestad Courier*."

"That's right."

"I'd like to have access to their photographic archive. From 1966."

Vanger set down his glass of milk and wiped his upper lip.

"Mikael, what have you discovered?"

He looked the old man straight in the eye.

"Nothing solid. But I think we may have made a mistake about the chain of events."

He showed Vanger the photograph and told him what he was thinking. Vanger sat saying nothing for a long time.

"If I'm right, we have to look as far as we still can at what happened in Hedestad that day, not just at what happened on Hedeby Island," Blomkvist said. "I don't know how to go about it after such a long time, but a lot of photographs must have been taken of the Children's Day celebrations which were never published. Those are the ones I want to look at."

Vanger used the telephone in the kitchen. He called Martin, explained what he wanted, and asked who the pictures editor was these days. Within ten minutes the right people had been located and access had been arranged.

The pictures editor of the *Hedestad Courier* was Madeleine Blomberg, called Maja. She was the first woman pictures editor Blomkvist had met in journalism, where photography was still primarily a male art form.

Since it was Saturday, the newsroom was empty, but Maja Blomberg turned out to live only five minutes away, and she met Blomkvist at the office entrance. She had worked at the *Hedestad Courier* for most of her life. She started as a proof-reader in 1964, changed to photo-finisher and spent a number of years in the darkroom, while occasionally being sent out as a photographer when the usual resources were insufficient. She had gained the position of editor, earned a full-time post on the picture desk, and ten years ago, when the old pictures editor retired, she took over as head of the department.

Blomkvist asked how the picture archive was arranged.

"To tell you the truth, the archive is rather a mess. Since we got computers and digital photographs, the current archive is on CDs. We've had an intern here who spent some time scanning in important older pictures, but only a small percentage of what's in the stacks have been catalogued. Older pictures are arranged by date in negative folders. They're either here in the newsroom or in the attic storeroom."

"I'm interested in photographs taken of the Children's Day parade in 1966, but also in any photographs that were taken that week."

Fröken Blomberg gave him a quizzical look.

"You mean the week that Harriet Vanger disappeared?"

"You know the story?"

"You couldn't work at the *Courier* your whole life without knowing about it, and when Martin Vanger calls me early in the morning on my day off, I draw my own conclusions. Has something new turned up?"

Blomberg had a nose for news. Blomkvist shook his head with a little smile and gave her his cover story.

"No, and I don't suppose anyone will ever find the solution to that puzzle. It's rather confidential, but the fact is that I'm ghostwriting Henrik Vanger's autobiography. The story of the missing girl is an odd topic, but it's also a chapter that can't really be ignored. I'm looking for something that hasn't been used before that might illustrate that day—of Harriet and her friends."

Blomberg looked dubious, but the explanation was reasonable and she was not going to question his story, given his role.

A photographer at a newspaper takes between two and ten rolls of film a day. For big events, it can be double that. Each roll contains thirty-six negatives; so it's not unusual for a local newspaper to accumulate over three hundred-plus images each day, of which only a very few are published. A well-organised department cuts up the rolls of film and places the negatives in six-frame sleeves. A roll takes up about one page in a negative binder. A binder holds about 110 rolls. In a year, about twenty-five binders are filled up. Over the years a huge number of binders is accumulated, which generally lack any commercial value and overflow the shelves in the photographic department. On the other hand, every photographer and pictures department is convinced that the pictures contain a *historical documentation of incalculable value*, so they never throw anything away.

The *Hedestad Courier* was founded in 1922, and the pictures department had existed since 1937. The *Courier*'s attic storeroom contained about 1,200 binders, arranged, as Blomberg said, by date. The negatives from September 1966 were kept in four cheap cardboard storage binders.

"How do we go about this?" Blomkvist said. "I really need to sit at a light table and be able to make copies of anything that might be of interest."

"We don't have a darkroom any more. Everything is scanned in. Do you know how to work a negative scanner?"

"Yes, I've worked with images and have an Agfa neg. scanner of my own. I work in PhotoShop."

"Then you use the same equipment we do."

Blomberg took him on a quick tour of the small office, gave him a chair at a light table, and switched on a computer and scanner. She showed him where the coffee machine was in the canteen area. They agreed that Blomkvist could work by himself, but that he had to call her when he wanted to leave the office so that she could come in and set the alarm system. Then she left him with a cheerful "Have fun."

The *Courier* had had two photographers back then. The one who had been on duty that day was Kurt Nylund, whom Blomkvist actually knew. Nylund was in his twenties in 1966. Then he moved to Stockholm and became a famous photographer working both freelance and as an employee of Scanpix Sweden in Marieberg. Blomkvist had crossed paths with Kurt Nylund several times in the nineties, when *Millennium* had used images from Scanpix. He remembered him as an angular man with thinning hair. On the day of the parade Nylund had used a daylight film, not too fast, one which many news photographers used.

Blomkvist took out the negatives of the photographs by the young Nylund and put them on the light table. With a magnifying glass he studied them frame by frame. Reading negatives is an art form, requiring experience, which Blomkvist lacked. To determine whether the photograph contained information of value he was going to have to scan in each image and examine it on the computer screen. That would take hours. So first he did a quite general survey of the photographs he might be interested in.

He began by running through all the ones that had been taken of the accident. Vanger's collection was incomplete. The person who had copied the collection—possibly Nylund himself—had left out about thirty photographs that were either blurred or of such poor quality that they were not considered publishable.

Blomkvist switched off the *Courier*'s computer and plugged the Agfa scanner into his own iBook. He spent two hours scanning in the rest of the images.

One caught his eye at once. Some time between 3:10 and 3:15 p.m., just at the time when Harriet vanished, someone had opened the window in her room. Vanger had tried in vain to find out who it was. Blomkvist had a photograph on his screen that must have been taken at exactly the moment the window was opened. There were a figure and a face, albeit out of focus. He decided that a detailed analysis could wait until he had first scanned all the images.

Then he examined the images of the Children's Day celebrations. Nylund had put in six rolls, around two hundred shots. There was an endless stream of children with balloons, grownups, street life with hot dog vendors, the parade itself, an artist on a stage, and an award presentation of some sort.

Blomkvist decided to scan in the entire collection. Six hours later he had a portfolio of ninety images, but he was going to have to come back.

At 9:00 he called Blomberg, thanked her, and took the bus home to Hedeby Island.

He was back at 9:00 on Sunday morning. The offices were still empty when Blomberg let him in. He had not realised that it was the Whitsuntide holiday weekend, and that there would not be a newspaper until Tuesday. He spent the entire day scanning images. At 6:00 in the evening there were still forty shots left of Children's Day. Blomkvist had inspected the negatives and decided that close-ups of cute children's faces or pictures of a painter appearing on stage were simply not germane to his objective. What he had scanned in was the street life and crowds.

Blomkvist spent the Whitsuntide holiday going over the new material. He made two discoveries. The first filled him with dismay. The second made his pulse beat faster.

The first was the face in Harriet Vanger's window. The photograph had a slight motion blur and was thus excluded from the original set. The photographer had stood on the church hill and sighted towards the bridge. The buildings were in the background. Mikael cropped the image to include the window alone, and then he experimented with adjusting the contrast and increasing the sharpness until he achieved what he thought was the best quality he could get.

The result was a grainy picture with a minimal greyscale that showed a curtain, part of an arm, and a diffuse half-moon-shaped face a little way inside the room.

The face was not Harriet Vanger's, who had raven-black hair, but a person with lighter hair colour.

It was impossible to discern clear facial features, but he was certain it was a woman; the lighter part of the face continued down to shoulder level and indicated a woman's flowing hair, and she was wearing light-coloured clothes.

He calculated her height in relation to the window: it was a woman about five foot seven.

He clicked on to other images from behind the accident and one person fitted the description—the twenty-year-old Cecilia Vanger.

Nylund had taken eighteen shots from the window of Sundström's Haberdashery. Harriet was in seventeen of them.

She and her classmates had arrived at Järnvägsgatan at the same time Nylund had begun taking his pictures. Blomkvist reckoned that the photographs were shot over a period of five minutes. In the first pictures, Harriet and her friends were coming down the street into the frame. In photographs 2–7 they were standing still and watching the parade. Then they had moved about six yards down the street. In the last picture, which may have been taken after some time had passed, the girls had gone.

Blomkvist edited a series of pictures in which he cropped the top half of Harriet and processed them to achieve the best contrast. He put the pictures in a separate folder, opened the Graphic Converter programme, and started the slide show function. The effect was a jerky silent film in which each image was shown for two seconds.

Harriet arrives, image in profile. Harriet stops and looks down at the street. Harriet turns her face towards the street. Harriet opens her mouth to say something to her friend. Harriet laughs. Harriet touches her ear with her left hand. Harriet smiles. Harriet suddenly looks surprised, her face at a 20° angle to the left of the camera. Harriet's eyes widen and she has stopped smiling. Harriet's mouth becomes a thin line. Harriet focuses her gaze. In her face can be read . . . what? Sorrow, shock, fury? Harriet lowers her eyes. Harriet is gone.

Blomkvist played the sequence over and over.

It confirmed with some force the theory he had formulated. Something happened on Järnvägsgatan.

She sees something—someone—on the other side of the street. She reacts with shock. She contacts Vanger for a private conversation which never happens. She vanishes without a trace.

Something happened, but the photographs did not explain what.

At 2:00 on Tuesday morning Blomkvist had coffee and sandwiches at the kitchen bench. He was simultaneously downhearted and exhilarated. Against all expectations he had turned up new evidence. The only problem was that although it shed light on the chain of events it brought him not one iota closer to solving the mystery.

He thought long and hard about what role Cecilia Vanger might have played in the drama. Vanger had relentlessly charted the activities of all persons involved that day, and Cecilia had been no exception. She was living in Uppsala, but she arrived in Hedeby two days before that fateful Saturday. She stayed with Isabella Vanger. She had said that she might possibly have seen Harriet early that morning, but that she had not spoken to her. She had driven into Hedestad on some errand. She had not seen Harriet there, and she came back to Hedeby Island around 1:00, about the time Nylund was taking his pictures on Järnvägsgatan. She changed and at about 2:00 helped to set the table for the banquet that evening.

As an alibi—if that is what it was—it was rather feeble. The times were approximate, especially the matter of when she had got back to Hedeby Island, but Vanger had not found anything to indicate that she was lying. Cecilia Vanger was one of those people in the family that Vanger liked best. And she had been his lover. How could he be objective? He certainly could not imagine her as a murderer.

Now a hitherto unknown photograph was telling him that she had lied when she said that she had never been in Harriet's room that day. Blomkvist wrestled with the possible significance of that.

And if you lied about that, what else did you lie about?

He went through in his mind what he knew about Cecilia. An introverted person obviously affected by her past. Lived alone, had no sex life, had difficulty getting close to people. Kept her distance, and when she let loose there was no restraint. She chose a stranger for a lover. Had said that she ended it because she was unable to live with the idea that he would go from her life as unexpectedly as he had appeared. Blomkvist supposed that the reason she had dared to start an affair with him was precisely that he was only there for a while. She did not have to be afraid he would change her life in any long-term way.

He sighed and pushed the amateur psychology aside.

He made the second discovery during the night. The key to the mystery was what it was that Harriet had seen in Hedestad. He would never find that out unless he could invent a time machine and stand behind her, looking over her shoulder.

And then he had a thought. He slapped his forehead and opened his iBook. He clicked on to the uncropped images in the series on Järnvägsgatan and . . . *there!*

Behind Harriet and about a yard to her right were a young couple, the man in a striped sweater and the woman in a pale jacket. She was holding a camera. When Blomkvist enlarged the image it looked to be a Kodak Instamatic with flash—a cheap holiday camera for people who know nothing about photography.

The woman was holding the camera at chin level. Then she raised it and took a picture of the clowns, just as Harriet's expression changed.

Blomkvist compared the camera's position with Harriet's line of vision. The woman had taken a picture of exactly what Harriet was looking at.

His heart was beating hard. He leaned back and plucked his cigarettes out of his breast pocket. *Someone had taken a picture.* How would he identify and find the woman? Could he get hold of her snapshot? Had the roll ever been developed, and if so did the prints still exist?

He opened the folder with Nylund's photographs from the crowd. For the next couple of hours he enlarged each one and scrutinised it one square inch at a time. He did not see the couple again until the very last pictures. Nylund had photographed another clown with balloons in his hand posing in front of his camera and laughing heartily. The photographs were taken in a car park by the entrance to the sports field where the celebration was being held. It must have been after 2:00 in the afternoon. Right after that Nylund had received the alarm about the crash on the bridge and brought his portraits of Children's Day to a rapid close.

The woman was almost hidden, but the man in the striped sweater was clearly visible, in profile. He had keys in his hand and was bending to open a car door. The focus was on the clown in the foreground, and the car was a bit fuzzy. The number plate was partly hidden but he could see that it started with "AC3."

Number plates in the sixties began with a code indicating the county, and as a child Blomkvist had memorised the county codes. "AC" was for Västerbotten.

Then he spotted something else. On the back window was a

sticker of some sort. He zoomed in, but the text dissolved in a blur. He cropped out the sticker and adjusted the contrast and sharpness. It took him a while. He still could not read the words, but he attempted to figure out what the letters were, based on the fuzzy shapes. Many letters looked surprisingly similar. An "O" could be mistaken for a "D," a "B" for an "E," and so on. After working with a pen and paper and excluding certain letters, he was left with an unreadable text, in one line.

R JÖ NI K RIFA RIK

He stared at the image until his eyes began to water. Then he saw the text. "NORSJÖ SNICKERIFABRIK," followed by figures in a smaller size that were utterly impossible to read, probably a telephone number.

CHAPTER 17

Wednesday, June 11–Saturday, June 14

Blomkvist got help with the third jigsaw piece from an unexpected quarter.

After working on the images practically all night he slept heavily until well into the afternoon. He awoke with a headache, took a shower, and walked to Susanne's for breakfast. He ought to have gone to see Vanger and report what he had discovered. Instead, when he came back, he went to Cecilia's house and knocked on the door. He needed to ask her why she had lied to him about being in Harriet's room. No-one came to the door.

He was just leaving when he heard: "Your whore isn't home."

Gollum had emerged from his cave. He was once tall, almost six foot six, but now so stooped with age that his eyes were level with Blomkvist's. His face and neck were splotched with dark liver spots. He was in his pyjamas and a brown dressing gown, leaning on a cane. He looked like a Central Casting nasty old man.

"What did you say?"

"I said that your whore isn't home."

Blomkvist stepped so close that he was almost nose to nose with Harald Vanger.

"You're talking about your own daughter, you fucking pig."

"I'm not the one who comes sneaking over here in the night," Harald said with a toothless smile. He smelled foul. Blomkvist sidestepped him and went down the road without looking back. He found Vanger in his office.

"I've just had the pleasure of meeting your brother," Mikael said.

"Harald? Well, well, so, he's ventured out. He does that a couple of times a year."

"I was knocking on Cecilia's door when this voice behind me said, quote, Your whore isn't home, unquote."

"That sounds like Harald," Vanger said calmly.

"He called his own daughter a whore, for God's sake."

"He's been doing that for years. That's why they don't talk much."

"Why does he call her that?"

"Cecilia lost her virginity when she was twenty-one. It happened here in Hedestad after a summer romance, the year after Harriet disappeared."

"And?"

"The man she fell in love with was called Peter Samuelsson. He was a financial assistant at the Vanger Corporation. A bright boy. Today he works for ABB. The kind of man I would have been proud to have as my son-in-law if she were my daughter. Harald measured his skull or checked his family tree or something and discovered that he was one-quarter Jewish."

"Good Lord."

"He's called her a whore ever since."

"He knew that Cecilia and I have . . ."

"Everybody in the village probably knows that with the possible exception of Isabella, because no-one in his right mind would tell her anything, and thank heavens she's nice enough to go to bed at 8:00 every night. Harald on the other hand has presumably been following every step you take."

Blomkvist sat down, looking foolish.

"You mean that everyone knows . . ."

"Of course."

"And you don't mind?"

"My dear Mikael, it's really none of my business."

"Where is Cecilia?"

"The school term is over. She went to London on Saturday to visit her sister, and after that she's having a holiday in . . . hmmm, I think it was Florida. She'll be back in about a month."

Blomkvist felt even more foolish.

"We've sort of put our relationship on hold for a while."

"So I understand, but it's still none of my business. How's your work coming along?"

Blomkvist poured himself a cup of coffee from Vanger's thermos.

"I think I've found some new material."

He took his iBook out of his shoulder bag and scrolled through the series of images showing how Harriet had reacted on Järnvägsgatan. He explained how he had found the other spectators with the camera and their car with the Norsjö Carpentry Shop sign. When he was finished Vanger wanted to see all the pictures again. When he looked up from the computer his face was grey. Blomkvist was suddenly alarmed and put a hand on Vanger's shoulder. Vanger waved him away and sat in silence for a while.

"You've done what I thought was impossible. You've turned up something completely new. What are you going to do next?"

"I am going to look for that snapshot, if it still exists."

He did not mention the face in the window.

• • •

Harald Vanger had gone back to his cave by the time Blomkvist came out. When he turned the corner he found someone quite different sitting on the porch of his cottage, reading a newspaper. For a fraction of a second he thought it was Cecilia, but the dark-haired girl on the porch was his daughter.

"Hi, Pappa," Pernilla Abrahamsson said.

He gave his daughter a long hug.

"Where in the world did you spring from?"

"From home, of course. I'm on my way to Skellefteå. Can I stay the night?"

"Of course you can, but how did you get here?"

"Mamma knew where you were. And I asked at the café if they knew where you were staying. The woman told me exactly how to get here. Are you glad to see me?"

"Certainly I am. Come in. You should have given me some warning so I could buy some good food or something."

"I stopped on impulse. I wanted to welcome you home from prison, but you never called."

"I'm sorry."

"That's OK. Mamma told me how you're always getting lost in your own thoughts."

"Is that what she says about me?"

"More or less. But it doesn't matter. I still love you."

"I love you too, but you know . . ."

"I know. I'm pretty grown-up by now."

He made tea and put out pastries.

What his daughter had said was true. She was most assuredly no longer a little girl; she was almost seventeen, practically a grown woman. He had to learn to stop treating her like a child.

"So, how was it?"

"How was what?"

"Prison."

He laughed. "Would you believe me if I said that it was like having a paid holiday with all the time you wanted for thinking and writing?"

"I would. I don't suppose there's much difference between a prison and a cloister, and people have always gone to cloisters for self-reflection."

"Well, there you go. I hope it hasn't been a problem for you, your father being a gaolbird."

"Not at all. I'm proud of you, and I never miss a chance to brag about the fact that you went to prison for what you believe in."

"Believe in?"

"I saw Erika Berger on TV."

"Pernilla, I'm not innocent. I'm sorry that I haven't talked to you about what happened, but I wasn't unfairly sentenced. The court made their decision based on what they were told during the trial."

"But you never told your side of the story."

"No, because it turned out that I didn't have proof."

"OK. Then answer me one question: is Wennerström a scoundrel or isn't he?"

"He's one of the blackest scoundrels I've ever dealt with."

"That's good enough for me. I've got a present for you."

She took a package out of her bag. He opened it and found a CD, *The Best of Eurythmics*. She knew it was one of his favourite old bands. He put it in his iBook, and they listened to "Sweet Dreams" together.

"Why are you going to Skellefteå?"

"Bible school at a summer camp with a congregation called the Light of Life," Pernilla said, as if it were the most obvious choice in the world.

Blomkvist felt a cold fire run down the back of his neck. He realised how alike his daughter and Harriet Vanger were. Pernilla was sixteen, exactly the age Harriet was when she disappeared. Both had absent fathers. Both were attracted to the religious fanaticism of strange sects—Harriet to the Pentecostals and Pernilla to an offshoot of something that was just about as crackpot as the Word of Life.

He did not know how he should handle his daughter's new interest in religion. He was afraid of encroaching on her right to decide for herself. At the same time, the Light of Life was most definitely a sect of the type that he would not hesitate to lambast in *Millennium*. He would take the first opportunity to discuss this matter with her mother.

Pernilla slept in his bed while he wrapped himself in blankets on the bench in the kitchen. He woke with a crick in his neck and aching muscles. Pernilla was eager to get going, so he made breakfast and went with her to the station. They had a little time, so they bought coffee at the mini-mart and sat down on a bench at the end of the platform, chatting about all sorts of things. Until she said: "You don't like the idea that I'm going to Skellefteå, do you?"

He was nonplussed.

"It's not dangerous. But you're not a Christian, are you?"

"Well, I'm not a good Christian, at any rate."

"You don't believe in God?"

"No, I don't believe in God, but I respect the fact that you do. Everyone has to have something to believe in."

When her train arrived, they gave each other a long hug until Pernilla had to get on board. With one foot on the step, she turned.

"Pappa, I'm not going to proselytise. It doesn't matter to me what you believe, and I'll always love you. But I think you should continue your Bible studies."

"Why do you say that?"

"I saw the quotes you had on the wall," she said. "But why so gloomy and neurotic? Kisses. See you later."

She waved and was gone. He stood on the platform, baffled, watching the train pull away. Not until it vanished around the bend did the meaning sink in.

Mikael hurried out of the station. It would be almost an hour before the next bus left. He was too much on edge to wait that long. He ran to the taxi stand and found Hussein with the Norrland accent.

Ten minutes later he was in his office. He had taped the note above his desk.

Magda—32016
Sara—32109
R.J.—30112
R.L.—32027
Mari—32018

He looked around the room. Then he realised where he'd be able to find a Bible. He took the note with him, searched for the keys, which he had left in a bowl on the windowsill, and jogged the whole way to Gottfried's cabin. His hands were practically shaking as he took Harriet's Bible down from its shelf.

She had not written down telephone numbers. The figures indicated the chapter and verse in Leviticus, the third book of the Pentateuch.

(Magda) Leviticus, 20:16
"If a woman approaches any beast and lies with it, you shall kill the woman and the beast; they shall be put to death, their blood is upon them."

(Sara) Leviticus, 21:9
"And the daughter of any priest, if she profanes herself by playing the harlot, profanes her father; she shall be burned with fire."

(R.J.) Leviticus, 1:12
"And he shall cut it into pieces, with its head and its fat, and the priest shall lay them in order upon the wood that is on the fire upon the altar."

(R.L.) Leviticus, 20:27
"A man or a woman who is a medium or a wizard shall be put to death; they shall be stoned with stones, their blood shall be upon them."

(Mari) Leviticus, 20:18
"If a man lies with a woman having her sickness, and uncovers her nakedness, he has made naked her fountain, and she has uncovered the fountain of her blood; both of them shall be cut off from among their people."

He went out and sat on the porch. Each verse had been underlined in Harriet's Bible. He lit a cigarette and listened to the singing of birds nearby.

He had the numbers. But he didn't have the names. Magda, Sara, Mari, R.J., and R.L.

All of a sudden an abyss opened as Mikael's brain made an intuitive leap. He remembered the fire victim in Hedestad that Inspector Morell had told him about. The Rebecka case, which occurred in the late forties. The girl was raped and then killed by having her head placed on smouldering coals. *"And he shall cut it into pieces, with its head and its fat, and the priest shall lay them in order upon the wood that is on the fire upon the altar.*" Rebecka. R.J. What was her last name?

What in God's name had Harriet gotten herself mixed up in?

Vanger had been taken ill. He was in bed when Blomkvist knocked on his door. But Anna agreed to let him in, saying he could visit the old man for a few minutes.

"A summer cold," Henrik explained, sniffling. "What did you want?"

"I have a question."

"Yes?"

"Did you ever hear of a murder that took place in Hedestad sometime in the forties? A girl called Rebecka—her head was put on a fire."

"Rebecka Jacobsson," Henrik said without a second's hesitation. "That's a name I'll never forget, although I haven't heard it mentioned in years."

"But you know about the murder?"

"Indeed I do. Rebecka Jacobsson was twenty-three or twenty-four when she died. That must have been in . . . It was in 1949. There was a tremendous hue and cry, I had a small part in it myself."

"You did?"

"Oh yes. Rebecka was on our clerical staff, a popular girl and very attractive. But why are you asking?"

"I'm not sure, Henrik, but I may be on to something. I'm going to have to think this through."

"Are you suggesting that there's a connection between Harriet and Rebecka? There were . . . almost seventeen years separating the two."

"Let me do my thinking and I'll come back and see you tomorrow if you're feeling better."

Blomkvist did not see Vanger the following day. Just before 1:00 a.m. he was still at the kitchen table, reading Harriet's Bible, when he heard the sound of a car making its way at high speed across the bridge. He looked out the window and saw the flashing blue lights of an ambulance.

Filled with foreboding, he ran outside. The ambulance parked by Vanger's house. On the ground floor all the lights were on. He dashed up the porch steps in two bounds and found a shaken Anna in the hall.

"It's his heart," she said. "He woke me a little while ago, complaining of pains in his chest. Then he collapsed."

Blomkvist put his arms around the housekeeper, and he was still there when the medics came out with an unconscious Vanger on a stretcher. Martin Vanger, looking decidedly stressed, walked behind. He had been in bed when Anna called. His bare feet were stuck in a pair of slippers, and he hadn't zipped his fly. He gave Mikael a brief greeting and then turned to Anna.

"I'll go with him to the hospital. Call Birger and see if you can reach Cecilia in London in the morning," he said. "And tell Dirch."

"I can go to Frode's house," Blomkvist said. Anna nodded gratefully.

It took several minutes before a sleepy Frode answered Blomkvist's ring at his door.

"I have bad news, Dirch. Henrik has been taken to the hospital. It seems to be a heart attack. Martin wanted me to tell you."

"Good Lord," Frode said. He glanced at his watch. "It's Friday the thirteenth," he said.

Not until the next morning, after he'd had a brief talk with Dirch Frode on his mobile and been assured that Vanger was still alive, did he call Berger with the news that *Millennium*'s new partner had been taken to the hospital with a heart attack. Inevitably, the news was received with gloom and anxiety.

Late in the evening Frode came to see him and give him the details about Henrik Vanger's condition.

"He's alive, but he's not doing well. He had a serious heart attack, and he's also suffering from an infection."

"Have you seen him?"

"No. He's in intensive care. Martin and Birger are sitting with him."

"What are his chances?"

Frode waved a hand back and forth.

"He survived the attack, and that's a good sign. Henrik is in excellent condition, but he's old. We'll just have to wait."

They sat in silence, deep in thought. Blomkvist made coffee. Frode looked wretchedly unhappy.

"I need to ask you about what's going to happen now," Blomkvist said.

Frode looked up.

"The conditions of your employment don't change. They're stipulated in a contract that runs until the end of this year, whether Henrik lives or dies. You don't have to worry."

"No, that's not what I meant. I'm wondering who I report to in his absence."

Frode sighed.

"Mikael, you know as well as I do that this whole story about Harriet is just a pastime for Henrik."

"Don't say that, Dirch."

"What do you mean?"

"I've found new evidence," Blomkvist said. "I told Henrik about some of it yesterday. I'm very much afraid that it may have helped to bring on his heart attack."

Frode looked at him with a strange expression.

"You're joking, you must be . . ."

Blomkvist shook his head.

"Over the past few days I've found significant material about Harriet's disappearance. What I'm worried about is that we never discussed who I should report to if Henrik is no longer here."

"You report to me."

"OK. I have to go on with this. Can I put you in the picture right now?"

Blomkvist described what he had found as concisely as possible, and he showed Frode the series of pictures from Järnvägsgatan. Then he explained how his own daughter had unlocked the mystery of the names in the date book. Finally, he proposed the connection, as he had for Vanger the day before, with the murder of Rebecka Jacobsson in 1949, R.J.

The only thing he kept to himself was Cecilia Vanger's face in Harriet's window. He had to talk to her before he put her in a position where she might be suspected of something.

Frode's brow was creased with concern.

"You really think that the murder of Rebecka has something to do with Harriet's disappearance?"

"It seems unlikely, I agree, but the fact remains that Harriet wrote the initials R.J. in her date book next to the reference to the Old Testament law about burnt offerings. Rebecka Jacobsson was burned to death. One connection with the Vanger family is inescapable—she worked for the corporation."

"But what is the connection with Harriet?"

"I don't know yet. But I want to find out. I will tell you everything I would have told Henrik. You have to make the decisions for him."

"Perhaps we ought to inform the police."

"No. At least not without Henrik's blessing. The statute of limitations has long since run out in the case of Rebecka, and the police investigation was closed. They're not going to reopen an investigation fifty-four years later."

"All right. What are you going to do?"

Blomkvist paced a lap around the kitchen.

"First, I want to follow up the photograph lead. If we could see what it was that Harriet saw . . . it might be the key. I need a car to go to Norsjö and follow that lead, wherever it takes me. And also, I want to research each of the Leviticus verses. We have one connection to one murder. We have four verses, possibly four other clues. To do this . . . I need some help."

"What kind of help?"

"I really need a research assistant with the patience to go through old newspaper archives to find 'Magda' and 'Sara' and the other names. If I'm right in thinking that Rebecka wasn't the only victim."

"You mean you want to let someone else in on . . ."

"There's a lot of work that has to be done and in a hurry. If I were a police officer involved in an active investigation, I could divide up the hours and resources and get people to dig for me. I need a professional who knows archive work and who can be trusted."

"I understand. . . . Actually I believe I know of an expert researcher," said Frode, and before he could stop himself, he added, "She was the one who did the background investigation on you."

"Who did *what*?" Blomkvist said.

"I was thinking out loud," Frode said. "It's nothing." I'm getting old, he thought.

"You had someone do an investigation on me?"

"It's nothing dramatic, Mikael. We wanted to hire you, and we just did a check on what sort of person you were."

"So that's why Henrik always seems to know exactly where he has me. How thorough was this investigation?"

"It was quite thorough."

"Did it look into *Millennium*'s problems?"

Frode shrugged. "It had a bearing."

Blomkvist lit a cigarette. It was his fifth of the day.

"A written report?"

"Mikael, it's nothing to get worked up about."

"I want to read the report," he said.

"Oh come on, there's nothing out of the ordinary about this. We wanted to check up on you before we hired you."

"I want to read the report," Mikael repeated.

"I couldn't authorise that."

"Really? Then here's what I say to you: either I have that report in my hands within the hour, or I quit. I'll take the evening train back to Stockholm. Where is the report?"

The two men eyed each other for several seconds. Then Frode sighed and looked away.

"In my office, at home."

Frode had put up a terrible fuss. It was not until 6:00 that evening that Blomkvist had Lisbeth Salander's report in his hand. It was almost eighty pages long, plus dozens of photocopied articles, certificates, and other records of the details of his life and career.

It was a strange experience to read about himself in what was part biography and part intelligence report. He was increasingly astonished at how detailed the report was. Salander had dug up facts that he thought had been long buried in the compost of history. She had dug up his youthful relationship with a woman who had been a flaming Syndicalist and who was now a politician. *Who in the world had she talked to?* She had found his rock band Bootstrap, which surely no-one today would remember.

She had scrutinised his finances down to the last öre. *How the hell had she done it?*

As a journalist, Blomkvist had spent many years hunting down information about people, and he could judge the quality of the work from a purely professional standpoint. There was no doubt that this Salander was one hell of an investigator. He doubted that even he could have produced a comparable report on any individual completely unknown to him.

It also dawned on him that there had never been any reason for him and Berger to keep their distance in Vanger's presence; he already knew of their long-standing relationship. The report came up with a disturbingly precise appraisal of *Millennium*'s financial position; Vanger knew just how shaky things were when he first contacted Berger. *What sort of game was he playing?*

The Wennerström affair was merely summarised, but whoever wrote the report had obviously been a spectator in court during part of the trial. The report questioned Blomkvist's refusal to comment during the trial. *Smart woman.*

The next second Mikael straightened up, hardly able to believe his eyes. Salander had written a brief passage giving her assessment of what would happen after the trial. She had reproduced virtually word for word the press release that he and Berger had submitted after he resigned as publisher of *Millennium.*

But Salander had used his original wording. He glanced again at the cover of the report. It was dated three days before Blomkvist was sentenced. *That was impossible.* The press release existed then in only one place in the whole world. In Blomkvist's computer. In his iBook, not on his computer at the office. The text was never printed out. Not even Berger had a copy, although they had talked about the subject.

Blomkvist put down Salander's report. He put on his jacket

and went out into the night, which was very bright one week before Midsummer. He walked along the shore of the sound, past Cecilia Vanger's property and the luxurious motorboat below Martin Vanger's villa. He walked slowly, pondering as he went. Finally he sat on a rock and looked at the flashing buoy lights in Hedestad Bay. There was only one conclusion.

"*You've been in my computer, Fröken Salander*," he said aloud. "*You're a fucking hacker.*"

CHAPTER 18

Wednesday, June 18

Salander awoke with a start from a dreamless slumber. She felt faintly sick. She did not have to turn her head to know that Mimmi had left already for work, but her scent still lingered in the stuffy air of the bedroom. Salander had drunk too many beers the night before with the Evil Fingers at the Mill. Mimmi had turned up not long before closing time and come home with her and into bed.

Salander—unlike Mimmi—had never thought of herself as a lesbian. She had never brooded over whether she was straight, gay, or even bisexual. She did not give a damn about labels, did not see that it was anyone else's business whom she spent her nights with. If she had to choose, she preferred guys—and they were in the lead, statistically speaking. The only problem was finding a guy who was not a jerk and one who was also good in bed; Mimmi was a sweet compromise, and she turned Salander on. They had met in a beer tent at the Pride Festival a year ago, and Mimmi was the only person that Salander had introduced to the Evil Fingers. But it was still just a casual affair for both of them. It was nice lying close to Mimmi's warm, soft body, and Salander did not mind waking up with her and their having breakfast together.

Her clock said it was 9:30, and she was wondering what could have woken her when the doorbell rang again. She sat up in surprise. *No-one* had *ever* rung her doorbell at this hour. Very few people rang her doorbell at all. She wrapped a sheet around her and walked unsteadily to the hall to open the door. She stared straight into the eyes of Mikael Blomkvist, felt panic race through her body, and took a step back.

"Good morning, Fröken Salander," he greeted her cheerfully. "It was a late night, I see. Can I come in?"

Without waiting for an answer, he walked in, closing the door behind him. He regarded with curiosity the pile of clothes on the hall floor and the rampart of bags filled with newspapers; then he peered through the bedroom door while Salander's world started spinning in the wrong direction. *How? What? Who?* Blomkvist looked at her bewilderment with amusement.

"I assumed that you would not have had breakfast yet, so I brought some filled bagels with me. I got one with roast beef, one with turkey and Dijon mustard, and one vegetarian with avocado, not knowing your preference." He marched into her kitchen and started rinsing her coffeemaker. "Where do you keep coffee?" he said. Salander stood in the hall as if frozen until she heard the water running out of the tap. She took three quick strides.

"Stop! Stop at once!" She realised that she was shouting and lowered her voice. "Damn it all, you can't come barging in here as if you owned the place. We don't even know each other."

Blomkvist paused, holding a jug and turned to look at her.

"Wrong! You know me better than almost anyone else does. Isn't that so?"

He turned his back on her and poured the water into the machine. Then he started opening her cupboards in search of coffee. "Speaking of which, I know how you do it. I know your secrets."

Salander shut her eyes, wishing that the floor would stop pitching under her feet. She was in a state of mental paralysis. She was hung over. This situation was unreal, and her brain was refusing to function. Never had she met one of her subjects face to face. *He knows where I live!* He was standing in her kitchen. This was impossible. It was outrageous. *He knows who I am!*

She felt the sheet slipping, and she pulled it tighter around her. He said something, but at first she didn't understand him. "We have to talk," he said again. "But I think you'd better take a shower first."

She tried to speak sensibly. "You listen to me—if you're thinking of making trouble, I'm not the one you should be talking to. I was just doing a job. You should talk to my boss."

He held up his hands. A universal sign of peace, or *I have no weapon.*

"I've already talked to Armansky. By the way, he wants you to ring him—you didn't answer his call last night."

She did not sense any threat, but she still stepped back a pace when he came closer, took her arm and escorted her to the bathroom door. She disliked having anyone touch her without her leave.

"I don't want to make trouble," he said. "But I'm quite anxious to talk to you. After you're awake, that is. The coffee will be ready by the time you put on some clothes. First, a shower. Vamoose!"

Passively she obeyed. *Lisbeth Salander is never passive,* she thought.

. . .

She leaned against the bathroom door and struggled to collect her thoughts. She was more shaken than she would have thought possible. Gradually she realised that a shower was not only good advice but a necessity after the tumult of the night. When she was done, she slipped into her bedroom and put on jeans, and a T-shirt with the slogan ARMAGEDDON WAS YESTERDAY—TODAY WE HAVE A SERIOUS PROBLEM.

After pausing for a second, she searched through her leather jacket that was slung over a chair. She took the taser out of the pocket, checked to see that it was loaded, and stuck it in the back pocket of her jeans. The smell of coffee was spreading through the apartment. She took a deep breath and went back to the kitchen.

"Do you never clean up?" he said.

He had filled the sink with dirty dishes and ashtrays; he had put the old milk cartons into a rubbish sack and cleared the table of five weeks of newspapers; he had washed the table clean and put out mugs and—he wasn't joking after all—bagels. *OK, let's see where this is heading.* She sat down opposite him.

"You didn't answer my question. Roast beef, turkey, or vegetarian?"

"Roast beef."

"Then I'll take the turkey."

They ate in silence, scrutinising each other. When she finished her bagel, she also ate half of the vegetarian one. She picked up a crumpled pack of cigarettes from the windowsill and dug one out.

He broke the silence. "I may not be as good as you at investigations, but at least I've found out that you're not a vegetarian or—as Herr Frode thought—anorexic. I'll include that information in my report."

Salander stared at him, but he looked so amused that she gave him a crooked smile. The situation was beyond all rhyme or reason. She sipped her coffee. He had kind eyes. She decided that whatever else he might be, he did not seem to be a malicious person. And there was nothing in the PI she had done that would indicate he was a vicious bastard who abused his girlfriends or anything like that. She reminded herself that *she* was the one who knew everything. *Knowledge is power.*

"What are you grinning at?" she said.

"I'm sorry. I had not in fact planned to make my entrance in this way. I didn't mean to alarm you. But you should have seen your face when you opened the door. It was priceless."

Silence. To her surprise, Salander found his uninvited intrusion acceptable—well, at least not unpleasant.

"You'll have to think of it as my revenge for your poking around in my personal life," he said. "Are you frightened?"

"Not the least bit," Salander said.

"Good. I'm not here to make trouble for you."

"If you even try to hurt me I'll have to do you an injury. You'll be sorry."

Blomkvist studied her. She was barely four foot eleven and did not look as though she could put up much resistance if he were an assailant who had forced his way into her apartment. But her eyes were expressionless and calm.

"Well, that won't be necessary," he said at last. "I only need to talk to you. If you want me to leave, all you have to do is say so. It's funny but . . . oh, nothing . . ."

"What?"

"This may sound crazy, but four days ago I didn't even know you existed. Then I read your analysis of me." He searched through his shoulder bag and brought out the report. "It was not entertaining reading."

He looked out of the kitchen window for a while. "Could I bum a cigarette?" She slid the pack across the table.

"You said before that we don't know each other, and I said

that yes, we do." He pointed at the report. "I can't compete with you. I've only done a rapid routine check, to get your address and date of birth, stuff like that. But you certainly know a great deal about me. Much of which is private, dammit, things that only my closest friends know. And now here I am, sitting in your kitchen and eating bagels with you. We have known each other half an hour, but I have the feeling that we've been friends for years. Does that make sense to you?"

She nodded.

"You have beautiful eyes," he said.

"You have nice eyes yourself," she said.

Long silence.

"Why are you here?" she said.

Kalle Blomkvist—she remembered his nickname and suppressed the impulse to say it out loud—suddenly looked serious. He also looked very tired. The self-confidence that he had shown when he first walked into her apartment was now gone. The clowning was over, or at least had been put aside. She felt him studying her closely.

Salander felt that her composure was barely skin-deep and that she really wasn't in complete control of her nerves. This totally unlooked-for visit had shaken her in a way that she had never experienced in connection with her work. Her bread and butter was spying on people. In fact she had never thought of what she did for Armansky as a real job; she thought of it more as a complicated pastime, a sort of hobby.

The truth was that she enjoyed digging into the lives of other people and exposing the secrets they were trying to hide. She had been doing it, in one form or another, for as long as she could remember. And she was still doing it today, not only when Armansky gave her an assignment, but sometimes for the sheer fun of it. It gave her a kick. It was like a complicated computer game, except that it dealt with real live people. And now one of her hobbies was sitting right here in her kitchen, feeding her bagels. It was totally absurd.

"I have a fascinating problem," Blomkvist said. "Tell me this, when you were doing your research on me for Herr Frode, did you have any idea what it was going to be used for?"

"No."

"The purpose was to find out all that information about me because Frode, or rather his employer, wanted to give me a freelance job."

"I see."

He gave her a faint smile.

"One of these days you and I should have a discussion about the ethics of snooping into other people's lives. But right now I have a different problem. The job I was offered, and which inexplicably I agreed to do, is without doubt the most bizarre assignment I've ever undertaken. Before I say more I need to be able to trust you, Lisbeth."

"What do you mean?"

"Armansky tells me you're 100 percent reliable. But I still want to ask you the question. Can I tell you confidential things without your telling them to anyone else, by any means, ever?"

"Wait a minute. You've talked to Dragan? Is he the one who sent you here?" *I'm going to kill you, you fucking stupid Armenian.*

"Not exactly. You're not the only one who can find out someone's address; I did that all on my own. I looked you up in the national registry. There are three Lisbeth Salanders, and the other two weren't a good match. But I had a long talk with Armansky yesterday. He too thought that I wanted to make trouble over your ferreting around in my private life. In the end I convinced him that I had a legitimate purpose."

"Which is what?"

"As I told you, Frode's employer hired me to do a job. I've reached a point where I need a skilled researcher. Frode told me about you and said that you were pretty good. He hadn't meant to identify you, it just slipped out. I explained to Armansky what I wanted. He OK'd the whole thing and tried to call you. And here I am. Call him if you want."

It took Salander a minute to find her mobile among the clothes that Mimmi had pulled off her. Blomkvist watched her embarrassed search with interest as he patrolled the apartment. All her furniture seemed to be strays. She had a state-of-the-art PowerBook on an apology for a desk in the living room. She had a CD player on a shelf. Her CD collection was a pitiful total of ten CDs by groups he had never heard of, and the musicians on the covers looked like vampires from outer space. Music was probably not her big interest.

Salander saw that Armansky had called her seven times the night before and twice this morning. She punched in his number while Blomkvist leaned against the door frame and listened to the conversation.

"It's me . . . sorry . . . yes . . . it was turned off . . . I know, he wants to hire me . . . no, he's standing in the middle of my fucking living room, for Christ's sake . . ." She raised her voice. "Dragan, I'm hung over and my head hurts, so please, no games, did you OK this job or not? . . . Thanks."

Salander looked through the door to the living room at Blomkvist pulling out CDs and taking books off the bookshelf. He had just found a brown pill bottle that was missing its label, and he was holding it up to the light. He was about to unscrew the top, so she reached out and took the bottle from him. She went back to the kitchen and sat down on a chair, massaging her forehead until he joined her.

"The rules are simple," she said. "Nothing that you discuss with me or with Armansky will be shared with anyone at all. There will be a contract which states that Milton Security pledges confidentiality. I want to know what the job is about before I decide whether I want to work for you or not. That also means that I agree to keep to myself everything you tell me, whether I take the job or not, provided that you're not conducting any sort of serious criminal activity. In which case, I'll report it to Dragan, who in turn will report it to the police."

"Fine." He hesitated. "Armansky may not be completely aware of what I want to hire you for . . ."

"Some historical research, he said."

"Well, yes, that's right. I want you to help me to identify a murderer."

It took Blomkvist an hour to explain all the intricate details in the Harriet Vanger case. He left nothing out. He had Frode's permission to hire her, and to do that he had to be able to trust her completely.

He told her everything about Cecilia Vanger and that he had found her face in Harriet's window. He gave Salander as good a description of her character as he could. She had moved high up on the list of suspects, his list. But he was still far from believing that she could be in any way associated with a murderer who was active when she was still a young woman.

He gave Salander a copy of the list in the date book: "Magda—32016; Sara—32109; R.J.—30112; R.L.—32027; Mari—32018." And he gave her a copy of the verses from Leviticus.

"What do you want me to do?"

"I've identified the R.J., Rebecka Jacobsson." He told her what the five-figure numbers stood for. "If I'm right, then we're going to find four more victims—Magda, Sara, Mari, and R.L."

"You think they're all murdered?"

"What I think is that we are looking for someone who—if the other numbers and initials also prove to be shorthand for four more killings—is a murderer who was active in the fifties and maybe also in the sixties. And who is in some way linked to Harriet Vanger. I've gone through back issues of the *Hedestad Courier*. Rebecka's murder is the only grotesque crime that I could find with a connection to Hedestad. I want you to keep digging, all over Sweden if necessary, until you make sense of the other names and verses."

Salander thought in expressionless silence for such a long time that Blomkvist began to grow impatient. He was wondering whether he had chosen the wrong person when she at last raised her head.

"I'll take the job. But first you have to sign a contract with Armansky."

Armansky printed out the contract that Blomkvist would take back to Hedestad for Frode's signature. When he returned to Salander's office, he saw how she and Blomkvist were leaning over her PowerBook. He had his hand on her shoulder—*he was touching her*—and pointing. Armansky paused in the corridor.

Blomkvist said something that seemed to surprise Salander. Then she laughed out loud.

Armansky had never once heard her laugh before, and for years he had been trying to win her trust. Blomkvist had known her for five minutes and she was practically giggling with him. He felt such a loathing for Blomkvist at that moment that he surprised himself. He cleared his throat as he stood in the doorway and put down the folder with the contract.

Blomkvist paid a quick visit to the *Millennium* office in the afternoon. It was his first time back. It felt very odd to be running up those familiar stairs. They had not changed the code on the door, and he was able to slip in unnoticed and stand for a moment, looking around.

Millennium's offices were arranged in an L shape. The entry was a hall that took up a lot of space without being able to be put to much use. There were two sofas there, so it was by way of being a reception area. Beyond was a lunchroom kitchenette, then cloakroom/toilets, and two storage rooms with bookshelves and filing cabinets. There was also a desk for an intern. To the right of the entry was the glass wall of Malm's studio, which took up about 500 square feet, with its own entrance from the landing. To the left was the editorial office, encompassing about 350 square feet, with the windows facing Götgatan.

Berger had designed everything, putting in glass partitions to make separate quarters for three of the employees and an open plan for the others. She had taken the largest room at the very back for herself, and given Blomkvist his own room at the opposite end. It was the only room that you could look into from the entry. No-one had moved into it, it seemed.

The third room was slightly apart from the others, and it was occupied by Sonny Magnusson, who had been for several years *Millennium*'s most successful advertising salesman. Berger had handpicked him; she offered him a modest salary and a commission. Over the past year, it had not made any difference how energetic he was as a salesman, their advertising income had taken a beating and Magnusson's income with it. But instead of looking elsewhere, he had tightened his belt and loyally stayed put. Unlike me, who caused the whole landslide, Blomkvist thought.

He gathered his courage and walked into the office. It was almost deserted. He could see Berger at her desk, telephone pressed to her ear. Monika Nilsson was at her desk, an experienced general reporter specialising in political coverage; she could be the most jaded cynic he had ever met. She'd been at *Millennium* for nine years and was thriving. Henry Cortez was the youngest employee on the editorial staff. He had come as an intern straight out of JMK two years ago, saying that he wanted to work at *Millennium* and nowhere else. Berger had no budget to hire him, but she offered him a desk in a corner and soon took him on as a permanent dogsbody, and anon as a staff reporter.

Both uttered cries of delight. He received kisses on the cheek and pats on the back. At once they asked him if he was returning to work. No, he had just stopped by to say hello and have a word with the boss.

Berger was glad to see him. She asked about Vanger's condition. Blomkvist knew no more than what Frode could tell him: his condition was inescapably serious.

"So what are you doing in the city?"

Blomkvist was embarrassed. He had been at Milton Security, only a few streets away, and he had decided on sheer impulse to come in. It seemed too complicated to explain that he had been there to hire a research assistant who was a security consultant who had hacked into his computer. Instead he shrugged and said he had come to Stockholm on Vanger-related business, and he would have to go back north at once. He asked how things were going at the magazine.

"Apart from the good news on the advertising and the subscription fronts, there is one cloud on the horizon."

"Which is?"

"Janne Dahlman."

"Of course."

"I had a talk with him in April, after we released the news that Henrik had become a partner. I don't know if it's just Janne's nature to be negative or if there's something more serious going on, if he's playing some sort of game."

"What happened?"

"It's nothing I can put a finger on, rather that I no longer trust him. After we signed the agreement with Vanger, Christer and I had to decide whether to inform the whole staff that we were no longer at risk of going under this autumn, or . . ."

"Or to tell just a chosen few."

"Exactly. I may be paranoid, but I didn't want to risk having Dahlman leak the story. So we decided to inform the whole staff on the same day the agreement was made public. Which meant that we kept the lid on it for over a month."

"And?"

"Well, that was the first piece of good news they'd had in a year. Everyone cheered except for Dahlman. I mean—we don't have the world's biggest editorial staff. There were three people cheering, plus the intern, and one person who got his nose out of joint because we hadn't told everybody earlier."

"He had a point . . ."

"I know. But the thing is, he kept on bitching about the issue day after day, and morale in the office was affected. After two weeks of this shit I called him into my office and told him to his face that my reason for not having informed the staff earlier was that I didn't trust him to keep the news secret."

"How did he take it?"

"He was terribly upset, of course. I stood my ground and gave him an ultimatum—either he had to pull himself together or start looking for another job."

"And?"

"He pulled himself together. But he keeps to himself, and there's a tension between him and the others. Christer can't stand him, and he doesn't hide it."

"What do you suspect Dahlman of doing?"

"I don't know. We hired him a year ago, when we were first talking about trouble with Wennerström. I can't prove a thing, but I have a nasty feeling that he's not working for us."

"Trust your instincts."

"Maybe he's just a square peg in a round hole who just happens to be poisoning the atmosphere."

"It's possible. But I agree that we made a mistake when we hired him."

Half an hour later he was on his way north across the locks at Slussen in the car he had borrowed from Frode's wife. It was a ten-year-old Volvo she never used. Blomkvist had been given leave to borrow it whenever he liked.

It was the tiny details that he could easily have missed if he had not been alert: some papers not as evenly stacked as he remembered; a binder not quite flush on the shelf; his desk drawer closed all the way—he was positive that it was an inch open when he left.

Someone had been inside his cottage.

He had locked the door, but it was an ordinary old lock that almost anyone could pick with a screwdriver, and who knew how many keys were in circulation. He systematically searched his office, looking for what might be missing. After a while he decided that everything was still there.

Nevertheless someone had been in the cottage and gone through his papers and binders. He had taken his computer with him, so they had not been able to access that. Two questions arose: who was it? and how much had his visitor been able to find out?

The binders belonged to the part of Vanger's collection that he brought back to the guest house after returning from prison. There was nothing of the new material in them. His notebooks in the desk would read like code to the uninitiated—but was the person who had searched his desk uninitiated?

In a plastic folder on the middle of the desk he had put a

copy of the date book list and a copy of the verses. That was serious. It would tell whoever it was that the date book code was cracked.

So who was it?

Vanger was in the hospital. He did not suspect Anna. Frode? He had already told him all the details. Cecilia Vanger had cancelled her trip to Florida and was back from London—along with her sister. Blomkvist had only seen her once, driving her car across the bridge the day before. Martin Vanger. Harald Vanger. Birger Vanger—he had turned up for a family gathering to which Blomkvist had not been invited on the day after Vanger's heart attack. Alexander Vanger. Isabella Vanger.

Whom had Frode talked to? What might he have let slip this time? How many of the anxious relatives had picked up on the fact that Blomkvist had made a breakthrough in his investigation?

It was after 8:00. He called the locksmith in Hedestad and ordered a new lock. The locksmith said that he could come out the following day. Blomkvist said he would pay double if he came at once. They agreed that he would come at around 10:30 that night and install a new deadbolt lock.

Blomkvist drove to Frode's house. His wife showed him into the garden behind the house and offered him a cold Pilsner, which he gratefully accepted. He asked how Henrik Vanger was.

Frode shook his head.

"They operated on him. He had blockages in his coronary arteries. The doctors say that the next few days are critical."

They thought about this for a while as they drank their Pilsners.

"You haven't talked to him, I suppose?"

"No. He's not well enough to talk. How did it go in Stockholm?"

"The Salander girl accepted the job. Here's the contract from Milton Security. You have to sign it and put it in the post."

Frode read through the document.

"She's expensive," he said.

"Henrik can afford it."

Frode nodded. He took a pen out of his breast pocket and scrawled his name.

"It's a good thing that I'm signing it while he's still alive. Could you put it in the letter box at Konsum on your way home?"

Blomkvist was in bed by midnight, but he could not sleep. Until now his work on Hedeby Island had seemed like research on a historical curiosity. But if someone was sufficiently interested in what he was doing to break into his office, then the solution had to be closer to the present than he had thought.

Then it occurred to him that there were others who might be interested in what he was working on. Vanger's sudden appearance on the board of *Millennium* had not gone unnoticed by Wennerström. Or was this paranoia?

Mikael got out of bed and went to stand naked at the kitchen window, gazing at the church on the other side of the bridge. He lit a cigarette.

He couldn't figure out Lisbeth Salander. She was altogether odd. Long pauses in the middle of the conversation. Her apartment was messy, bordering on chaotic. Bags filled with newspapers in the hall. A kitchen that had not been cleaned or tidied in years. Clothes were scattered in heaps on the floor. She had obviously spent half the night in a bar. She had love bites on her neck and she had clearly had company overnight. She had heaven knows how many tattoos and two piercings on her face and maybe in other places. She was weird.

Armansky assured him that she was their very best researcher, and her report on him was excruciatingly thorough. *A strange girl.*

Salander was sitting at her PowerBook, but she was thinking about Mikael Blomkvist. She had never in her adult life allowed anyone to cross her threshold without an express invitation, and she could count those she had invited on one hand. Blomkvist had nonchalantly barged into her life, and she had uttered only a few lame protests.

Not only that, he had teased her.

Under normal circumstances that sort of behaviour would have made her mentally cock a pistol. But she had not felt an iota of threat or any sort of hostility from his side. He had good reason to read her the riot act, even report her to the police. Instead he had treated even her hacking into his computer as a joke.

That had been the most sensitive part of their conversation. Blomkvist seemed to be deliberately not broaching the subject, and finally she could not help asking the question.

"You said that you knew what I did."

"You've been inside my computer. You're a hacker."

"How do you know that?" Salander was absolutely positive that she had left no traces and that her trespassing could not be discovered by anyone unless a top security consultant sat down and scanned the hard drive at the same time as she was accessing the computer.

"You made a mistake."

She had quoted from a text that was only on his computer.

Salander sat in silence. Finally she looked up at him, her eyes expressionless.

"How did you do it?" he asked.

"My secret. What are you thinking of doing about it?"

Mikael shrugged.

"What can I do?"

"It's exactly what you do as a journalist."

"Of course. And that's why we journalists have an ethics committee that keeps track of the moral issues. When I write an article about some bastard in the banking industry, I leave out, for instance, his or her private life. I don't say that a forger is a lesbian or gets turned on by having sex with her dog or anything like that, even if it happens to be true. Bastards too have a right to their private lives. Does that make sense?"

"Yes."

"So you encroached on my integrity. My employer doesn't need to know who I have sex with. That's my business."

Salander's face was creased by a crooked smile.

"You think I shouldn't have mentioned that?"

"In my case it didn't make a lot of difference. Half the city knows about my relationship with Erika. But it's a matter of principle."

"In that case, it might amuse you to know that I also have principles comparable to your ethics committee's. I call them *Salander's Principles*. One of them is that a bastard is always a bastard, and if I can hurt a bastard by digging up shit about him, then he deserves it."

"OK," Blomkvist said. "My reasoning isn't too different from yours, but . . ."

"But the thing is that when I do a PI, I also look at what I think about the person. I'm not neutral. If the person seems like a good sort, I might tone down my report."

"Really?"

"In your case I toned it down. I could have written a book about your sex life. I could have mentioned to Frode that Erika Berger has a past in Club Xtreme and played around with

BDSM in the eighties—which would have prompted certain unavoidable notions about your sex life and hers."

Blomkvist met Salander's gaze. After a moment he laughed.

"You're really meticulous, aren't you? Why didn't you put it in the report?"

"You are adults who obviously like each other. What you do in bed is nobody's business, and the only thing I would have achieved by talking about her was to hurt both of you, or to provide someone with blackmail material. I don't know Frode—the information could have ended up with Wennerström."

"And you don't want to provide Wennerström with information?"

"If I had to choose between you and him, I'd probably end up in your court."

"Erika and I have a . . . our relationship is . . ."

"Please, I really don't give a toss about what sort of relationship you have. But you haven't answered my question: what do you plan to do about my hacking into your computer?"

"Lisbeth, I'm not here to blackmail you. I'm here to ask you to help me do some research. You can say yes or no. If you say no, fine, I'll find someone else and you'll never hear from me again."

CHAPTER 19

Thursday, June 19–
Sunday, June 29

While he waited for word on whether Vanger was going to pull through or not, Blomkvist spent the days going over his materials. He kept in close touch with Frode. On Thursday evening Frode brought him the news that the immediate crisis seemed to be over.

"I was able to talk to him for a while today. He wants to see you as soon as possible."

So it was that, around 1:00 on the afternoon of Midsummer Eve, Blomkvist drove to Hedestad Hospital and went in search of the ward. He encountered an angry Birger Vanger, who blocked his way. Henrik could not possibly receive visitors, he said.

"That's odd," Blomkvist said, "Henrik sent word saying that he expressly wanted to see me today."

"You're not a member of the family; you have no business here."

"You're right. I'm not a member of the family. But I'm working for Henrik Vanger, and I take orders only from him."

This might have led to a heated exchange if Frode had not at that moment come out of Vanger's room.

"Oh, there you are. Henrik has been asking after you."

Frode held open the door and Blomkvist walked past Birger into the room.

Vanger looked to have aged ten years. He was lying with his eyes half closed, an oxygen tube in his nose, and his hair more dishevelled than ever. A nurse stopped Blomkvist, putting a hand firmly on his arm.

"Two minutes. No more. And don't upset him." Blomkvist sat on a visitor's chair so that he could see Vanger's face. He felt a tenderness that astonished him, and he stretched out his hand to gently squeeze the old man's hand.

"Any news?" The voice was weak.

Blomkvist nodded.

"I'll give you a report as soon as you're better. I haven't solved the mystery yet, but I've found more new stuff and I'm following up a number of leads. In a week, perhaps two, I'll be able to tell the results."

The most Vanger could manage was to blink, indicating that he understood.

"I have to be away for a few days."

Henrik raised his eyebrows.

"I'm not jumping ship. I have some research to do. I've reached an agreement with Dirch that I should report to him. Is that OK with you?"

"Dirch is . . . my man . . . in all matters."

Blomkvist squeezed Vanger's hand again.

"Mikael . . . if I don't . . . I want you to . . . finish the job."

"I will finish the job."

"Dirch has . . . full . . ."

"Henrik, I want you to get better. I'd be furious with you if you went and died after I've made such progress."

"Two minutes," the nurse said.

"Next time we'll have a long talk."

Birger Vanger was waiting for him when he came out. He stopped him by laying a hand on his shoulder.

"I don't want you bothering Henrik any more. He's very ill, and he's not supposed to be upset or disturbed."

"I understand your concern, and I sympathise. And I'm not going to upset him."

"Everyone knows that Henrik hired you to poke around in his little hobby . . . Harriet. Dirch said that Henrik became very upset after a conversation you had with him before he had the heart attack. He even said that you thought you had caused the attack."

"I don't think so any more. Henrik had severe blockages in his arteries. He could have had a heart attack just by having a pee. I'm sure you know that by now."

"I want full disclosure into this lunacy. This is my family you're mucking around in."

"I told you, I work for Henrik, not for the family."

Birger Vanger was apparently not used to having anyone stand up to him. For a moment he stared at Blomkvist with an expression that was presumably meant to instil respect, but which made him look more like an inflated moose. Birger turned and went into Vanger's room.

Blomkvist restrained the urge to laugh. This was no place for laughter, in the corridor outside Vanger's sickbed, which might also turn out to be his deathbed. But he thought of a verse from Lennart Hyland's rhyming alphabet. It was the letter *M*. *And all alone the moose he stood, laughing in a shot-up wood.*

In the hospital lobby he ran into Cecilia Vanger. He had tried calling her mobile a dozen times since she came back from her interrupted holiday, but she had never answered or returned his calls. And she was never home at her place on Hedeby Island whenever he walked past and knocked on the door.

"Hi, Cecilia," he said. "I'm so sorry about all this with Henrik."

"Thanks," she said.

"We need to talk."

"I'm sorry that I've shut you out like this. I can understand that you must be cross, but I'm not having an easy time of it these days."

Mikael put his hand on her arm and smiled at her.

"Wait, you've got it wrong, Cecilia. I'm not cross at all. I am still hoping that we can be friends. Can we have a cup of coffee?" He nodded in the direction of the hospital cafeteria.

Cecilia Vanger hesitated. "Not today. I need to go and see Henrik."

"OK, but I still need to talk to you. It's purely professional."

"What does that mean?" She was suddenly alert.

"Do you remember the first time we met, when you came to the cottage in January? I said that we were talking off the record, and that if I needed to ask you any real questions, I would tell you. It has to do with Harriet."

Cecilia Vanger's face was suddenly flushed with anger.

"You really are the fucking pits."

"Cecilia, I've found some things that I really do have to talk to you about."

She took a step away from him.

"Don't you realise that this bloody hunt for that cursed Harriet is just occupational therapy for Henrik? Don't you see that he might be up there dying, and that the very last thing he needs is to get upset again and be filled with false hopes and . . ."

"It may be a hobby for Henrik, but there is now more material to go on than anyone has had to work with in a very long time. There are questions that do now need to be answered."

"If Henrik dies, that investigation is going to be over awfully damned fast. Then you'll be out on your grubby, snivelling investigative backside," Cecilia said, and she walked away.

Everything was closed. Hedestad was practically deserted, and the inhabitants seemed to have retreated to their Midsummer poles at their summer cottages. Blomkvist made for the Stadshotel terrace, which was actually open, and there he was able to order coffee and a sandwich and read the evening papers. Nothing of importance was happening in the world.

He put the paper down and thought about Cecilia Vanger. He had told no-one—apart from the Salander girl—that she was the one who had opened the window in Harriet's room. He was afraid that it would make her a suspect, and the last thing he wanted to do was hurt her. But the question was going to have to be asked, sooner or later.

He sat on the terrace for an hour before he decided to set the whole problem aside and devote Midsummer Eve to something other than the Vanger family. His mobile was silent. Berger was away amusing herself somewhere with her husband, and he had no-one to talk to.

He went back to Hedeby Island at around 4:00 in the afternoon and made another decision—to stop smoking. He had been working out regularly ever since he did his military service, both at the gym and by running along Söder Mälarstrand, but had fallen out of the habit when the problems with Wennerström began. It was at Rullåker Prison that he had starting pumping iron again, mostly as therapy. But since his release he had taken almost no exercise. It was time to start again. He put on his tracksuit and set off at a lazy pace along the road to Gottfried's cabin, turned off towards the Fortress, and took a rougher course cross country. He had done no orienteering since he was in the military, but he had always thought it was more fun to run through a wooded terrain than on a flat track. He followed the fence around Östergården back to the village. He was aching all over and out of breath by the time he took the last steps up to the guest house.

At 6:00 he took a shower. He boiled some potatoes and had open sandwiches of pickled herring in mustard sauce with chives and egg on a rickety table outside the cottage, facing the bridge. He poured himself a shot of aquavit and drank a toast to himself. After that he opened a crime novel by Val McDermid entitled *The Mermaids Singing*.

At around 7:00 Frode drove up and sat heavily in the chair across from him. Blomkvist poured him a shot of Skåne aquavit.

"You stirred up some rather lively emotions today," Frode said.

"I could see that."

"Birger is a conceited fool."

"I know that."

"But Cecilia is not a conceited fool, and she's furious."

Mikael nodded.

"She has instructed me to see that you stop poking around in the family's affairs."

"I see. And what did you say to her?"

Frode looked at his glass of Skåne and downed the liquor in one gulp.

"My response was that Henrik has given me clear instructions about what he wants you to do. As long as he doesn't change those instructions, you will continue to be employed under the terms of your contract. I expect you to do your best to fulfil your part of the contract."

Blomkvist looked up at the sky, where rain clouds had begun to gather.

"Looks like a storm is brewing," Frode said. "If the winds get too strong, I'll have to back you up."

"Thank you."

They sat in silence for a while.

"Could I have another drink?"

Only minutes after Frode had gone home, Martin Vanger drove up and parked his car by the road in front of the cottage. He came over and said hello. Mikael wished him a happy Midsummer and asked if he'd like a drink.

"No, it's better if I don't. I'm just here to change my clothes and then I'm going to drive back to town to spend the evening with Eva."

Blomkvist waited.

"I've talked to Cecilia. She's a little traumatised just now—she and Henrik have always been close. I hope you'll forgive her if she says anything . . . unpleasant."

"I'm very fond of Cecilia."

"I know that. But she can be difficult. I just want you to know that she's very much against your going on digging into our past."

Blomkvist sighed. Everyone in Hedestad seemed to know why Vanger had hired him.

"What's your feeling?"

"This thing with Harriet has been Henrik's obsession for decades. I don't know . . . Harriet was my sister, but somehow it feels all so far away. Dirch says that you have a contract that only Henrik can break, and I'm afraid that in his present condition it would do more harm than good."

"So you want me to continue?"

"Have you made any progress?"

"I'm sorry, Martin, but it would be a breach of that contract if I told you anything without Henrik's permission."

"I understand." Suddenly he smiled. "Henrik is a bit of a conspiracy fanatic. But above all, I don't want you to get his hopes up unnecessarily."

"I won't do that."

"Good . . . By the way, to change the subject, we now have another contract to consider as well. Given that Henrik is ill and can't in the short term fulfil his obligations on the *Millennium* board, it's my responsibility to take his place."

Mikael waited.

"I suppose we should have a board meeting to look at the situation."

"That's a good idea. But as far as I know, it's been decided that the next board meeting won't be held until August."

"I know that, but maybe we should hold it earlier."

Blomkvist smiled politely.

"You're really talking to the wrong person. At the moment I'm not on the board. I left in December. You should get in touch with Erika Berger. She knows that Henrik has been taken ill."

Martin Vanger had not expected this response.

"You're right, of course. I'll talk to her." He patted Blomkvist on the shoulder to say goodbye and was gone.

Nothing concrete had been said, but the threat hung in the air. Martin Vanger had set *Millennium* on the balance tray. After a moment Blomkvist poured himself another drink and picked up his Val McDermid.

The mottled brown cat came to say hello and rubbed on his leg. He lifted her up and scratched behind her ears.

"The two of us are having a very boring Midsummer Eve, aren't we?" he said.

When it started to rain, he went inside and went to bed. The cat preferred to stay outdoors.

Salander got out her Kawasaki on Midsummer Eve and spent the day giving it a good overhaul. A lightweight 125cc might not be the toughest bike in the world, but it was hers, and she could handle it. She had restored it, one nut at a time, and she had souped it up just a bit over the legal limit.

In the afternoon she put on her helmet and leather suit and drove to Äppelviken Nursing Home, where she spent the evening in the park with her mother. She felt a pang of concern and guilt. Her mother seemed more remote than ever before. During three hours they exchanged only a few words, and when they did speak, her mother did not seem to know who she was talking to.

Blomkvist wasted several days trying to identify the car with the AC plates. After a lot of trouble and finally by consulting a retired mechanic in Hedestad, he came to the conclusion that the car was a Ford Anglia, a model that he had never heard of before. Then he contacted a clerk at the motor vehicle department and enquired about the possibility of getting a list of all the Ford Anglias in 1966 that had a licence plate beginning AC3. He was eventually told that such an archaeological excavation in the records presumably could be done, but that it would take time and it was beyond the boundaries of what could be considered public information.

Not until several days after Midsummer did Blomkvist get into his borrowed Volvo and drive north on the E4. He drove at a leisurely pace. Just short of the Härnösand Bridge he stopped to have coffee at the Vesterlund pastry shop.

The next stop was Umeå, where he pulled into an inn and had the daily special. He bought a road atlas and continued on to Skellefteå, where he turned towards Norsjö. He arrived around 6:00 in the evening and took a room in the Hotel Norsjö.

He began his search early the next morning. The Norsjö Carpentry Shop was not in the telephone book. The Polar Hotel desk clerk, a girl in her twenties, had never heard of the business.

"Who should I ask?"

The clerk looked puzzled for a few seconds until her face lit up and she said that she would call her father. Two minutes later she came back and explained that the Norsjö Carpentry Shop closed in the early eighties. If he needed to talk to someone who knew more about the business, he should go and see a certain Burman, who had been the foreman and who now lived on a street called Solvändan.

Norsjö was a small town with one main street, appropriately enough called Storgatan, that ran through the whole community. It was lined with shops with residential side streets off it. At the east end there was a small industrial area and a stable; at the western end stood an uncommonly beautiful wooden church. Blomkvist noted that the village also had a Missionary church and a Pentecostal church. A poster on a bulletin board at the bus station advertised a hunting museum and a skiing museum. A leftover flyer announced that Veronika would sing at the fairgrounds at Midsummer. He could walk from one end of the village to the other in less than twenty minutes.

The street called Solvändan consisted of single-family homes and was about five minutes from the hotel. There was no answer when Blomkvist rang the bell. It was 9:30, and he assumed that Burman had left for work or, if he was retired, was out on an errand.

His next stop was the hardware store on Storgatan. He

reasoned that anyone living in Norsjö would sooner or later pay a visit to the hardware store. There were two sales clerks in the shop. Blomkvist chose the older one, maybe fifty or so.

"Hi. I'm looking for a couple who probably lived in Norsjö in the sixties. The man might have worked for the Norsjö Carpentry Shop. I don't know their name, but I have two pictures that were taken in 1966."

The clerk studied the photographs for a long time but finally shook his head, saying he could not recognise either the man or the woman.

At lunchtime he had a burger at a hot-dog stand near the bus station. He had given up on the shops and had made his way through the municipal office, the library, and the pharmacy. The police station was empty, and he had started approaching older people at random. Early in the afternoon he asked two young women: they did not recognise the couple in the photographs, but they did have a good idea.

"If the pictures were taken in 1966, the people would have to be in their sixties today. Why don't you go over to the retirement home on Solbacka and ask there?"

Blomkvist introduced himself to a woman at the front desk of the retirement home, explaining what he wanted to know. She glared at him suspiciously but finally allowed herself to be persuaded. She led him to the day room, where he spent half an hour showing the pictures to a group of elderly people. They were very helpful, but none of them could identify the couple.

At 5:00 he went back to Solvändan and knocked on Burman's door. This time he had better luck. The Burmans, both the man and the wife, were retired, and they had been out all day. They invited Blomkvist into their kitchen, where his wife promptly made coffee while Mikael explained his errand. As with all his other attempts that day, he again drew a blank. Burman scratched his head, lit a pipe, and then concluded after a moment that he did not recognise the couple in the photographs. The Burmans spoke in a distinct Norsjö dialect to each other, and Blomkvist occasionally had difficulty understanding what they were saying. The wife meant "curly hair" when she remarked that the woman in the picture had *knövelhära*.

"But you're quite right that it's a sticker from the carpentry shop," her husband said. "That was clever of you to recognise it. But the problem was that we handed out those stickers left and right. To contractors, people who bought or delivered timber, joiners, machinists, all sorts."

"It's turning out to be harder to find this couple than I thought."

"Why do you want to find them?"

Blomkvist had decided to tell the truth if anyone asked him. Any attempt to make up a story about the couple in the pictures would just sound false and create confusion.

"It's a long story. I'm investigating a crime that occurred in Hedestad in 1966, and I think there's a possibility, although a very small one, that the people in the photographs might have seen what happened. They're not in any way under suspicion, and I don't think they're even aware that they might have information that could solve the crime."

"A crime? What kind of crime?"

"I'm sorry, but I can't tell you any more than that. I know it sounds bizarre that someone would come here almost forty years later, trying to find this couple, but the crime is still unsolved, and it's only lately that new facts have come to light."

"I see. Yes, this is certainly an unusual assignment that you're on."

"How many people worked at the carpentry shop?"

"The normal work force was forty or so. I worked there from the age of seventeen in the mid-fifties until the shop closed. Then I became a contractor." Burman thought for a moment.

"This much I can tell you. The guy in your pictures never worked there. He might have been a contractor, but I think I'd recognise him if he was. But there is one other possibility. Maybe his father or some other relative worked at the shop and that's not his car."

Mikael nodded. "I realise there are lots of possibilities. Can you suggest anyone I could talk to?"

"Yes," said Burman, nodding. "Come by tomorrow morning and we'll go and have a talk with some of the old guys."

Salander was facing a methodology problem of some significance. She was an expert at digging up information on just about anybody, but her starting point had always been a name and a social security number for a living person. If the individual was listed in a computer file, which everyone inevitably was, then the subject quickly landed in her spider's web. If the individual owned a computer with an Internet connection, an email address, and maybe even a personal website, which nearly everyone did who came under her special type of research, she could sooner or later find out their innermost secrets.

The work she had agreed to do for Blomkvist was altogether different. This assignment, in simple terms, was to identify four social security numbers based on extremely vague data. In addition, these individuals most likely died several decades ago. So probably they would not be on any computer files.

Blomkvist's theory, based on the Rebecka Jacobsson case, was that these individuals had fallen victim to a murderer. This meant that they should be found in various unsolved police investigations. There was no clue as to when or where these murders had taken place, except that it had to be before 1966. In terms of research, she was facing a whole new situation.

So, how do I go about this?

She pulled up the Google search engine, and typed in the keywords [Magda] + [murder]. That was the simplest form of research she could do. To her surprise, she made an instant breakthrough in the investigation. Her first hit was the programme listings for TV Värmland in Karlstad, advertising a segment in the series "Värmland Murders" that was broadcast in 1999. After that she found a brief mention in a TV listing in *Värmlands Folkblad*.

> In the series "Värmland Murders" the focus now turns to Magda Lovisa Sjöberg in Ranmoträsk, a gruesome murder mystery that occupied the Karlstad police several decades ago. In April 1960, the 46-year-old farmer's wife was found murdered in the family's barn. The reporter Claes Gunnars describes the last hours of her life and the fruitless search for the killer. The murder caused a great stir at the time, and many theories have been presented about who the guilty party was. A young relative will appear on the show to talk about how his life was destroyed when he was accused of the murder. 8:00 p.m.

She found more substantial information in the article "The Lovisa Case Shook the Whole Countryside," which was published in the magazine *Värmlandskultur*. All of the magazine's texts had been loaded on to the Net. Written with obvious glee and in a chatty and titillating tone, the article described how Lovisa Sjöberg's husband, the lumberjack Holger Sjöberg, had found his wife dead when he came home from work around 5:00. She had been subjected to gross sexual assault, stabbed, and finally murdered with the prongs of a pitchfork. The murder occurred in the family barn, but what aroused the most attention was the fact that the perpetrator, after committing the murder, had tied her up in a kneeling position inside a horse stall.

It was later discovered that one of the animals on the farm, a cow, had suffered a stab wound on the side of its neck.

Initially the husband was suspected of the murder, but he had been in the company of his work colleagues from 6:00 in the morning at a clearing twenty-five miles from his home. It could be verified that Lovisa Sjöberg had been alive as late as 10:00 in the morning, when she had a visit from a woman friend. No-one had seen or heard anything; the farm was five hundred yards from its nearest neighbour.

After dropping the husband as a suspect, the police investigation focused on the victim's twenty-three-year-old nephew. He had repeatedly fallen foul of the law, was extremely short of cash, and many times had borrowed small sums from his aunt. The nephew's alibi was significantly weaker, and he was taken into custody for a while, but released for lack of evidence. Even so, many people in the village thought it highly probable that he was guilty.

The police followed another lead. A part of the investigation concerned the search for a pedlar who was seen in the area; there was also a rumour that a group of "thieving gypsies" had carried out a series of raids. Why they should have committed a savage, sexually related murder without stealing anything was never explained.

For a time suspicion was directed at a neighbour in the village, a bachelor who in his youth was suspected of an allegedly homosexual crime—this was back when homosexuality was still a punishable offence—and according to several statements, he had a reputation for being "odd." Why someone who was supposedly homosexual would commit a sex crime against a woman was not explained either. None of these leads, or any others, led to a charge.

Salander thought there was a clear link to the list in Harriet Vanger's date book. Leviticus 20:16 said: *"If a woman approaches any beast and lies with it, you shall kill the woman and the beast; they shall be put to death, their blood is upon them.*" It couldn't be a coincidence that a farmer's wife by the name of Magda had been found murdered in a barn, with her body so arranged and tied up in a horse stall.

The question was why had Harriet Vanger written down the name Magda instead of Lovisa, which was apparently the name the victim went under. If her full name had not been printed in the TV listing, Salander would have missed it.

And, of course, the more important question was: was there a link between Rebecka's murder in 1949, the murder of Magda Lovisa in 1960, and Harriet Vanger's disappearance in 1966?

On Saturday morning Burman took Blomkvist on an extensive tour of Norsjö. In the morning they called on five former employees who lived within walking distance of Burman's house. Everyone offered them coffee. All of them studied the photographs and shook their heads.

After a simple lunch at the Burman home, they got in the car for a drive. They visited four villages near Norsjö, where former employees of the carpentry shop lived. At each stop Burman was greeted with warmth, but no-one was able to help them. Blomkvist was beginning to despair.

At 4:00 in the afternoon, Burman parked his car outside a typical red Västerbotten farm near Norsjövallen, just north of Norsjö, and introduced Mikael to Henning Forsman, a retired master carpenter.

"Yes, that's Assar Brännlund's lad," Forsman said as soon as Blomkvist showed him the photographs. *Bingo.*

"Oh, so that's Assar's boy," Burman said. "Assar was a buyer."

"How can I find him?"

"The lad? Well, you'll have to dig. His name was Gunnar, and he worked at the Boliden mine. He died in a blasting accident in the mid-seventies."

Blomkvist's heart sank.

"But his wife is still alive. The one in the picture here. Her name is Mildred, and she lives in Bjursele."

"Bjursele?"

"It's about six miles down the road to Bastuträsk. She lives in the long red house on the right-hand side as you're coming into the village. It's the third house. I know the family well."

"Hi, my name is Lisbeth Salander, and I'm writing my thesis on the criminology of violence against women in the twentieth century. I'd like to visit the police district in Landskrona and read through the documents of a case from 1957. It has to do with the murder of a woman by the name of Rakel Lunde. Do you have any idea where those documents are today?"

Bjursele was like a poster for the Västerbotten country village. It consisted of about twenty houses set relatively close together in a semicircle at one end of a lake. In the centre of the village was a crossroads with an arrow pointing towards Hemmingen, 10½ miles, and another pointing towards Bastuträsk, 7 miles. Near the crossroads was a small bridge with a creek that Blomkvist assumed was the water, the *sel*. At the height of summer, it was as pretty as a postcard.

He parked in the courtyard in front of a Konsum that was no longer open, almost opposite the third house on the right-hand side. When he knocked on the door, no-one answered.

He took an hour-long walk along the road towards Hemmingen. He passed a spot where the stream became rushing rapids.

He met two cats and saw a deer, but not a single person, before he turned around. Mildred Brännlund's door was still shut.

On a post near the bridge he found a peeling flyer announcing the BTCC, something that could be deciphered as the Bjursele Tukting Car Championship 2002. "Tukting" a car was apparently a winter sport that involved smashing up a vehicle on the ice-covered lake.

He waited until 10:00 p.m. before he gave up and drove back to Norsjö, where he had a late dinner and then went to bed to read the denouement of Val McDermid's novel.

It was grisly.

At 10:00 Salander added one more name to Harriet Vanger's list. She did so with some hesitation.

She had discovered a shortcut. At quite regular intervals articles were published about unsolved murders, and in a Sunday supplement to the evening newspaper she had found an article from 1999 with the headline "Many Murderers of Women Go Free." It was a short article, but it included the names and photographs of several noteworthy murder victims. There was the Solveig case in Norrtälje, the Anita murder in Norrköping, Margareta in Helsingborg, and a number of others.

The oldest case to be recounted was from the sixties, and none of the murders matched the list that Salander had been given by Blomkvist. But one case did attract her attention.

In June 1962 a prostitute by the name of Lea Persson from Göteborg had gone to Uddevalla to visit her mother and her nine-year-old son, whom her mother was taking care of. On a Sunday evening, after a visit of several days, Lea had hugged her mother, said goodbye, and caught the train back to Göteborg. She was found two days later behind a container on an industrial site no longer in use. She had been raped, and her body had been subjected to extraordinary violence.

The Lea murder aroused a great deal of attention as a summer serial story in the newspaper, but no killer had ever been identified. There was no Lea on Harriet Vanger's list. Nor did the manner of her death fit with any of Harriet's Bible quotes.

On the other hand, there was such a bizarre coincidence that Salander's antennae instantly buzzed. About ten yards from where Lea's body was found lay a flowerpot with a pigeon inside. Someone had tied a string round the pigeon's neck and pulled it through the hole in the bottom of the pot. Then the pot was put on a little fire that had been laid between two bricks. There was no certainty that this cruelty had any connection with the Lea murder. It could have been a child playing a horrible game, but the press dubbed the murder the Pigeon Murder.

Salander was no Bible reader—she did not even own one—but that evening she went over to Högalid Church and with some difficulty she managed to borrow a Bible. She sat on a park bench outside the church and read Leviticus. When she reached Chapter 12, verse 8, her eyebrows went up. Chapter 12 dealt with the purification of women after childbirth.

> *And if she cannot afford a lamb, then she shall take two turtledoves or two young pigeons, one for a burnt offering and the other for a sin offering; and the priest shall make atonement for her, and she shall be clean.*

Lea could very well have been included in Harriet's date book as: Lea—31208.

Salander thought that no research she had ever done before had contained even a fraction of the scope of this assignment.

. . .

Mildred Brännlund, remarried and now Mildred Berggren, opened the door when Blomkvist knocked around 10:00 on Sunday morning. The woman was much older, of course, and had by now filled out a good deal, but he recognised her at once.

"Hi, my name is Mikael Blomkvist. You must be Mildred Berggren."

"That's right."

"I'm sorry for knocking on your door like this, but I've been trying to find you, and it's rather complicated to explain." He smiled at her. "I wonder if I could come in and take up a small amount of your time."

Mildred's husband and a son who was about thirty-five were home, and without much hesitation she invited Blomkvist to come and sit in their kitchen. He shook hands with each of them. He had drunk more coffee during the past twenty-four hours than at any time in his life, but by now he had learned that in Norrland it was rude to say no. When the coffee cups were on the table, Mildred sat down and asked with some curiosity how she could help him. It was obvious that he did not easily understand her Norsjö dialect, so she switched to standard Swedish.

Blomkvist took a deep breath. "This is a long and peculiar story," he said. "In September 1966 you were in Hedestad with your then husband, Gunnar Brännlund."

She looked surprised. He waited for her to nod before he laid the photograph from Järnvägsgatan on the table in front of her.

"When was this picture taken? Do you remember the occasion?"

"Oh, my goodness," Mildred Berggren said. "That was a lifetime ago."

Her present husband and son came to stand next to her to look at the picture.

"We were on our honeymoon. We had driven down to

Stockholm and Sigtuna and were on our way home and happened to stop somewhere. Was it in Hedestad, you said?"

"Yes, Hedestad. This photograph was taken at about 1:00 in the afternoon. I've been trying to find you for some time now, and it hasn't been a simple task."

"You see an old photograph of me and then actually track me down. I can't imagine how you did it."

Blomkvist put the photograph from the car park on the table.

"I was able to find you thanks to this picture, which was taken a little later in the day." He explained how, via the Norsjö Carpentry Shop, he had found Burman, who in turn had led him to Henning Forsman in Norsjövallen.

"You must have a good reason for this long search."

"I do. This girl standing close to you in this photograph is called Harriet. That day she disappeared, and she was never seen or heard of again. The general assumption is that she fell prey to a murderer. Can I show you some more photographs?"

He took out his iBook and explained the circumstances while the computer booted up. Then he played her the series of images showing how Harriet's facial expression changed.

"It was when I went through these old images that I found you, standing with a camera right behind Harriet, and you seem to be taking a picture in the direction of whatever it is she's looking at, whatever caused her to react in that way. I know that this is a really long shot, but the reason I've been looking for you is to ask you if by any miracle you still have the pictures from that day."

He was prepared for Mildred Berggren to dismiss the idea and tell him that the photographs had long since vanished. Instead she looked at him with her clear blue eyes and said, as if it were the most natural thing in the world, that of course she still had her old honeymoon pictures.

She went to another room and came back after several minutes with a box in which she had stored a quantity of pictures in various albums. It took a while to find the honeymoon ones. She had taken three photographs in Hedestad. One was blurry and showed the main street. Another showed her husband at the time. The third showed the clowns in the parade.

Blomkvist eagerly leaned forward. He could see a figure on the other side of the street behind a clown. But the photograph told him absolutely nothing.

CHAPTER 20

Tuesday, July 1–
Wednesday, July 2

The first thing Blomkvist did the morning he returned to Hedestad was to go to Frode's house to ask about Vanger's condition. He learned to his delight that the old man had improved quite a bit during the past week. He was weak still, and fragile, but now he could sit up in bed. His condition was no longer regarded as critical.

"Thank God," he said. "I realised that I actually like him."

Frode said: "I know that. And Henrik likes you too. How was Norrland?"

"Successful yet unsatisfying. I'll explain a little later. Right now I have a question."

"Go ahead."

"What realistically will happen to your interest in *Millennium* if Henrik dies?"

"Nothing at all. Martin will take his place on the board."

"Is there any risk, hypothetically speaking, that Martin might create problems for *Millennium* if I don't put a stop to the investigation of Harriet's disappearance?"

Frode gave him a sharp look.

"What's happened?"

"Nothing, actually." Mikael told him about the conversation he had had with Martin Vanger on Midsummer Eve. "When I was in Norsjö Erika told me that Martin had called her and said that he thought I was very much needed back at the office."

"I understand. My guess is that Cecilia was after him. But I don't think that Martin would put pressure on you like that on his own. He's much too savvy. And remember, I'm also on the board of the little subsidiary we formed when we bought into *Millennium*."

"But what if a ticklish situation came up—how would you act then?"

"Contracts exist to be honoured. I work for Henrik. Henrik and I have been friends for forty-five years, and we are in complete agreement in such matters. If Henrik should die it is in point of fact I—not Martin—who would inherit Henrik's share in the subsidiary. We have a contract in which we have undertaken to back *Millennium* for three years. Should Martin wish to start any mischief—which I don't believe he will—then theoretically he could put the brakes on a small number of new advertisers."

"The lifeblood of *Millennium*'s existence."

"Yes, but look at it this way—worrying about such trivia is a waste of time. Martin is presently fighting for his industrial survival and working fourteen hours a day. He doesn't have time for anything else."

"May I ask—I know it's none of my business—what is the general condition of the corporation?"

Frode looked grave.

"We have problems."

"Yes, even a common financial reporter like myself can see that. I mean, how serious is it?"

"Off the record?"

"Between us."

"We've lost two large orders in the electronics industry in the past few weeks and are about to be ejected from the Russian market. In September we're going to have to lay off 1,600 employees in Örebro and Trollhättan. Not much of a reward to give to people who've worked for the company for many years. Each time we shut down a factory, confidence in the company is further undermined."

"Martin is under pressure."

"He's pulling the load of an ox and walking on eggshells."

Blomkvist went back to his cottage and called Berger. She was not at the office, so he spoke to Malm.

"Here's the deal: Erika called when I was in Norsjö. Martin Vanger has been after her and has, how shall I put it, encouraged her to propose that I start to take on editorial responsibility."

"I think you should too," Malm said.

"I know that. But the thing is, I have a contract with Henrik Vanger that I can't break, and Martin is acting on behalf of someone up here who wants me to stop what I am doing and leave town. So his proposal amounts to an attempt to get rid of me."

"I see."

"Say hi to Erika and tell her I'll come back to Stockholm when I'm finished here. Not before."

"I understand. You're stark raving mad, of course, but I'll give her the message."

"Christer. Something is going on up here, and I have no intention of backing out."

Blomkvist knocked on Martin Vanger's door. Eva Hassel opened it and greeted him warmly.

"Hi. Is Martin home?"

As if in reply to the question, Martin Vanger came walking out with a briefcase in his hand. He kissed Eva on the cheek and said hello to Mikael.

"I'm on my way to the office. Do you want to talk to me?"

"We can do it later if you're in a hurry."

"Let's hear it."

"I won't be going back to *Millennium*'s editorial board before I'm finished with the assignment that Henrik gave me. I'm informing you of this now so that you won't count on me being on the board before New Year's."

Martin Vanger teetered back and forth for a bit.

"I see. You think I want to get rid of you." He paused. "Mikael, we'll have to talk about this later. I don't really have time to devote to my hobby on *Millennium*'s board, and I wish I'd never agreed to Henrik's proposal. But believe me—I'm going to do my best to make sure that *Millennium* survives."

"I've never had any doubt about that," Blomkvist said.

"If we make an appointment for sometime next week we can go over the finances and I can give you my views on the matter. But my basic attitude is that *Millennium* cannot actually afford to have one of its key people sitting up here on Hedeby Island twiddling his thumbs. I like the magazine and I think we can make it stronger together, but you're crucial to that task. I've wound up in a conflict of loyalties here. Either I follow Henrik's wishes or carry out my job on *Millennium*'s board."

. . .

Blomkvist changed into his tracksuit and went for a run out to the Fortress and down to Gottfried's cabin before he headed home at a slower pace along the water. Frode was sitting at the garden table. He waited patiently as Mikael drank a bottle of water and towelled the sweat from his face.

"That doesn't look so healthy in this heat."

"Oh, come on," Blomkvist said.

"I was wrong. Cecilia isn't the main person who's after Martin. It's Isabella. She's busy mobilising the Vanger clan to tar and feather you and possibly burn you at the stake too. She's being backed up by Birger."

"Isabella?"

"She's a malicious, petty woman who doesn't like other people in general. Right now it seems that she detests you in particular. She's spreading stories that you're a swindler who duped Henrik into hiring you, and that you got him so worked up that he had a heart attack."

"I hope no-one believes that?"

"There's always someone willing to believe malicious rumours."

"I'm trying to work out what happened to her daughter—and she hates me. If Harriet were my daughter, I would have reacted a bit differently."

At 2:00 in the afternoon, his mobile rang.

"Hello, my name is Conny Torsson and I work at the *Hedestad Courier*. Do you have time to answer a few questions? We got a tip that you're living here in Hedeby."

"Well, Herr Torsson, your tip machine is a little slow. I've been living here since the first of the year."

"I didn't know that. What are you doing in Hedestad?"

"Writing. And taking a sort of sabbatical."

"What are you working on?"

"You'll find out when I publish it."

"You were just released from prison . . ."

"Yes?"

"Do you have a view on journalists who falsify material?"

"Journalists who falsify material are idiots."

"So in your opinion you're an idiot?"

"Why should I think that? I've never falsified material."

"But you were convicted of libel."

"So?"

Torsson hesitated long enough that Blomkvist had to give him a push.

"I was convicted of libel, not of falsifying material."

"But you published the material."

"If you're calling to discuss the judgement against me, I have no comment."

"I'd like to come out and do an interview with you."

"I have nothing to say to you on this topic."

"So you don't want to discuss the trial?"

"That's correct," he said, and hung up. He sat thinking for a long time before he went back to his computer.

Salander followed the instructions she had received and drove her Kawasaki across the bridge to Hedeby Island. She stopped at the first little house on the left. She was really out in the sticks. But as long as her employer was paying, she did not mind if she went to the North Pole. Besides, it was great to give her bike its head on a long ride up the E4. She put the bike on its stand and loosened the strap that held her overnight duffel bag in place.

Blomkvist opened the door and waved to her. He came out and inspected her motorcycle with obvious astonishment.

He whistled. "You're riding a motorbike!"

Salander said nothing, but she watched him intently as he touched the handlebars and tried the accelerator. She did not like anyone touching her stuff. Then she saw his childlike, boyish smile, which she took for a redeeming feature. Most people who were into motorcycles usually laughed at her lightweight bike.

"I had a motorbike when I was nineteen," he said, turning to her. "Thanks for coming up. Come in and let's get you settled."

He had borrowed a camp bed from the Nilssons. Salander took a tour around the cabin, looking suspicious, but she seemed to relax when she could find no immediate signs of any insidious trap. He showed her where the bathroom was.

"In case you want to take a shower and freshen up."

"I have to change. I am not going to wander around in my leathers."

"OK, while you change I'll make dinner."

He sautéed lamb chops in red wine sauce and set the table outdoors in the afternoon sun while Salander showered and changed. She came out barefoot wearing a black camisole and a short, worn denim skirt. The food smelled good, and she put away two stout helpings. Fascinated, Blomkvist sneaked a look at the tattoos on her back.

"Five plus three," Salander said. "Five cases from your Harriet's list and three cases that I think should have been on the list."

"Tell me."

"I've only been on this for eleven days, and I haven't had a chance to dig up all the reports. In some cases the police reports had been put in the national archive, and in others they're still stored in the local police district. I made three day trips to different police districts, but I didn't have time to get to all of them. The five are identified."

Salander put a solid heap of paper on the kitchen table, around 500 pages. She quickly sorted the material into different stacks.

"Let's take them in chronological order." She handed Blomkvist a list.

1949—REBECKA JACOBSSON, *Hedestad* (30112)
1954—MARI HOLMBERG, *Kalmar* (32018)
1957—RAKEL LUNDE, *Landskrona* (32027)
1960—(MAGDA) LOVISA SJÖBERG, *Karlstad* (32016)
1960—LIV GUSTAVSSON, *Stockholm* (32016)
1962—LEA PERSSON, *Uddevalla* (31208)
1964—SARA WITT, *Ronneby* (32109)
1966—LENA ANDERSSON, *Uppsala* (30112)

"The first case in this series is Rebecka Jacobsson, 1949, the details of which you already know. The next case I found was Mari Holmberg, a thirty-two-year-old prostitute in Kalmar who was murdered in her apartment in October 1954. It's not clear exactly when she was killed, since her body wasn't found right away, probably nine or ten days later."

"And how do you connect her to Harriet's list?"

"She was tied up and badly abused, but the cause of death was strangulation. She had a sanitary towel down her throat."

Blomkvist sat in silence for a moment before he looked up the verse that was Leviticus 20:18.

"If a man lies with a woman having her sickness, and uncovers her nakedness, he has made naked her fountain, and she has uncovered the fountain of her blood; both of them shall be cut off from among their people."

Salander nodded.

"Harriet Vanger made the same connection. OK. Next?"

"May 1957, Rakel Lunde, forty-five. She worked as a cleaning woman and was a bit of a happy eccentric in the village. She was a fortune-teller and her hobby was doing Tarot readings, palms, et cetera. She lived outside Landskrona in a house a long way from anywhere, and she was murdered there some time early in the morning. She was found naked and tied to a laundry-drying frame in her back garden, with her mouth taped shut. Cause of death was a heavy rock being repeatedly thrown at her. She had countless contusions and fractures."

"Jesus Christ. Lisbeth, this is fucking disgusting."

"It gets worse. The initials R.L. are correct—you found the Bible quote?"

"Overly explicit. *A man or a woman who is a medium or a wizard shall be put to death; they shall be stoned with stones, their blood shall be upon them.*"

"Then there's Sjöberg in Ranmo outside Karlstad. She's the one Harriet listed as Magda. Her full name was Magda Lovisa, but people called her Lovisa."

Blomkvist listened while Salander recounted the bizarre details of the Karlstad murder. When she lit a cigarette he pointed at the pack, and she pushed it over to him.

"So the killer attacked the animal too?"

"The Leviticus verse says that if a woman has sex with an animal, both must be killed."

"The likelihood of this woman having sex with a cow must be . . . well, non-existent."

"The verse can be read literally. It's enough that she 'approaches' the animal, which a farmer's wife would undeniably do every day."

"Understood."

"The next case on Harriet's list is Sara. I've identified her as

Sara Witt, thirty-seven, living in Ronneby. She was murdered in January 1964, found tied to her bed, subjected to aggravated sexual assault, but the cause of death was asphyxiation; she was strangled. The killer also started a fire, with the probable intention of burning the whole house down to the ground, but part of the fire went out by itself, and the rest was taken care of by the fire service, who were there in a very short time."

"And the connection?"

"Listen to this. Sara Witt was both the daughter of a pastor and married to a pastor. Her husband was away that weekend."

"*And the daughter of any priest, if she profanes herself by playing the harlot, profanes her father; she shall be burned with fire.* OK. That fits on the list. You said you'd found more cases."

"I've found three other women who were murdered under such similarly strange circumstances and they could have been on Harriet's list. The first is a young woman named Liv Gustavsson. She was twenty-two and lived in Farsta. She was a horse-loving girl—she rode in competitions and was quite a promising talent. She also owned a small pet shop with her sister. She was found in the shop. She had worked late on the bookkeeping and was there alone. She must have let the killer in voluntarily. She was raped and strangled to death."

"That doesn't sound quite like Harriet's list, does it?"

"Not exactly, if it weren't for one thing. The killer concluded his barbarities by shoving a parakeet up her vagina and then let all the animals out into the shop. Cats, turtles, white mice, rabbits, birds. Even the fish in the aquarium. So it was quite an appalling scene her sister encountered in the morning."

Blomkvist made a note.

"She was murdered in August 1960, four months after the murder of the farmer's wife Magda Lovisa in Karlstad. In both instances they were women who worked professionally with animals, and in both cases there was an animal sacrifice. The cow in Karlstad may have survived—but I can imagine it would be difficult to stab a cow to death with a knife. A parakeet is more straightforward. And besides, there was an additional animal sacrifice."

"What?"

Salander told the story of the "pigeon murder" of Lea Persson. Blomkvist sat for so long in silence and in thought that even Salander grew impatient.

"I'll buy your theory," he said at last. "There's one case left."

"A case that I discovered by chance. I don't know how many I may have missed."

"Tell me about it."

"February 1966 in Uppsala. The victim was a seventeen-year-old gymnast called Lena Andersson. She disappeared after a class party and was found three days later in a ditch on the Uppsala plain, quite a way out of town. She had been murdered somewhere else and her body dumped there. This murder got a lot of attention in the media, but the true circumstances surrounding her death were never reported. The girl had been grotesquely tortured. I read the pathologist's report. She was tortured with fire. Her hands and breasts were atrociously burned, and she had been burned repeatedly at various spots all over her body. They found paraffin stains on her, which showed that candles had been used, but her hands were so charred that they must have been held over a more powerful fire. Finally, the killer sawed off her head and tossed it next to the body."

Blomkvist blanched. "Good Lord," he said.

"I can't find any Bible quote that fits, but there are several passages that deal with a fire offering and a sin offering, and in some places it's recommended that the sacrificial animal—most often a bull—be cut up in such a way that *the head is severed from the fat*. Fire also reminds me of the first murder, of Rebecka here in Hedestad."

. . .

Towards evening when the mosquitoes began to swarm they cleared off the garden table and moved to the kitchen to go on with their talk.

"The fact that you didn't find an exact Bible quotation doesn't mean much. It's not a matter of quotations. This is a grotesque parody of what is written in the Bible—it's more like associations to quotations pulled out of context."

"I agree. It isn't even logical. Take for example the quote that both have to be cut off from their people if someone has sex with a girl who's having her period. If that's interpreted literally, the killer should have committed suicide."

"So where does all this lead?" Blomkvist wondered aloud.

"Your Harriet either had quite a strange hobby or else she must have known that there was a connection between the murders."

"Between 1949 and 1966, and maybe before and after as well. The idea that an insanely sick sadistic serial killer was slaughtering women for at least seventeen years without anyone seeing a connection sounds utterly unbelievable to me."

Salander pushed back her chair and poured more coffee from the pot on the stove. She lit a cigarette. Mikael cursed himself and stole another from her.

"No, it's not so unbelievable," she said, holding up one finger. "We have several dozen unsolved murders of women in Sweden during the twentieth century. That professor of criminology, Persson, said once on TV that serial killers are very rare in Sweden, but that probably we have had some that were never caught."

She held up another finger.

"These murders were committed over a very long period of time and all over the country. Two occurred close together in 1960, but the circumstances were quite different—a farmer's wife in Karlstad and a twenty-two-year-old in Stockholm."

Three fingers.

"There is no immediately apparent pattern. The murders were carried out at different places and there is no real signature, but there are certain things that do recur. Animals. Fire. Aggravated sexual assault. And, as you pointed out, a parody of Biblical quotations. But it seems that not one of the investigating detectives interpreted any of the murders in terms of the Bible."

Blomkvist was watching her. With her slender body, her black camisole, the tattoos, and the rings piercing her face, Salander looked out of place, to say the least, in a guest cottage in Hedeby. When he tried to be sociable over dinner, she was taciturn to the point of rudeness. But when she was working she sounded like a professional to her fingertips. Her apartment in Stockholm might look as if a bomb had gone off in it, but mentally Salander was extremely well organised.

"It's hard to see the connection between a prostitute in Uddevalla who's killed in an industrial yard and a pastor's wife who is strangled in Ronneby and has her house set on fire. If you don't have the key that Harriet gave us, that is."

"Which leads to the next question," Salander said.

"How on earth did Harriet get mixed up in all this? A sixteen-year-old girl who lived in a really sheltered environment."

"There's only one answer," Salander said. "There must be some connection to the Vanger family."

By 11:00 that night they had gone over the series of murders and discussed the conceivable connections and the tiny details of similarity and difference so often that Blomkvist's head was spinning. He rubbed his eyes and stretched and asked Salander if she felt like a walk. Her expression suggested that she thought such practices were a waste of time, but she agreed. Blomkvist advised her to change into long trousers because of the mosquitoes.

They strolled past the small-boat harbour and then under the bridge and out towards Martin Vanger's point. Blomkvist pointed out the various houses and told her about the people who lived in them. He had some difficulty when they came to Cecilia Vanger's house. Salander gave him a curious look.

They passed Martin Vanger's motor yacht and reached the point, and there they sat on a rock and shared a cigarette.

"There's one more connection," Blomkvist said suddenly. "Maybe you've already thought of it."

"What?"

"Their names."

Salander thought for a moment and shook her head.

"They're all Biblical names."

"Not true," she said. "Where is there a Liv or Lena in the Bible?"

"They are there. Liv means to live, in other words Eva. And come on—what's Lena short for?"

Salander grimaced in annoyance. He had been quicker than she was. She did not like that.

"Magdalena," she said.

"The whore, the first woman, the Virgin Mary . . . they're all there in this group. This is so freaky it'd make a psychologist's head spin. But there's something else I thought of with regard to the names."

Salander waited patiently.

"They're obviously all traditional Jewish names. The Vanger family has had more than its share of fanatical anti-Semites, Nazis, and conspiracy theorists. The only time I met Harald Vanger he was standing in the road snarling that his own daughter was a whore. He certainly has problems with women."

· · ·

When they got back to the cabin they made a midnight snack and heated up the coffee. Mikael took a look at the almost 500 pages that Dragan Armansky's favourite researcher had produced for him.

"You've done a fantastic job of digging up these facts in such a short time," he said. "Thanks. And thanks also for being nice enough to come up here and report on it."

"What happens now?" Salander wanted to know.

"I'm going to talk to Dirch Frode tomorrow and arrange for your fee to be paid."

"That wasn't what I meant."

Blomkvist looked at her.

"Well . . . I reckon the job I hired you for is done," he said.

"I'm not done with this."

Blomkvist leaned back against the kitchen wall and met her gaze. He couldn't read anything at all in her eyes. For half a year he had been working alone on Harriet's disappearance, and here was another person—an experienced researcher—who grasped the implications. He made the decision on impulse.

"I know. This story has got under my skin too. I'll talk to Frode. We'll hire you for a week or two more as . . . a research assistant. I don't know if he'll want to pay the same rate he pays to Armansky, but we should be able to arrange a basic living wage for you."

Salander suddenly gave him a smile. She had no wish to be shut out and would have gladly done the job for free.

"I'm falling asleep," she said, and without further ado she went to her room and closed the door.

Two minutes later she opened the door and put out her head.

"I think you're wrong. It's not an insane serial killer who read his Bible wrong. It's just a common or garden bastard who hates women."

CHAPTER 21

Thursday, July 3–Thursday, July 10

Salander was up before Blomkvist, around 6:00. She put on some water for coffee and went to take a shower. When Blomkvist woke at 7:30, she was reading his summary of the Harriet Vanger case on his iBook. He came out to the kitchen with a towel round his waist, rubbing the sleep out of his eyes.

"There's coffee on the stove," she said.

He looked over her shoulder.

"That document was password protected, dammit," he said.

She turned and peered up at him.

"It takes thirty seconds to download a programme from the Net that can crack Word's encryption protection."

"We need to have a talk on the subject of what's yours and what's mine," he said, and went to take a shower.

When he came back, Salander had turned off his computer and put it back in its place in his office. She had booted up her own PowerBook. Blomkvist felt sure that she had already transferred the contents of his computer to her own.

Salander was an information junkie with a delinquent child's take on morals and ethics.

He had just sat down to breakfast when there was a knock at the front door. Martin Vanger looked so solemn that for a second Blomkvist thought he had come to bring the news of his uncle's death.

"No, Henrik's condition is the same as yesterday. I'm here for a quite different reason. Could I come in for a moment?"

Blomkvist let him in, introducing him to "my research assistant" Lisbeth Salander. She gave the captain of industry barely a glance and a quick nod before she went back to her computer. Martin Vanger greeted her automatically but looked so distracted that he hardly seemed to notice her. Blomkvist poured him a cup of coffee and invited him to have a seat.

"What's this all about?"

"You don't subscribe to the *Hedestad Courier*?"

"No. But sometimes I see it at Susanne's Bridge Café."

"Then you haven't read this morning's paper."

"You make it sound as if I ought to."

Martin Vanger put the day's paper on the table in front of him. He had been given two columns on the front page, continued on page four. "Convicted Libel Journalist Hiding Here." A photograph taken with a telephoto lens from the church hill on the other side of the bridge showed Blomkvist coming out of the cottage.

The reporter, Torsson, had cobbled together a scurrilous piece. He recapitulated the Wennerström affair and explained that Blomkvist had left *Millennium* in disgrace and that he had recently served a prison term. The article ended with the usual line that Blomkvist had declined to comment to the *Hedestad Courier*. Every self-respecting resident of Hedestad was put on notice that an Olympic-class shit from Stockholm was skulking around the area. None of the claims in the article was libellous, but they were slanted to present Blomkvist in an unflattering light; the layout and type style was of the kind that such newspapers used to discuss political terrorists. *Millennium* was described as a magazine with low credibility "bent on agitation," and Blomkvist's book on financial journalism was presented as a collection of "controversial claims" about other more respected journalists.

"Mikael . . . I don't have words to express what I felt when I read this article. It's repulsive."

"It's a put-up job," Blomkvist said calmly.

"I hope you understand that I didn't have the slightest thing to do with this. I choked on my morning coffee when I read it."

"Then who did?"

"I made some calls. This Torsson is a summer work experience kid. He did the piece on orders from Birger."

"I thought Birger had no say in the newsroom. After all, he *is* a councillor and political figure."

"Technically he has no influence. But the editor in chief of the *Courier* is Gunnar Karlman, Ingrid's son, who's part of the Johan Vanger branch of the family. Birger and Gunnar have been close for many years."

"I see."

"Torsson will be fired forthwith."

"How old is he?"

"To tell you the truth, I don't know. I've never met him."

"Don't fire him. When he called me he sounded like a very young and inexperienced reporter."

"This can't be allowed to pass without consequences."

"If you want my opinion, the situation seems a bit absurd, when the editor in chief of a publication owned by the Vanger family goes on the attack against another publication in which Henrik Vanger is a part owner and on whose board you sit. Your editor, Karlman, is attacking you and Henrik."

"I see what you mean, and I ought to lay the blame where it belongs. Karlman is a part owner in the corporation and has always taken potshots at me, but this seems more like Birger's revenge because you had a run-in with him at the hospital. You're a thorn in his side."

"I believe it. That's why I think Torsson is the last person to blame. It takes a lot for an intern to say no when the boss instructs him to write something in a certain way."

"I could demand that you be given an apology tomorrow."

"Better not. It would just turn into a long, drawn-out squabble that would make the situation worse."

"So you don't think I should do anything?"

"It wouldn't be any use. Karlman would kick up a fuss and in the worst case you'd be painted as a villain who, in his capacity as owner, is trying to stamp on the freedom of expression."

"Pardon me, Mikael, but I don't agree with you. As a matter of fact, I also have the right to express my opinion. My view is that this article stinks—and I intend to make my own point of view clear. However reluctantly, I'm Henrik's replacement on *Millennium*'s board, and in that role I am not going to let an offensive article like this one pass unchallenged."

"Fair enough."

"So I'm going to demand the right to respond. And if I make Karlman look like an idiot, he has only himself to blame."

"You must do what you believe is right."

"For me, it's also important that you absolutely understand that I have nothing whatsoever to do with this vitriolic attack."

"I believe you," Blomkvist said.

"Besides—I didn't really want to bring this up now, but this just serves to illustrate what we've already discussed. It's important to re-install you on *Millennium*'s editorial board so that we can show a united front to the world. As long as you're away, the gossip will continue. I believe in *Millennium,* and I'm convinced that we can win this fight together."

"I see your point, but now it's my turn to disagree with you. I can't break my contract with Henrik, and the fact is that I wouldn't want to break it. You see, I really like him. And this thing with Harriet . . ."

"Yes?"

"I know it's a running sore for you and I realise that Henrik has been obsessed with it for many years."

"Just between the two of us—I do love Henrik and he is my mentor—but when it comes to Harriet, he's almost off his rocker."

"When I started this job I couldn't help thinking that it was a waste of time. But I think we're on the verge of a breakthrough and that it might now be possible to know what really happened."

Blomkvist read doubt in Martin Vanger's eyes. At last he made a decision.

"OK, in that case the best thing we can do is to solve the mystery of Harriet as quickly as possible. I'll give you all the support I can so that you finish the work to your satisfaction—and, of course, Henrik's—and then return to *Millennium.*"

"Good. So I won't have to fight with you too."

"No, you won't. You can ask for my help whenever you run into a problem. I'll make damn sure that Birger won't put any sort of obstacles in your way. And I'll try to talk to Cecilia, to calm her down."

"Thank you. I need to ask her some questions, and she's been resisting my attempts at conversation for a month now."

Martin Vanger laughed. "Perhaps you have other issues to iron out. But I won't get involved in that."

They shook hands.

. . .

Salander had listened to the conversation. When Martin Vanger left she reached for the *Hedestad Courier* and scanned the article. She put the paper down without making any comment.

Blomkvist sat in silence, thinking. Gunnar Karlman was born in 1948 and would have been eighteen in 1966. He was one of the people on the island when Harriet disappeared.

After breakfast he asked his research assistant to read through the police report. He gave her all the photographs of the accident, as well as the long summary of Vanger's own investigations.

Blomkvist then drove to Frode's house and asked him kindly to draw up an agreement for Salander as a research assistant for the next month.

By the time he returned to the cottage, Salander had decamped to the garden and was immersed in the police report. Blomkvist went in to heat up the coffee. He watched her through the kitchen window. She seemed to be skimming, spending no more than ten or fifteen seconds on each page. She turned the pages mechanically, and Blomkvist was amazed at her lack of concentration; it made no sense, since her own report was so meticulous. He took two cups of coffee and joined her at the garden table.

"Your notes were done before you knew we were looking for a serial killer."

"That's true. I simply wrote down questions I wanted to ask Henrik, and some other things. It was quite unstructured. Up until now I've really been struggling in the dark, trying to write a story—a chapter in the autobiography of Henrik Vanger."

"And now?"

"In the past all the investigations focused on Hedeby Island. Now I'm sure that the story, the sequence of events that ended in her disappearance, started in Hedestad. That shifts the perspective."

Salander said: "It was amazing what you discovered with the pictures."

Blomkvist was surprised. Salander did not seem the type to throw compliments around, and he felt flattered. On the other hand—from a purely journalistic point of view—it *was* quite an achievement.

"It's your turn to fill in the details. How did it go with that picture you were chasing up in Norsjö?"

"You mean you didn't check the images in my computer?"

"There wasn't time. I needed to read the résumés, your situation reports to yourself."

Blomkvist started his iBook and clicked on the photograph folder.

"It's fascinating. The visit to Norsjö was a sort of progress, but it was also a disappointment. I found the picture, but it doesn't tell us much.

"That woman, Mildred Berggren, had saved all her holiday pictures in albums. The picture I was looking for was one of them. It was taken on cheap colour film and after thirty-seven years the print was incredibly faded—with a strong yellow tinge. But, would you believe, she still had the negative in a shoebox. She let me borrow all the negatives from Hedestad and I've scanned them in. This is what Harriet saw."

He clicked on an image which now had the filename HAR RIET/bd-19.eps.

Salander immediately understood his dismay. She saw an unfocused image that showed clowns in the foreground of the Children's Day parade. In the background could be seen the corner of Sundström's Haberdashery. About ten people were standing on the pavement in front of Sundström's.

"I think this is the person she saw. Partly because I tried to triangulate what she was looking at, judging by the angle that her face was turned—I made a drawing of the crossroads there—and partly because this is the only person who seems to be looking straight into the camera. Meaning that—perhaps—he was staring at Harriet."

What Salander saw was a blurry figure standing a little bit behind the spectators, almost in the side street. He had on a dark padded jacket with a red patch on the shoulders and dark trousers, possibly jeans. Blomkvist zoomed in so that the figure from the waist up filled the screen. The photograph became instantly fuzzier still.

"It's a man. He's about five-foot eleven, normal build. He has dark-blond, semi-long hair and is clean-shaven. But it's impossible to make out his facial features or even estimate his age. He could be anywhere between his teens and middle age.

"You could manipulate the image . . ."

"I *have* manipulated the image, dammit. I even sent a copy to the image processing wizard at *Millennium*." Blomkvist clicked up a new shot. "This is the absolute best I can get out of it. The camera is simply too lousy and the distance too far."

"Have you shown the picture to anyone? Someone might recognise the man's bearing or . . ."

"I showed it to Frode. He has no idea who the man is."

"Herr Frode probably isn't the most observant person in Hedestad."

"No, but I'm working for him and Henrik Vanger. I want to show the picture to Henrik before I cast the net wider."

"Perhaps he's nothing more than a spectator."

"That's possible. But he managed to trigger a strange response from Harriet."

During the next several days Blomkvist and Salander worked on the Harriet case virtually every waking moment. Salander went on reading the police report, rattling off one question after another. There could only be one truth, and each vague answer or uncertainty led to more intense interrogation. They spent one whole day examining timetables for the cast of characters at the scene of the accident on the bridge.

Salander became more and more of an enigma to him. Despite the fact that she only skimmed the documents in the report, she always seemed to settle on the most obscure and contradictory details.

They took a break in the afternoons, when the heat made it unbearable out in the garden. They would swim in the channel or walk up to the terrace at Susanne's Bridge Café. Susanne now treated Blomkvist with an undisguised coolness. He realised that Salander looked barely legal and she was obviously living at his cottage, and that—in Susanne's eyes—made him a dirty old middle-aged man. It was not pleasant.

Blomkvist went out every evening for a run. Salander made no comment when he returned out of breath to the cottage. Running was obviously not her thing.

"I'm over forty," he said. "I have to exercise to keep from getting too fat around the middle."

"I see."

"Don't you ever exercise?"

"I box once in a while."

"You box?"

"Yeah, you know, with gloves."

"What weight do you box in?" he said, when he emerged from the shower.

"None at all. I spar a little now and then against the guys in a club in Söder."

Why is that no surprise? he thought. But at least she had told him something about herself. He knew no basic facts about her. How did she come to be working for Armansky? What sort of education did she have? What did her parents do? As soon as

Blomkvist tried to ask about her life she shut up like a clam, answered in single syllables, or ignored him.

One afternoon Salander suddenly put down a binder, frowning. "What do you know about Otto Falk? The pastor."

"Not much. I met the present incumbent a few times earlier in the year, and she told me that Falk lives in some geriatric home in Hedestad. Alzheimer's."

"Where did he come from?"

"From Hedestad. He studied in Uppsala."

"He was unmarried. And Harriet hung out with him."

"Why do you ask?"

"I'm just saying that Morell went pretty easy on him in the interview."

"In the sixties pastors enjoyed a considerably different status in society. It was natural for him to live out here on the island, close to the power brokers, so to speak."

"I wonder how carefully the police searched the parsonage. In the photographs it looks like it was a big wooden house, and there must have been plenty of places to hide a body for a while."

"That's true, but there's nothing in the material to indicate that he would have any connection to the serial murders or to Harriet's disappearance."

"Actually, there is," Salander said, with a wry smile. "First of all he was a pastor, and pastors more than anyone else have a special relationship to the Bible. Second, he was the last person known to have seen and talked with Harriet."

"But he went down to the scene of the accident and stayed there for several hours. He's in lots of the pictures, especially during the time when Harriet must have vanished."

"All right, I can't crack his alibi. But I was actually thinking about something else. This story is about a sadistic killer of women."

"So?"

"I was . . . I had a little time to myself this spring and read quite a bit about sadists in a rather different context. One of the things I read was an FBI manual. It claimed that a striking portion of convicted serial killers came from dysfunctional homes and tortured animals in their childhood. Some of the convicted American serial killers were also arrested for arson. Tortured animals and arson crop up in several of Harriet's murder cases, but what I was really thinking about was the fact that the parsonage burned down in the late seventies."

"It's a long shot," Blomkvist said.

Lisbeth nodded. "Agreed. But I find nothing in the police report about the cause of the fire, and it would be very interesting to know if there were other unexplained fires hereabouts in the sixties. It would also be worth checking to see if there were any cases of animal abuse or mutilation in the area back then."

When Salander went to bed on her seventh night in Hedeby, she was mildly irritated with Blomkvist. For almost a week she had spent practically every waking minute with him. Normally seven minutes of another person's company was enough to give her a headache, so she set things up to live as a recluse. She was perfectly content as long as people left her in peace. Unfortunately society was not very smart or understanding; she had to protect herself from social authorities, child welfare authorities, guardianship authorities, tax authorities, police, curators, psychologists, psychiatrists, teachers, and bouncers, who (apart from the guys watching the door at Kvarnen, who by this time knew who she was) would never let her into the bar even though she was twenty-five. There was a whole army of people who seemed not to have anything better to do than to try to disrupt her life, and, if they were given the opportunity, to correct the way she had chosen to live it.

It did no good to cry, she had learned that early on. She had also learned that every time she tried to make someone aware of something in her life, the situation just got worse. Consequently it was up to her to solve her problems by herself, using whatever methods she deemed necessary. Something that Advokat Bjurman had found out the hard way.

Blomkvist had the same tiresome habit as everyone else, poking around in her life and asking questions. On the other hand, he did not react at all like most other men she had met.

When she ignored his questions he simply shrugged and left her in peace. Astounding.

Her immediate move, when she got hold of his iBook that first morning, had naturally been to transfer all the information to her own computer. That way it was OK if he dumped her from the case; she would still have access to the material.

She had expected a furious outburst when he appeared for his breakfast. Instead he had looked almost resigned, muttered something sarcastic, and gone off to the shower. Then he began discussing what she had read. A strange guy. She might even be deluded into thinking that he trusted her.

That he knew about her propensities as a hacker was serious. Salander was aware that the legal description of the kind of hacking she did, both professionally and as a hobby, was "unlawful data trespassing" and could earn her two years in prison. She did not want to be locked up. In her case a prison sentence would mean that her computers would be taken from her, and with them the only occupation that she was really good at. She had never told Armansky how she gathered the information they were paying her to find.

With the exception of Plague and a few people on the Net who, like her, devoted themselves to hacking on a professional level—and most of them knew her only as "Wasp" and did not know who she was or where she lived—Kalle Blomkvist was the only one who had stumbled on to her secret. He had come to her because she made a blunder that not even a twelve-year-old would commit, which only proved that her brain was being eaten up by worms and that she deserved to be flogged. But instead of going crazy with rage he had hired her.

Consequently she was mildly irritated with him.

When they had a snack just before she went to bed, he had suddenly asked her if she was a good hacker.

To her own surprise she replied, "I'm probably the best in Sweden. There may be two or three others at about my level."

She did not doubt the accuracy of her reply. Plague had once been better than she was, but she had passed him long ago.

On the other hand, it felt funny to say the words. She had never done it before. She had never had an outsider to have this sort of conversation with, and she enjoyed the fact that he seemed impressed by her talents. Then he had ruined the feeling by asking another question: how had she taught herself hacking?

What could she say? *I've always been able to do it.* Instead she went to bed without saying goodnight.

Irritating her yet further, he did not react when she left so abruptly. She lay listening to him moving about in the kitchen, clearing the table and washing the dishes. He had always stayed up later than she did, but now he was obviously on his way to bed too. She heard him in the bathroom, and then he went into his bedroom and shut the door. After a while she heard the bed creak when he got into it, not a yard away from her own but on the other side of the wall.

She had been sharing a house with him for a week, and he

had not once flirted with her. He had worked with her, asked her opinion, slapped her on the knuckles figuratively speaking when she was on the wrong track, and acknowledged that she was right when she corrected him. Dammit, he had treated her like a human being.

She got out of bed and stood by the window, restlessly peering into the dark. The hardest thing for her was to show herself naked to another person for the first time. She was convinced that her skinny body was repulsive. Her breasts were pathetic. She had no hips to speak of. She did not have much to offer. Apart from that she was a quite normal woman, with the same desires and sex drive as every other woman. She stood there for the next twenty minutes before she made up her mind.

Blomkvist was reading a novel by Sara Paretsky when he heard the door handle turn and looked up to see Salander. She had a sheet wrapped round her body and stood in the doorway for a moment.

"You OK?" he said.

She shook her head.

"What is it?"

She went over to his bed, took the book, and put it on the bedside table. Then she bent down and kissed him on the mouth. She quickly got into his bed and sat looking at him, searching him. She put her hand on the sheet over his stomach. When he did not protest she leaned over and bit him on the nipple.

Blomkvist was flabbergasted. He took her shoulders and pushed her away a little so that he could see her face.

"Lisbeth . . . I don't know if this is such a good idea. We have to work together."

"I want to have sex with you. And I won't have any problem

working with you, but I will have a hell of a problem with you if you kick me out."

"But we hardly know each other."

She laughed, an abrupt laugh that sounded almost like a cough.

"You've never let anything like that stand in your way before. In fact, as I didn't say in my background report, you're one of these guys who can't keep his hands off women. So what's wrong? Aren't I sexy enough for you?"

Blomkvist shook his head and tried to think of something clever to say. When he couldn't she pulled the sheet off him and sat astride him.

"I don't have any condoms," he said.

"Screw it."

When he woke up, he heard her in the kitchen. It was not yet 7:00. He may only have slept for two hours, and he stayed in bed, dozing.

This woman baffled him. At absolutely no point had she even with a glance indicated that she was the least bit interested in him.

"Good morning," she said from the doorway. She even had the hint of a smile.

"Hi."

"We are out of milk. I'll go to the petrol station. They open at seven." And she was gone.

He heard her go out of the front door. He shut his eyes. Then he heard the front door open again and seconds later she was back in the doorway. This time she was not smiling.

"You'd better come and look at this," she said in a strange voice.

Blomkvist was on his feet at once and pulled on his jeans.

During the night someone had been to the cottage with an unwelcome present. On the porch lay the half-charred corpse of a cat. The cat's legs and head had been cut off, then the body had been flayed and the guts and stomach removed, flung next to the corpse, which seemed to have been roasted over a fire. The cat's head was intact, on the saddle of Salander's motorcycle. He recognised the reddish-brown fur.

CHAPTER 22

Thursday, July 10

They ate breakfast in the garden in silence and without milk in their coffee. Salander had taken out a Canon digital camera and photographed the macabre tableau before Blomkvist got a rubbish sack and cleaned it away. He put the cat in the boot of the Volvo. He ought to file a police report for animal cruelty, possibly intimidation, but he did not think he would want to explain why the intimidation had taken place.

At 8:30 Isabella Vanger walked past and on to the bridge. She did not see them or at least pretended not to.

"How are you doing?" Blomkvist said.

"Oh, I'm fine." Salander looked at him, perplexed. *OK, then. He expects me to be upset.* "When I find the motherfucker who tortured an innocent cat to death just to send us a warning, I'm going to clobber him with a baseball bat."

"You think it's a warning?"

"Have you got a better explanation? It definitely means something."

"Whatever the truth is in this story, we've worried somebody enough for that person to do something really sick. But there's another problem too."

"I know. This is an animal sacrifice in the style of 1954 and 1960 and it doesn't seem credible that someone active fifty years ago would be putting tortured animal corpses on your doorstep today."

Blomkvist agreed.

"The only ones who could be suspected in that case are Harald Vanger and Isabella Vanger. There are a number of older relatives on Johan Vanger's side, but none of them live in the area."

Blomkvist sighed.

"Isabella is a repulsive bitch who could certainly kill a cat, but I doubt she was running around killing women in the fifties. Harald Vanger . . . I don't know, he seems so decrepit he can hardly walk, and I can't see him sneaking over here last night, catching a cat, and doing all this."

"Unless it was two people. One older, one younger."

Blomkvist heard a car go by and looked up and saw Cecilia driving away over the bridge. *Harald and Cecilia,* he thought, but they hardly spoke. Despite Martin Vanger's promise to talk to her, Cecilia had still not answered any of his telephone messages.

"It must be somebody who knows we're doing this work and that we're making progress," Salander said, getting up to go inside. When she came back out she had put on her leathers.

"I'm going to Stockholm. I'll be back tonight."

"What are you going to do?"

"Pick up some gadgets. If someone is crazy enough to kill a cat in that disgusting way, he or she could attack us next time. Or set the cottage on fire while we're asleep. I want you to go into Hedestad and buy two fire extinguishers and two smoke alarms today. One of the fire extinguishers has to be halon."

Without another word, she put on her helmet, kick-started the motorcycle, and roared off across the bridge.

Blomkvist hid the corpse and the head and guts in the rubbish bin beside the petrol station before he drove into Hedestad to do his errands. He drove to the hospital. He had made an appointment to meet Frode in the cafeteria, and he told him what had happened that morning. Frode blanched.

"Mikael, I never imagined that this story could take this turn."

"Why not? The job was to find a murderer, after all."

"But this is disgusting and inhuman. If there's a danger to your life or to Fröken Salander's life, we are going to call it off. Let me talk to Henrik."

"No. Absolutely not. I don't want to risk his having another attack."

"He asks me all the time how things are going with you."

"Say hello from me, please, and tell him I'm moving forward."

"What is next, then?"

"I have a few questions. The first incident occurred just after Henrik had his heart attack and I was down in Stockholm for the day. Somebody went through my office. I had printed out the Bible verses, and the photographs from Järnvägsgatan were on my desk. You knew and Henrik knew. Martin knew a part of it since he organised for me to get into the *Courier* offices. How many other people knew?"

"Well, I don't know who Martin talked to. But both Birger and Cecilia knew about it. They discussed your hunting in the pictures archive between themselves. Alexander knew about it too. And, by the way, Gunnar and Helena Nilsson did too. They were up to say hello to Henrik and got dragged into the conversation. And Anita Vanger."

"Anita? The one in London?"

"Cecilia's sister. She came back with Cecilia when Henrik had his heart attack but stayed at a hotel; as far as I know, she hasn't been out to the island. Like Cecilia, she doesn't want to see her father. But she flew back when Henrik came out of intensive care."

"Where's Cecilia living? I saw her this morning as she drove across the bridge, but her house is always dark."

"She's not capable of doing such a thing, is she?"

"No, I just wonder where she's staying."

"She's staying with her brother, Birger. It's within walking distance to visit Henrik."

"Do you know where she is right now?"

"No. She's not visiting Henrik, at any rate."

"Thanks," Blomkvist said, getting up.

The Vanger family was hovering around Hedestad Hospital. In the reception Birger Vanger passed on his way to the lifts. Blomkvist waited until he was gone before he went out to the reception. Instead he ran into Martin Vanger at the entrance, at exactly the same spot where he had run into Cecilia on his previous visit. They said hello and shook hands.

"Have you been up to see Henrik?"

"No, I just happened to meet Dirch Frode."

Martin looked tired and hollow-eyed. It occurred to Mikael that he had aged appreciably during the six months since he had met him.

"How are things going with you, Mikael?" he said.

"More interesting with every day that passes. When Henrik is feeling better I hope to be able to satisfy his curiosity."

. . .

Birger Vanger's was a white-brick terrace house a five-minute walk from the hospital. He had a view of the sea and the Hedestad marina. No-one answered when Blomkvist rang the doorbell. He called Cecilia's mobile number but got no answer there either. He sat in the car for a while, drumming his fingers on the steering wheel. Birger Vanger was the wild card in the deck; born in 1939 and so ten years old when Rebecka Jacobsson was murdered; twenty-seven when Harriet disappeared.

According to Henrik, Birger and Harriet hardly ever saw each other. He had grown up with his family in Uppsala and only moved to Hedestad to work for the firm. He jumped ship after a couple of years and devoted himself to politics. But he had been in Uppsala at the time Lena Andersson was murdered.

The incident with the cat gave him an ominous feeling, as if he were about to run out of time.

Otto Falk was thirty-six when Harriet vanished. He was now seventy-two, younger than Henrik Vanger but in a considerably worse mental state. Blomkvist sought him out at the Svalan convalescent home, a yellow-brick building a short distance from the Hede River at the other end of the town. Blomkvist introduced himself to the receptionist and asked to be allowed to speak with Pastor Falk. He knew, he explained, that the pastor suffered from Alzheimer's and enquired how lucid he was now. A nurse replied that Pastor Falk had first been diagnosed three years earlier and that alas the disease had taken an aggressive course. Falk could communicate, but he had a very feeble short-term memory, and did not recognise all of his relatives. He was on the whole slipping into the shadows. He was also prone to anxiety attacks if he was confronted with questions he could not answer.

Falk was sitting on a bench in the garden with three other

patients and a male nurse. Blomkvist spent an hour trying to engage him in conversation.

He remembered Harriet Vanger quite well. His face lit up, and he described her as a charming girl. But Blomkvist was soon aware that the pastor had forgotten that she had been missing these last thirty-seven years. He talked about her as if he had seen her recently and asked Blomkvist to say hello to her and urge her to come and see him. Blomkvist promised to do so.

He obviously did not remember the accident on the bridge. It was not until the end of their conversation that he said something which made Blomkvist prick up his ears.

It was when Blomkvist steered the talk to Harriet's interest in religion that Falk suddenly seemed hesitant. It was as though a cloud passed over his face. Falk sat rocking back and forth for a while and then looked up at Blomkvist and asked who he was. Blomkvist introduced himself again and the old man thought for a while. At length he said: "She's still a seeker. She has to take care of herself and you have to warn her."

"What should I warn her about?"

Falk grew suddenly agitated. He shook his head with a frown.

"She has to read *sola scriptura* and understand *sufficientia scripturae*. That's the only way that she can maintain *sola fide*. Josef will certainly exclude them. They were never accepted into the canon."

Blomkvist understood nothing of this, but took assiduous notes. Then Pastor Falk leaned towards him and whispered, "I think she's a Catholic. She loves magic and has not yet found her God. She needs guidance."

The word "Catholic" obviously had a negative connotation for Pastor Falk.

"I thought she was interested in the Pentecostal movement?"

"No, no, no, not the Pentecostals. She's looking for the forbidden truth. She is not a good Christian."

Then Pastor Falk seemed to forget all about Blomkvist and started talking with the other patients.

He got back to Hedeby Island just after 2:00. He walked over to Cecilia Vanger's and knocked on the door, but without success. He tried her mobile number again but no answer.

He attached one smoke alarm to a wall in the kitchen and one next to the front door. He put one fire extinguisher next to the woodstove beside the bedroom door and another one beside the bathroom door. Then he made himself lunch, which consisted of coffee and open sandwiches, and sat in the garden, where he was typing up the notes of his conversation with Pastor Falk. When that was done, he raised his eyes to the church.

Hedeby's new parsonage was quite an ordinary modern dwelling a few minutes' walk from the church. Blomkvist knocked on the door at 4:00 and explained to Pastor Margareta Strandh that he had come to seek advice on a theological matter. Margareta Strandh was a dark-haired woman of about his own age, dressed in jeans and a flannel shirt. She was barefoot and had painted toenails. He had run into her before at Susanne's Bridge Café on a couple of occasions and talked to her about Pastor Falk. He was given a friendly reception and invited to come and sit in her courtyard.

Blomkvist told her that he had interviewed Otto Falk and what the old man had said. Pastor Strandh listened and then asked him to repeat it word for word.

"I was sent to serve here in Hedeby only three years ago, and I've never actually met Pastor Falk. He retired several years before that, but I believe that he was fairly high-church. What he said to you meant something on the lines of 'keep to Scripture alone'—*sola scriptura*—and that it is *sufficientia scripturae*. This latter is an expression that establishes the sufficiency of

Scripture among literal believers. *Sola fide* means faith alone or the true faith."

"I see."

"All this is basic dogma, so to speak. In general it's the platform of the church and nothing unusual at all. He was saying quite simply: '*Read the Bible—it will provide sufficient knowledge and vouches for the true faith.*' "

Mikael felt a bit embarrassed.

"Now I have to ask you in what connection this conversation occurred," she said.

"I was asking him about a person he had met many years ago, someone I'm writing about."

"A religious seeker?"

"Something along that line."

"OK. I think I understand the context. You told me that Pastor Falk said two other things—that '*Josef will certainly exclude them*' and that '*they were never accepted into the canon.*' Is it possible that you misunderstood and that he said Josefus instead of Josef? It's actually the same name."

"That's possible," Blomkvist said. "I taped the conversation if you want to listen to it."

"No, I don't think that's necessary. These two sentences establish fairly unequivocally what he was alluding to. Josefus was a Jewish historian, and the sentence '*they were never accepted into the canon*' may have meant that they were never in the Hebrew canon."

"And that means?"

She laughed.

"Pastor Falk was saying that this person was enthralled by esoteric sources, specifically the Apocrypha. The Greek word *apokryphos* means 'hidden,' and the Apocrypha are therefore the hidden books which some consider highly controversial and others think should be included in the Old Testament. They are

Tobias, Judith, Esther, Baruch, Sirach, the books of the Maccabees, and some others."

"Forgive my ignorance. I've heard about the books of the Apocrypha but have never read them. What's special about them?"

"There's really nothing special about them at all, except that they came into existence somewhat later than the rest of the Old Testament. The Apocrypha were deleted from the Hebrew Bible—not because Jewish scholars mistrusted their content but simply because they were written after the time when God's revelatory work was concluded. On the other hand, the Apocrypha are included in the old Greek translation of the Bible. They're not considered controversial in, for example, the Roman Catholic Church."

"I see."

"However, they *are* controversial in the Protestant Church. During the Reformation, theologians looked to the old Hebrew Bible. Martin Luther deleted the Apocrypha from the Reformation's Bible and later Calvin declared that the Apocrypha absolutely must not serve as the basis for convictions in matters of faith. Thus their contents contradict or in some way conflict with *claritas scripturae*—the clarity of Scripture."

"In other words, censored books."

"Quite right. For example, the Apocrypha claim that magic can be practised and that lies in certain cases may be permissible, and such statements, of course, upset dogmatic interpreters of Scripture."

"So if someone has a passion for religion, it's not unthinkable that the Apocrypha will pop up on their reading list, or that someone like Pastor Falk would be upset by this."

"Exactly. Encountering the Apocrypha is almost unavoidable if you're studying the Bible or the Catholic faith, and it's equally probable that someone who is interested in esoterica in general might read them."

"You don't happen to have a copy of the Apocrypha, do you?"

She laughed again. A bright, friendly laugh.

"Of course I do. The Apocrypha were actually published as a state report from the Bible Commission in the eighties."

Armansky wondered what was going on when Salander asked to speak to him in private. He shut the door behind her and motioned her to the visitor's chair. She told him that her work for Mikael Blomkvist was done—the lawyer would be paying her before the end of the month—but that she had decided to keep on with this particular investigation. Blomkvist had offered her a considerably higher salary for a month.

"I am self-employed," Salander said. "Until now I've never taken a job that you haven't given me, in keeping with our agreement. What I want to know is what will happen to our relationship if I take a job on my own?"

Armansky shrugged.

"You're a freelancer, you can take any job you want and charge what you think it's worth. I'm just glad you're making your own money. It would, however, be disloyal of you to take on clients you find through us."

"I have no plans to do that. I've finished the job according to the contract we signed with Blomkvist. What this is about is that I want to stay on the case. I'd even do it for nothing."

"Don't ever do anything for nothing."

"You know what I mean. I want to know where this story is going. I've convinced Blomkvist to ask the lawyer to keep me on as a research assistant."

She passed the agreement over to Armansky, who read rapidly through it.

"With this salary you might as well be working for free. Lisbeth, you've got talent. You don't have to work for small change. You know you can make a hell of a lot more with me if you come on board full-time."

"I don't want to work full-time. But, Dragan, my loyalty is to you. You've been great to me since I started here. I want to know if a contract like this is OK with you, that there won't be any friction between us."

"I see." He thought for a moment. "It's 100 percent OK. Thanks for asking. If any more situations like this crop up in the future I'd appreciate it if you asked me so there won't be any misunderstandings."

Salander thought over whether she had anything to add. She fixed her gaze on Armansky, saying not a word. Instead she just nodded and then stood up and left, as usual with no farewell greeting.

She got the answer she wanted and instantly lost interest in Armansky. He smiled to himself. That she had even asked him for advice marked a new high point in her socialisation process.

He opened a folder with a report on security at a museum where a big exhibition of French Impressionists was opening soon. Then he put down the folder and looked at the door through which Salander had just gone. He thought about how she had laughed with Blomkvist in her office and wondered if she was finally growing up or whether it was Blomkvist who was the attraction. He also felt a strange uneasiness. He had never been able to shake off the feeling that Lisbeth Salander was a perfect victim. And here she was, hunting a madman out in the back of beyond.

On the way north again, Salander took on impulse a detour by way of Äppelviken Nursing Home to see her mother. Except for the visit on Midsummer Eve, she had not seen her mother since

Christmas, and she felt bad for so seldom taking the time. A second visit within the course of a few weeks was quite unusual.

Her mother was in the day room. Salander stayed a good hour and took her mother for a walk down to the duck pond in the grounds of the hospital. Her mother was still muddling Lisbeth with her sister. As usual, she was hardly present, but she seemed troubled by the visit.

When Salander said goodbye, her mother did not want to let go of her hand. Salander promised to visit her again soon, but her mother gazed after her sadly and anxiously.

It was as if she had a premonition of some approaching disaster.

Blomkvist spent two hours in the garden behind his cabin going through the Apocrypha without gaining a single insight. But a thought had occurred to him. How religious had Harriet Vanger actually been? Her interest in Bible studies had started the last year before she vanished. She had linked a number of Bible quotes to a series of murders and then had methodically read not only her Bible but also the Apocrypha, and she had developed an interest in Catholicism.

Had she really done the same investigation that Blomkvist and Salander were doing thirty-seven years later? Was it the hunt for a murderer that had spurred her interest rather than religiosity? Pastor Falk had indicated that in his eyes she was more of a seeker, less a good Christian.

He was interrupted by Berger calling him on his mobile.

"I just wanted to tell you that Greger and I are leaving on holiday next week. I'll be gone for four weeks."

"Where are you going?"

"New York. Greger has an exhibition, and then we thought we'd go to the Caribbean. We have a chance to borrow a house on Antigua from a friend of Greger's and we're staying there two weeks."

"That sounds wonderful. Have a great time. And say hi to Greger."

"The new issue is finished and we've almost wrapped up the next one. I wish you could take over as editor, but Christer has said he will do it."

"He can call me if he needs any help. How's it going with Janne Dahlman?"

She hesitated.

"He's also going on holiday. I've pushed Henry into being the acting managing editor. He and Christer are minding the store."

"OK."

"I'll be back on August seventh."

In the early evening Blomkvist tried five times to telephone Cecilia Vanger. He sent her a text asking her to call him. But he received no answer.

He put away the Apocrypha and got into his tracksuit, locking the door before he set off.

He followed the narrow path along the shore and then turned into the woods. He ground his way through thickets and around uprooted trees as fast as he could go, emerging exhausted at the Fortress with his pulse racing. He stopped by one of the old artillery batteries and stretched for several minutes.

Suddenly he heard a sharp crack and the grey concrete wall next to his head exploded. Then he felt the pain as fragments of concrete and shrapnel tore a deep gash in his scalp.

For what seemed an eternity Blomkvist stood paralysed. Then he threw himself into the artillery trench, landing hard on his shoulder and knocking the wind out of himself. A second round came at the instant he dived. The bullet smacked into the concrete foundation.

He got to his feet and looked all around. He was in the middle of the Fortress. To the right and left narrow, overgrown passages a yard deep ran to the batteries that were spread along a line of 250 yards. In a crouch, he started running south through the labyrinth.

He suddenly heard an echo of Captain Adolfsson's inimitable voice from winter manoeuvres at the infantry school in Kiruna. *Blomkvist, keep your fucking head down if you don't want to get your arse shot off.* Years later he still remembered the extra practise drills that Captain Adolfsson used to devise.

He stopped to catch his breath, his heart pounding. He could hear nothing but his own breathing. *The human eye perceives motion much quicker than shapes and figures. Move slowly when you're scouting.* Blomkvist slowly peeked an inch over the top edge of the battery. The sun was straight ahead and made it impossible to make out details, but he could see no movement.

He pulled his head back down and ran on to the next battery. *It doesn't matter how good the enemy's weapons are. If he can't see you, he can't hit you. Cover, cover, cover. Make sure you're never exposed.*

He was 300 yards from the edge of Östergården farm. Some 40 yards from where he knelt there was an almost impenetrable thicket of low brush. But to reach the thicket he would have to sprint down a grass slope from the artillery battery, and he would be completely exposed. It was the only way. At his back was the sea.

He was suddenly aware of pain in his temple and discovered that he was bleeding and that his T-shirt was drenched with blood. *Scalp wounds never stop bleeding,* he thought before he again concentrated on his position. One shot could just have been an accident, but two meant that somebody was trying to kill him. He had no way of knowing if the marksman was waiting for him to reappear.

He tried to be calm, think rationally. The choice was to wait or to get the hell out. If the marksman was still there, the latter alternative was assuredly not a good idea. If he waited where he was, the marksman would calmly walk up to the Fortress, find him, and shoot him at close range.

He (or she?) can't know if I've gone to the right or left. Rifle, maybe a moose rifle. Probably with telescopic sights. Which would mean that the marksman would have a limited field of vision if he was looking for Mikael through the sights.

If you're in a tight spot—take the initiative. Better than waiting. He watched and listened for sounds for two minutes; then he clambered out of the battery and raced down the slope as fast as he could.

He was halfway down the slope as a third shot was fired, but he only heard a vague smack behind him. He threw himself flat through the curtain of brush and rolled through a sea of stinging nettles. Then he was on his feet and moving away from the direction of the fire, crouching, running, stopping every fifty yards, listening. He heard a branch crack somewhere between him and the Fortress. He dropped to his stomach.

Crawl using your elbows was another of Captain Adolfsson's favourite expressions. Blomkvist covered the next 150 yards on his knees and toes and elbows through the undergrowth. He pushed aside twigs and branches. Twice he heard sudden cracks in the thicket behind him. The first seemed to be very close, maybe twenty paces to the right. He froze, lay perfectly still. After a while he cautiously raised his head and looked around, but he could see no-one. He lay still for a long time, his nerves on full alert, ready to flee or possibly make a desperate counterattack if the enemy came at him. The next crack was from farther away. Then silence.

He knows I'm here. Has he taken up a position somewhere, waiting for me to start moving, or has he retreated?

Blomkvist kept crawling through the undergrowth until he reached the Östergården's fence.

This was the next critical moment. A path ran inside the fence. He lay stretched out on the ground, watching. The farmhouse was 400 yards down a gentle slope. To the right of the house he saw cows grazing. *Why hadn't anyone heard the shots and come to investigate? Summer. Maybe nobody is at home right now.*

There was no question of crossing the pasture—there he would have no cover at all. The straight path beside the fence was the place he himself would have picked for a clear field of fire. He retreated into the brush until he came out on the other side into a sparse pine wood.

He took the long way around Östergården's fields and Söderberget to reach home. When he passed Östergården he could see that their car was gone. At the top of Söderberget he stopped and looked down on Hedeby. In the old fishing cabins by the marina there were summer visitors; women in bathing suits were sitting talking on a dock. He smelled something cooking on an outdoor grill. Children were splashing in the water near the docks in the marina.

Just after 8:00. It was fifty minutes since the shots had been fired. Nilsson was watering his lawn, wearing shorts and no shirt. *How long have you been there?* Vanger's house was empty but for Anna. Harald Vanger's house looked deserted as always. Then he saw Isabella Vanger in her back garden. She was sitting there, obviously talking to someone. It took a second for Blomkvist to realise it was the sickly Gerda Vanger, born in 1922 and living with her son, Alexander, in one of the houses beyond Henrik's. He had never met her, but he had seen her a few times. Cecilia Vanger's house looked empty, but then Mikael saw a movement in her kitchen. *She's home. Was the marksman a woman?* He knew that Cecilia could handle a gun. He could see Martin Vanger's car in the drive in front of his house. *How long have you been home?*

Or was it someone else that he had not thought of yet? Frode? Alexander? Too many possibilities.

He climbed down from Söderberget and followed the road into the village; he got home without encountering anyone. The first thing he saw was that the door of the cottage was ajar. He went into a crouch almost instinctively. Then he smelled coffee and saw Salander through the kitchen window.

She heard him come in the front door and turned towards him. She stiffened. His face looked terrible, smeared with blood that had begun to congeal. The left side of his white T-shirt was crimson. He was holding a sodden red handkerchief to his head.

"It's bleeding like hell, but it's not dangerous," Blomkvist said before she could ask.

She turned and got the first-aid kit from the cupboard; it contained two packets of elastic bandages, a mosquito stick, and a little roll of surgical tape. He pulled off his clothes and dropped them on the floor; then he went to the bathroom.

The wound on his temple was a gash so deep that he could lift up a big flap of flesh. It was still bleeding and it needed stitches, but he thought it would probably heal if he taped it closed. He ran a towel under the cold tap and wiped his face.

He held the towel against his temple while he stood under

the shower and closed his eyes. Then he slammed his fist against the tile so hard that he scraped his knuckles. *Fuck you, whoever you are,* he thought. *I'm going to find you, and I will get you.*

When Salander touched his arm he jumped as if he had had an electric shock and stared at her with such anger in his eyes that she took a step back. She handed him the soap and went back to the kitchen without a word.

He put on three strips of surgical tape. He went into the bedroom, pulled on a clean pair of jeans and a new T-shirt, taking the folder of printed-out photographs with him. He was so furious he was almost shaking.

"Stay here, Lisbeth," he shouted.

He walked over to Cecilia Vanger's house and rang the doorbell. It was half a minute before she opened the door.

"I don't want to see you," she said. Then she saw his face, where blood was already seeping through the tape.

"Let me in. We have to talk."

She hesitated. "We have nothing to talk about."

"We do now, and you can discuss it here on the steps or in the kitchen."

Blomkvist's tone was so determined that Cecilia stepped back and let him in. He sat at her kitchen table.

"What have you done?" she said.

"You claim that my digging for the truth about Harriet Vanger is some futile form of occupational therapy for Henrik. That's possible, but an hour ago someone bloody nearly shot my head off, and last night someone—maybe the same humourist—left a horribly dead cat on my porch."

Cecilia opened her mouth, but Blomkvist cut her off.

"Cecilia, I don't give a shit about your hang-ups or what you worry about or the fact that you suddenly hate the sight of me. I'll never come near you again, and you don't have to worry that I'm going to bother you or run after you. Right this minute I wish I'd never heard of you or anyone else in the Vanger family. But I require answers to my questions. The sooner you answer them, the sooner you'll be rid of me."

"What do you want to know?"

"Number one: where were you an hour ago?"

Cecilia's face clouded over.

"An hour ago I was in Hedestad."

"Can anyone confirm where you were?"

"Not that I can think of, and I don't have to account to you."

"Number two: why did you open the window in Harriet's room the day she disappeared?"

"What?"

"You heard me. For all these years Henrik has tried to work out who opened the window in Harriet's room during those critical minutes. Everybody has denied doing it. Someone is lying."

"And what in hell makes you think it was me?"

"This picture," Blomkvist said, and flung the blurry photograph onto her kitchen table.

Cecilia walked over to the table and studied the picture. Blomkvist thought he could read shock on her face. She looked up at him. He felt a trickle of blood run down his cheek and drop onto his shirt.

"There were sixty people on the island that day," he said. "And twenty-eight of them were women. Five or six of them had shoulder-length blonde hair. Only one of those was wearing a light-coloured dress."

She stared intently at the photograph.

"And you think that's supposed to be me?"

"If it isn't you, I'd like you to tell me who you think it is. Nobody knew about this picture before. I've had it for weeks and tried to talk to you about it. I may be an idiot, but I haven't showed it to Henrik or anyone else because I'm deathly afraid of casting suspicion on you or doing you wrong. But I do have to have an answer."

"You'll get your answer." She held out the photograph to him. "I didn't go into Harriet's room that day. It's not me in the picture. I didn't have the slightest thing to do with her disappearance."

She went to the front door.

"You have your answer. Now please go. But I think you should have a doctor look at that wound."

Salander drove him to Hedestad Hospital. It took only two stitches and a good dressing to close the wound. He was given cortisone salve for the rash from the stinging nettles on his neck and hands.

After they left the hospital Blomkvist sat for a long time wondering whether he ought to go to the police. He could see the headlines now. "*Libel Journalist in Shooting Drama.*" He shook his head. "Let's go home," he said.

It was dark when they arrived back at Hedeby Island, and that suited Salander fine. She lifted a sports bag on to the kitchen table.

"I borrowed this stuff from Milton Security, and it's time we made use of it."

She planted four battery-operated motion detectors around the house and explained that if anyone came closer than twenty feet, a radio signal would trigger a small chirping alarm that she set up in Blomkvist's bedroom. At the same time, two light-sensitive video cameras that she had put in trees at the front and back of the cabin would send signals to a PC laptop that she set in the cupboard by the front door. She camouflaged the cameras with dark cloth.

She put a third camera in a birdhouse above the door. She

drilled a hole right through the wall for the cable. The lens was aimed at the road and the path from the gate to the front door. It took a low-resolution image every second and stored them all on the hard drive of another PC laptop in the wardrobe.

Then she put a pressure-sensitive doormat in the entrance. If someone managed to evade the infrared detectors and got into the house, a 115-decibel siren would go off. Salander demonstrated for him how to shut off the detectors with a key to a box in the wardrobe. She had also borrowed a night-vision scope.

"You don't leave a lot to chance," Blomkvist said, pouring coffee for her.

"One more thing. No more jogging until we crack this."

"Believe me, I've lost all interest in exercise."

"I'm not joking. This may have started out as a historical mystery, but what with dead cats and people trying to blow your head off we can be sure we're on somebody's trail."

They ate dinner late. Blomkvist was suddenly dead tired and had a splitting headache. He could hardly talk any more, so he went to bed.

Salander stayed up reading the report until 2:00.

CHAPTER 23

Friday, July 11

He awoke at 6:00 with the sun shining through a gap in the curtains right in his face. He had a vague headache, and it hurt when he touched the bandage. Salander was asleep on her stomach with one arm flung over him. He looked down at the dragon on her shoulder blade.

He counted her tattoos. As well as a wasp on her neck, she had a loop around one ankle, another loop around the biceps of her left arm, a Chinese symbol on her hip, and a rose on one calf.

He got out of bed and pulled the curtains tight. He went to the bathroom and then padded back to bed, trying to get in without waking her.

A couple of hours later over breakfast Blomkvist said, "How are we going to solve this puzzle?"

"We sum up the facts we have. We try to find more."

"For me, the only question is: why? Is it because we're trying to solve the mystery about Harriet, or because we've uncovered a hitherto unknown serial killer?"

"There must be a connection," Salander said. "If Harriet realised that there was a serial killer, it can only have been someone she knew. If we look at the cast of characters in the sixties, there were at least two dozen possible candidates. Today hardly any of them are left except Harald Vanger, who is not running around in the woods of Fröskogen at almost ninety-three with a gun. Everybody is either too old to be of any danger today, or too young to have been around in the fifties. So we're back to square one."

"Unless there are two people who are collaborating. One older and one younger."

"Harald and Cecilia? I don't think so. I think she was telling the truth when she said that she wasn't the person in the window."

"Then who was that?"

They turned on Blomkvist's iBook and spent the next hour studying in detail once again all the people visible in the photographs of the accident on the bridge.

"I can only assume that everyone in the village must have been down there, watching all the excitement. It was September. Most of them are wearing jackets or sweaters. Only one person has long blonde hair and a light-coloured dress."

"Cecilia Vanger is in a lot of the pictures. She seems to be everywhere. Between the buildings and the people who are looking at the accident. Here she's talking to Isabella. Here she's standing next to Pastor Falk. Here she's with Greger Vanger, the middle brother."

"Wait a minute," Blomkvist said. "What does Greger have in his hand?"

"Something square-shaped. It looks like a box of some kind."

"It's a Hasselblad. So he too had a camera."

They scrolled through the photographs one more time. Greger was in more of them, though often blurry. In one it could be clearly seen that he was holding a square-shaped box.

"I think you're right. It's definitely a camera."

"Which means that we go on another hunt for photographs."

"OK, but let's leave that for a moment," Salander said. "Let me propose a theory."

"Go ahead."

"What if someone of the younger generation knows that someone of the older generation is a serial killer, but they don't want it acknowledged. The family's honour and all that crap. That would mean that there are two people involved, but not that they're in it together. The murderer could have died years ago, while our nemesis just wants us to drop the whole thing and go home."

"But why, in that case, put a mutilated cat on our porch? It's an unmistakable reference to the murders." Blomkvist tapped Harriet's Bible. "Again a parody of the laws regarding burnt offerings."

Salander leaned back and looked up at the church as she quoted from the Bible. It was as if she were talking to herself.

"Then he shall kill the bull before the Lord; and Aaron's sons the priests shall present the blood, and they shall throw the blood round about against the altar that is the door of the tent of meeting. And he shall flay the burnt offering and cut it into pieces."

She fell silent, aware that Blomkvist was watching her with a tense expression. He opened the Bible to the first chapter of Leviticus.

"Do you know verse twelve too?"

Salander did not reply.

"And he shall . . ." he began, nodding at her.

"And he shall cut it into pieces, with its head and its fat, and the

priest shall lay them in order upon the wood that is on the fire upon the altar." Her voice was ice.

"And the next verse?"

Abruptly she stood up.

"Lisbeth, you have a photographic memory," Mikael exclaimed in surprise. "That's why you can read a page of the investigation in ten seconds."

Her reaction was almost explosive. She fixed her eyes on Blomkvist with such fury that he was astounded. Then her expression changed to despair, and she turned on her heel and ran for the gate.

"Lisbeth," he shouted after her.

She disappeared up the road.

Mikael carried her computer inside, set the alarm, and locked the front door before he set out to look for her. He found her twenty minutes later on a jetty at the marina. She was sitting there, dipping her feet in the water and smoking. She heard him coming along the jetty, and he saw her shoulders stiffen. He stopped a couple of paces away.

"I don't know what I did, but I didn't mean to upset you."

He sat down next to her, tentatively placing a hand on her shoulder.

"Please, Lisbeth. Talk to me."

She turned her head and looked at him.

"There's nothing to talk about," she said. "I'm just a freak, that's all."

"I'd be overjoyed if my memory was what yours is."

She tossed the cigarette end into the water.

Mikael sat in silence for a long time. *What am I supposed to say? You're a perfectly ordinary girl. What does it matter if you're a little different? What kind of self-image do you have, anyway?*

"I thought there was something different about you the instant I saw you," he said. "And you know what? It's been a really long time since I've had such a spontaneous good impression of anyone from the very beginning."

Some children came out of a cabin on the other side of the harbour and jumped into the water. The painter, Eugen Norman, with whom Blomkvist still had not exchanged a single word, was sitting in a chair outside his house, sucking on his pipe as he regarded Blomkvist and Salander.

"I really want to be your friend, if you'll let me," he said. "But it's up to you. I'm going back to the house to put on some more coffee. Come home when you feel like it."

He got up and left her in peace. He was only halfway up the hill when he heard her footsteps behind him. They walked home together without exchanging a word.

She stopped him just as they reached the house.

"I was in the process of formulating a theory . . . We talked about the fact that all this is a parody of the Bible. It's true that he took a cat apart, but I suppose it would be hard to get hold of an ox. But he's following the basic story. I wonder . . ." She looked up at the church again. "*And they shall throw the blood round about against the altar that is the door of the tent of meeting . . .*"

They walked over the bridge to the church. Blomkvist tried the door, but it was locked. They wandered around for a while, looking at headstones until they came to the chapel, which stood a short distance away, down by the water. All of a sudden Blomkvist opened his eyes wide. It was not a chapel, it was a crypt. Above the door he could read the name Vanger chiselled into the stone, along with a verse in Latin, but he could not decipher it.

" 'Slumber to the end of time,' " Salander said behind him.

Blomkvist turned to look at her. She shrugged.

"I happened to see that verse somewhere."

Blomkvist roared with laughter. She stiffened and at first she looked furious, but then she relaxed when she realised that he was laughing at the comedy of the situation.

Blomkvist tried the door. It was locked. He thought for a moment, then told Salander to sit down and wait for him. He walked over to see Anna Nygren and knocked. He explained that he wanted to have a closer look at the family crypt, and he wondered where Henrik might keep the key. Anna looked doubtful, but she collected the key from his desk.

As soon as they opened the door, they knew that they had been right. The stench of burned cadaver and charred remains hung heavy in the air. But the cat torturer had not made a fire. In one corner stood a blowtorch, the kind used by skiers to melt the wax on their skis. Salander got the camera out of the pocket of her jeans skirt and took some pictures. Then, gingerly, she picked up the blowtorch.

"This could be evidence. He might have left fingerprints," she said.

"Oh sure, we can ask the Vanger family to line up and give us their fingerprints." Blomkvist smiled. "I would love to watch you get Isabella's."

"There are ways," Salander said.

There was a great deal of blood on the floor, not all of it dry, as well as a bolt cutter, which they reckoned had been used to cut off the cat's head.

Blomkvist looked around. A raised sarcophagus belonged to Alexandre Vangeersad, and four graves in the floor housed the remains of the earliest family members. More recently the Vangers had apparently settled for cremation. About thirty niches on the wall had the names of the clan ancestors.

Blomkvist traced the family chronicle forward in time, wondering where they buried family members who were not given space inside the crypt—those not deemed important enough.

"Now we know," Blomkvist said as they were re-crossing the bridge. "We're hunting for the complete lunatic."

"What do you mean?"

Blomkvist paused in the middle of the bridge and leaned on the rail.

"If this was some run-of-the-mill crackpot who was trying to frighten us, he would have taken the cat down to the garage or even out into the woods. But he went to the crypt. There's something compulsive about that. Just think of the risk. It's summer and people are out and about at night, going for walks. The road through the cemetery is a main road between the north and south of Hedeby. Even if he shut the door behind him, the cat must have raised Cain, and there must have been a burning smell."

"He?"

"I don't think that Cecilia Vanger would be creeping around here in the night with a blowtorch."

Salander shrugged.

"I don't trust any last one of them, including Frode or your friend Henrik. They're all part of a family that would swindle you if they had the chance. So what do we do now?"

Blomkvist said, "I've discovered a lot of secrets about you. How many people, for example, know that you're a hacker?"

"No-one."

"No-one except me, you mean."

"What are you getting at?"

"I want to know if you're OK with me. If you trust me."

She looked at him for a long moment. Finally, for an answer, she only shrugged.

"There's nothing I can do about it."

"Do you trust me?" Blomkvist persisted.

"For the time being," she said.

"Good. Let's go over to see Frode."

This was the first time Advokat Frode's wife had met Salander. She gave her a wide-eyed look at the same time as she smiled politely. Frode's face lit up when he saw Salander. He stood to welcome them.

"How nice to see you," he said. "I've been feeling guilty that I never properly expressed my gratitude for the extraordinary work you did for us. Both last winter and now, this summer."

Salander gave him a suspicious glare.

"I was paid," she said.

"That's not it. I made some assumptions about you when I first saw you. You would be kind to pardon me in retrospect."

Blomkvist was surprised. Frode was capable of asking a twenty-five-year-old pierced and tattooed girl to forgive him for something for which he had no need to apologise! The lawyer climbed a few notches in Blomkvist's eyes. Salander stared straight ahead, ignoring him.

Frode looked at Blomkvist.

"What did you do to your head?"

They sat down. Blomkvist summed up the developments of the past twenty-four hours. As he described how someone had shot at him out near the Fortress, Frode leaped to his feet.

"This is barking mad." He paused and fixed his eyes on Blomkvist. "I'm sorry, but this has to stop. I can't have it. I am going to talk to Henrik and break the contract."

"Sit down," said Blomkvist.

"You don't understand . . ."

"What I understand is that Lisbeth and I have got so close

that whoever is behind all of this is reacting in a deranged manner, in panic. We've got some questions. First of all: how many keys are there to the Vanger family crypt and who has one?"

"It's not my province, and I have no idea," Frode said. "I would suppose that several family members would have access to the crypt. I know that Henrik has a key, and that Isabella sometimes goes there, but I can't tell you whether she has her own key or whether she borrows Henrik's."

"OK. You're still on the main board. Are there any corporate archives? A library or something like that, where they've collected press clippings and information about the firm over the years?"

"Yes, there is. At the Hedestad main office."

"We need access to it. Are there any old staff newsletters or anything like that?"

"Again I have to concede that I don't know. I haven't been to the archives myself in thirty years. You need to talk to a woman named Bodil Lindgren."

"Could you call her and arrange that Lisbeth has access to the archives this afternoon? She needs all the old press clippings about the Vanger Corporation."

"That's no problem. Anything else?"

"Yes. Greger Vanger was holding a Hasselblad in his hand on the day the bridge accident occurred. That means that he also might have taken some pictures. Where would the pictures have ended up after his death?"

"With his widow or his son, logically. Let me call Alexander and ask him."

"What am I looking for?" Salander said when they were on their way back to the island.

"Press clippings and staff newsletters. I want you to read through everything around the dates when the murders in the fifties and sixties were committed. Make a note of anything that strikes you. Better if you do this part of the job. It seems that your memory . . ."

She punched him in the side.

Five minutes later her Kawasaki was clattering across the bridge.

Blomkvist shook hands with Alexander Vanger. He had been away for most of the time that Blomkvist had been in Hedeby. He was twenty when Harriet disappeared.

"Dirch said that you wanted to look at old photographs."

"Your father had a Hasselblad, I believe."

"That's right. It's still here, but no-one uses it."

"I expect you know that Henrik has asked me to study again what happened to Harriet."

"That's what I understand. And there are plenty of people who aren't happy about that."

"Apparently so, and of course you don't have to show me anything."

"Please . . . What would you like to see?"

"If your father took any pictures on the day of the accident, the day that Harriet disappeared."

They went up to the attic. It took several minutes before Alexander was able to identify a box of unsorted photographs.

"Take home the whole box," he said. "If there are any at all, they'll be in there."

•

As illustrations for the family chronicle, Greger Vanger's box held some real gems, including a number of Greger together with Sven Olof Lindholm, the big Swedish Nazi leader in the forties. Those he set aside.

He found envelopes of pictures that Greger had taken of family gatherings as well as many typical holiday photographs—fishing in the mountains and a journey in Italy.

He found four pictures of the bridge accident. In spite of his exceptional camera, Greger was a wretched photographer. Two pictures were close-ups of the tanker truck itself, two were of spectators, taken from behind. He found only one in which Cecilia Vanger was visible in semi-profile.

He scanned in the pictures, even though he knew that they would tell him nothing new. He put everything back in the box and had a sandwich lunch as he thought things over. Then he went to see Anna.

"Do you think Henrik had any photograph albums other than the ones he assembled for his investigation about Harriet?"

"Yes, Henrik has always been interested in photography—ever since he was young, I've been told. He has lots of albums in his office."

"Could you show me?"

Her reluctance was plain to see. It was one thing to lend Blomkvist the key to the family crypt—God was in charge there, after all—but it was another matter to let him into Henrik Vanger's office. God's writ did not extend there. Blomkvist suggested that Anna should call Frode. Finally she agreed to allow him in. Almost three feet of the very bottom shelf was taken up with photograph albums. He sat at the desk and opened the first album.

Vanger had saved every last family photograph. Many were obviously from long before his time. The oldest pictures dated back to the 1870s, showing gruff men and stern women. There were pictures of Vanger's parents. One showed his father celebrating Midsummer with a large and cheerful group in Sandhamn in 1906. Another Sandhamn photograph showed Fredrik Vanger and his wife, Ulrika, with Anders Zorn and Albert

Engström sitting at a table. Other photographs showed workers on the factory floor and in offices. He found Captain Oskar Granath who had transported Vanger and his beloved Edith Lobach to safety in Karlskrona.

Anna came upstairs with a cup of coffee. He thanked her. By then he had reached modern times and was paging through images of Vanger in his prime, opening factories, shaking hands with Tage Erlander, one of Vanger and Marcus Wallenberg—the two capitalists staring grimly at each other.

In the same album he found a spread on which Vanger had written in pencil "Family Council 1966." Two colour photographs showed men talking and smoking cigars. He recognised Henrik, Harald, Greger, and several of the male in-laws in Johan Vanger's branch of the family. Two photographs showed the formal dinner, forty men and women seated at the table, all looking into the camera. The pictures were taken after the drama at the bridge was over but before anyone was aware that Harriet had disappeared. He studied their faces. This was the dinner she should have attended. Did any of the men know that she was gone? The photographs provided no answer.

Then suddenly he choked on his coffee. He started coughing and sat up straight in his chair.

At the far end of the table sat Cecilia Vanger in her light-coloured dress, smiling into the camera. Next to her sat another blonde woman with long hair and an identical light-coloured dress. They were so alike that they could have been twins. And suddenly the puzzle piece fell into place. Cecilia wasn't the one in Harriet's window—it was her sister, Anita, two years her junior and now living in London.

What was it Salander had said? *Cecilia Vanger is in a lot of the pictures.* Not at all. There were two girls, and as chance would have it—until now—they had never been seen in the same frame. In the black-and-white photographs, from a distance, they looked identical. Vanger had presumably always been able to tell the sisters apart, but for Blomkvist and Salander the girls looked so alike that they had assumed it was one person. And no-one had ever pointed out their mistake because they had never thought to ask.

Blomkvist turned the page and felt the hairs on the back of his neck stand on end. It was as if a cold gust of wind passed through the room.

There were pictures taken the next day, when the search for Harriet had begun. A young Inspector Morell was giving instructions to a search party consisting of two uniformed police officers and ten men wearing boots who were about to set out. Vanger was wearing a knee-length raincoat and a narrow-brimmed English hat.

On the left of the photograph stood a young, slightly stout young man with light, longish hair. He had on a dark padded jacket with a red patch at the shoulder. The image was very clear. Blomkvist recognised him at once—and the jacket—but, just to make sure, he removed the photograph and went down to ask Anna if she recognised the man.

"Yes, of course, that's Martin."

Salander ploughed through year after year of press cuttings, moving in chronological order. She began in 1949 and worked her way forward. The archive was huge. The company was mentioned in the media nearly every day during the relevant time period—not only in the local press but also in the national media. There were financial analyses, trade union negotiations, the threat of strikes, factory openings and factory closings, annual reports, changes in managers, new products that were launched . . . There was a flood of news. *Click. Click. Click.* Her brain was working at high speed as she focused and absorbed the information from the yellowing pages.

After several hours she had an idea. She asked the archives manager if there was a chart showing where the Vanger Corporation had factories or companies during the fifties and sixties.

Bodil Lindgren looked at Salander with undisguised coldness. She was not at all happy giving a total stranger permission to enter the inner sanctum of the firm's archives, being obliged to allow her to look through whatever documents she liked. And besides, this girl looked like some sort of half-witted fifteen-year-old anarchist. But Herr Frode had given her instructions that could not be misinterpreted. This slip of a girl was to be free to look at anything she pleased. And it was urgent. She brought out the printed annual reports for the years that Salander wanted to see; each report contained a chart of the firm's divisions throughout Sweden.

Salander looked at the charts and saw that the firm had many factories, offices, and sales outlets. At every site where a murder was committed, there was also a red dot, sometimes several, indicating the Vanger Corporation.

She found the first connection in 1957. Rakel Lunde, Landskrona, was found dead the day after the V. & C. Construction Company clinched an order worth several million to build a galleria in the town. V. & C. stood for Vanger and Carlén Construction. The local paper had interviewed Gottfried Vanger, who had come to town to sign the contract.

Salander recalled something she had read in the police investigation in the provincial record office in Landskrona. Rakel Lunde, fortune-teller in her free time, was an office cleaner. She had worked for V. & C. Construction.

. . .

At 7:00 in the evening Blomkvist called Salander a dozen times and each time her mobile was turned off. She did not want to be disturbed.

He wandered restlessly through the house. He had pulled out Vanger's notes on Martin's activities at the time of Harriet's disappearance.

Martin Vanger was in his last year at the preparatory school in Uppsala in 1966. *Uppsala. Lena Andersson, seventeen-year-old preparatory school pupil. Head separated from the fat.*

Vanger had mentioned this at one point, but Blomkvist had to consult his notes to find the passage. Martin had been an introverted boy. They had been worried about him. After his father drowned, Isabella had decided to send him to Uppsala—a change of scene where he was given room and board with Harald Vanger. *Harald and Martin?* It hardly felt right.

Martin Vanger was not with Harald in the car going to the gathering in Hedestad, and he had missed a train. He arrived late in the afternoon and so was among those stranded on the wrong side of the bridge. He only arrived on the island by boat some time after 6:00. He was received by Vanger himself, among others. Vanger had put Martin far down the list of people who might have had anything to do with Harriet's disappearance.

Martin said that he had not seen Harriet on that day. He was lying. He had arrived in Hedestad earlier in the day and he was on Järnvägsgatan, face to face with his sister. Blomkvist could prove the lie with photographs that had been buried for almost forty years.

Harriet Vanger had seen her brother and reacted with shock. She had gone out to Hedeby Island and tried to talk to Henrik, but she was gone before any conversation could take place. *What were you thinking of telling him? Uppsala? But Lena Andersson, Uppsala, was not on the list. You could not have known about it.*

The story still did not make sense to Blomkvist. Harriet had disappeared around 3:00 in the afternoon. Martin was unquestionably on the other side of the water at that time. He could be seen in the photograph from the church hill. He could not possibly have hurt Harriet on the island. One puzzle piece was still missing. *An accomplice? Anita Vanger?*

From the archives Salander could see that Gottfried Vanger's position within the firm had changed over the years. At the age of twenty in 1947, he met Isabella and immediately got her pregnant; Martin Vanger was born in 1948, and with that there was no question but that the young people would marry.

When Gottfried was twenty-two, he was brought into the main office of the Vanger Corporation by Henrik Vanger. He was obviously talented and they may have been grooming him to take over. He was promoted to the board at the age of twenty-five, as the assistant head of the company's development division. A rising star.

Sometime in the mid-fifties his star began to plummet. *He drank. His marriage to Isabella was on the rocks. The children, Harriet and Martin, were not doing well. Henrik drew the line.* Gottfried's career had reached its zenith. In 1956 another appointment was made, another assistant head of development. Two assistant heads: one who did the work while Gottfried drank and was absent for long periods of time.

But Gottfried was still a Vanger, as well as charming and eloquent. From 1957 on, his work seemed to consist of travelling around the country to open factories, resolve local conflicts, and spread an image that company management really did care.

We're sending out one of our own sons to listen to your problems. We do take you seriously.

Salander found a second connection. Gottfried Vanger had participated in a negotiation in Karlstad, where the Vanger Corporation had bought a timber company. On the following day a farmer's wife, Magda Lovisa Sjöberg, was found murdered.

Salander discovered the third connection just fifteen minutes later. Uddevalla, 1962. The same day that Lea Persson disappeared, the local paper had interviewed Gottfried Vanger about a possible expansion of the harbour.

When Fru Lindgren had wanted to close up and go home at 5:30, Salander had snapped at her that she was a long way from finished yet. She could go home as long as she left the key, and Salander would lock up. By that time the archives manager was so infuriated that a girl like this one could boss her around that she called Herr Frode. Frode told her that Salander could stay all night if she wanted to. Would Fru Lindgren please notify security at the office so that they could let Salander out when she wanted to leave?

Three hours later, getting on for 8:30, Salander had concluded that Gottfried Vanger had been close to where at least five of the eight murders were committed, either during the days before or after the event. She was still missing information about the murders in 1949 and 1954. She studied a newspaper photograph of him. A slim, handsome man with dark blond hair; he looked rather like Clark Gable in *Gone with the Wind*.

In 1949 Gottfried was twenty-two years old. The first murder took place in his home territory. Hedestad. Rebecka Jacobsson, who worked at the Vanger Corporation. Where did the two of you meet? What did you promise her?

Salander bit her lip. The problem was that Gottfried Vanger had drowned when he was drunk in 1965, while the last murder was committed in Uppsala in February 1966. She wondered if she was mistaken when she had added Lena Andersson, the seventeen-year-old schoolgirl, to the list. *No. It might not be the same signature, but it was the same Bible parody. They must be connected.*

By 9:00 it was getting dark. The air was cool and it was drizzling. Mikael was sitting in the kitchen, drumming his fingers on the table, when Martin Vanger's Volvo crossed the bridge and turned out towards the point. That somehow brought matters to a head.

He did not know what he should do. His whole being was burning with a desire to ask questions—to initiate a confrontation. It was certainly not a sensible attitude to have if he suspected Martin Vanger of being an insane murderer who had killed his sister and a girl in Uppsala, and who had also very nearly succeeded in killing him too. But Martin was also a magnet. And he did not know that Blomkvist knew; he could go and see him with the pretext that . . . well, he wanted to return the key to Gottfried Vanger's cabin. Blomkvist locked the door behind him and strolled out to the point.

Harald Vanger's house was pitch dark, as usual. In Henrik's house the lights were off except in one room facing the courtyard. Anna had gone to bed. Isabella's house was dark. Cecilia wasn't at home. The lights were on upstairs in Alexander's house, but they were off in the two houses occupied by people who were not members of the Vanger family. He did not see a soul.

He paused irresolutely outside Martin Vanger's house, took out his mobile, and punched in Salander's number. Still no answer. He turned off his mobile so that it would not start ringing.

There were lights on downstairs. Blomkvist walked across

the lawn and stopped a few yards from the kitchen window, but he could see no-one. He continued on around the house, pausing at each window, but there was no sign of Martin. On the other hand, he did discover that the small side door into the garage was slightly open. *Don't be a damn fool.* But he could not resist the temptation to look.

The first thing he saw on the carpenter's bench was an open box of ammunition for a moose rifle. Then he saw two gasoline cans on the floor under the bench. *Preparations for another nocturnal visit, Martin?*

"Come in, Mikael. I saw you on the road."

Blomkvist's heart skipped a beat. Slowly he turned his head and saw Martin Vanger standing in the dark by a door leading into the house.

"You simply couldn't stay away, could you?"

His voice was calm, almost friendly.

"Hi, Martin," Blomkvist said.

"Come in," Martin repeated. "This way."

He took a step forward and to the side, holding out his left hand in an inviting gesture. He raised his right hand, and Blomkvist saw the reflection of dull metal.

"I have a Glock in my hand. Don't do anything stupid. At this distance I won't miss."

Blomkvist slowly moved closer. When he reached Martin, he stopped and looked him in the eye.

"I had to come here. There are so many questions."

"I understand. Through the door."

Blomkvist entered the house. The passage led to the hall near the kitchen, but before he got that far, Martin Vanger stopped him by putting a hand lightly on Blomkvist's shoulder.

"No, not that way. To your right. Open the door."

The basement. When Blomkvist was halfway down the steps, Martin Vanger turned a switch and the lights went on. To the right of him was the boiler room. Ahead he could smell the scents of laundry. Martin guided him to the left, into a storage room with old furniture and boxes, at the back of which was a steel security door with a deadbolt lock.

"Here," Martin said, tossing a key ring to Blomkvist. "Open it."

He opened the door.

"The switch is on the left."

Blomkvist had opened the door to hell.

Around 9:00 Salander went to get some coffee and a plastic-wrapped sandwich from the vending machine in the corridor outside the archives. She kept on paging through old documents, looking for any trace of Gottfried Vanger in Kalmar in 1954. She found nothing.

She thought about calling Blomkvist, but decided to go through the staff newsletters before she called it a day.

The space was approximately ten by twenty feet. Blomkvist assumed that it was situated along the north side of the house.

Martin Vanger had contrived his private torture chamber with great care. On the left were chains, metal eyelets in the ceiling and floor, a table with leather straps where he could restrain his victims. And then the video equipment. A taping studio. In the back of the room was a steel cage for his guests. To the right of the door was a bench, a bed, and a TV corner with videos on a shelf.

As soon as they entered the room, Martin Vanger aimed the pistol at Blomkvist and told him to lie on his stomach on the floor. Blomkvist refused.

"Very well," Martin said. "Then I'll shoot you in the kneecap."

He took aim. Blomkvist capitulated. He had no choice.

He had hoped that Martin would relax his guard just a tenth of a second—he knew he would win any sort of fight with him. He had had half a chance in the passage upstairs when Martin put his hand on his shoulder, but he had hesitated. After that Martin had not come close. With a bullet in his kneecap he would have lost his chance. He lay down on the floor.

Martin approached from behind and told him to put his hands on his back. He handcuffed him. Then he kicked Mikael in the crotch and punched him viciously and repeatedly.

What happened after that seemed like a nightmare. Martin swung between rationality and pure lunacy. For a time quite calm, the next instant he would be pacing back and forth like an animal in a cage. He kicked Blomkvist several times. All Blomkvist could do was try to protect his head and take the blows in the soft parts of his body.

For the first half hour Martin did not say a word, and he appeared to be incapable of any sort of communication. After that he seemed to recover control. He put a chain round Blomkvist's neck, fastening it with a padlock to a metal eyelet on the floor. He left Blomkvist alone for about fifteen minutes. When he returned, he was carrying a litre bottle of water. He sat on a chair and looked at Blomkvist as he drank.

"Could I have some water?" Blomkvist said.

Martin leaned down and let him take a good long drink from the bottle. Blomkvist swallowed greedily.

"Thanks."

"Still so polite, *Kalle Blomkvist*."

"Why all the punching and kicking?" Blomkvist said.

"Because you make me very angry indeed. You deserve to be punished. Why didn't you just go home? You were needed at *Millennium*. I was serious—we could have made it into a great magazine. We could have worked together for years."

Blomkvist grimaced and tried to shift his body into a more comfortable position. He was defenceless. All he had was his voice.

"I assume you mean that the opportunity has passed," Blomkvist said.

Martin Vanger laughed.

"I'm sorry, Mikael. But, of course, you know perfectly well that you're going to die down here."

Blomkvist nodded.

"How the hell did you find me, you and that anorexic spook that you dragged into this?"

"You lied about what you were doing on the day that Harriet disappeared. You were in Hedestad at the Children's Day parade. You were photographed there, looking at Harriet."

"Was that why you went to Norsjö?"

"To get the picture, yes. It was taken by a honeymoon couple who happened to be in Hedestad."

He shook his head.

"That's a crass lie," Martin said.

Blomkvist thought hard: what to say to prevent or postpone his execution.

"Where's the picture now?"

"The negative? It's in a safe-deposit box at Handelsbanken here in Hedestad . . . You didn't know that I have a safe-deposit box?" He lied easily. "There are copies in various places. In my computer and in the girl's, on the server at *Millennium*, and on the server at Milton Security, where the girl works."

Martin waited, trying to work out whether or not Blomkvist was bluffing.

"How much does the girl know?"

Blomkvist hesitated. Salander was right now his only hope of rescue. What would she think when she came home and found him not there? He had put the photograph of Martin Vanger wearing the padded jacket on the kitchen table. Would she make the connection? Would she sound the alarm? *She is not going to call the police.* The nightmare was that she would come to Martin Vanger's house and ring the bell, demanding to know where Blomkvist was.

"Answer me," Martin said, his voice ice-cold.

"I'm thinking. She knows almost as much as I do, maybe even a little more. Yes, I would reckon she knows more than I do. She's bright. She's the one who made the link to Lena Andersson."

"Lena Andersson?" Martin sounded perplexed.

"The girl you tortured and killed in Uppsala in 1966. Don't tell me you've forgotten?"

"I don't know what you're talking about." But for the first time he sounded shaken. It was the first time that anyone had made that connection—Lena Andersson was not included in Harriet's date book.

"Martin," Blomkvist said, making his voice as steady as he could. "It's over. You can kill me, but it's finished. Too many people know."

Martin started pacing back and forth again.

I have to remember that he's irrational. The cat. He could have brought the cat down here, but he went to the family crypt. Martin stopped.

"I think you're lying. You and Salander are the only ones who know anything. You obviously haven't talked to anyone, or the police would have been here by now. A nice little blaze in the guest cottage and the proof will be gone."

"And if you're wrong?"

"If I'm wrong, then it really is over. But I don't think it is. I'll bet that you're bluffing. And what other choice do I have? I'll give that some thought. It's that anorexic little cunt who's the weak link."

"She went to Stockholm at lunchtime."

Martin laughed.

"Bluff away, Mikael. She has been sitting in the archives at the Vanger Corporation offices all evening."

Blomkvist's heart skipped a beat. *He knew. He's known all along.*

"That's right. The plan was to visit the archive and then go to Stockholm," Blomkvist said. "I didn't know she stayed there so long."

"Stop all this crap, Mikael. The archives manager rang to tell me that Dirch had let the girl stay there as late as she liked. Which means she'll certainly be home. The night watchman is going to call me when she leaves."

PART 4

Hostile Takeover

JULY 11 TO DECEMBER 30

Ninety-two percent of women in Sweden who have been subjected to sexual assault have not reported the most recent violent incident to the police.

CHAPTER 24

Friday, July 11–Saturday, July 12

Martin Vanger bent down and went through Mikael's pockets. He took the key.

"Smart of you to change the lock," he said. "I'm going to take care of your girlfriend when she gets back."

Blomkvist reminded himself that Martin was a negotiator experienced from many industrial battles. He had already seen through one bluff.

"Why?"

"Why what?"

"Why all of this?" Blomkvist gestured vaguely at the space around him.

Martin bent down and put one hand under Blomkvist's chin, lifting his head so their eyes met.

"Because it's so easy," he said. "Women disappear all the time. Nobody misses them. Immigrants. Whores from Russia. Thousands of people pass through Sweden every year."

He let go of Blomkvist's head and stood up.

Martin's words hit Blomkvist like a punch in the face.

Christ Almighty. This is no historical mystery. Martin Vanger is murdering women today. And I wandered right into it . . .

"As it happens, I don't have a guest right now. But it might amuse you to know that while you and Henrik sat around babbling this winter and spring, there was a girl down here. Irina from Belarus. While you sat and ate dinner with me, she was locked up in the cage down here. It was a pleasant evening as I remember, no?"

Martin perched on the table, letting his legs dangle. Blomkvist shut his eyes. He suddenly felt acid in his throat and he swallowed hard. The pain in his gut and in his ribs seemed to swell.

"What do you do with the bodies?"

"I have my boat at the dock right below here. I take them a long way out to sea. Unlike my father, I don't leave traces. But he was smart too. He spread his victims out all over Sweden."

The puzzle pieces were falling into place.

Gottfried Vanger. From 1949 until 1965. Then Martin Vanger, starting in 1966 in Uppsala.

"You admire your father."

"He was the one who taught me. He initiated me when I was fourteen."

"Uddevalla. Lea Persson."

"Aren't you clever? Yes, I was there. I only watched, but I was there."

"1964. Sara Witt in Ronneby."

"I was sixteen. It was the first time I had a woman. My father taught me. I was the one who strangled her."

He's bragging. Good Lord, what a revoltingly sick family.

"You can't have any notion of how demented this is."

"You are a very ordinary little person, Mikael. You would not be able to understand the godlike feeling of having absolute control over someone's life and death."

"You enjoy torturing and killing women, Martin."

"I don't think so really. If I do an intellectual analysis of my condition, I'm more of a serial rapist than a serial murderer. In fact, most of all I'm a serial kidnapper. The killing is a natural consequence, so to speak, because I have to hide my crime.

"Of course my actions aren't socially acceptable, but my crime is first and foremost a crime against the conventions of society. Death doesn't come until the end of my guests' visits here, after I've grown weary of them. It's always so fascinating to see their disappointment."

"Disappointment?"

"Exactly. *Disappointment*. They imagine that if they please me, they'll live. They adapt to my rules. They start to trust me and develop a certain camaraderie with me, hoping to the very end that this camaraderie means something. The disappointment comes when it finally dawns on them that they've been well and truly screwed."

Martin walked around the table and leaned against the steel cage.

"You with your bourgeois conventions would never grasp this, but the excitement comes from planning a kidnapping. They're not done on impulse—those kinds of kidnappers invariably get caught. It's a science with thousands of details that I have to weigh. I have to identify my prey, map out her life, who is she, where does she come from, how can I make contact with her, what do I have to do to be alone with my *prey* without revealing my name or having it turn up in any future police investigation?"

Shut up, for God's sake, Blomkvist thought.

"Are you really interested in all this, Mikael?"

He bent down and stroked Blomkvist's cheek. The touch was almost tender.

"You realise that this can only end one way? Will it bother you if I smoke?"

"You could offer me a cigarette," he said.

Martin lit two cigarettes and carefully placed one of them between Blomkvist's lips, letting him take a long drag.

"Thanks," Blomkvist said, automatically.

Martin Vanger laughed again.

"You see. You've already started to adapt to the submission principle. I hold your life in my hands, Mikael. You know that I can dispatch you at any second. You pleaded with me to improve your quality of life, and you did so by using reason and a little good manners. And you were rewarded."

Blomkvist nodded. His heart was pounding so hard it was almost unbearable.

At 11:15 Lisbeth Salander drank the rest of the water from her PET bottle as she turned the pages. Unlike Blomkvist, who earlier in the day had choked on his coffee, she didn't get the water down the wrong way. On the other hand, she did open her eyes wide when she made the connection.

Click!

For two hours she had been wading through the staff newsletters from all points of the compass. The main newsletter was *Company Information.* It bore the Vanger logo—a Swedish banner fluttering in the wind, with the point forming an arrow. The publication was presumably put together by the firm's advertising department, and it was filled with propaganda that was supposed to make the employees feel that they were members of one big family.

In association with the winter sports holiday in February 1967, Henrik Vanger, in a magnanimous gesture, had invited fifty employees from the main office and their families to a week's skiing holiday in Härjedalen. The company had made record profits during the previous year. The PR department went too and put together a picture report.

Many of the pictures with amusing captions were from the slopes. Some showed groups in the bar, with laughing employees hoisting beer mugs. Two photographs were of a small morning function when Henrik Vanger proclaimed Ulla-Britt Mogren to be the Best Office Worker of the Year. She was given a bonus of five hundred kronor and a glass bowl.

The ceremony was held on the terrace of the hotel, clearly right before people were thinking of heading back to the slopes. About twenty people were in the picture.

On the far right, just behind Henrik Vanger, stood a man with long blond hair. He was wearing a dark padded jacket with a distinctive patch at the shoulder. Since the publication was in black-and-white, the colour wasn't identifiable, but Salander was willing to bet her life that the shoulder patch was red.

The caption explained the connection. . . . *far right, Martin Vanger (19), who is studying in Uppsala. He is already being discussed as someone with a promising future in the company's management.*

"Gotcha," Salander said in a low voice.

She switched off the desk lamp and left the newsletters in piles all over the desk—*something for that slut Lindgren to take care of tomorrow.*

She went out to the car park through a side door. As it closed behind her, she remembered that she had promised to tell the night watchman when she left. She stopped and let her eyes sweep over the car park. The watchman's office was on the other side of the building. That meant that she would have to walk all the way round to the other side. *Let sleeping dogs lie,* she decided.

Before she put on her helmet, she turned on her mobile and called Blomkvist's number. She got a message saying that the subscriber could not be reached. But she also saw that he had tried to call her no fewer than thirteen times between 3:30 and 9:00. In the last two hours, no call.

Salander tried the cottage number, but there was no answer. She frowned, strapped on her computer, put on her helmet, and kick-started the motorcycle. The ride from the main office at the entrance to Hedestad's industrial district out to Hedeby Island took ten minutes. A light was on in the kitchen.

Salander looked around. Her first thought was that Blomkvist had gone to see Frode, but from the bridge she had already noticed that the lights were off in Frode's house on the other side of the water. She looked at her watch: 11:40.

She went into the cottage, opened the wardrobe, and took out the two PCs that she was using to store the surveillance pictures from the cameras she had installed. It took her a while to run up the sequence of events.

At 15:32 Blomkvist entered the cabin.

At 16:03 he took his coffee cup out to the garden. He had a folder with him, which he studied. He made three brief telephone calls during the hour he spent out in the garden. The three calls corresponded exactly to calls she had not answered.

At 17:21 Blomkvist left the cottage. He was back less than fifteen minutes later.

At 18:20 he went to the gate and looked in the direction of the bridge.

At 21:03 he went out. He had not come back.

Salander fast-forwarded through the pictures from the other PC, which photographed the gate and the road outside the front door. She could see who had gone past during the day.

At 19:12 Nilsson came home.

At 19:42 the Saab that belonged to Östergården drove towards Hedestad.

At 20:02 the Saab was on its way back.

At 21:00 Martin Vanger's car went by. Three minutes later Blomkvist left the house.

At 21:50, Martin Vanger appeared in the camera's viewfinder. He stood at the gate for over a minute, looking at the house, then peering through the kitchen window. He went up to the porch and tried the door, taking out a key. He must have discovered that they had put in a new lock. He stood still for a moment before he turned on his heel and left the house.

Salander felt an ice-cold fear in her gut.

Martin Vanger once again left Blomkvist alone. He was still in his uncomfortable position with his hands behind his back and his neck fastened by a thin chain to an eyelet in the floor. He fiddled with the handcuffs, but he knew that he would not be able to get them off. The cuffs were so tight that his hands were numb.

He had no chance. He shut his eyes.

He did not know how much time had passed when he heard Martin's footsteps again. He appeared in Blomkvist's field of vision. He looked worried.

"Uncomfortable?" he said.

"Very," said Blomkvist.

"You've only got yourself to blame. You should have gone back to Stockholm."

"Why do you kill, Martin?"

"It's a choice that I made. I could discuss the moral and intellectual aspects of what I do; we could talk all night, but it wouldn't change anything. Try to look at it this way: a human being is a shell made of skin keeping the cells, blood, and chemical components in place. Very few end up in the history books. Most people succumb and disappear without a trace."

"You kill women."

"Those of us who murder for pleasure—I'm not the only one with this hobby—we live a complete life."

"But why Harriet? Your own sister?"

In a second Martin grabbed him by the hair.

"What happened to her, you little bastard? *Tell me.*"

"What do you mean?" Blomkvist gasped. He tried to turn his head to lessen the pain in his scalp. The chain tightened round his neck.

"You and Salander. What have you come up with?"

"Let go, for heaven's sake. We're talking."

Martin Vanger let go of his hair and sat cross-legged in front of Blomkvist. He took a knife from his jacket and opened it. He set the point against the skin just below Blomkvist's eye. Blomkvist forced himself to meet Martin's gaze.

"What the hell happened to her, bastard?"

"I don't understand. I thought you killed her."

Martin Vanger stared at Blomkvist for a long moment. Then he relaxed. He got up and wandered around the room, thinking. He threw the knife on the floor and laughed before he came back to face Blomkvist.

"Harriet, Harriet, always Harriet. We tried . . . to talk to her. Gottfried tried to teach her. We thought that she was one of us and that she would accept her duty, but she was just an ordinary . . . *cunt.* I had her under control, or so I thought, but she was planning to tell Henrik, and I realised that I couldn't trust her. Sooner or later she was going to tell someone about me."

"You killed her."

"I *wanted* to kill her. I *thought* about it, but I arrived too late. I couldn't get over to the island."

Blomkvist's brain was with difficulty trying to absorb this information, but it felt as if a message had popped up with the words INFORMATION OVERLOAD. Martin Vanger did not know what had happened to his sister.

All of a sudden Martin pulled his mobile telephone out of his pocket, glanced at the display, and put it on the chair next to the pistol.

"It's time to stop all this. I have to dispose of your anorexic bitch tonight too."

He took out a narrow leather strap from a cupboard and slipped it around Blomkvist's neck, like a noose. He loosened the chain that held him shackled to the floor, hauled him to his feet, and shoved him towards the wall. He slipped the leather strap through a loop above Blomkvist's head and then tightened it so that he was forced to stand on tiptoes.

"Is that too tight? Can you breathe?" He loosened it a notch and locked the other end of the strap in place, further down the wall. "I don't want you to suffocate all at once."

The noose was cutting so hard into Blomkvist's throat that he was incapable of uttering a word. Martin looked at him attentively.

Abruptly he unzipped Blomkvist's trousers and tugged them down, along with his boxer shorts. As he pulled them off, Blomkvist lost his foothold and dangled for a second from the noose before his toes again made contact with the floor. Martin went over to a cupboard and took out a pair of scissors. He cut off Blomkvist's T-shirt and tossed the bits on the floor. Then he took up a position some distance away from Mikael and regarded his victim.

"I've never had a boy in here," Martin said in a serious voice. "I've never touched another man, as a matter of fact . . . except for my father. That was my duty."

Blomkvist's temples were pounding. He could not put his weight on his feet without being strangled. He tried to use his fingers to get a grip on the concrete wall behind him, but there was nothing to hold on to.

"It's time," Martin Vanger said.

He put his hand on the strap and pulled down. Blomkvist instantly felt the noose cutting into his neck.

"I've always wondered how a man tastes."

He increased the pressure on the noose and leaned forward to kiss Blomkvist on the lips at the same time that a cold voice cut through the room.

"Hey, you fucking creep, in this shithole I've got a monopoly on that one."

Blomkvist heard Salander's voice through a red fog. He managed to focus his eyes enough to see her standing in the doorway. She was looking at Martin Vanger without expression.

"No . . . run," he croaked.

He could not see the look on Martin's face, but he could almost physically feel the shock when he turned around. For a second, time stood still. Then Martin reached for the pistol he had left on the chair.

Salander took three swift strides forward and swung a golf club she had hidden at her side. The iron flew in a wide arc and hit Martin on the collarbone near his shoulder. The blow had a terrible force, and Blomkvist heard something snap. Martin howled.

"Do you like pain, creep?" Salander said.

Her voice was as rough as sandpaper. As long as Blomkvist lived, he would never forget her face as she went on the attack. Her teeth were bared like a beast of prey. Her eyes were glittering, black as coal. She moved with the lightning speed of a tarantula and seemed totally focused on her prey as she swung the club again, striking Martin in the ribs.

He stumbled over the chair and fell. The pistol tumbled to the floor at Salander's feet. She kicked it away.

Then she struck for the third time, just as Martin Vanger was trying to get to his feet. She hit him with a loud smack on the hip. A horrible cry issued from Martin's throat. The fourth blow struck him from behind, between the shoulder blades.

"Lis . . . uuth . . ." Blomkvist gasped.

He was about to pass out, and the pain in his temples was almost unbearable.

She turned to him and saw that his face was the colour of a tomato, his eyes were open wide, and his tongue was popping out of his mouth.

She looked about her and saw the knife on the floor. Then she spared a glance at Martin Vanger, who was trying to crawl away from her, one arm hanging. He would not be making any trouble for the next few seconds. She let go of the golf club and picked up the knife. It had a sharp point but a dull edge. She stood on her toes and frantically sawed at the leather strap to get it off. It took several seconds before Blomkvist sank to the floor. But the noose was pulled tighter round his neck.

Salander looked again at Martin Vanger. He was on his feet but doubled over. She tried to dig her fingers under the noose. At first she did not dare cut it, but finally she slipped the point of the knife underneath, scoring Blomkvist's neck as she tried to expand the noose. At last it loosened and Blomkvist took several shaky, wheezing breaths.

For a moment Blomkvist had a sensation of his body and soul uniting. He had perfect vision and could make out every speck of dust in the room. He had perfect hearing and registered every breath, every rustle of clothing, as if they were entering his ears through a headset, and he was aware of the odour of Salander's sweat and the smell of leather from her jacket. Then the illusion burst as blood began streaming to his head.

Salander turned her head just as Martin Vanger disappeared out the door. She got up, grabbed the pistol, checked the magazine and flicked off the safety. She looked around and focused on the keys to the handcuffs, which lay in plain sight on the table.

"I'm going to take him," she said, running for the door. She grabbed the keys as she passed the table and tossed them back-handed to the floor next to Blomkvist.

He tried to shout to her to wait, but he managed only a rasping sound and by then she had vanished.

Salander had not forgotten that Martin Vanger had a rifle somewhere, and she stopped, holding the pistol ready to fire in front of her, as she came upstairs to the passageway between the garage and the kitchen. She listened, but she could hear no sound telling her where her prey was. She moved stealthily towards the kitchen, and she was almost there when she heard a car starting up in the courtyard.

From the drive she saw a pair of tail lights passing Henrik Vanger's house and turning down to the bridge, and she ran as fast as her legs could carry her. She stuffed the pistol in her jacket pocket and did not bother with the helmet as she started her motorcycle. Seconds later she was crossing the bridge.

He had maybe a ninety-second start when she came into the roundabout at the entrance to the E4. She could not see his car. She braked and turned off the motor to listen.

The sky was filled with heavy clouds. On the horizon she saw a hint of the dawn. Then she heard the sound of an engine and caught a glimpse of tail lights on the E4, going south. Salander kicked the motorcycle, put it into gear, and raced under the viaduct. She was doing 40 miles per hour as she took the curve of the entrance ramp. She saw no traffic and accelerated to full speed and flew forward. When the road began to curve along a ridge, she was doing 90 mph, which was about the fastest her souped-up lightweight bike could manage going downhill. After two minutes she saw the lights about 650 yards ahead.

Analyse consequences. What do I do now?

She decelerated to a more reasonable seventy-five and kept pace with him. She lost sight of him for several seconds when they took several bends. Then they came on to a long straight; she was only two hundred yards behind him.

He must have seen the headlight from her motorcycle, and he sped up when they took a long curve. She accelerated again but lost ground on the bends.

She saw the headlights of a truck approaching. Martin Vanger did too. He increased his speed again and drove straight into the oncoming lane. Salander saw the truck swerve and flash its lights, but the collision was unavoidable. Martin Vanger drove straight into the truck and the sound of the crash was terrible.

Salander braked. She saw the trailer start to jackknife across her lane. At the speed she was going, it took two seconds for her to cover the distance up to the accident site. She accelerated and steered on to the hard shoulder, avoiding the hurtling back of the truck by two yards as she flew past. Out of the corner of her eye she saw flames coming from the front of the truck.

She rode on, braking and thinking, for another 150 yards before she stopped and turned around. She saw the driver of the truck climb out of his cab on the passenger side. Then she accelerated again. At Åkerby, about a mile south, she turned left and took the old road back north, parallel to the E4. She went up a hill past the scene of the crash. Two cars had stopped. Big flames were boiling out of the wreckage of Martin's car, which was wedged underneath the truck. A man was spraying the flames with a small fire extinguisher.

She was soon rolling across the bridge at a low speed. She

parked outside the cottage and walked back to Martin Vanger's house.

Mikael was still fumbling with the handcuffs. His hands were so numb that he could not get a grip on the key. Salander unlocked the cuffs for him and held him tight as the blood began to circulate in his hands again.

"Martin?" he said in a hoarse voice.

"Dead. He drove slap into the front of a truck a couple of miles south on the E4."

Blomkvist stared at her. She had only been gone a few minutes.

"We have to . . . call the police," he whispered. He began coughing hard.

"Why?" Salander said.

For ten minutes Blomkvist was incapable of standing up. He was still on the floor, naked, leaning against the wall. He massaged his neck and lifted the water bottle with clumsy fingers. Salander waited patiently until his sense of touch started to return. She spent the time thinking.

"Put your trousers on."

She used Blomkvist's cut-up T-shirt to wipe fingerprints from the handcuffs, the knife, and the golf club. She picked up her PET bottle.

"What are you doing?"

"Get dressed and hurry up. It's getting light outside."

Blomkvist stood on shaky legs and managed to pull on his boxers and jeans. He slipped on his trainers. Salander stuffed his socks into her jacket pocket and then stopped him.

"What exactly did you touch down here?"

Blomkvist looked around. He tried to remember. At last he said that he had touched nothing except the door and the keys. Salander found the keys in Martin Vanger's jacket, which he had hung over the chair. She wiped the door handle and the switch and turned off the light. She helped Blomkvist up the basement stairs and told him to wait in the passageway while she put the golf club back in its proper place. When she came back she was carrying a dark T-shirt that belonged to Martin Vanger.

"Put this on. I don't want anyone to see you scampering about with a bare chest tonight."

Blomkvist realised that he was in a state of shock. Salander had taken charge, and passively he obeyed her instructions. She led him out of Martin's house. She held on to him the whole time. As soon as they stepped inside the cottage, she stopped him.

"If anyone sees us and asks what we were doing outside tonight, you and I went out to the point for a nighttime walk, and we had sex out there."

"Lisbeth, I can't . . ."

"Get in the shower. *Now.*"

She helped him off with his clothes and propelled him to the bathroom. Then she put on water for coffee and made half a dozen thick sandwiches on rye bread with cheese and liver sausage and dill pickles. She sat down at the kitchen table and was thinking hard when he came limping back into the room. She studied the bruises and scrapes on his body. The noose had been so tight that he had a dark red mark around his neck, and the knife had made a bloody gash in his skin on the left side.

"Get into bed," she said.

She improvised bandages and covered the wound with a makeshift compress. Then she poured the coffee and handed him a sandwich.

"I'm really not hungry," he said.

"I don't give a damn if you're hungry. Just eat," Salander commanded, taking a big bite of her own cheese sandwich.

Blomkvist closed his eyes for a moment, then he sat up and took a bite. His throat hurt so much that he could scarcely swallow.

Salander took off her leather jacket and from the bathroom brought a jar of Tiger Balm from her sponge bag.

"Let the coffee cool for a while. Lie face down."

She spent five minutes massaging his back and rubbing him with the liniment. Then she turned him over and gave him the same treatment on the front.

"You're going to have some serious bruises for a while."

"Lisbeth, we have to call the police."

"No," she replied with such vehemence that Blomkvist opened his eyes in surprise. "If you call the police, I'm leaving. I don't want to have anything to do with them. Martin Vanger is dead. He died in a car accident. He was alone in the car. There are witnesses. Let the police or someone else discover that fucking torture chamber. You and I are just as ignorant about its existence as everyone else in this village."

"Why?"

She ignored him and started massaging his aching thighs.

"Lisbeth, we can't just . . ."

"If you go on nagging, I'll drag you back to Martin's grotto and chain you up again."

As she said this, Blomkvist fell asleep, as suddenly as if he had fainted.

CHAPTER 25

Saturday, July 12–Monday, July 14

Blomkvist woke with a start at 5:00 in the morning, scrabbling at his neck to get rid of the noose. Salander came in and took hold of his hands, keeping him still. He opened his eyes and looked at her blearily.

"I didn't know that you played golf," he said, closing his eyes again. She sat with him for a couple of minutes until she was sure he was asleep. While he slept, Salander had gone back to Martin Vanger's basement to examine and photograph the crime scene. In addition to the torture instruments, she had found a collection of violent pornographic magazines and a large number of Polaroid photographs pasted into albums.

There was no diary. On the other hand, she did find two A4 binders with passport photographs and handwritten notes about the women. She put the binders in a nylon bag along with Martin's Dell PC laptop, which she found on the hall table upstairs. While Blomkvist slept she continued her examination of Martin's computer and binders. It was after 6:00 by the time she turned off the computer. She lit a cigarette.

Together with Mikael Blomkvist she had taken up the hunt for what they thought was a serial killer from the past. They had found something appallingly different. She could hardly imagine the horrors that must have played out in Martin Vanger's basement, in the midst of this well-ordered, idyllic spot.

She tried to understand.

Martin Vanger had been killing women since the sixties, during the past fifteen years one or two victims per year. The killing had been done so discreetly and was so well planned that no-one was even aware that a serial killer was at work. How was that possible?

The binders provided a partial answer.

His victims were often new arrivals, immigrant girls who had no friends or social contacts in Sweden. There were also prostitutes and social outcasts, with drug abuse or other problems in their background.

From her own studies of the psychology of sexual sadism, Salander had learned that this type of murderer usually collected souvenirs from his victims. These souvenirs functioned as reminders that the killer could use to re-create some of the pleasure he had experienced. Martin Vanger had developed this peculiarity by keeping a "death book." He had catalogued and graded his victims. He had described their suffering. He had documented his killings with videotapes and photographs.

The violence and the killing were the goal, but Salander concluded that it was the hunt that was Martin Vanger's primary interest. In his laptop he had created a database with a list of more than a hundred women. There were employees from the Vanger Corporation, waitresses in restaurants where he regularly ate, reception staff in hotels, clerks at the social security office, the secretaries of business associates, and many other women. It seemed as if Martin had pigeonholed practically every woman he had ever come into contact with.

He had killed only a fraction of these women, but every woman anywhere near him was a potential victim. The cataloguing had the mark of a passionate hobby, and he must have devoted countless hours to it.

Is she married or single? Does she have children and family? Where does she work? Where does she live? What kind of car does she drive? What sort of education does she have? Hair colour? Skin colour? Figure?

The gathering of personal information about potential victims must have been a significant part of Martin Vanger's sexual fantasies. He was first of all a stalker, and second a murderer.

When she had finished reading, she discovered a small envelope in one of the binders. She pulled out two much-handled and faded Polaroid pictures. In the first picture a dark-haired girl was sitting at a table. The girl had on dark jeans and had a bare torso with tiny, pointed breasts. She had turned her face away from the camera and was in the process of lifting one arm in a gesture of defence, almost as if the photographer had surprised her. In the second picture she was completely naked. She was lying on her stomach on a blue bedspread. Her face was still turned away from the camera.

Salander stuffed the envelope with the pictures into her jacket pocket. After that she carried the binders over to the woodstove and struck a match. When she was done with the fire, she stirred the ashes. It was pouring down with rain when she took a short walk and, kneeling as if to tie a shoelace, discreetly dropped Martin Vanger's laptop into the water under the bridge.

When Frode marched through the open door at 7:30 that morning, Salander was at the kitchen table smoking a cigarette and drinking coffee. Frode's face was ashen, and he looked as if he had had a cruel awakening.

"Where's Mikael?" he said.

"He's still asleep."

Frode sat down heavily on a kitchen chair. Salander poured coffee and pushed the cup over to him.

"Martin . . . I just found out that Martin was killed in a car accident last night."

"That's sad," Salander said, taking a sip of her own coffee.

Frode looked up. At first he stared at her, uncomprehending. Then his eyes opened wide.

"What . . . ?"

"He crashed. How annoying."

"What do you know about this?"

"He drove his car right into the front of a truck. He committed suicide. The press, the stress, a floundering financial empire, dot, dot, dot, too much for him. At least that's what I suppose it will say on the placards."

Frode looked as if he were about to have a cerebral haemorrhage. He stood up swiftly and walked unsteadily to the bedroom.

"Let him sleep," Salander snapped.

Frode looked at the sleeping figure. He saw the black and blue marks on Blomkvist's face and the contusions on his chest. Then he saw the flaming line where the noose had been. Salander touched his arm and closed the door. Frode backed out and sank on to the kitchen bench.

Lisbeth Salander told him succinctly what had happened during the night. She told him what Martin Vanger's chamber of horrors looked like and how she had found Mikael with a noose around his neck and the CEO of the Vanger Corporation standing in front of his naked body. She told him what she had found in the company's archives the day before and how she had established a possible link between Martin's father and the murders of at least seven women.

Frode interrupted her recitation only once. When she stopped talking, he sat mutely for several minutes before he took a deep breath and said: "What are we going to do?"

"That's not for me to say," Salander said.

"But . . ."

"As I see it, I've never set foot in Hedestad."

"I don't understand."

"Under no circumstances do I want my name in any police report. I don't exist in connection with any of this. If my name is mentioned in connection with this story, I'll deny that I've ever been here, and I'll refuse to answer a single question."

Frode gave her a searching look.

"I don't understand."

"You don't need to understand."

"Then what should I do?"

"You'll have to work that out for yourself. Only leave me and Mikael out of it."

Frode was deathly pale.

"Look at it this way: the only thing you know is that Martin Vanger died in a traffic accident. You have no idea that he was also an insane, nauseating serial killer, and you've never heard about the room in his basement."

She put the key on the table between them.

"You've got time—before anyone is going to clean out Martin's house and discover the basement."

"We have to go to the police about this."

"Not *we*. *You* can go to the police if you like. It's your decision."

"This can't be brushed under a carpet."

"I'm not suggesting that it should be brushed anywhere, just that you leave me and Mikael out of it. When you discover the room, you draw your own conclusions and decide for yourself who you want to tell."

"If what you say is true, it means that Martin has kidnapped and murdered women . . . there must be families that are desperate because they don't know where their children are. We can't just . . ."

"That's right. But there's just one problem. The bodies are gone. Maybe you'll find passports or ID cards in some drawer. Maybe some of the victims can be identified from the videotapes. But you don't need to decide today. Think it over."

Frode looked panic-stricken.

"Oh, dear God. This will be the death blow for the company. Think of how many families will lose their livelihood if it gets out that Martin . . ."

Frode rocked back and forth, juggling with a moral dilemma.

"That's one issue. If Isabella Vanger is to inherit, you may think it would be inappropriate if she were the first one to light upon her son's hobby."

"I have to go and see . . ."

"I think you should stay away from that room today," Salander said sharply. "You have a lot of things to take care of. You have to go and tell Henrik, and you have to call a special meeting of the board and do all those things you chaps do when your CEO dies."

Frode thought about what she was saying. His heart was thumping. He was the old attorney and problem-solver who was expected to have a plan ready to meet any eventuality, yet he felt powerless to act. It suddenly dawned on him that here he was, taking orders from a child. She had somehow seized control of the situation and given him the guidelines that he himself was unable to formulate.

"And Harriet . . . ?"

"Mikael and I are not finished yet. But you can tell Herr Vanger that I think now that we're going to solve it."

Martin Vanger's unexpected demise was the top story on the 9:00 news on the radio when Blomkvist woke up. Nothing was reported about the night's events other than to say that the industrialist had inexplicably and at high speed crossed to the wrong side of the E4, travelling south. He had been alone in the car.

The local radio ran a story that dealt with concern for the future of the Vanger Corporation and the consequences that this death would inevitably have for the company.

A hastily composed lunchtime update from the TT wire service had the headline A TOWN IN SHOCK, and it summed up the problems of the Vanger Corporation. It escaped no-one's notice that in Hedestad alone more than 3,000 of the town's 21,000 inhabitants were employed by the Vanger Corporation or were otherwise dependent on the prosperity of the company. The firm's CEO was dead, and the former CEO was seriously ill after a heart attack. There was no natural heir. All this at a time considered to be among the most critical in the company's history.

Blomkvist had had the option of going to the police in Hedestad and telling them what had happened that night, but Salander had already set a certain process in motion. Since he had not immediately called the police, it became harder to do so with each hour that passed. He spent the morning in gloomy silence, sitting on the kitchen bench, watching the rain outside. Around 10:00 there was another cloudburst, but by lunchtime the rain had stopped and the wind had died down a bit. He went out and wiped off the garden furniture and then sat there with a mug of coffee. He was wearing a shirt with the collar turned up.

Martin's death cast a shadow, of course, over the daily life of Hedeby. Cars began parking outside Isabella Vanger's house as the clan gathered to offer condolences. Salander observed the procession without emotion.

"How are you feeling?" she said at last.

"I think I'm still in shock," he said. "I was helpless. For several hours I was convinced that I was going to die. I felt the fear of death and there wasn't a thing I could do."

He stretched out his hand and placed it on her knee.

"Thank you," he said. "But for you, I *would* be dead."

Salander smiled her crooked smile.

"All the same . . . I don't understand how you could be such an idiot as to tackle him on your own. I was chained to the floor down there, praying that you'd see the picture and put two and two together and call the police."

"If I'd waited for the police, you wouldn't have survived. I wasn't going to let that motherfucker kill you."

"Why don't you want to talk to the police?"

"I never talk to the authorities."

"Why not?"

"That's my business. But in your case, I don't think it would be a terrific career move to be hung out to dry as the journalist who was stripped naked by Martin Vanger, the famous serial killer. If you don't like 'Kalle Blomkvist,' you can think up a whole new epithet. Just don't take it out of this chapter of your heroic life."

Blomkvist gave her a searching look and dropped the subject.

"We do still have a problem," she said.

Blomkvist nodded. "What happened to Harriet. Yes."

Salander laid the two Polaroid pictures on the table in front of him. She explained where she'd found them. Mikael studied the pictures intently for a while before he looked up.

"It might be her," he said at last. "I wouldn't swear to it, but the shape of her body and the hair remind me of the pictures I've seen."

They sat in the garden for an hour, piecing together the details. They discovered that each of them, independently and from different directions, had identified Martin Vanger as the missing link.

Salander never did find the photograph that Blomkvist had left on the kitchen table. She had come to the conclusion that Blomkvist had done something stupid after studying the pictures from the surveillance cameras. She had gone over to Martin Vanger's house by way of the shore and looked in all the windows and seen no-one. She had tried all the doors and windows on the ground floor. Finally she had climbed in through an open balcony door upstairs. It had taken a long time, and she had moved extremely cautiously as she searched the house, room by room. Eventually she found the stairs down to the basement. Martin had been careless. He left the door to his chamber of horrors ajar, and she was able to form a clear impression of the situation.

Blomkvist asked her how much she had heard of what Martin said.

"Not much. I got there when he was asking you about what happened to Harriet, just before he hung you up by the noose. I left for a few minutes to go back and find a weapon."

"Martin had no idea what happened to Harriet," Blomkvist said.

"Do you believe that?"

"Yes," Blomkvist said without hesitation. "Martin was dafter than a syphilitic polecat—where do I get these metaphors from?—but he confessed to all the crimes he had committed. I think that he wanted to impress me. But when it came to Harriet, he was as desperate as Henrik Vanger to find out what happened."

"So . . . where does that take us?"

"We know that Gottfried was responsible for the first series of murders, between 1949 and 1965."

"OK. And he brought on little Martin."

"Talk about a dysfunctional family," Blomkvist said. "Martin really didn't have a chance."

Salander gave him a strange look.

"What Martin told me—even though it was rambling—was that his father started his apprenticeship after he reached puberty. He was there at the murder of Lea in Uddevalla in 1962. He was fourteen, for God's sake. He was there at the murder of Sara in 1964 and that time he took an active part. He was sixteen."

"And?"

"He said that he had never touched another man—except his father. That made me think that . . . well, the only possible conclusion is that his father raped him. Martin called it 'his duty.' The sexual assaults must have gone on for a long time. He was raised by his father, so to speak."

"Bullshit," Salander said, her voice as hard as flint.

Blomkvist stared at her in astonishment. She had a stubborn look in her eyes. There was not an ounce of sympathy in it.

"Martin had exactly the same opportunity as anyone else to strike back. He killed and he raped because he liked doing it."

"I'm not saying otherwise. But Martin was a repressed boy and under the influence of his father, just as Gottfried was cowed by his father, the Nazi."

"So you're assuming that Martin had no will of his own and that people become whatever they've been brought up to be."

Blomkvist smiled cautiously. "Is this a sensitive issue?"

Salander's eyes blazed with fury. Blomkvist quickly went on. "I'm only saying that I think that a person's upbringing does play a role. Gottfried's father beat him mercilessly for years. That leaves its mark."

"Bullshit," Salander said again. "Gottfried isn't the only kid who was ever mistreated. That doesn't give him the right to murder women. He made that choice himself. And the same is true of Martin."

Blomkvist held up his hand.

"Can we not argue?"

"I'm not arguing. I just think that it's pathetic that creeps always have to have someone else to blame."

"They have a personal responsibility. We'll work it all out later. What matters is that Martin was seventeen when Gottfried died, and he didn't have anyone to guide him. He tried to continue in his father's footsteps. In February 1966, in Uppsala."

Blomkvist reached for one of Salander's cigarettes.

"I won't speculate about what impulses Gottfried was trying to satisfy or how he himself interpreted what he was doing. There's some sort of Biblical gibberish that a psychiatrist might be able to figure out, something to do with punishment and purification in a figurative sense. It doesn't matter what it was. He was a cut and dried serial killer.

"Gottfried wanted to kill women and clothe his actions in some sort of pseudo-religious clap-trap. Martin didn't even pretend to have an excuse. He was organised and did his killing systematically. He also had money to put into his hobby. And he was shrewder than his father. Every time Gottfried left a body behind, it led to a police investigation and the risk that someone might track him down, or at least link together the various murders."

"Martin Vanger built his house in the seventies," Salander said pensively.

"I think Henrik mentioned it was in 1978. Presumably he ordered a safe room put in for important files or some such purpose. He got a soundproofed, windowless room with a steel door."

"He's had that room for twenty-five years."

They fell silent for a while as Blomkvist thought about what atrocities must have taken place there for a quarter of a century. Salander did not need to think about the matter; she had seen the videotapes. She noticed that Blomkvist was unconsciously touching his neck.

"Gottfried hated women and taught his son to hate women at the same time as he was raping him. But there's also some sort of undertone . . . I think Gottfried fantasised that his children would share his, to put it mildly, perverted world view. When I asked about Harriet, his own sister, Martin said: 'We tried to talk to her. But she was just an ordinary cunt. She was planning to tell Henrik.' "

"I heard him. That was about when I got down to the basement. And that means that we know what her aborted conversation with Henrik was to have been about."

Blomkvist frowned. "Not really. Think of the chronology. We don't know when Gottfried first raped his son, but he took Martin with him when he murdered Lea Persson in Uddevalla in 1962. He drowned in 1965. Before that, he and Martin tried to *talk to* Harriet. Where does that lead us?"

"Martin wasn't the only one that Gottfried assaulted. He also assaulted Harriet."

"Gottfried was the teacher. Martin was the pupil. Harriet was what? Their plaything?"

"Gottfried taught Martin to screw his sister." Salander pointed at the Polaroid prints. "It's hard to determine her attitude from these two pictures because we can't see her face, but she's trying to hide from the camera."

"Let's say that it started when she was fourteen, in 1964. She defended herself—couldn't accept it, as Martin put it. That was what she was threatening to tell Henrik about. Martin undoubtedly had nothing to say in this connection; he just did what his father told him. But he and Gottfried had formed some sort of . . . pact, and they tried to initiate Harriet into it too."

Salander said: "In your notes you wrote that Henrik had let Harriet move into his house in the winter of 1964."

"Henrik could see there was something wrong in her family. He thought it was the bickering and friction between Gottfried and Isabella that was the cause, and he took her in so that she could have some peace and quiet and concentrate on her studies."

"An unforeseen obstacle for Gottfried and Martin. They couldn't get their hands on her as easily or control her life. But eventually . . . Where did the assault take place?"

"It must have been at Gottfried's cabin. I'm almost positive that these pictures were taken there—it should be possible to check. The cabin is in a perfect location, isolated and far from the village. Then Gottfried got drunk one last time and died in a most banal way."

"So Harriet's father had attempted to have sex with her, but my guess is that he didn't initiate her into the killing."

Blomkvist realised that this was a weak point. Harriet had made note of the names of Gottfried's victims, pairing them up with Bible quotes, but her interest in the Bible did not emerge until the last year, and by then Gottfried was already dead. He paused, trying to come up with a logical explanation.

"Sometime along the way Harriet discovered that Gottfried had not only committed incest, but he was also a serial sex murderer," he said.

"We don't know when she found out about the murders. It could have been right before Gottfried drowned. It might also have been after he drowned, if he had a diary or had saved press cuttings about them. Something put her on his track."

"But that wasn't what she was threatening to tell Henrik," Blomkvist said.

"It was Martin," Salander said. "Her father was dead, but Martin was going on abusing her."

"Exactly."

"But it was a year before she took any action."

"What would you do if you found out that your father was a murderer who had been raping your brother?"

"I'd kill the fucker," Salander said in such a sober tone that Blomkvist believed her. He remembered her face as she was attacking Martin Vanger. He smiled joylessly.

"OK, but Harriet wasn't like you. Gottfried died before she managed to do anything. That also makes sense. When Gottfried died, Isabella sent Martin to Uppsala. He might have come home for Christmas or other holidays, but during that following year he didn't see Harriet very often. She was able to get some distance from him."

"And she started studying the Bible."

"And in light of what we now know, it didn't have to be for any religious reasons. Maybe she simply wanted to know what her father had been up to. She brooded over it until the Children's Day celebration in 1966. Then suddenly she sees her brother on Järnvägsgatan and realises that he's back. We don't know if they talked to each other or if he said anything. But no matter what happened, Harriet had an urge to go straight home and talk to Henrik."

"And then she disappeared."

After they had gone over the chain of events, it was not hard to understand what the rest of the puzzle must have looked like.

Blomkvist and Salander packed their bags. Before they left, Blomkvist called Frode and told him that he and Salander had to go away for a while, but that he absolutely wanted to see Henrik Vanger before they left.

Blomkvist needed to know what Frode had told Henrik. The man sounded so stressed on the telephone that Blomkvist felt concerned for him. Frode said that he had only told him that Martin had died in a car accident.

It was thundering again when Blomkvist parked outside Hedestad Hospital, and the sky was filled once more with heavy rain clouds. He hurried across the car park just as it started to rain.

Vanger was wearing a bathrobe, sitting at a table by the window of his room. His illness had left its mark, but Vanger had regained some colour in his face and looked as if he were on the path to recovery. They shook hands. Blomkvist asked the nurse to leave them alone for a few minutes.

"You've been avoiding me," Vanger said.

Mikael nodded. "On purpose. Your family didn't want me to come at all, but today everyone is over at Isabella's house."

"Poor Martin," Vanger said.

"Henrik. You gave me an assignment to dig up the truth about what happened to Harriet. Did you expect the truth to be painless?"

The old man looked at him. Then his eyes widened.

"Martin?"

"He's part of the story."

Henrik closed his eyes.

"Now I have got a question for you," Blomkvist said.

"Tell me."

"Do you still want to know what happened? Even if it turns out to be painful and even if the truth is worse than you imagined?"

Henrik gave Blomkvist a long look. Then he said, "I want to know. That was the point of your assignment."

"OK. I think I know what happened to Harriet. But there's one last piece of the puzzle missing before I'm sure."

"Tell me."

"No. Not today. What I want you to do right now is to rest. The doctors say that the crisis is over and that you're getting better."

"Don't you treat me like a child, young man."

"I haven't worked it all out yet. What I have is a theory. I am going out to find the last piece of the puzzle. The next time you see me, I'll tell you the whole story. It may take a while, but I want you to know that I'm coming back and that you'll know the truth."

Salander pulled a tarpaulin over her motorcycle and left it on the shady side of the cabin. Then she got into Blomkvist's borrowed car. The thunderstorm had returned with renewed force, and just south of Gävle there was such a fierce downpour that Blomkvist could hardly see the road. Just to be safe, he pulled into a petrol station. They waited for the rain to let up, so they did not arrive in Stockholm until 7:00 that evening. Blomkvist gave Salander the security code to his building and dropped her off at the central tunnelbana. His apartment seemed unfamiliar.

He vacuumed and dusted while Salander went to see Plague in Sundbyberg. She arrived at Blomkvist's apartment at around midnight and spent ten minutes examining every nook and cranny of it. Then she stood at the window for a long time, looking at the view facing the Slussen locks.

They got undressed and slept.

. . .

At noon the next day they landed at London's Gatwick Airport. They were met with rain. Blomkvist had booked a room at the Hotel James near Hyde Park, an excellent hotel compared to all the one-star places in Bayswater where he had always ended up on his previous trips to London.

At 5:00 p.m. they were standing at the bar when a youngish man came towards them. He was almost bald, with a blond beard, and he was wearing jeans and a jacket that was too big for him.

"Wasp?"

"Trinity?" she said. They nodded to each other. He did not ask for Blomkvist's name.

Trinity's partner was introduced as Bob the Dog. He was in an old VW van around the corner. They climbed in through the sliding doors and sat down on folding chairs fastened to the sides. While Bob navigated through the London traffic, Wasp and Trinity talked.

"Plague said this had to do with some crash-bang job."

"Telephone tapping and checking emails in a computer. It might go fast, or it could take a couple of days, depending on how much pressure he applies." Lisbeth gestured towards Blomkvist with her thumb. "Can you do it?"

"Do dogs have fleas?" Trinity said.

Anita Vanger lived in a terrace house in the attractive suburb of St. Albans, about an hour's drive north. From the van they saw her arrive home and unlock the door some time after 7:30 that evening. They waited until she had settled, had her supper, and was sitting in front of the TV before Blomkvist rang the doorbell.

An almost identical copy of Cecilia Vanger opened the door, her expression politely questioning.

"Hi, Anita. My name is Mikael Blomkvist. Henrik Vanger

asked me to come and see you. I assume that you've heard the news about Martin."

Her expression changed from surprise to wariness. She knew exactly who Mikael Blomkvist was. But Henrik's name meant that she was forced to open the door. She showed Blomkvist into her living room. He noticed a signed lithograph by Anders Zorn over the fireplace. It was altogether a charming room.

"Forgive me for bothering you out of the blue, but I happened to be in St. Albans, and I tried to call you during the day."

"I understand. Please tell me what this is about?"

"Are you planning to be at the funeral?"

"No, as a matter of fact, I'm not. Martin and I weren't close, and anyway, I can't get away at the moment."

Anita Vanger had stayed away from Hedestad for thirty years. After her father moved back to Hedeby Island, she had hardly set foot there.

"I want to know what happened to Harriet Vanger, Anita. It's time for the truth."

"Harriet? I don't know what you mean."

Blomkvist smiled at her feigned surprise.

"You were Harriet's closest friend in the family. You were the one she turned to with her horrible story."

"I can't think what you're talking about," Anita said.

"Anita, you were in Harriet's room that day. I have photographic proof of it, in spite of what you said to Inspector Morell. In a few days I'm going to report to Henrik, and he'll take it from there. It would be better to tell me what happened."

Anita Vanger stood up.

"Get out of my house this minute."

Blomkvist got up.

"Sooner or later you're going to have to talk to me."

"I have nothing now, nor ever will have, anything to say to you."

"Martin is dead," Blomkvist said. "You never liked Martin. I think that you moved to London not only to avoid seeing your father but also so that you wouldn't have to see Martin. That means that you also knew about Martin, and the only one who could have told you was Harriet. The question is: what did you do with that knowledge?"

Anita Vanger slammed her front door in his face.

Salander smiled with satisfaction as she unfastened the microphone from under his shirt.

"She picked up the telephone about twenty seconds after she nearly took the door off its hinges," she said.

"The country code is Australia," Trinity said, putting down the earphones on the little desk in the van. "I need to check the area code." He switched on his laptop. "OK, she called the following number, which is a telephone in a town called Tennant Creek, north of Alice Springs in the Northern Territory. Do you want to hear the conversation?"

Blomkvist nodded. "What time is it in Australia right now?"

"About 5:00 in the morning." Trinity started the digital player and attached a speaker. Mikael counted eight rings before someone picked up the telephone. The conversation took place in English.

"Hi. It's me."

"Hmm, I know I'm a morning person but . . ."

"I thought of calling you yesterday . . . Martin is dead. He seems to have driven his car into a truck the day before yesterday."

Silence. Then what sounded like someone clearing their throat, but it might have been: "Good."

"But we have got a problem. A disgusting journalist that Henrik dug up from somewhere has just knocked on my door, here in St. Albans. He's asking questions about what happened in 1966. He knows something."

Again silence. Then a commanding voice.

"Anita. Put down the telephone right now. We can't have any contact for a while."

"But . . ."

"Write a letter. Tell me what's going on." Then the conversation was over.

"Sharp chick," Salander said.

They returned to their hotel just before 11:00. The front desk manager helped them to reserve seats on the next available flight to Australia. Soon they had reservations on a plane leaving at 7:05 the following evening, destination Melbourne, changing in Singapore.

This was Salander's first visit to London. They spent the morning walking from Covent Garden through Soho. They stopped to have a caffe latte on Old Compton Street. Around 3:00 they were back at the hotel to collect their luggage. While Blomkvist paid the bill, Salander turned on her mobile. She had a text message.

"Armansky says to call at once."

She used a telephone in the lobby. Blomkvist, who was standing a short distance away, noticed Salander turn to him with a frozen expression on her face. He was at her side at once.

"What is it?"

"My mother died. I have to go home."

Salander looked so unhappy that he put his arms around her. She pushed him away.

They sat in the hotel bar. When Blomkvist said that he would cancel the reservations to Australia and go back to Stockholm with her, she shook her head.

"No," she said. "We can't screw up the job now. You'll have to go by yourself."

They parted outside the hotel, each of them making for a different airport.

CHAPTER 26

Tuesday, July 15–Thursday, July 17

Blomkvist flew from Melbourne to Alice Springs. After that he had to choose either to charter a plane or to rent a car for the remaining 250-mile trip north. He chose to go by car.

An unknown person with the biblical signature of Joshua, who was part of Plague's or possibly Trinity's mysterious international network, had left an envelope for him at the central information desk at Melbourne airport.

The number that Anita had called belonged to a place called Cochran Farm. It was a sheep station. An article pulled off the Internet gave a snapshot guide.

Australia: population of 18 million; sheep farmers, 53,000; approx. 120 million head of sheep. The export of wool approx. 3.5 billion dollars annually. Australia exports 700 million tons of mutton and lamb, plus skins for clothing. Combined meat and wool production one of the country's most important industries . . .

Cochran Farm, founded 1891 by Jeremy Cochran, Australia's

fifth largest agricultural enterprise, approx. 60,000 Merino sheep (wool considered especially fine). The station also raised cattle, pigs, and chickens. Cochran Farm had impressive annual exports to the U.S.A., Japan, China, and Europe.

The personal biographies were fascinating.

In 1972 Cochran Farm passed down from Raymond Cochran to Spencer Cochran, educ. Oxford. Spencer d. in 1994, and farm run by widow. Blomkvist found her in a blurry, low-resolution photograph downloaded from the Cochran Farm website. It showed a woman with short blonde hair, her face partially hidden, shearing a sheep.

According to Joshua's note, the couple had married in Italy in 1971.

Her name was Anita Cochran.

Blomkvist stopped overnight in a dried-up hole of a town with the hopeful name of Wannado. At the local pub he ate roast mutton and downed three pints along with some locals who all called him "mate."

Last thing before he went to bed he called Berger in New York.

"I'm sorry, Ricky, but I've been so busy that I haven't had time to call."

"What the hell is going on?" she exploded. "Christer called and told me that Martin Vanger had been killed in a car accident."

"It's a long story."

"And why don't you answer your telephone? I've been calling like crazy for two days."

"It doesn't work here."

"Where is here?"

"Right now I'm about one hundred twenty-five miles north of Alice Springs. In Australia, that is."

Mikael had rarely managed to surprise Berger. This time she was silent for nearly ten seconds.

"And what are you doing in Australia? If I might ask."

"I'm finishing up the job. I'll be back in a few days. I just called to tell you that my work for Henrik Vanger is almost done."

He arrived at Cochran Farm around noon the following day, to be told that Anita Cochran was at a sheep station near a place called Makawaka seventy-five miles farther west.

It was 4:00 in the afternoon by the time Mikael found his way there on dusty back roads. He stopped at a gate where some sheep ranchers were gathered around the hood of a Jeep having coffee. Blomkvist got out and explained that he was looking for Anita Cochran. They all turned towards a muscular young man, clearly the decision-maker of the group. He was bare chested and very brown except for the parts normally covered by his T-shirt. He was wearing a wide-brimmed hat.

"The boss is about eighteen miles off in that direction," he said, pointing with his thumb.

He cast a sceptical glance at Blomkvist's vehicle and said that it might not be such a good idea to go on in that Japanese toy car. Finally the tanned athlete said that he was heading that way and would drive Blomkvist in his Jeep. Blomkvist thanked him and took along his computer case.

The man introduced himself as Jeff and said that he was the "studs manager" at the station. Blomkvist asked him to explain what that meant. Jeff gave him a sidelong look and concluded that Blomkvist was not from these parts. He explained that a studs manager was rather the equivalent of a financial manager in a bank, although he administered sheep, and that a "station" was the Australian word for ranch.

They continued to converse as Jeff cheerfully steered the Jeep at about ten kilometres an hour down into a ravine with a 20° slope. Blomkvist thanked his lucky stars that he had not attempted the drive in his rental car. He asked what was down in the ravine and was told that it was the pasture land for 700 head of sheep.

"As I understand it, Cochran Farm is one of the bigger ranches."

"We're one of the largest in all of Australia," Jeff said with a certain pride in his voice. "We run about 9,000 sheep here in the Makawaka district, but we have stations in both New South Wales and Western Australia. We have 60,000 plus head."

They came out from the ravine into a hilly but gentler landscape. Blomkvist suddenly heard shots. He saw sheep cadavers, big bonfires, and a dozen ranch hands. Several men seemed to be carrying rifles. They were apparently slaughtering sheep.

Involuntarily, he thought of the biblical sacrificial lambs.

Then he saw a woman with short blonde hair wearing jeans and a red-and-white checked shirt. Jeff stopped a few yards away from her.

"Hi, Boss. We've got a tourist," he said.

Blomkvist got out of the Jeep and looked at her. She looked back with an inquisitive expression.

"Hi, Harriet. It's been a long time," he said in Swedish.

None of the men who worked for Anita Cochran understood what he said, but they all saw her reaction. She took a step back, looking shocked. The men saw her response, stopped their joking, and straightened up, ready to intervene against this odd stranger. Jeff's friendliness suddenly evaporated and he advanced towards Blomkvist.

Blomkvist was keenly aware how vulnerable he was. A word from Anita Cochran and he would be done for.

Then the moment passed. Harriet Vanger waved her hand in a peaceful gesture and the men moved back. She came over to Blomkvist and met his gaze. Her face was sweaty and dirty. Her blonde hair had darker roots. Her face was older and thinner, but she had grown into the beautiful woman that her confirmation portrait had promised.

"Have we met before?" she said.

"Yes, we have. I am Mikael Blomkvist. You were my babysitter one summer when I was three years old. You were twelve or thirteen at the time."

It took a few seconds for her puzzled expression to clear, and then he saw that she remembered. She looked surprised.

"What do you want?"

"Harriet, I'm not your enemy. I'm not here to make trouble for you. But I need to talk with you."

She turned to Jeff and told him to take over, then signalled to Blomkvist to follow her. They walked a few hundred feet over to a group of white canvas tents in a grove of trees. She motioned him to a camp stool at a rickety table and poured water into a basin. She rinsed her face, dried it, and went inside the tent to change her shirt. She got two beers out of a cooler.

"So. Talk."

"Why are you shooting the sheep?"

"We have a contagious epidemic. Most of these sheep are probably healthy, but we can't risk it spreading. We're going to have to slaughter more than six hundred in the coming week. So I'm not in a very good mood."

Blomkvist said: "Your brother crashed his car into a truck a few days ago. He must have died instantaneously."

"I heard that."

"From Anita, who called you."

She scrutinised him for a long moment. Then she nodded. She knew that it was pointless to deny the fact.

"How did you find me?"

"We tapped Anita's telephone." Blomkvist did not think there was any reason to lie. "I saw your brother a few minutes before he died."

Harriet Vanger frowned. He met her gaze. Then he took off the ridiculous scarf he was wearing, turned down his collar, and showed her the stripe left from the noose. It was still red and inflamed, and he would probably always have a scar to remind him of Martin Vanger.

"Your brother had hung me from a hook, but by the grace of God my partner arrived in time to stop him killing me."

Harriet's eyes suddenly burned.

"I think you'd better tell me the story from the beginning."

It took more than an hour. He told her who he was and what he was working on. He described how he came to be given the assignment by Henrik Vanger. He explained how the police's investigation had come to a dead end, and he told her of Henrik's long investigation, and finally he told her how a photograph of her with friends in Järnvägsgatan in Hedestad had led to the uncovering of the sorrows behind the mystery of her disappearance and its appalling sequel, which had ended with Martin Vanger's suicide.

As he talked, dusk set in. The men quit work for the day, fires were started, and pots began to simmer. Blomkvist noticed that Jeff stayed close to his boss and kept a watchful eye on him. The cook served them dinner. They each had another beer. When he was finished Harriet sat for a long time in silence.

At length she said: "I was so happy that my father was dead and the violence was over. It never occurred to me that Martin . . . I'm glad he's dead."

"I can understand that."

"Your story doesn't explain how you knew that I was alive."

"After we realised what had happened, it wasn't so difficult to work out the rest. To disappear, you needed help. Anita was your confidante and the only one you could even consider. You were friends, and she had spent the summer with you. You stayed out at your father's cabin. If there was anyone you had confided in, it had to be her—and also she had just got her driver's licence."

Harriet looked at him with an unreadable expression.

"So now that you know I'm alive, what are you going to do?"

"I have to tell Henrik. He deserves to know."

"And then? You're a journalist."

"I'm not thinking of exposing you. I've already breached so many rules of professional conduct in this whole dismal mess that the Journalists Association would undoubtedly expel me if they knew about it." He was trying to make light of it. "One more won't make any difference, and I don't want to make my old babysitter angry."

She was not amused.

"How many people know the truth?"

"That you're alive? Right now, you and me and Anita and my partner. Henrik's lawyer knows about two-thirds of the story, but he still thinks you died in the sixties."

Harriet Vanger seemed to be thinking something over. She stared out at the dark. Mikael once again had an uneasy feeling that he was in a vulnerable situation, and he reminded himself that Harriet Vanger's own rifle was on a camp bed three paces away. Then he shook himself and stopped imagining things. He changed the subject.

"But how did you come to be a sheep farmer in Australia? I

already know that Anita smuggled you off Hedeby Island, presumably in the boot of her car when the bridge re-opened the day after the accident."

"Actually, I lay on the floor of the back seat with a blanket over me. But no-one was looking. I went to Anita when she arrived on the island and told her that I had to escape. You guessed right that I confided in her. She helped me, and she's been a loyal friend all these years."

"Why Australia?"

"I stayed in Anita's room in Stockholm for a few weeks. Anita had her own money, which she generously lent me. She also gave me her passport. We looked almost exactly like each other, and all I had to do was dye my hair blonde. For four years I lived in a convent in Italy—I wasn't a nun. There are convents where you can rent a room cheap, to have peace and quiet to think. Then I met Spencer Cochran. He was some years older; he'd just finished his degree in England and was hitchhiking around Europe. I fell in love. He did too. That's all there was to it. 'Anita' Vanger married him in 1971. I've never had any regrets. He was a wonderful man. Very sadly, he died eight years ago, and I became the owner of the station."

"But your passport—surely someone should have discovered that there were two Anita Vangers?"

"No, why should they? A Swedish girl named Anita Vanger who's married to Spencer Cochran. Whether she lives in London or Australia makes no difference. The one in London has been Spencer Cochran's estranged wife. The one in Australia was his very much present wife. They don't match up computer files between Canberra and London. Besides, I soon got an Australian passport under my married name. The arrangement functioned perfectly. The only thing that could have upset the story was if Anita herself wanted to get married. My marriage had to be registered in the Swedish national registration files."

"But she never did."

"She claims that she never found anyone. But I know that she did it for my sake. She's been a true friend."

"What was she doing in your room?"

"I wasn't very rational that day. I was afraid of Martin, but as long as he was in Uppsala, I could push the problem out of my mind. Then there he was in Hedestad, and I realised that I'd never be safe the rest of my life. I went back and forth between wanting to tell Uncle Henrik and wanting to flee. When Henrik didn't have time to talk to me, I just wandered restlessly around the village. Of course I know that the accident on the bridge overshadowed everything else for everyone, but not for me. I had my own problems, and I was hardly even aware of the accident. Everything seemed unreal. Then I ran into Anita, who was staying in a guest cottage in the compound with Gerda and Alexander. That was when I made up my mind. I stayed with her the whole time and didn't dare go outside. But there was one thing I had to take with me—I had written down everything that happened in a diary, and I needed a few clothes. Anita got them for me."

"I suppose she couldn't resist the temptation to look out at the accident scene." Blomkvist thought for a moment. "What I don't understand is why you didn't just go to Henrik, as you had intended."

"Why do you think?"

"I really don't know. Henrik would certainly have helped you. Martin would have been removed immediately—probably sent to Australia for some sort of therapy or treatment."

"You haven't understood what happened."

Up to this point Blomkvist had only referred to Gottfried's sexual assault on Martin, leaving Harriet's role out of it.

"Gottfried molested Martin," he said cautiously. "I suspect that he also molested you."

. . .

Harriet Vanger did not move a muscle. Then she took a deep breath and buried her face in her hands. It took five seconds before Jeff was beside her, asking if everything was all right. Harriet looked at him and gave him a faint smile. Then she astonished Blomkvist by standing up and giving her studs manager a hug and a kiss on the cheek. She turned to Blomkvist with her arm around Jeff's shoulder.

"Jeff, this is Mikael, an old . . . friend from the past. He's brought problems and bad news, but we're not going to shoot the messenger. Mikael, this is Jeff Cochran, my oldest son. I also have another son and a daughter."

Blomkvist stood up to shake hands with Jeff, saying that he was sorry to have brought bad news which had upset his mother. Harriet exchanged a few words with Jeff and then sent him away. She sat down again and seemed to have made a decision.

"No more lies. I accept that it's all over. In some sense I've been waiting for this day since 1966. For years I was terrified that someone might come up to me and say my name. But you know what? All of a sudden I don't care any more. My crime falls outside the statute of limitations. And I don't give a shit what people think about me."

"Crime?" said Mikael.

She gave him an urgent look, but he still didn't understand what she was talking about.

"I was sixteen. I was scared. I was ashamed. I was desperate. I was all alone. The only ones who knew the truth were Anita and Martin. I had told Anita about the sexual assaults, but I didn't have the courage to tell her that my father was also an insane killer of women. Anita had never known about that. But I did tell her about the crime that I committed myself. It was so horrible that when it came down to it, I didn't dare tell Henrik. I prayed to God to forgive me. And I hid inside a convent for several years."

"Harriet, your father was a rapist and a murderer. It wasn't your fault."

"I know that. My father molested me for a year. I did everything to avoid . . . but he was my father and I couldn't refuse to have anything to do with him without giving him some explanation. So I lied and played a role and tried to pretend that everything was OK. And I made sure that someone else was always around when I saw him. My mother knew what he was doing, of course, but she didn't care."

"Isabella *knew*?"

Harriet's voice took on a new harshness.

"Of course she knew. Nothing ever happened in our family without Isabella knowing. But she ignored everything that was unpleasant or showed her in a bad light. My father could have raped me in the middle of the living room right before her eyes and she wouldn't have noticed. She was incapable of acknowledging that anything was wrong in her life or mine."

"I've met her. She's not my favourite in the family."

"She's been like that her whole life. I've often wondered about my parents' relationship. I realised that they rarely or maybe never had sex with each other after I was born. My father had women, but for some strange reason he was afraid of Isabella. He stayed away from her, but he couldn't get a divorce."

"No-one does in the Vanger family."

She laughed for the first time.

"No, they don't. But the point is that I couldn't bring myself to say anything. The whole world would have found out. My schoolmates, all my relatives . . ."

"Harriet, I'm so sorry."

"I was fourteen when he raped me the first time. And during the next year he would take me out to his cabin. Many times Martin came along. He forced both me and Martin to do things with him. And he held my arms while Martin . . . had his way with me. When my father died, Martin was ready to take over his role. He expected me to become his lover and he thought it was perfectly natural for me to submit to him. At that time I no longer had any choice. I was forced to do what Martin said. I was rid of one tormentor only to land in the clutches of another, and the only thing I could do was to make sure there was never an occasion when I was alone with him . . ."

"Henrik would have . . ."

"You still don't understand."

She raised her voice. Blomkvist saw that several of the men at the next tent were looking at him. She lowered her voice again and leaned towards him.

"All the cards are on the table. You'll have to work out the rest."

She stood up and got two more beers. When she came back, Mikael said a single word to her.

"Gottfried."

She nodded.

"On August 7, 1965, my father forced me to go out to his cabin. Henrik was away. My father was drinking, and he tried to force himself on me. But he couldn't get it up and he flew into a drunken rage. He was always . . . rough and violent towards me when we were alone, but this time he crossed the line. *He urinated on me.* Then he started telling me what he was going to do to me. That night he told me about the women he had killed. He was bragging about it. He quoted from the Bible. This went on for an hour. I didn't understand half of what he was saying, but I realised that he was totally, absolutely sick."

She took a gulp of her beer.

"Sometime around midnight he had a fit. He was totally

insane. We were up in the sleeping loft. He put a T-shirt around my neck and pulled it as tight as he could. I blacked out. I don't have the slightest doubt that he really was trying to kill me, and for the first time that night he managed to complete the rape."

Harriet looked at Blomkvist. Her eyes entreated him to understand.

"But he was so drunk that somehow I managed to get away. I jumped down from the loft and fled. I was naked and I ran without thinking, and ended up on the jetty by the water. He came staggering after me."

Blomkvist suddenly wished that she would not tell him anything more.

"I was strong enough to shove an old drunk into the water. I used an oar to hold him under until he wasn't struggling any more. It didn't take long."

When she stopped, the silence was deafening.

"And when I looked up, there stood Martin. He looked terrified, but at the same time he was grinning. I don't know how long he was outside the cabin, spying on us. From that moment I was at his mercy. He came up to me, grabbed me by the hair, and led me back to the cabin—to Gottfried's bed. He tied me up and raped me while our father was still floating in the water. And I couldn't even offer any resistance."

Blomkvist closed his eyes. He was terribly ashamed and wished that he had left Harriet Vanger in peace. But her voice had taken on a new force.

"From that day on, I was in his power. I did what he told me to do. I felt paralysed, and the only thing that saved my sanity was that Isabella—or maybe it was Uncle Henrik—decided that Martin needed a change of scenery after his father's tragic death, so she sent him to Uppsala. Of course this was because she knew what he was doing to me, and it was her way of solving the problem. You can bet that Martin was disappointed. During the next year he was home only for the Christmas holiday. I managed to keep away from him. I went with Henrik on a trip to Copenhagen between Christmas and New Year's. And during the summer holiday, Anita was there. I confided in her, and she stayed with me the whole time, making sure that he didn't come near me."

"Until you saw him on Järnvägsgatan."

"I was told that he wouldn't be coming to the family gathering, that he was staying in Uppsala. But obviously he changed his mind, and suddenly there he was on the other side of the street, staring at me. He smiled at me. It felt like a hideous dream. I had murdered my father, and I realised that I would never be free of my brother. Up until then, I had thought about killing myself. I chose instead to flee." She gave Blomkvist what was almost a look of relief. "It feels fantastic to tell the truth. So now you know."

CHAPTER 27

Saturday, July 26–
Monday, July 28

Blomkvist picked up Salander by her front door on Lundagatan at 10:00 and drove her to the Norra crematorium. He stayed at her side during the ceremony. For a long time they were the only mourners along with the pastor, but when the funeral began Armansky slipped in. He nodded curtly to Blomkvist and stood behind Salander, gently putting a hand on her shoulder. She nodded without looking at him, as if she knew who was standing there. Then she ignored them both.

Salander had told him nothing about her mother, but the pastor had apparently spoken to someone at the nursing home where she died, and Blomkvist understood that the cause of death was a cerebral haemorrhage. Salander did not say a word during the ceremony. The pastor lost her train of thought twice when she turned directly to her. Salander looked her straight in the eye without expression. When it was over she turned on her heel and left without saying thank you or goodbye. Blomkvist and Armansky took a deep breath and looked at each other.

"She's feeling really bad," Armansky said.

"I know that," Blomkvist said. "It was good of you to come."

"I'm not so sure about that."

Armansky fixed Blomkvist with his gaze.

"If you two are driving back north, keep an eye on her."

He promised to do that. They said goodbye, and to the pastor, at the church door. Salander was already in the car, waiting.

She had to go back with him to Hedestad to get her motorcycle and the equipment she had borrowed from Milton Security. Not until they had passed Uppsala did she break her silence and ask how the trip to Australia had gone. Blomkvist had landed at Arlanda late the night before and had slept only a few hours. During the drive he told her Harriet Vanger's story. Salander sat in silence for half an hour before she opened her mouth.

"Bitch," she said.

"Who?"

"Harriet Fucking Vanger. If she had done something in 1966, Martin Vanger couldn't have kept killing and raping for thirty-seven years."

"Harriet knew about her father murdering women, but she had no idea that Martin had anything to do with it. She fled from a brother who raped her and then threatened to reveal that she had drowned her father if she didn't do what he said."

"Bullshit."

After that they sat in silence all the way to Hedestad. Blomkvist was late for his appointment and dropped her at the turnoff to Hedeby Island; he asked if she would please be there when he came back.

"Are you thinking of staying overnight?" she said.

"I think so."

"Do you want me to be here?"

He climbed out of the car and went around and put his arms around her. She pushed him away, almost violently. Blomkvist took a step back.

"Lisbeth, you're my friend."

"Do you want me to stay here so you'll have somebody to fuck tonight?"

Blomkvist gave her a long look. Then he turned and got into the car and started the engine. He wound down the window. Her hostility was palpable.

"I want to be your friend," he said. "If you want otherwise, then you don't need to be here when I get home."

Henrik Vanger was sitting up, dressed, when Dirch Frode let him into the hospital room.

"They're thinking of letting me out for Martin's funeral tomorrow."

"How much has Dirch told you?"

Henrik looked down at the floor.

"He told me about what Martin and Gottfried got up to. This is far, far worse than I could have imagined."

"I know what happened to Harriet."

"Tell me: how did she die?"

"She didn't die. She's still alive. And if you like, she really wants to see you."

Both men stared at him as if their world had just been turned upside down.

"It took a while to convince her to come, but she's alive, she's doing fine, and she's here in Hedestad. She arrived this morning and can be here in an hour. If you want to see her, that is."

. . .

Blomkvist had to tell the story from beginning to end. A couple of times Henrik interrupted with a question or asked him to repeat something. Frode said not a word.

When the story was done, Henrik sat in silence. Blomkvist had been afraid that it would be too much for the old man, but Henrik showed no sign of emotion, except that his voice might have been a bit thicker when he broke his silence

"Poor, poor Harriet. If only she had come to me."

Blomkvist glanced at the clock. It was five minutes to four.

"Do you want to see her? She's still afraid that you won't want to after you found out what she did."

"What about the flowers?" Henrik said.

"I asked her that on the plane coming home. There was one person in the family, apart from Anita, whom she loved, and that was you. She, of course, was the one who sent the flowers. She said that she hoped you would understand that she was alive and that she was doing fine, without having to make an appearance. But since her only channel of information was Anita, who moved abroad as soon as she finished her studies and never visited Hedestad, Harriet's awareness about what went on here was limited. She never knew how terribly you suffered or that you thought it was her murderer taunting you."

"I assume it was Anita who posted the flowers."

"She worked for an airline and flew all over the world. She posted them from wherever she happened to be."

"But how did you know Anita was the one who helped her?"

"She was the one in Harriet's window."

"But she could have been mixed up in . . . she could have been the murderer instead. How did you find out that Harriet was alive?"

Blomkvist gave Henrik a long look. Then he smiled for the first time since he had returned to Hedestad.

"Anita was involved in Harriet's disappearance, but she couldn't have killed her."

"How could you be sure of that?"

"Because this isn't some damned locked-room mystery novel. If Anita had murdered Harriet, you would have found the body years ago. So the only logical thing was that she helped Harriet escape and hide. Do you want to see her?"

"Of course I want to see her."

Blomkvist found Harriet by the lift in the lobby. At first he did not recognise her. Since they had parted at Arlanda Airport the night before she had dyed her hair brown again. She was dressed in black trousers, a white blouse, and an elegant grey jacket. She looked radiant, and Blomkvist bent down to give her an encouraging hug.

Henrik got up from his chair when Mikael opened the door. She took a deep breath.

"Hi, Henrik," she said.

The old man scrutinised her from top to toe. Then Harriet went over and kissed him. Blomkvist nodded to Frode and closed the door.

Salander was not in the cottage when Blomkvist returned to Hedeby Island. The video equipment and her motorcycle were gone, as well as the bag with her extra clothes and her sponge bag. The cottage felt empty. It suddenly seemed alien and unreal. He looked at the stacks of paper in the office, which he would have to pack up in boxes and carry back to Henrik's house. But he could not face starting the process. He drove to Konsum and bought bread, milk, cheese, and something for supper. When he returned he put on water for coffee, sat in the garden, and read the evening papers without thinking of anything else.

At 5:30 a taxi drove across the bridge. After three minutes it went back the way it came. Blomkvist caught a glimpse of Isabella Vanger in the back seat.

Around 7:00 he had dozed off in the garden chair when Frode woke him up.

"How's it going with Henrik and Harriet?" he said.

"This unhappy cloud has its silver lining," Frode said with a restrained smile. "Isabella, would you believe, came rushing into Henrik's hospital room. She'd obviously seen that you'd come back and was completely beside herself. She screamed at him that there had to be an end to this outrageous fuss about her Harriet, adding that *you* were the one who drove her son to his death with your snooping."

"Well, she's right, in a way."

"She commanded Henrik to dismiss you forthwith and run you off the property for good. And would he, once and for all, stop searching for ghosts."

"Wow!"

"She didn't even glance at the woman sitting beside the bed talking to Henrik. She must have thought it was one of the staff. I will never forget the moment when Harriet stood up and said, 'Hello, Mamma.' "

"What happened?"

"We had to call a doctor to check Isabella's vital signs. Right now she's refusing to believe that it's Harriet. You are accused of dragging in an impostor."

Frode was on his way to visit Cecilia and Alexander to give them the news that Harriet had risen from the dead. He hurried away, leaving Blomkvist to his solitary musings.

. . .

Salander stopped and filled her tank at a petrol station north of Uppsala. She had been riding doggedly, staring straight ahead. She paid quickly and got back on her bike. She started it up and rode to the exit, where she stopped, undecided.

She was still in a terrible mood. She was furious when she left Hedeby, but her rage had slowly dissolved during the ride. She could not make up her mind why she was so angry with Blomkvist, or even if he was the one she was angry with.

She thought of Martin Vanger and Harriet Fucking Vanger and Dirch Fucking Frode and the whole damned Vanger clan sitting in Hedestad reigning over their little empire and plotting against each other. They had needed her help. Normally they wouldn't even have said hello to her in the street, let alone entrust her with their repellent secrets.

Fucking riff-raff.

She took a deep breath and thought about her mother, whom she had consigned to ashes that very morning. She would never be able to mend things. Her mother's death meant that the wound would never heal, since she would never now get an answer to the questions she had wanted to ask.

She thought about Armansky standing behind her at the crematorium. She should have said something to him. At least given him some sign that she knew he was there. But if she did that, he would have taken it as a pretext for trying to structure her life. If she gave him her little finger he'd take her whole arm. And he would never understand.

She thought about the lawyer, Bjurman, who was still her guardian and who, at least for the time being, had been neutralised and was doing as he was told.

She felt an implacable hatred and clenched her teeth.

And she thought about Mikael Blomkvist and wondered

what he would say when he found out that she was a ward of the court and that her entire life was a fucking rats' nest.

It came to her that she really was not angry with him. He was just the person on whom she had vented her anger when what she had wanted most of all was to murder somebody, several people. Being angry with *him* was pointless.

She felt strangely ambivalent towards him.

He stuck his nose in other people's business and poked around in her life and . . . but . . . she had also enjoyed working with him. Even that was an odd feeling—to work *with* somebody. She wasn't used to that, but it had been unexpectedly painless. He did not mess with her. He did not try to tell her how to live her life.

She was the one who had seduced him, not vice versa.

And besides, it had been satisfying.

So why did she feel as if she wanted to kick him in the face?

She sighed and unhappily raised her eyes to see an intercontinental roar past on the E4.

Blomkvist was still in the garden at 8:00 when he was roused by the rattle of the motorcycle crossing the bridge and saw Salander riding towards the cottage. She put her bike on its stand and took off her helmet. She came up to the garden table and felt the coffeepot, which was empty and cold. Blomkvist stood up, gazing at her in surprise. She took the coffeepot and went into the kitchen. When she came back out she had taken off her leathers and sat down in jeans and a T-shirt with the slogan I CAN BE A REGULAR BITCH. JUST TRY ME.

"I thought you'd be in Stockholm by now," he said.

"I turned round in Uppsala."

"Quite a ride."

"I'm sore."

"Why did you turn around?"

No answer. He waited her out while they drank coffee. After ten minutes she said, reluctantly, "I like your company."

Those were words that had never before passed her lips.

"It was . . . interesting to work with you on this case."

"I enjoyed working with you too," he said.

"Hmm."

"The fact is, I've never worked with such a brilliant researcher. OK, I know you're a hacker and hang out in suspect circles in which you can set up an illegal wiretap in London in twenty-four hours, but you get results."

She looked at him for the first time since she had sat at the table. He knew so many of her secrets.

"That's just how it is. I know computers. I've never had a problem with reading a text and absorbing what it said."

"Your photographic memory," he said softly.

"I admit it. I just have no idea how it works. It's not only computers and telephone networks, but the motor in my bike and TV sets and vacuum cleaners and chemical processes and formulae in astrophysics. I'm a nut case, I admit it: a freak."

Blomkvist frowned. He sat quietly for a long time.

Asperger's syndrome, he thought. *Or something like that. A talent for seeing patterns and understanding abstract reasoning where other people perceive only white noise.*

Salander was staring down at the table.

"Most people would give an eye tooth to have such a gift."

"I don't want to talk about it."

"We'll drop it. Are you glad you came back?"

"I don't know. Maybe it was a mistake."

"Lisbeth, can you define the word friendship for me?"

"It's when you like somebody."

"Sure, but what is it that makes you like somebody?"

She shrugged.

"Friendship—my definition—is built on two things," he said. "Respect and trust. Both elements have to be there. And it has to be mutual. You can have respect for someone, but if you don't have trust, the friendship will crumble."

She was still silent.

"I understand that you don't want to discuss yourself with me, but someday you're going to have to decide whether you trust me or not. I want us to be friends, but I can't do it all by myself."

"I like having sex with you."

"Sex has nothing to do with friendship. Sure, friends can have sex, but if I had to choose between sex and friendship when it comes to you, there's no doubt which I would pick."

"I don't get it. Do you want to have sex with me or not?"

"You shouldn't have sex with people you're working with," he muttered. "It just leads to trouble."

"Did I miss something here, or isn't it true that you and Erika Berger fuck every time you get the chance? And she's married."

"Erika and I . . . have a history that started long before we started working together. The fact that she's married is none of your business."

"Oh, I see, all of a sudden you're the one who doesn't want to talk about yourself. And there I was, learning that friendship is a matter of trust."

"What I mean is that I don't discuss a friend behind her back. I'd be breaking her trust. I wouldn't discuss you with Erika behind your back either."

Salander thought about that. This had become an awkward conversation. She did not like awkward conversations.

"I do like having sex with you," she said.

"I like it too . . . but I'm still old enough to be your father."

"I don't give a shit about your age."

"No, you can't ignore our age difference. It's no sort of basis for a lasting relationship."

"Who said anything about lasting?" Salander said. "We just finished up a case in which men with fucked-up sexuality played a prominent role. If I had to decide, men like that would be exterminated, every last one of them."

"Well, at least you don't compromise."

"No," she said, giving him her crooked non-smile. "But at least you're not like them." She got up. "Now I'm going in to take a shower, and then I think I'll get into your bed naked. If you think you're too old, you'll have to go and sleep on the camp bed."

Whatever hang-ups Salander had, modesty certainly was not one of them. He managed to lose every argument with her. After a while he washed up the coffee things and went into the bedroom.

They got up at 10:00, took a shower together, and ate breakfast out in the garden. At 11:00 Dirch Frode called and said that the funeral would take place at 2:00 in the afternoon, and he asked if they were planning to attend.

"I shouldn't think so," said Mikael.

Frode asked if he could come over around 6:00 for a talk. Mikael said that would be fine.

He spent a few hours sorting the papers into the packing crates and carrying them over to Henrik's office. Finally he was left with only his own notebooks and the two binders about the Hans-Erik Wennerström affair that he hadn't opened in six months. He sighed and stuffed them into his bag.

Frode rang to say he was running late and did not reach the cottage until 8:00. He was still in his funeral suit and looked harried when he sat down on the kitchen bench and gratefully accepted the cup of coffee that Salander offered him. She sat at the side table with her computer while Blomkvist asked how Harriet's reappearance had been received by the family as a whole.

"You might say that it has overshadowed Martin's demise. Now the media have found out about her too."

"And how are you explaining the situation?"

"Harriet talked with a reporter from the *Courier*. Her story is that she ran away from home because she didn't get along with her family, but that she obviously has done well in the world since she's the head of a very substantial enterprise."

Blomkvist whistled.

"I discovered that there was money in Australian sheep, but I didn't know the station was doing that well."

"Her sheep station is going superbly, but that isn't her only source of income. The Cochran Corporation is in mining, opals, manufacturing, transport, electronics, and a lot of other things too."

"Wow! So what's going to happen now?"

"Honestly, I don't know. People have been turning up all day, and the family has been together for the first time in years. They're here from both Fredrik and Johan Vanger's sides, and quite a few from the younger generation too—the ones in their twenties and up. There are probably around forty Vangers in Hedestad this evening. Half of them are at the hospital wearing out Henrik; the other half are at the Grand Hotel talking to Harriet."

"Harriet must be the big sensation. How many of them know about Martin?"

"So far it's just me, Henrik, and Harriet. We had a long talk together. Martin and . . . your uncovering of his unspeakable life, it's overshadowing just about everything for us at the moment. It has brought an enormous crisis for the company to a head."

"I can understand that."

"There is no natural heir, but Harriet is staying in Hedestad for a while. The family will work out who owns what, how the inheritance is to be divided, and so on. She actually has a share of it that would have been quite large if she had been here the whole time. It's a nightmare."

Mikael laughed. Frode was not laughing at all.

"Isabella had a collapse at the funeral. She's in the hospital now. Henrik says he won't visit her."

"Good for Henrik."

"However, Anita is coming over from London. I am to call a family meeting for next week. It will be the first time in twenty-five years that she's participated."

"Who will be the new CEO?"

"Birger is after the job, but he's out of the question. What's going to happen is that Henrik will step in as CEO pro tem from his sickbed until we hire either someone from outside or someone from within the family . . ."

Blomkvist raised his eyebrows.

"Harriet? You can't be serious."

"Why not? We're talking about an exceptionally competent and respected businesswoman."

"She has a company in Australia to look after."

"True, but her son Jeff Cochran is minding the store in her absence."

"He's the studs manager on a sheep ranch. If I understood the matter correctly, he sees to it that the correct sheep mate with each other."

"He also has a degree in economics from Oxford and a law degree from Melbourne."

Blomkvist thought about the sweaty, muscular man with his

shirt off who had driven him into and through the ravine; he tried to imagine him in a pinstripe suit. Why not?

"All of this will take time to work out," Frode said. "But she would be a perfect CEO. With the right support team she could represent a whole new deal for the company."

"She doesn't have the experience . . ."

"That's true. She can't just pop up out of more or less nowhere and start micro-managing the company. But the Vanger Corporation is international, and we could certainly have an American CEO who doesn't speak a word of Swedish . . . it's only business, when all's said and done."

"Sooner or later you're going to have to face up to the problem of Martin's basement."

"I know. But we can't say anything without destroying Harriet . . . I'm glad I'm not the one who has to make the decision about this."

"Damn it, Dirch, you won't be able to bury the fact that Martin was a serial killer."

"Mikael, I'm in a . . . very uncomfortable position."

"Tell me."

"I have a message from Henrik. He thanks you for the outstanding work you did and says that he considers the contract fulfilled. That means he is releasing you from any further obligations and that you no longer have to live or work here in Hedestad, etc. So, taking effect immediately, you can move back to Stockholm and devote yourself to your other pursuits."

"He wants me to vanish from the scene, is that the gist of it?"

"Absolutely not. He wants you to visit him for a conversation about the future. He says he hopes that his involvement on the board of *Millennium* can proceed without restrictions. But . . ."

Frode looked even more uncomfortable, if that was possible.

"Don't tell me, Dirch . . . he no longer wants me to write a history of the Vanger family."

Dirch Frode nodded. He picked up a notebook, opened it, and pushed it over to Mikael.

"He wrote you this letter."

Dear Mikael,

I have nothing but respect for your integrity, and I don't intend to insult you by trying to tell you what to write. You may write and publish whatever you like, and I won't exert any pressure on you whatsoever.

Our contract remains valid, if you want to continue. You have enough material to finish the chronicle of the Vanger family.

Mikael, I've never begged anyone for anything in my entire life. I've always thought that a person should follow his morals and his convictions. This time I have no choice.

I am, with this letter, begging you, both as a friend and as part owner of Millennium, *to refrain from publishing the truth about Gottfried and Martin. I know that's wrong, but I see no way out of this darkness. I have to choose between two evils, and in this case there are no winners.*

I beg you not to write anything that would further hurt Harriet. You know first-hand what it's like to be the subject of a media campaign. The campaign against you was of quite modest proportions. You can surely imagine what it would be like for Harriet if the truth were to come out. She has been tormented for forty years and shouldn't have to suffer any more for the deeds that her brother and her father committed. And I beg you to think through the consequences this story might have for the thousands of employees in the company. This could crush her and annihilate us.

Henrik

"Henrik also says that if you require compensation for financial losses that may arise from your refraining from publishing the story, he is entirely open to discussion. You can set any financial demands you think fit."

"Henrik Vanger is trying to shut me up. Tell him that I wish he had never given me this offer."

"The situation is just as troublesome for Henrik as it is for you. He likes you very much and considers you his friend."

"Henrik Vanger is a clever bastard," Blomkvist said. He was suddenly furious. "He wants to hush up the story. He's playing on my emotions and he knows I like him too. And what he's also saying is that I have a free hand to publish, and if I do so he would have to revise his attitude towards *Millennium*."

"Everything changed when Harriet stepped on to the stage."

"And now Henrik is feeling out what my price tag might be. I don't intend to hang Harriet out to dry, but *somebody* has to say *something* about the women who died in Martin's basement. Dirch, we don't even know how many women he tortured and slaughtered. Who is going to speak up on their behalf?"

Salander looked up from her computer. Her voice was almost inaudible as she said to Frode, "Isn't there anyone in your company who's going to try to shut *me* up?"

Frode looked astonished. Once again he had managed to ignore her existence.

"If Martin Vanger were alive at this moment, I would have hung him out to dry," she went on. "Whatever agreement Mikael made with you, I would have sent every detail about him to the nearest evening paper. And if I could, I would have stuck him down in his own torture hole and tied him to that table and stuck needles through his balls. Unfortunately he's dead."

She turned to Blomkvist.

"I'm satisfied with the solution. Nothing we do can repair

the harm that Martin Vanger did to his victims. But an interesting situation has come up. You're in a position where you can continue to harm innocent women—especially that Harriet whom you so warmly defended in the car on the way up here. So my question to you is: which is worse—the fact that Martin Vanger raped her out in the cabin or that you're going to do it in print? You have a fine dilemma. Maybe the ethics committee of the Journalists Association can give you some guidance."

She paused. Blomkvist could not meet her gaze. He stared down at the table.

"But I'm not a journalist," she said at last.

"What do you want?" Dirch Frode asked.

"Martin videotaped his victims. I want you to do your damnedest to identify as many as you can and see to it that their families receive suitable compensation. And then I want the Vanger Corporation to donate 2 million kronor annually and in perpetuity to the National Organisation for Women's Crisis Centres and Girls' Crisis Centres in Sweden."

Frode weighed the price tag for a minute. Then he nodded.

"Can you live with that, Mikael?" Salander said.

Blomkvist felt only despair. His professional life he had devoted to uncovering things which other people had tried to hide, and he could not be party to the covering up of the appalling crimes committed in Martin Vanger's basement. He who had lambasted his colleagues for not publishing the truth, here he sat, discussing, negotiating even, the most macabre cover-up he had ever heard of.

He sat in silence for a long time. Then he nodded his assent.

"So be it," Frode said. "And with regard to Henrik's offer for financial compensation . . ."

"He can shove it up his backside, and Dirch, I want you to leave now. I understand your position, but right now I'm so furious with you and Henrik and Harriet that if you stay any longer we might not be friends any more."

Frode made no move to go.

"I can't leave yet. I'm not done. I have another message to deliver, and you're not going to like this one either. Henrik is insisting that I tell you tonight. You can go up to the hospital and flay him tomorrow morning if you wish."

Blomkvist looked up and stared at him.

Frode went on. "This has got to be the hardest thing I've ever done in my life. But I think that only complete candour with all the cards on the table can save the situation now."

"So it's candour at last, is it?"

"When Henrik convinced you to take the job last Christmas," Dirch said, ignoring his sarcasm, "neither he nor I thought that anything would come of it. That was exactly what he said, but he wanted to give it one last try. He had analysed your situation, particularly with the help of the report that Fröken Salander put together. He played on your isolation, he offered good pay, and he used the right bait."

"Wennerström."

Frode nodded.

"You were bluffing?"

"No, no," Frode said.

Salander raised an eyebrow with interest.

"Henrik is going to make good on everything he promised. He's arranging an interview and is going public with a direct assault on Wennerström. You can have all the details later, but roughly the situation is this: when Wennerström was employed in the finance department of the Vanger Corporation, he spent several million kronor speculating on foreign currency. This was long before foreign exchange futures became the rage. He did this without authority. One deal after another went bad, and he was sitting there with a loss of seven million kronor that he tried to cover up. Partly by cooking the books and partly by speculating even harder. It inevitably came to light and he was sacked."

"Did he make any profit himself?"

"Oh yes, he made off with about half a million kronor, which ironically enough became the seed money for the Wennerström Group. We have documentation for all of this. You can use the information however you like, and Henrik will back up the accusations publicly. But . . ."

"But, and it's a big but, Dirch, the information is worthless," Blomkvist said, slamming his fist on the table. "It all happened thirty-plus years ago and it's a closed book."

"You'll get confirmation that Wennerström is a crook."

"That will annoy Wennerström when it comes out, but it won't damage him any more than a direct hit from a peashooter. He's going to shuffle the deck by putting out a press release saying that Henrik Vanger is an old has-been who's still trying to steal some business from him, and then he'll probably claim that he was acting on orders from Henrik. Even if he can't prove his innocence, he can lay down enough smoke screens that no-one will take the story seriously."

Frode looked unhappy.

"You conned me," Blomkvist said.

"That wasn't our intention."

"I blame myself. I was grasping at straws, and I should have realised it was something like that." He laughed abruptly. "Henrik is an old shark. He was selling a product and told me what I wanted to hear. It's time you went, Dirch."

"Mikael . . . I'm sorry that . . ."

"Dirch. *Go*."

. . .

Salander did not know whether to go over to Blomkvist or to leave him in peace. He solved the problem for her by picking up his jacket without a word and slamming the door behind him.

For more than an hour she waited restlessly in the kitchen. She felt so bad that she cleared the table and washed the dishes—a role she usually left to Blomkvist. She went regularly to the window to see if there was any sign of him. Finally she was so nervous that she put on her jacket and went out to look for him.

First she walked to the marina, where lights were still on in the cabins, but there was no sign of him. She followed the path along the water where they usually took their evening walks. Martin Vanger's house was dark and already looked abandoned. She went out to the rocks at the point where they had often sat talking, and then she went back home. He still had not returned.

She went to the church. Still no sign. She was at a loss to know what to do. Then she went back to her motorcycle and got a flashlight from the saddlebag and set off along the water again. It took her a while to wind her way along the half-overgrown road, and even longer to find the path to Gottfried's cabin. It loomed out of the darkness behind some trees when she had almost reached it. He was not on the porch and the door was locked.

She had turned towards the village when she stopped and went back, all the way out to the point. She caught sight of Blomkvist's silhouette in the darkness on the end of the jetty where Harriet Vanger had drowned her father. She sighed with relief.

He heard her as she came out on to the jetty, and he turned around. She sat down next to him without a word. At last he broke the silence.

"Forgive me. I had to be alone for a while."

"I know."

She lit two cigarettes and gave him one. Blomkvist looked at her. Salander was the most asocial human being he had ever met. Usually she ignored any attempt on his part to talk about anything personal, and she had never accepted a single expression of sympathy. She had saved his life, and now she had tracked him out here in the night. He put an arm around her.

"Now I know what my price is," he said. "We've forsaken those girls. They're going to bury the whole story. Everything in Martin's basement will be vacuumed into oblivion."

Salander did not answer.

"Erika was right," he said. "I would have done more good if I'd gone to Spain for a month and then come home refreshed and taken on Wennerström. I've wasted all these months."

"If you'd gone to Spain, Martin Vanger would still be operating in his basement."

They sat together for a long time before he suggested that they go home.

Blomkvist fell asleep before Salander. She lay awake listening to him breathe. After a while she went to the kitchen and sat in the dark on the kitchen bench, smoking several cigarettes as she brooded. She had taken it for granted that Vanger and Frode might con him. It was in their nature. But it was Blomkvist's problem, not hers. Or was it?

At last she made a decision. She stubbed out her cigarette and went into the bedroom, turned on the lamp, and shook Mikael awake. It was 2:30 in the morning.

"What?"

"I've got a question. Sit up."

Blomkvist sat up, drunk with sleep.

"When you were indicted, why didn't you defend yourself?"

Blomkvist rubbed his eyes. He looked at the clock.

"It's a long story, Lisbeth."

"I've got time. Tell me."

He sat for a long while, pondering what he should say. Finally he decided on the truth.

"I had no defence. The information in the article was wrong."

"When I hacked your computer and read your email exchange with Berger, there were plenty of references to the Wennerström affair, but you two kept discussing practical details about the trial and nothing about what actually happened. What was it that went wrong?"

"Lisbeth, I can't let the real story get out. I fell into a trap. Erika and I are quite clear that it would damage our credibility even further if we told anyone what really happened."

"Listen, Kalle Blomkvist, yesterday afternoon you sat here preaching about friendship and trust and stuff. I'm not going to put the story on the Net."

Blomkvist protested. It was the middle of the night. He could not face thinking about the whole thing now. She went on stubbornly sitting there until he gave in. He went to the bathroom and washed his face and put the coffeepot on. Then he came back to the bed and told her about how his old schoolfriend Robert Lindberg, in a yellow Mälar-30 in the guest marina in Arholma, had aroused his curiosity.

"You mean that your buddy was lying?"

"No, not at all. He told me exactly what he knew, and I could verify each and every word in documents from the audit at SIB. I even went to Poland and photographed the sheet-metal shack where this huge big Minos Company was housed. I interviewed several of the people who had been employed at the company. They all said exactly the same thing."

"I don't get it."

Blomkvist sighed. It was a while before he spoke again.

"I had a damned good story. I still hadn't confronted Wennerström himself, but the story was airtight; if I had published it at that moment I really would have shook him up. It might not have led to an indictment for fraud—the deal had already been approved by the auditors—but I would have damaged his reputation."

"What went wrong?"

"Somewhere along the way somebody heard about what I was poking my nose into, and Wennerström was made aware of my existence. And all of a sudden a whole bunch of strange things started happening. First I was threatened. Anonymous calls from card telephones that were impossible to trace. Erika was also threatened. It was the usual nonsense: lie down or else we're going to nail you to a barn door, and so on. She, of course, was mad as a hellcat."

He took a cigarette from Salander.

"Then something extremely unpleasant happened. Late one night when I left the office I was attacked by two men who just walked up to me and gave me a couple of punches. I got a fat lip and fell down in the street. I couldn't identify them, but one of them looked like an old biker."

"So, next . . ."

"All these goings-on, of course, only had the effect of making Erika very cross indeed, and I got stubborn. We beefed up security at *Millennium*. The problem was that the harassment was out of all proportion to the content of the story. We couldn't fathom why all this was happening."

"But the story you published was something quite different."

"Exactly. Suddenly we made a breakthrough. We found a source, a Deep Throat in Wennerström's circle. This source was literally scared to death, and we were only allowed to meet him in hotel rooms. He told us that the money from the Minos affair had been used for weapons deals in the war in Yugoslavia. Wennerström had been making deals with the right-wing Ustashe in Croatia. Not only that, the source was able to give us copies of documents to back it up."

"You believed him?"

"He was clever. He only ever gave us enough information to lead us to the next source, who would confirm the story. We were even given a photograph of one of Wennerström's closest colleagues shaking hands with the buyer. It was detailed blockbuster material, and everything seemed verifiable. So we published."

"And it was a fake."

"It was all a fake from beginning to end. The documents were skilful forgeries. Wennerström's lawyer was able to prove that the photograph of Wennerström's subordinate and the Ustashe leader was a montage of two different images."

"Fascinating," Salander said.

"In hindsight it was very easy to see how we had been manipulated. Our original story really had damaged Wennerström. Now that story was drowned in a clever forgery. We published a story that Wennerström could pick apart point by point and prove his innocence."

"You couldn't back down and tell the truth? You had absolutely no proof that Wennerström had committed the falsification?"

"If we had tried to tell the truth and accused Wennerström of being behind the whole thing, nobody would have believed us. It would have looked like a desperate attempt to shift the blame from our stupidity on to an innocent leader of industry."

"I see."

"Wennerström had two layers of protection. If the fake had been revealed, he would have been able to claim that it was one of his enemies trying to slander him. And we at *Millennium* would once again have lost all credibility, since we fell for something that turned out to be false."

"So you chose not to defend yourself and take the prison sentence."

"I deserved it," Blomkvist said. "I had committed libel. Now you know. Can I go back to sleep now?"

He turned off the lamp and shut his eyes. Salander lay down next to him.

"Wennerström is a gangster."

"I know."

"No, I mean, I *know* that he's a gangster. He works with everybody from the Russian mafia to the Colombian drug cartels."

"What do you mean?"

"When I turned in my report to Frode he gave me an extra assignment. He asked me to try to find out what really happened at the trial. I had just started working on it when he called Armansky and cancelled the job."

"I wonder why."

"I assume that they scrapped the investigation as soon as you accepted Henrik Vanger's assignment. It would no longer have been of immediate interest."

"And?"

"Well, I don't like leaving things unresolved. I had a few weeks . . . free last spring when Armansky didn't have any jobs for me, so I did some digging into Wennerström for fun."

Blomkvist sat up and turned on the lamp and looked at Salander. He met her eyes. She actually looked guilty.

"Did you find out anything?"

"I have his entire hard disk on my computer. You can have as much proof as you need that he's a gangster."

CHAPTER 28

Tuesday, July 29–
Friday, October 24

Blomkvist had been poring over Salander's computer printouts for three days—boxes full of papers. The problem was that the subjects kept changing all the time. An option deal in London. A currency deal in Paris through an agent. A company with a post-office box in Gibraltar. A sudden doubling of funds in an account at the Chase Manhattan Bank in New York.

And then all those puzzling question marks: a trading company with 200,000 kronor in an untouched account registered five years earlier in Santiago, Chile—one of nearly thirty such companies in twelve different countries—and not a hint of what type of activity was involved. A dormant company? *Waiting for what?* A front for some other kind of activity? The computer gave no clue as to what was going on in Wennerström's mind or what may have been perfectly obvious to him and so was never formulated in an electronic document.

Salander was persuaded that most of these questions would never be answered. They could see the message, but without a key they would never be able to interpret the meaning. Wennerström's empire was like an onion from which one layer after another could be removed; a labyrinth of enterprises owned by one another. Companies, accounts, funds, securities. They reckoned that nobody—perhaps not even Wennerström himself—could have a complete overview. Wennerström's empire had a life of its own.

But there was a pattern, or at least a hint of a pattern. A labyrinth of enterprises owned by each other. Wennerström's empire was variously valued at between 100 and 400 billion kronor, depending on whom you asked and how it was calculated. But if companies own each other's assets—what then would be their value?

They had left Hedeby Island in great haste early in the morning after Salander dropped the bomb that was now occupying every waking moment of Blomkvist's life. They drove to Salander's place and spent two days in front of her computer while she guided him through Wennerström's universe. He had plenty of questions. One of them was pure curiosity.

"Lisbeth, how are you able to operate his computer, from a purely practical point of view?"

"It's a little invention that my friend Plague came up with. Wennerström has an IBM laptop that he works on, both at home and at the office. That means that all the information is on a single hard drive. He has a broadband connection to his property at home. Plague invented a type of cuff that you fasten around the broadband cable, and I'm testing it out for him. Everything that Wennerström sees is registered by the cuff, which forwards the data to a server somewhere else."

"Doesn't he have a firewall?"

Salander smiled.

"Of course he has a firewall. But the point is that the cuff also functions as a type of firewall. It takes a while to hack the computer this way. Let's say that Wennerström gets an email; it goes first to Plague's cuff and we can read it before it even passes through his firewall. But the ingenious part is that the email is rewritten and a few bytes of source code are added. This is repeated every time he downloads anything to his computer. Pictures are even better. He does a lot of surfing on the Net. Each time he picks up a porn picture or opens a new home page, we add several rows of source code. After a while, in several hours or several days, depending on how much he uses the computer, Wennerström has downloaded an entire programme of approximately three megabytes in which each bit is linked to the next bit."

"And?"

"When the last bits are in place, the programme is integrated with his Internet browser. To him it will look as though his computer has locked up, and he has to restart it. During the restart a whole new software programme is installed. He uses Internet Explorer. The next time he starts Explorer, he's really starting a whole different programme that's invisible on his desktop and looks and functions just like Explorer, but it also does a lot of other things. First it takes control of his firewall and makes sure that everything is working. Then it starts to scan the computer and transmits bits of information every time he clicks the mouse while he's surfing. After a while, again depending on how much he surfs, we've accumulated a complete mirror image of the contents of his hard drive on a server somewhere. And then it's time for the HT."

"HT?"

"Sorry. Plague calls it the HT. Hostile Takeover."

"I see."

"The really subtle thing is what happens next. When the structure is ready, Wennerström has two complete hard drives, one on his own machine and one on our server. The next time he boots up his computer, it's actually the mirrored computer that's starting. He's no longer working on his own computer; in reality he's working on our server. His computer will run a little slower, but it's virtually not noticeable. And when I'm connected to the server, I can tap his computer in real time. Each time Wennerström presses a key on his computer I see it on mine."

"Your friend is also a hacker?"

"He was the one who arranged the telephone tap in London. He's a little out of it socially, but on the Net he's a legend."

"OK," Blomkvist said, giving her a resigned smile. "Question number two: why didn't you tell me about Wennerström earlier?"

"You never asked me."

"And if I never did ask you—let's suppose that I never met you—you would have sat here knowing that Wennerström was a gangster while *Millennium* went bankrupt?"

"Nobody asked me to expose Wennerström for what he is," Salander replied in a know-it-all voice.

"Yes, but what if?"

"I did tell you," she said.

Blomkvist dropped the subject.

Salander burned the contents of Wennerström's hard drive—about five gigabytes—on to ten CDs, and she felt as if she had more or less moved into Blomkvist's apartment. She waited patiently, answering all the questions he asked.

"I can't understand how he can be so fucking dim to put all his dirty laundry on one hard drive," he said. "If it ever got into the hands of the police . . ."

"People aren't very rational. He has to believe that the police would never think of confiscating his computer."

"Above suspicion. I agree that he's an arrogant bastard, but he must have security consultants telling him how to handle his computer. There's material on this machine going all the way back to 1993."

"The computer itself is relatively new. It was manufactured a year ago, but he seems to have transferred all his old correspondence and everything else on to the hard drive instead of storing it on CDs. But at least he's using an encryption programme."

"Which is totally useless if you're inside his computer and reading the passwords every time he types them in."

After they'd been back in Stockholm for four days, Malm called on Blomkvist's mobile at 3:00 in the morning.

"Henry Cortez was at a bar with his girlfriend tonight."

"Uh-huh," Blomkvist said, sleepily.

"On the way home they ended up at Centralen's bar."

"Not a very good place for a seduction."

"Listen. Dahlman is on holiday. Henry discovered him sitting at a table with some guy."

"And?"

"Henry recognised the man from his byline pic. Krister Söder."

"I don't think I recognise the name, but . . ."

"He works for *Monopoly Financial Magazine,* which is owned by the Wennerström Group."

Blomkvist sat up straight in bed.

"Are you there?"

"I'm here. That might not mean anything. Söder is a journalist, and he might be an old friend."

"Maybe I'm being paranoid. But a while ago *Millennium* bought a story from a freelancer. The week before we were going to publish it, Söder ran an exposé that was almost identical. It was the story about the mobile telephone manufacturer and the defective component."

"I hear what you're saying. But that sort of thing does happen. Have you talked to Erika?"

"No, she's not back until next week."

"Don't do anything. I'll call you back later," Blomkvist said.

"Problems?" Salander asked.

"*Millennium*," Blomkvist said. "I have to go there. Want to come along?"

The editorial offices were deserted. It took Salander three minutes to crack the password protection on Dahlman's computer, and another two minutes to transfer its contents to Blomkvist's iBook.

Most of Dahlman's emails were probably on his own laptop, and they did not have access to it. But through his desktop computer at *Millennium,* Salander was able to discover that Dahlman had a Hotmail account in addition to his millennium.se address. It took her six minutes to crack the code and download his correspondence from the past year. Five minutes later Blomkvist had evidence that Dahlman had leaked information about the situation at *Millennium* and kept the editor of *Monopoly Financial Magazine* updated on which stories Berger was planning for which issues. The spying had been going on at least since the previous autumn.

They turned off the computers and went back to Mikael's apartment to sleep for a few hours. He called Christer Malm at 10:00 a.m.

"I have proof that Dahlman is working for Wennerström."

"I knew it. Great, I'm going to fire that fucking pig today."

"No, don't. Don't do anything at all."

"Nothing?"

"Christer, trust me. Is Dahlman still on holiday?"

"Yes, he's back on Monday."

"How many are in the office today?"

"Well, about half."

"Can you call a meeting for 2:00? Don't say what it's about. I'm coming over."

There were six people around the conference table. Malm looked tired. Cortez looked like someone newly in love, the way that only twenty-four-year-olds can look. Nilsson looked on edge—Malm had not told anyone what the meeting was about, but she had been with the company long enough to know that something out of the ordinary was going on, and she was annoyed that she had been kept out of the loop. The only one who looked the same as usual was the part-timer Ingela Oskarsson, who worked two days a week dealing with simple administrative tasks, the subscriber list and the like; she had not looked truly relaxed since she became a mother two years ago. The other part-timer was the freelance reporter Lotta Karim, who had a contract similar to Cortez's and had just started back to work after her holiday. Malm had also managed to get Magnusson to come in, although he was still on holiday.

Blomkvist began by greeting everyone warmly and apologising for being so long absent.

"What we're going to discuss today is something that

Christer and I haven't taken up with Erika, but I can assure you that in this case I speak for her too. Today we're going to determine *Millennium*'s future."

He paused to let the words sink in. No-one asked any questions.

"The past year has been rough. I'm surprised and proud that none of you has reconsidered and found a job somewhere else. I have to assume that either you're stark raving mad or wonderfully loyal and actually enjoy working on this magazine. That's why I'm going to lay the cards on the table and ask you for one last effort."

"One *last* effort?" Nilsson said. "That sounds as if you're thinking of shutting down the magazine."

"Exactly, Monika," Blomkvist said. "And thank you for that. When she gets back Erika is going to gather us all together for a gloomy editorial meeting and to tell us that *Millennium* will fold at Christmas and that you're all fired."

Now alarm began spreading through the group. Even Malm thought for a moment that Blomkvist was serious. Then they all noticed his broad smile.

"What you have to do this autumn is play a double game. The disagreeable fact is that our dear managing editor, Janne Dahlman, is moonlighting as an informer for Hans-Erik Wennerström. This means that the enemy is being kept informed of exactly what's going on in our editorial offices. This explains a number of setbacks we've experienced. You especially, Sonny, when advertisers who seemed positive pulled out without warning."

Dahlman had never been popular in the office, and the revelation was apparently not a shock to anyone. Blomkvist cut short the murmuring that started up.

"The reason that I'm telling you this is because I have absolute confidence in all of you. I know that you've all got your heads screwed on straight. That's why I also know that you'll play along with what takes place this autumn. It's very important that Wennerström believes that *Millennium* is on the verge of collapse. It will be your job to make sure he does."

"What's our real situation?" Cortez said.

"OK, here it is: by all accounts *Millennium* should be on its way to the grave. I give you my word that that's not going to happen. *Millennium* is stronger today than it was a year ago. When this meeting is over, I'm going to disappear again for about two months. Towards the end of October I'll be back. Then we're going to clip Wennerström's wings."

"How are we going to do that?" Nilsson said.

"Sorry, Monika. I don't want to give you the details, but I'm writing a new story, and this time we're going to do it right. I'm thinking of having roast Wennerström for the Christmas party and various critics for dessert."

The mood turned cheerful. Blomkvist wondered how he would have felt if he were one of them sitting listening to all this. Dubious? Most likely. But apparently he still had some "trust capital" among *Millennium*'s small group of employees. He held up his hand.

"If this is going to work, it's important that Wennerström believes that *Millennium* is on the verge of collapse because I don't want him to start some sort of retaliation or indeed get rid of the evidence which we mean to expose. So we're going to start writing a script that you'll follow during the coming months. First of all, it's important that nothing we discuss here today is written down or is referred to in emails. We don't know to what if any extent Dahlman has been digging around in our computers, and I've become aware that it's alarmingly simple to read co-workers' private email. So—we're going to do this orally. If you feel the need to air anything, go and see Christer at home. Very discreetly."

Blomkvist wrote "no email" on the whiteboard.

"Second, I want you to start squabbling among yourselves, complaining about me when Dahlman is around. Don't exaggerate. Just give your natural bitchy selves full rein. Christer, I want you and Erika to have a serious disagreement. Use your imagination and be secretive about the cause."

He wrote "start bitching" on the whiteboard.

"Third, when Erika comes home, her job will be to see to it that Janne Dahlman thinks our agreement with the Vanger Corporation—which is in fact giving us its full support—has fallen through because Henrik Vanger is seriously ill and Martin Vanger died in a car crash."

He wrote the word "disinformation."

"But the agreement really is solid?" Nilsson said.

"Believe me," Blomkvist said, "the Vanger Corporation will go to great lengths to ensure that *Millennium* survives. In a few weeks, let's say at the end of August, Erika will call a meeting to warn you about layoffs. You all know that it's a scam, and that the only one who's going to be leaving is Dahlman. But start talking about looking for new jobs and say what a lousy reference it is to have *Millennium* on your C.V."

"And you really think that this game will end up saving *Millennium*?" Magnusson said.

"I know it will. And Sonny, I want you to put together a fake report each month showing falling advertising sales and showing that the number of subscribers has also dropped."

"This sounds fun," Nilsson said. "Should we keep it internal here in the office, or should we leak it to other media too?"

"Keep it internal. If the story shows up anywhere, we'll know who put it there. In a very few months, if anyone asks us about it, we'll be able to tell them: you've been listening to baseless rumours, and we've never considered closing *Millennium* down. The best thing that could happen is for Dahlman to go out and tip off the other mass media. If you're able to give Dahlman a tip about a plausible but fundamentally idiotic story, so much the better."

They spent an hour concocting a script and dividing up the various roles.

After the meeting Blomkvist had coffee with Malm at Java on Horngatspuckeln.

"Christer, it's really important that you pick up Erika at the airport and fill her in. You have to convince her to play along with the game. If I know her, she'll want to confront Dahlman instantly—but that can't happen. I don't want Wennerström to hear any kind of buzz and then manage to bury the evidence."

"Will do."

"And see to it that Erika stays away from her email until she installs the PGP encryption programme and learns how to use it. It's pretty likely that through Dahlman, Wennerström is able to read everything we email to each other. I want you and everyone else in the editorial offices to install PGP. Do it in a natural way. Get the name of a computer consultant to contact and have him come over to inspect the network and all the computers in the office. Let him install the software as if it were a perfectly natural part of the service."

"I'll do my best. But Mikael—what *are* you working on?"

"Wennerström."

"What exactly?"

"For the time being, that has to remain my secret."

Malm looked uncomfortable. "I've always trusted you, Mikael. Does this mean that you don't trust me?"

Blomkvist laughed.

"Of course I trust you. But right now I'm involved in rather serious criminal activities that could get me two years in prison. It's the nature of my research that's a little dubious . . . I'm playing with the same underhand methods as Wennerström uses. I don't want you or Erika or anyone else at *Millennium* to be involved in any way."

"You're making me awfully nervous."

"Stay cool, Christer, and tell Erika that the story is going to be a big one. Really big."

"Erika will insist on knowing what you're working on . . ."

Mikael thought for a second. Then he smiled.

"Tell her that she made it very clear to me in the spring when she signed a contract with Henrik Vanger behind my back that I'm now just an ordinary mortal freelancer who no longer sits on the board and has no influence on *Millennium* policy. Which means that I no longer have any obligation to keep her informed. But I promise that if she behaves herself, I'll give her first option on the story."

"She's going to go through the roof," Malm said cheerfully.

Blomkvist knew that he had not been entirely honest with Malm. He was deliberately avoiding Berger. The most natural thing would have been to contact her at once and tell her about the information in his possession. But he did not want to talk to her. A dozen times he had stood with his mobile in his hand, starting to call her. Each time he changed his mind.

He knew what the problem was. He could not look her in the eyes.

The cover-up in which he had participated in Hedestad was unforgivable from a professional point of view. He had no idea how he could explain it to her without lying, and if there was one thing he had never thought of doing, it was lying to Erika Berger.

Above all, he did not have the energy to deal with that problem at the same time as he was tackling Wennerström. So he put off seeing her, turned off his mobile, and avoided talking to her. But he knew that the reprieve could only be temporary.

Right after the editorial meeting, Mikael moved out to his cabin in Sandhamn; he hadn't been there in over a year. His baggage included two boxes of printouts and the CDs that Salander had given him. He stocked up on food, locked the door, opened his iBook, and started writing. Each day he took a short walk, bought the newspapers, and shopped for groceries. The guest marina was still filled with yachts, and young people who had borrowed their father's boat were usually sitting in the Divers' Bar, drinking themselves silly. Blomkvist scarcely took in his surroundings. He sat in front of his computer more or less from the moment he opened his eyes until he fell into bed at night, exhausted.

> Encrypted email from editor in chief <erika.berger@millennium.se> to publisher on leave of absence <mikael.blomkvist@millennium.se>:
>
> Mikael. I want to know what's going on—good grief, I've come back from holiday to total chaos. The news about Janne Dahlman and this double game you've come up with. Martin Vanger dead. Harriet Vanger alive. What's going on in Hedeby? Where are you? Is there a story? Why don't you answer your mobile? /E.

P.S. I understood the insinuation that Christer relayed with such glee. You're going to have to eat your words. Are you seriously cross with me?

P.P.S. I am trusting you for the time being, but you are going to have to give proof—you remember, the stuff that stands up in court—on J.D.

From <mikael.blomkvist@millennium.se>
To <erika.berger@millennium.se>:

Hi Ricky. No, for God's sake, I'm not cross. Forgive me for not keeping you updated, but the past few months of my life have been topsy-turvy. I'll tell you everything when we see each other, but not by email. I'm at Sandhamn. There is a story, but the story is not Harriet Vanger. I'm going to be glued to my computer here for a while. Then it'll be over. Trust me. Hugs and kisses. M.

From <erika.berger@millennium.se>
To <mikael.blomkvist@millennium.se>:

Sandhamn? I'm coming to see you immediately.

From <mikael.blomkvist@millennium.se>
To <erika.berger@millennium.se>:

Not right now. Wait a couple of weeks, at least until I've got the story organised. Besides, I'm expecting company.

From <erika.berger@millennium.se>
To <mikael.blomkvist@millennium.se>:

In that case, of course I'll stay away. But I have to know what's going on. Henrik Vanger has become CEO again, and he doesn't answer my calls. If the deal with Vanger is off, I absolutely need to know. Ricky

P.S. Who is she?

From <mikael.blomkvist@millennium.se>
To <erika.berger@millennium.se>

First of all: no question of Henrik pulling out. But he is still working only a short day, and I'm guessing that the chaos after Martin's death and Harriet's resurrection is taking its toll on his strength.

Second: *Millennium* will survive. I'm working on the most important report of our lives, and when we publish it, it's going to sink Wennerström once and for all.

Third: My life is up and down right now, but as for you and me and *Millennium*—nothing has changed. Trust me. Kisses / Mikael.

P.S. I'll introduce you as soon as an opportunity presents itself.

When Salander went out to Sandhamn she found an unshaven and hollow-eyed Blomkvist, who gave her a quick hug and asked her to make some coffee and wait while he finished what he was writing.

Salander looked around his cabin and decided almost at once that she liked it. It was right next to a jetty, with the water three paces from the door. It was only fifteen by eighteen feet but it had such a high ceiling that there was space for a sleeping loft. She could stand up straight there, just. Blomkvist would have to stoop. The bed was wide enough for both of them.

The cabin had one large window facing the water, right next to the front door. That was where his kitchen table stood, doubling as his desk. On the wall near the desk was a shelf with a CD player and a big collection of Elvis and hard rock, which was not Salander's first choice.

In a corner was a woodstove made of soapstone with a glazed front. The rest of the sparse furnishings consisted of a large wardrobe for clothes and linen and a sink that also functioned as a washing alcove behind a shower curtain. Near the sink was a small window on one side of the cabin. Under the spiral stairs to the loft Blomkvist had built a separate space for a composting toilet. The whole cabin was arranged like the cabin on a boat, with clever cubbyholes for stowing things.

During her personal investigation of Mikael Blomkvist, Salander had found out that he had remodelled the cabin and built the furniture himself—a conclusion drawn from the comments of an acquaintance who had sent Mikael an email after visiting Sandhamn and was impressed by his handiwork. Everything was clean, unpretentious, and simple, bordering on spartan. She could see why he loved this cabin in Sandhamn so much.

After two hours she managed to distract Mikael enough that he turned off his computer in frustration, shaved, and took her out for a guided tour. It was raining and windy, and they quickly retreated to the inn. Blomkvist told her what he was writing, and Salander gave him a CD with updates from Wennerström's computer.

Then she took him up to the loft and managed to get his clothes off and distract him even further. She woke up late that night to find herself alone. She peered down from the loft and saw him sitting hunched over his computer. She lay there for a long time, leaning on one hand, watching him. He seemed happy, and she too felt strangely content with life.

Salander stayed only five days before she went back to Stockholm to do a job for Armansky. She spent eleven days on the assignment, made her report, and then returned to Sandhamn. The stack of printed pages next to Mikael's iBook was growing.

This time she stayed for four weeks. They fell into a routine. They got up at 8:00, ate breakfast, and spent an hour together. Then Mikael worked intently until late in the afternoon, when they took a walk and talked. Salander spent most of the days in bed, either reading books or surfing the Net using Blomkvist's ADSL modem. She tried not to disturb him during the day. They ate dinner rather late and only then did Salander take the initiative and force him up to the sleeping loft, where she saw to it that he devoted all his attention to her.

It was as if she were on the very first holiday of her life.

Encrypted email from <erika.berger@millennium.se>
To <mikael.blomkvist@millennium.se>:

Hi M. It's now official. Janne Dahlman has resigned and starts working at *Monopoly Financial Magazine* in three weeks. I've done as you asked and said nothing, and everyone is going around playing monkey games. E.

P.S. They seem to be having fun. Henry and Lotta had a fight and started throwing things at each other a couple of days ago. They've been messing with Dahlman's head so blatantly that I can't understand how he can miss seeing that it's all a put-up job.

From <mikael.blomkvist@millennium.se>
To <erika.berger@millennium.se>:

Wish him good luck from me, will you, and let him go straight away. But lock up the silverware. Hugs and kisses / M.

From <erika.berger@millennium.se>
To <mikael.blomkvist@millennium.se>:

I have no managing editor two weeks before we go to press, and my investigative reporter is sitting out in Sandhamn refusing to talk to me. Micke, I'm on my knees. Can you come in? / Erika.

From <mikael.blomkvist@millennium.se>
To <erika.berger@millennium.se>:

Hold out another couple of weeks, then we'll be home free. And start planning for a December issue that's going to be unlike anything we've ever done. The piece will take up 40 pages. M.

From <erika.berger@millennium.se>
To <mikael.blomkvist@millennium.se>:

40 PAGES!!! Are you out of your mind?

From <mikael.blomkvist@millennium.se>
To <erika.berger@millennium.se>:

It's going to be a special issue. I need three more weeks. Could you do the following: (1) register a publishing company under the *Millennium* name, (2) get an ISBN number, (3) ask Christer to put together a cool logo for our new publishing company, and (4) find a good printer that can produce a paperback quickly and cheaply. And by the way, we're going to need capital to print our first book. Kisses / Mikael

----

From <erika.berger@millennium.se>
To <mikael.blomkvist@millennium.se>:

Special issue. Book publisher. Money. Yes, master. Anything else I can do for you? Dance naked at Slussplan? / E.

P.S. I assume you know what you're doing. But what do I do about Dahlman?

From <mikael.blomkvist@millennium.se>
To <erika.berger@millennium.se>:

Don't do anything about Dahlman. Tell him he's free to go right away and you aren't sure you can pay his wages anyway. *Monopoly* isn't going to survive for long. Bring in more freelance material for this issue. And hire a new managing editor, for God's sake. / M.

P.S. Slussplan? It's a date.

From <erika.berger@millennium.se>
To <mikael.blomkvist@millennium.se>:

Slussplan—in your dreams. But we've always done the hiring together. / Ricky.

From <mikael.blomkvist@millennium.se>
To <erika.berger@millennium.se>:

And we've always agreed about who we should hire. We will this time too, no matter who you choose. We're going to scupper Wennerström. That's the whole story. Just let me finish this in peace. / M.

In early October Salander read an article on the Internet edition of the *Hedestad Courier*. She told Blomkvist about it. Isabella Vanger had died after a short illness. She was mourned by her daughter, Harriet Vanger, lately returned from Australia.

Encrypted email from <erika.berger@millennium.se>
To <mikael.blomkvist@millennium.se>:

Hi Mikael.

Harriet Vanger came to see me at the office today. She called five minutes before she arrived, and I was totally unprepared. A beautiful woman, elegant clothes and a cool gaze.

She came to tell me that she'll be replacing Martin Vanger as Henrik's representative on our board. She was polite and friendly and assured me that the Vanger Corporation had no plans to back out of the agreement. On the contrary, the family stands fully behind Henrik's obligations to the magazine. She asked for a tour of the editorial offices, and she wanted to know how I see the situation.

I told her the truth. That it feels as if I don't have solid ground under my feet, that you have forbidden me to come to Sandhamn, and that I don't know what you're working on, other than that you are planning to sink Wennerström. (I assumed it was OK to say that. She is on the board, after all.) She raised an eyebrow and smiled and asked if I had doubts that you'd succeed. What was I supposed to say to that? I said that I would sleep a little easier if I knew exactly what you were writing. Jeez, of course I trust you. But you're driving me crazy.

I asked her if *she* knew what you were working on. She denied it but said that it was her impression that you were extremely resourceful, with an innovative way of thinking. (Her words.)

I said that I also gathered that something dramatic had happened up in Hedestad and that I was ever so slightly curious about the story regarding Harriet Vanger herself. In short, I felt like an idiot. She asked me whether you really hadn't told me anything. She said that she understood that you and I have a special relationship and that you would undoubtedly tell me the story when you had time. Then she asked if she could trust me. What was I supposed to say? She's on the *Millennium* board, and you've left me here totally in the dark.

Then she said something odd. She asked me not to judge either her or you too harshly. She said she owed you some sort of debt of gratitude, and she would really like it if she and I could also be friends. Then she promised to tell me the story someday if you couldn't do it. Half an hour ago she left, and I'm still in a daze. I think I like her, but who *is* this person? / Erika

P.S. I miss you. I have a feeling that something nasty happened in Hedestad. Christer says that you have a strange mark on your neck.

From <mikael.blomkvist@millennium.se>
To <erika.berger@millennium.se>:

Hi Ricky. The story about Harriet is so miserably awful that you can't even imagine it. It would be great if she could tell you about it herself. I can hardly bring myself to think about it.

By the way, you can trust her. She was telling the truth when she said that she owes a debt of gratitude to me—and believe me, she will never do anything to harm *Millennium*. Be her friend if you like her. She deserves respect. And she's a hell of a businesswoman. / M.

The next day Mikael received another email.

From <harriet.vanger@vangerindustries.com>
To <mikael.blomkvist@millennium.se>:

Hi Mikael. I've been trying to find time to write to you for several weeks now, but it seems there are never enough hours in the day. You left so suddenly from Hedeby that I never had a chance to say goodbye.

Since my return to Sweden, my days have been filled with bewildering impressions and hard work. The Vanger Corporation is in chaos, and along with Henrik I've been working hard to put its affairs in order. Yesterday I visited the *Millennium* offices; I'll be Henrik's representative on the board. Henrik has filled me in on all the details of the magazine's situation and yours.

I hope that you will accept having me show up like this. If you don't want me (or anyone else from the family) on the board, I'll understand, but I do assure you that I'll do all I can to support *Millennium*. I am in great debt to you, and I will always have the best of intentions in this regard.

I met your colleague Erika Berger. I'm not sure what she thought of me, and I was surprised to hear that you hadn't told her about what happened.

I would very much like to be your friend. If you can stand to have anything more to do with the Vanger family. Best regards, Harriet

P.S. I understood from Erika that you're planning to tackle Wennerström again. Dirch Frode told me how Henrik pulled a swifty on you, as they say in Australia. What can I say? I'm sorry. If there's anything I can do, let me know.

From <mikael.blomkvist@millennium.se>
To <harriet.vanger@vangerindustries.com>:

Hi Harriet. I left Hedeby in a big hurry and am now working on what I really should have been spending my time on this year. You'll be advised in plenty of time before the article goes to press, but I think I can say that the problems of the past year will soon be over.

I hope you and Erika will be friends, and, of course, I have no problem with you being on *Millennium*'s board. I'll tell Erika about what happened, if you think that's wise. Henrik wanted me never to say anything to anyone. Let's see, but right now I don't have the time or the energy and I need a little distance first.

Let's keep in touch. Best / Mikael

Salander was not especially interested in what Mikael was writing. She looked up from her book when Blomkvist said something, but at first she could not make it out.

"Sorry. I was talking aloud. I said that this is horrible."

"What's horrible?"

"Wennerström had an affair with a twenty-two-year-old

waitress and he got her pregnant. Have you read his correspondence with his lawyer?"

"My dear Mikael—you have ten years of correspondence, emails, agreements, travel arrangements, and God knows what on that hard drive. I don't find Wennerström so fascinating that I'd cram six gigs of garbage into my head. I read through a fraction of it, mostly to satisfy my curiosity, and that was enough to tell me that he's a gangster."

"OK. He got her pregnant in 1997. When she wanted compensation, his lawyer got someone to try to convince her to have an abortion. I assume the intention was to offer her a sum of money, but she wasn't interested. Then the persuading ended up with the heavy holding her underwater in a bath until she agreed to leave Wennerström in peace. And Wennerström's idiot writes all this to the lawyer in an email—of course encrypted, but even so . . . It doesn't say much for the IQ of this bunch."

"What happened to the girl?"

"She had an abortion, and Wennerström was pleased."

Salander said nothing for ten minutes. Her eyes had suddenly turned dark.

"One more man who hates women," she muttered at last.

She borrowed the CDs and spent the next few days reading through Wennerström's emails and other documents. While Blomkvist kept working, Salander was up in the sleeping loft with her PowerBook on her knees, pondering Wennerström's peculiar empire.

An idea had occurred to her and she could not let it go. Most of all she wondered why it had not occurred to her sooner.

In late October Mikael turned off his computer when it was only 11:00 in the morning. He climbed up to the sleeping loft and handed Salander what he had written. Then he fell asleep. She woke him that evening and gave him her opinion of the article.

Just after 2:00 in the morning, Blomkvist made the last backup of his work.

The next day he closed the shutters on the windows and locked up. Salander's holiday was over. They went back to Stockholm together.

He brought up the subject as they were drinking coffee from paper cups on the Vaxholm ferry.

"What the two of us need to decide is what to tell Erika. She's going to refuse to publish this if I can't explain how I got hold of the material."

Erika Berger. Blomkvist's editor in chief and long-time lover. Salander had never met her and was not sure that she wanted to either. Berger seemed like some indefinable disturbance in her life.

"What does she know about me?"

"Nothing." He sighed. "The fact is that I've been avoiding her ever since the summer. She's very frustrated about the fact that I couldn't tell her what happened in Hedestad. She knows, of course, that I've been staying out at Sandhamn and writing this story, but she doesn't know what it's about."

"Hmm."

"In a couple of hours she'll have the manuscript. Then she's going to give me the third degree. The question is, what should I tell her?"

"What do you want to tell her?"

"I'd like to tell her the truth."

Salander frowned.

"Lisbeth, Erika and I argue almost all the time. It seems to be part of how we communicate. But she's absolutely trustworthy. You're a source. She would rather die than reveal who you are."

"How many others would you have to tell?"

"Absolutely no-one. It will go to the grave with me and Erika. But I won't tell her your secret if you don't want me to. On the other hand, it's not an option for me to lie to Erika, make up some source that doesn't exist."

Salander thought about it until they docked by the Grand Hotel. Analysis of consequences. Reluctantly she finally gave Blomkvist permission to introduce her to Erika. He switched on his mobile and made the call.

Berger was lunching with Malin Eriksson, whom she was considering hiring as managing editor. Eriksson was twenty-nine years old and had been working as a temp for five years. She had never held a permanent job and had started to doubt that she ever would. Berger called her on the very day that Malin's latest temp job ended to ask if she would like to apply for the *Millennium* position.

"It's a temporary post for three months," Berger said. "But if things work out, it could be permanent."

"I've heard rumours that *Millennium* is having a difficult time."

Berger smiled.

"You shouldn't believe rumours."

"This Dahlman that I would be replacing . . ." Eriksson hesitated. "He's going to work at a magazine owned by Hans-Erik Wennerström . . ."

Berger nodded. "It's hardly a trade secret that we're in conflict with Wennerström. He doesn't like people who work for *Millennium*."

"So if I take the job at *Millennium,* I would end up in that category too."

"It's very likely, yes."

"But Dahlman got a job with *Monopoly Financial Magazine,* didn't he?"

"You might say that it's Wennerström's way of paying for services rendered. Are you still interested?"

Eriksson nodded.

"When do you want me to start?"

That's when Blomkvist called.

She used her own key to open the door to his apartment. It was the first time since his brief visit to the office at Midsummer that she was meeting him face to face. She went into the living room and found an anorexically thin girl sitting on the sofa, wearing a worn leather jacket and with her feet propped up on the coffee table. At first she thought the girl was about fifteen, but that was before she looked into her eyes. She was still looking at this creature when Blomkvist came in with a coffeepot and coffee cake.

"Forgive me for being completely impossible," he said.

Berger tilted her head. There was something different about him. He looked haggard, thinner than she remembered. His eyes had a shamed expression, and for a moment he avoided her gaze. She glanced at his neck. She saw a pale red line, clearly distinguishable.

"I've been avoiding you. It's a very long story, and I'm not proud of my role in it. But we'll talk about that later . . . Now I want to introduce you to this young woman. Erika, this is Lisbeth Salander. Lisbeth, Erika Berger, editor in chief of *Millennium* and my best friend."

Salander studied Berger's elegant clothes and self-confident

. . .

manner and decided after ten seconds that she was most likely not going to be her best friend.

Their meeting lasted five hours. Berger twice made calls to cancel other meetings. She spent an hour reading parts of the manuscript that Blomkvist put in her hands. She had a thousand questions but realised that it would take weeks before she got them answered. The important thing was the manuscript, which she finally put down. If even a fraction of these claims were accurate, a whole new situation had emerged.

Berger looked at Blomkvist. She had never doubted that he was an honest person, but now she felt dizzy and wondered whether the Wennerström affair had broken him—that what he had been working on was all a figment of his imagination. Blomkvist was at that moment unpacking two boxes of printed-out source material. Berger blanched. She wanted, of course, to know how it had come into his possession.

It took a while to convince her that this odd girl, who had said not one word during the meeting, had unlimited access to Wennerström's computer. And not just his—she had also hacked into the computers of several of his lawyers and close associates.

Berger's immediate reaction was that they could not use the material since it had been obtained through illegal means.

But, of course, they could use it. Blomkvist pointed out that they had no obligation to explain how they had acquired the material. They could just as well have a source with access to Wennerström's computer who had burned everything on his hard drive to a CD.

Finally Berger realised what a weapon she had in her hands. She felt exhausted and still had questions, but she did not know where to begin. At last she leaned back against the sofa and threw out her hands.

"Mikael, what happened up in Hedestad?"

Salander looked up sharply. Blomkvist answered with a question.

"How are you getting along with Harriet Vanger?"

"Fine. I think. I've met her twice. Christer and I drove up to Hedestad for a board meeting last week. We got drunk on wine."

"And the board meeting?"

"She kept her word."

"Ricky, I know you're frustrated that I've been ducking you and coming up with excuses not to tell you what happened. You and I have never had secrets from each other, and all of a sudden there's six months of my life that I'm . . . not prepared to tell you about."

Berger met Blomkvist's gaze. She knew him inside and out, but what she saw in his eyes was something she had never seen before. He was begging her not to ask. Salander watched their wordless dialogue. She was no part of it.

"Was it that bad?"

"It was worse. I've been dreading this conversation. I promise to tell you, but I've spent several months suppressing my feelings while Wennerström has absorbed all my attention . . . I'm still not ready. I'd prefer it if Harriet told you instead."

"What's that mark around your neck?"

"Lisbeth saved my life up there. If it weren't for her, I'd be dead."

Berger's eyes widened. She stared at the girl in the leather jacket.

"And right now you need to come to an agreement with her. She is our source."

Berger sat for a time, thinking. Then she did something that astonished Blomkvist and startled Salander; she surprised even herself. The whole time she had been sitting at Mikael's living-room table, she had felt Salander's eyes on her. A taciturn girl with hostile vibrations.

Berger stood up and went around the table and threw her arms around the girl. Salander squirmed like a worm about to be put on a hook.

CHAPTER 29

Saturday, November 1–
Tuesday, November 25

Salander was surfing through Wennerström's cyber-empire. She had been staring at her computer screen for almost eleven hours. The idea that had materialised in some unexplored nook of her brain during the last week at Sandhamn had grown into a manic preoccupation. For four weeks she had isolated herself in her apartment and ignored any communication from Armansky. She had spent twelve hours a day in front of her computer, some days more, and the rest of her waking hours she had brooded over the same problem.

During the past month she had had intermittent contact with Blomkvist. He too was preoccupied, busy at the *Millennium* offices. They had conferred by telephone a couple of times each week, and she had kept him updated on Wennerström's correspondence and other activities.

For the hundredth time she went over every detail. She was not afraid that she had missed anything, but she was not sure that she had understood how every one of the intricate connections fitted together.

This much-discussed empire was like a living, formless, pulsating organism that kept changing shape. It consisted of options, bonds, shares, partnerships, loan interest, income interest, deposits, bank accounts, payment transfers, and thousands of other elements. An incredibly large proportion of the assets was deposited in post-office-box companies that owned one another.

The financial pundits' most inflated analyses of the Wennerström Group estimated its value at more than 900 billion kronor. That was a bluff, or at least a figure that was grossly exaggerated. Obviously Wennerström himself was by no means poor. She calculated the real assets to be worth between 90 and 100 billion kronor, which was nothing to sneeze at. A thorough audit of the entire corporation would take years. All in all Salander had identified close to three thousand separate accounts and bank holdings all over the world. Wennerström was devoting himself to fraud that was so extensive it was no longer merely criminal—it was business.

Somewhere in the Wennerström organism there was also substance. Three assets kept showing up in the hierarchy. The fixed Swedish assets were unassailable and genuine, available to public scrutiny, balance sheets, and audits. The American firm was solid, and a bank in New York served as the base for all liquid capital. The story was in the business with the post-office-box companies in places such as Gibraltar and Cyprus and Macao. Wennerström was like a clearing house for the illegal weapons trade, money laundering for suspect enterprises in Colombia, and extremely unorthodox businesses in Russia.

An anonymous account in the Cayman Islands was unique; it was personally controlled by Wennerström but was not connected to any companies. A few hundredths of a percent of every deal that Wennerström made would be siphoned into the Cayman Islands via the post-office-box companies.

Salander worked in a trance-like state. The account—*click*—email—*click*—balance sheets—*click*. She noted down the latest transfers. She tracked a small transaction in Japan to Singapore and on via Luxembourg to the Cayman Islands. She understood how it worked. It was as if she were part of the impulses in cyberspace. Small changes. The latest email. One brief message of somewhat peripheral interest was sent at 10:00 p.m. The PGP encryption programme (rattle, rattle) was a joke for anyone who was already inside his computer and could read the message in plain text:

> Berger has stopped arguing about the ads. Has she given up or does she have something cooking? Your source at the editorial offices assured us that they were on the brink of ruin, but it sounds as if they just hired a new person. Find out what's happening. Blomkvist has been working at Sandhamn for the past few weeks, but no-one knows what he's writing. He's been seen at the editorial offices the past few days. Can you arrange for an advance copy of the next issue?/HEW/

Nothing dramatic. Let him worry. *Your goose is cooked, old man.*

At 5:30 in the morning she turned off her computer and got out a new pack of cigarettes. She had drunk four, no, five Cokes during the night, and now she got out a sixth and went to sit on the sofa. She was wearing only knickers and a washed-out camouflage shirt advertising *Soldier of Fortune* magazine, with the slogan KILL THEM ALL AND LET GOD SORT THEM OUT. She realised that she was cold, so she reached for a blanket, which she wrapped around herself.

She felt high, as if she had consumed some inappropriate and presumably illegal substance. She focused her gaze on the street lamp outside the window and sat still while her brain worked at top speed. Mamma—*click*—sister—*click*—Mimmi—*click*—Holger Palmgren. Evil Fingers. And Armansky. The job. Harriet Vanger. *Click*. Martin Vanger. *Click*. The golf club. *Click*. The lawyer Bjurman. *Click*. Every single fucking detail that she couldn't forget even if she tried.

She wondered whether Bjurman would ever take his clothes off in front of a woman again, and if he did, how was he going to explain the tattoos on his stomach? And the next time he went to the doctor how would he avoid taking off his clothes?

And Mikael Blomkvist. *Click*.

She considered him to be a good person, possibly with a Practical Pig complex that was sometimes a little too apparent. And he was unbearably naive with regard to certain elementary moral issues. He had an indulgent and forgiving personality that looked for explanations and excuses for the way people behaved, and he would never get it that the raptors of the world understood only one language. She felt almost awkwardly protective whenever she thought of him.

She did not remember falling asleep, but she woke up at 9:00 a.m. with a crick in her neck and with her head leaning against the wall behind the sofa. She tottered to the bedroom and fell back to sleep.

It was without a doubt the biggest story of their lives. For the first time in a year and a half, Berger was happy in the way that only an editor who has a spectacular scoop in the oven can be.

She and Blomkvist were polishing the article one last time when Salander called him on his mobile.

"I forgot to say that Wennerström is starting to get worried about what you've been doing lately, and he's asked for an advance copy of the next issue."

"How do you know . . . ah, forget that. Any idea what he plans to do?"

"Nix. Just one logical guess."

Blomkvist thought for a few seconds. "The printer," he exclaimed.

Berger raised her eyebrows.

"If you're keeping a lid on the editorial offices, there aren't many other possibilities. Provided none of his thugs is planning to pay you a nighttime visit."

Blomkvist turned to Berger. "Book a new printer for this issue. Now. And call Dragan Armansky—I want security here at night for the next week." Back to Salander. "Thanks."

"What's it worth?"

"What do you mean?"

"What's the tip worth?"

"What would you like?"

"I'd like to discuss it over coffee. Right now."

They met at Kaffebar on Hornsgatan. Salander looked so serious when Blomkvist sat down on the bench next to her that he felt a pang of concern. As usual, she came straight to the point.

"I need to borrow some money."

Blomkvist gave her one of his most foolish grins and reached for his wallet.

"Sure. How much?"

"120,000 kronor."

"Steady, steady." He put his wallet away.

"I'm not kidding. I need to borrow 120,000 kronor for . . . let's say six weeks. I have a chance to make an investment, but I don't have anyone else to turn to. You've got roughly 140,000 kronor in your current account right now. You'll get your money back."

No point commenting on the fact that Salander had hacked his bank password.

"You don't have to borrow the money from me," he replied. "We haven't discussed your share yet, but it's more than enough to cover what you want to borrow."

"My share?"

"Lisbeth, I have an insane fee to cash in from Henrik Vanger, and we're going to finalise the deal at the end of the year. Without you, there wouldn't be a me and *Millennium* would have gone under. I'm planning to split the fee with you. Fifty-fifty."

Salander gave him a searching look. A frown had appeared on her brow. Blomkvist was used to her silences. Finally she shook her head.

"I don't want your money."

"But . . ."

"I don't want one single krona from you, unless it comes in the form of presents on my birthday."

"Come to think of it, I don't even know when your birthday is."

"You're a journalist. Check it out."

"I'm serious, Lisbeth. About splitting the money."

"I'm serious too. I only want to borrow it, and I need it tomorrow."

She didn't even ask how much her share would be. "I'll be happy to go to the bank with you today and lend you the amount you need. But at the end of the year let's have another talk about your share." He held up his hand. "And by the way, when is your birthday?"

"On Walpurgis Night," she replied. "Very fitting, don't you think? That's when I gad around with a broom between my legs."

She landed in Zürich at 7:30 in the evening and took a taxi to the Matterhorn Hotel. She had booked a room under the name of Irene Nesser, and she identified herself using a Norwegian passport in that name. Irene Nesser had shoulder-length blonde hair. Salander had bought a wig in Stockholm and used 10,000 kronor of what she had borrowed from Blomkvist to buy two passports through one of the contacts in Plague's international network.

She went to her room, locked the door, and got undressed. She lay on the bed and looked up at the ceiling in the room that cost 1,600 kronor per night. She felt empty. She had already run through half the sum she'd borrowed, and even though she had added in every krona of her own savings, she was still on a tight budget. She stopped thinking and fell asleep almost at once.

She awoke just after 5:00 in the morning. She showered and spent a long time masking the tattoo on her neck with a thick layer of skin-coloured lotion and powder over it. The second item on her checklist was to make an appointment at the beauty salon in the lobby of a significantly more expensive hotel for 6:30 that morning. She bought another blonde wig, this one in a page-boy style, and then she had a manicure, getting pink nails attached to her own chewed ones. She also got false eyelashes, more powder, rouge, and finally lipstick and other make-up. No change from 8,000 kronor.

She paid with a credit card in the name of Monica Sholes, and she showed them her British passport with that name.

Next stop was Camille's House of Fashion down the street. After an hour she came out wearing black boots, a sand-coloured skirt with matching blouse, black tights, a waist-length jacket, and a beret. Every item bore an expensive designer label. She had let the sales girl make the selection. She had also chosen an exclusive leather briefcase and a small Samsonite suitcase. The crowning touches were discreet earrings and a simple gold chain around her neck. The credit card had been debited 44,000 kronor.

For the first time in her life Salander had a bustline that made her—when she glanced at herself in the full-length mirror—catch her breath. The breasts were as fake as Monica Sholes' identity. They were made of latex and had been bought in Copenhagen where the transvestites shopped.

She was ready for battle.

Just after 9:00 she walked two blocks to the venerable Zimmertal Hotel, where she booked a room in Monica Sholes' name. She gave a generous tip to a boy who carried up her suitcase (which contained her travel bag). The suite was a small one, costing 22,000 kronor a day. She had booked it for one night. When she was alone she took a look around. She had a dazzling view of Lake Zürich, which didn't interest her in the least. But she did spend close to five minutes examining herself in the mirror. She saw a total stranger. Big-busted Monica Sholes in a blonde page-boy wig, wearing more make-up than Lisbeth Salander dreamed of using in a whole month. She looked . . . different.

At 9:30 she had breakfast in the hotel bar: two cups of coffee and a bagel with jam. The cost was 210 kronor. *Are these people soft in the head?*

Just before 10:00 Monica Sholes set down her coffee cup, opened her mobile, and punched in the number of a modem uplink in Hawaii. After three rings, the handshaking tone began. The modem was connected. Monica Sholes replied by punching in a six-digit code on her mobile and texting a message containing instructions to start a programme that Salander had written especially for this purpose.

In Honolulu the programme came to life on an anonymous home page on a server that was officially located at the university. The programme was simple. Its only function was to send instructions to start another programme in another server, which in this case was a perfectly ordinary commercial ISP offering Internet services in Holland. The function of that programme, in turn, was to look for the mirrored hard drive belonging to Hans-Erik Wennerström and take command of the programme that showed the contents of his approximately 3,000 bank accounts around the world.

There was only one account of any interest. Salander had noted that Wennerström looked at the account a couple of times each week. If he turned on his computer and looked at that particular file, everything would appear to be normal. The programme showed small changes, which were to be expected, based on normal fluctuations in the account during the past six months. If during the next forty-eight hours Wennerström should go in and ask to have the funds paid out or moved from the account, the programme would dutifully report that it had been done. In reality, the change would have occurred only on the mirrored hard drive in Holland.

Monica Sholes switched off her mobile the moment she heard four short tones confirming that the programme had started.

She left the Zimmertal Hotel and walked over to Bank Hauser General, across the street, where she had made an appointment to see Herr Wagner, the general manager, at 10:00. She was there three minutes ahead of schedule, and she spent the waiting time posing in front of the surveillance camera, which took her picture as she walked into the department with offices for discreet private consultations.

"I need some assistance with a number of transactions," she said in Oxford English. When she opened her briefcase, she let drop a pen from the Zimmertal Hotel, and Herr Wagner politely retrieved it for her. She gave him an arch smile and wrote an account number on the notepad on the desk in front of her.

Herr Wagner pigeonholed her as the spoiled daughter, or possibly mistress, of some bigshot.

"There are a number of accounts at the Bank of Kroenenfeld in the Cayman Islands. Automatic transfer can be done by sequential clearing codes," she said.

"Fräulein Sholes, naturally you have all the required clearing codes?" he asked.

"*Aber natürlich*," she replied with such a heavy accent that it was obvious she had only school-level German.

She started reciting several series of sixteen-digit numbers without once referring to any papers. Herr Wagner saw that it was going to be a long morning, but for a 4 percent commission on the transactions, he was prepared to skip lunch, and he was going to have to revise his pigeonhole for Fräulein Sholes.

She did not leave Bank Hauser General until just past noon, slightly later than planned, and she walked back to the Zimmertal. She put in an appearance at the front desk before she went up to her room and took off the clothes she had bought. She kept on the latex breasts but replaced the page-boy wig with Irene Nesser's shoulder-length blonde hair. She put on more familiar clothes: boots with stiletto heels, black trousers, a simple shirt, and a nice black leather jacket from Malungsboden in

Stockholm. She studied herself in the mirror. Not unkempt by any means, but she was no longer an heiress. Before Irene Nesser left the room, she sorted through a number of bonds, which she placed inside a thin portfolio.

At 1:05, a few minutes behind schedule, she went into Bank Dorffmann, about seventy yards away from Bank Hauser General. Irene Nesser had made an appointment in advance with a Herr Hasselmann. She apologised for being late. She spoke impeccable German with a Norwegian accent.

"No problem at all, Fräulein," Herr Hasselmann said. "How can I be of service?"

"I would like to open an account. I have a number of private bonds that I'd like to convert."

Irene Nesser placed her portfolio on the desk in front of him.

Herr Hasselmann examined the contents, hastily at first, and then more slowly. He raised an eyebrow and smiled politely.

She opened five numbered accounts, which she could access via the Internet and which were owned by an apparently anonymous post-office-box company in Gibraltar. A broker had set them up for her for 50,000 kronor of the money she had borrowed from Blomkvist. She cashed in fifty of the bonds and deposited the money in the accounts. Each bond was worth the equivalent of one million kronor.

Her business at the Bank Dorffmann also took more time than expected, so now she was even more behind on her schedule. She had no chance to take care of her final transactions before the banks closed for the day. So Irene Nesser returned to the Matterhorn Hotel, where she spent an hour hanging around to establish her presence. But she had a headache and went to bed early. She bought some aspirin at the front desk and ordered a wake-up call for 8:00 a.m. Then she went back to her room.

It was close to 5:00 p.m., and all the banks in Europe were closed for business. But the banks in North and South America were open. She booted up her PowerBook and uplinked to the Net through her mobile. She spent an hour emptying the numbered accounts she had opened at Bank Dorffmann earlier in the day.

She divided the money up into small amounts and used it to pay invoices for a large number of fictional companies around the world. When she was done, the money had strangely enough been transferred back to the Bank of Kroenenfeld in the Cayman Islands, but this time to an entirely different account than the one from which it had been withdrawn earlier that day.

Irene Nesser considered this first stage to be secure and almost impossible to trace. She made one payment from the account: the sum of nearly one million kronor was deposited into an account linked to a credit card that she had in her wallet. The account was owned by Wasp Enterprises, registered in Gibraltar.

Several minutes later a girl with blonde page-boy hair left the Matterhorn by a door into the hotel bar. Monica Sholes walked to the Zimmertal Hotel, nodded politely to the desk clerk, and took the lift up to her room.

There she took her time putting on Monica Sholes' combat uniform, touching up her make-up, and applying an extra layer of skin cream to the tattoo before she went down to the hotel restaurant and had an insanely delicious fish dinner. She ordered a bottle of vintage wine that she had never heard of before though it cost 1,200 kronor, drank one glass, and nonchalantly left the rest before she went into the hotel bar. She left absurd tips, which certainly made the staff notice her.

She spent quite a while allowing herself to be picked up by a drunk young Italian with an aristocratic name which she did not bother to remember. They shared two bottles of champagne, of which she drank almost one glass.

Around 11:00 her intoxicated suitor leaned forward and boldly squeezed her breast. She moved his hand down to the table, feeling pleased. He did not seem to have noticed that he was squeezing soft latex. At times they were so loud that they caused a certain amount of irritation among the other guests. Just before midnight, when Monica Sholes noticed that a hall porter was keeping a stern eye on them, she helped her Italian boyfriend up to his room.

When he went to the bathroom, she poured one last glass of wine. She opened a folded piece of paper and spiked the wine with a crushed Rohypnol sleeping tablet. He passed out in a miserable heap on the bed within a minute after she drank a toast with him. She loosened his tie, pulled off his shoes, and drew a cover over him. She wiped the bottle clean, then washed the glasses in the bathroom and wiped them off too before going back to her room.

Monica Sholes had breakfast in her room at 6:00 and checked out of the Zimmertal at 6:55. Before leaving her room, she spent five minutes wiping off fingerprints from the door handles, wardrobes, toilet, telephone, and other objects in the room that she had touched.

Irene Nesser checked out of the Matterhorn around 8:30, shortly after the wake-up call. She took a taxi and left her luggage in a locker at the railway station. Then she spent the next few hours visiting nine private banks, where she distributed some of the private bonds from the Cayman Islands. By 3:00 in the afternoon she had converted about 10 percent of the bonds into cash, which she deposited in thirty numbered accounts. The rest of the bonds she bundled up and put in a safe-deposit box.

Irene Nesser would need to make several more visits to Zürich, but there was no immediate hurry.

At 4:30 that afternoon Irene Nesser took a taxi to the airport, where she went into the ladies' room and cut up Monica Sholes' passport into little pieces, flushing them down the toilet. The credit card she also cut up and put the bits in five different rubbish bins, and the scissors too. After September 11 it was not a good idea to attract attention by having any sharp objects in your baggage.

Irene Nesser took Lufthansa flight GD890 to Oslo and caught the airport bus to the Oslo train station, where she went into the ladies' room and sorted through her clothes. She placed all items belonging to the Monica Sholes persona—the pageboy wig and the designer clothes—in three plastic bags and tossed them into three different rubbish containers and wastebaskets in the train station. She put the empty Samsonite suitcase in an unlocked locker. The gold chain and earrings were designer jewellery that could be traced; they disappeared down a drain in the street outside the station.

After a moment of anxious hesitation, Irene Nesser decided to keep the fake latex breasts.

By then she did not have much time and took on some fuel in the form of a hamburger from McDonald's while she transferred the contents of the luxury leather briefcase to her travel bag. When she left, the empty briefcase remained under the table. She bought a latte to go at a kiosk and ran to catch the night train to Stockholm. She arrived as the doors were closing. She had booked a private sleeping berth.

When she locked the door to her compartment, she could feel that for the first time in two days, her adrenaline levels had returned to normal. She opened the compartment window and defied the no-smoking regulations. She stood there sipping at her coffee as the train rolled out of Oslo.

She ran through her checklist to be sure that she had forgotten no detail. After a moment she frowned and rummaged through her jacket pockets. She took out the complimentary pen from the Zimmertal Hotel and studied it for several minutes before she tossed it out of the window.

After fifteen minutes she crept into bed and fell asleep.

EPILOGUE: FINAL AUDIT

Thursday, November 27–Tuesday, December 30

Millennium's special report on Hans-Erik Wennerström took up all of forty-six pages of the magazine and exploded like a time bomb the last week of November. The main story appeared under the joint byline of Mikael Blomkvist and Erika Berger. For the first few hours the media did not know how to handle the scoop. A similar story just a year earlier had resulted in Blomkvist being convicted of libel, and it had also apparently resulted in his being dismissed from *Millennium*. For that reason his credibility was regarded as rather low. Now the same magazine was back with a story by the same journalist containing much more serious allegations than the article for which he had run into so much trouble. Some parts of the report were so absurd that they defied common sense. The Swedish media sat and waited, filled with mistrust.

But that evening *She* on TV4 led off with an eleven-minute summary of the highlights in Blomkvist's accusations. Berger had lunched with the host several days earlier and given her an advance exclusive.

TV4's brutal profile scooped the state-run news channels, which did not clamber on to the bandwagon until the 9:00 news. By then the TT wire service had also sent out its first wire with the cautious headline: CONVICTED JOURNALIST ACCUSES FINANCIER OF SERIOUS CRIME. The text was a rewrite of the TV story, but the fact that TT addressed the subject at all unleashed feverish activity at the Conservative morning newspaper and at a dozen of the larger regional papers as they reset their front pages before the presses started rolling. Up until then, the papers had more or less decided to ignore the *Millennium* allegations.

The Liberal morning newspaper commented on *Millennium*'s scoop in the form of an editorial, written personally by the editor in chief, earlier in the afternoon. The editor in chief then went to a dinner party as TV4 started broadcasting its news programme. He dismissed his secretary's frantic calls that there "might be something" to Blomkvist's claims with these later famous words: "Nonsense—if there were, our financial reporters would have found out about it long ago." Consequently, the Liberal editor in chief's editorial was the only media voice in the country that butchered *Millennium*'s claims. The editorial contained phrases such as: *personal vendetta, criminally sloppy journalism,* and demands that *measures be taken against indictable allegations regarding decent citizens.* But that was the only contribution the editor in chief made during the debate.

That night the *Millennium* editorial offices were fully staffed. According to their plans, only Berger and the new managing editor, Malin Eriksson, were due to be there to handle any calls. But by 10:00 p.m. the entire staff was still there, and they had also been joined by no fewer than four former staff members and half a dozen regular freelancers. At midnight Malm opened a bottle of champagne. That was when an old acquaintance sent over an advance copy from one of the evening papers, which devoted sixteen pages to the Wennerström affair under the headline THE FINANCIAL MAFIA. When the evening papers came out the next day, a media frenzy erupted, the likes of which had seldom been seen before.

Eriksson concluded that she was going to enjoy working at *Millennium*.

During the following week, the Swedish Stock Exchange trembled as the securities fraud police began investigating, prosecutors were called in, and a panicky selling spree set in. Two days after the publication the Minister of Commerce made a statement on "the Wennerström affair."

The frenzy did not mean, however, that the media swallowed *Millennium*'s claims without criticism—the revelations were far too serious for that. But unlike the first Wennerström affair, this time *Millennium* could present a convincing burden of proof: Wennerström's own emails and copies of the contents of his computer, which contained balance sheets from secret bank assets in the Cayman Islands and two dozen other countries, secret agreements, and other blunders that a more cautious racketeer would never in his life have left on his hard drive. It soon became clear that if *Millennium*'s claims held up in a court of appeals—and everyone agreed that the case would end up there sooner or later—then it was by far the biggest bubble to burst in the Swedish financial world since the Kreuger crash of 1932. The Wennerström affair made all the Gotabank imbroglios and Trustor frauds pale in comparison. This was fraud on such a grand scale that no-one even dared to speculate on how many laws had been broken.

For the first time in Swedish financial reporting, the terms "organised crime," "Mafia," and "gangster empire" were used.

Wennerström and his young stockbrokers, partners, and Armani-clad lawyers emerged like a band of hoodlums.

During the first days of the media frenzy, Blomkvist was invisible. He did not answer his emails and could not be reached by telephone. All editorial comments on behalf of *Millennium* were made by Berger, who purred like a cat as she was interviewed by the Swedish national media and important regional newspapers, and eventually also by a growing number of overseas media. Each time she was asked how *Millennium* had come into possession of all those private and internal documents, she replied simply that she was unable to reveal the magazine's source.

When she was asked why the previous year's exposé of Wennerström had been such a fiasco, she was even more delphic. She never lied, but she may not always have told the whole truth. Off the record, when she did not have a microphone under her nose, she would utter a few mysterious catch phrases, which, if pieced together, led to some rather rash conclusions. That is how a rumour was born that soon assumed legendary proportions, claiming that Mikael Blomkvist had not presented any sort of defence at his trial and had voluntarily submitted to the prison sentence and heavy fines because otherwise his documentation would have led inevitably to the identification of his source. He was compared to role models in the American media who had accepted gaol rather than reveal their sources, and Blomkvist was described as a hero in such ludicrously flattering terms that he was quite embarrassed. But this was no time to deny the misunderstanding.

There was one thing that everyone agreed on: the person who had delivered the documentation had to be someone within Wennerström's most trusted circle. This led to a debate about who the "Deep Throat" was: colleagues with reason to be dissatisfied, lawyers, even Wennerström's cocaine-addicted daughter and other family members were put up as possible candidates. Neither Blomkvist nor Berger commented on the subject.

Berger smiled happily, knowing that they had won when an evening paper on the third day of the frenzy ran the headline MILLENNIUM'S REVENGE. The article was an ingratiating portrait of the magazine and its staff, including illustrations with a particularly favourable portrait of Berger. She was named the "queen of investigative journalism." That sort of thing won points in the rankings of the entertainment pages, and there was talk of the Big Journalism Prize.

Five days after *Millennium* fired the first salvo, Blomkvist's book *The Mafia Banker* appeared in bookshops. The book had been written during those feverish days at Sandhamn in September and October, and in great haste and under the utmost secrecy it was printed by Hallvigs Reklam in Morgongåva. It was the first book to be published under *Millennium*'s own logo. It was eccentrically dedicated: *To Sally, who showed me the benefits of the sport of golf.*

It was a brick of a book, 608 pages in paperback. The first edition of 2,000 copies was virtually guaranteed to be a losing proposition, but the print run actually sold out in a couple of days, and Berger ordered 10,000 more copies.

The reviewers concluded that this time, at any rate, Mikael Blomkvist had no intention of holding back since it was a matter of publishing extensive source references. In this regard they were right. Two-thirds of the book consisted of appendices that were actual copies of the documentation from Wennerström's computer. At the same time as the book was published,

Millennium put the texts from Wennerström's computer as source material in downloadable PDF files on their website.

Blomkvist's extraordinary absence was part of the media strategy that he and Berger had put together. Every newspaper in the country was looking for him. Not until the book was launched did he give an exclusive interview to *She* on TV4, once again scooping the state-run stations. But the questions were anything but sycophantic.

Blomkvist was especially pleased with one exchange when he watched a video of his appearance. The interview was broadcast live at the very moment when the Stockholm Stock Exchange found itself in freefall and a handful of financial yuppies were threatening to throw themselves out of windows. He was asked what was *Millennium*'s responsibility with regard to the fact that Sweden's economy was now headed for a crash.

"The idea that Sweden's economy is headed for a crash is nonsense," Blomkvist said.

The host of *She* on TV4 looked perplexed. His reply did not follow the pattern she had expected, and she was forced to improvise. Blomkvist got the follow-up question he was hoping for. "We're experiencing the largest single drop in the history of the Swedish stock exchange—and you think that's nonsense?"

"You have to distinguish between two things—the Swedish economy and the Swedish stock market. The Swedish economy is the sum of all the goods and services that are produced in this country every day. There are telephones from Ericsson, cars from Volvo, chickens from Scan, and shipments from Kiruna to Skövde. That's the Swedish economy, and it's just as strong or weak today as it was a week ago."

He paused for effect and took a sip of water.

"The Stock Exchange is something very different. There is no economy and no production of goods and services. There are only fantasies in which people from one hour to the next decide that this or that company is worth so many billions, more or less. It doesn't have a thing to do with reality or with the Swedish economy."

"So you're saying that it doesn't matter if the Stock Exchange drops like a rock?"

"No, it doesn't matter at all," Blomkvist said in a voice so weary and resigned that he sounded like some sort of oracle. His words would be quoted many times over the following year. Then he went on.

"It only means that a bunch of heavy speculators are now moving their shareholdings from Swedish companies to German ones. So it's the financial gnomes that some tough reporter should identify and expose as traitors. They're the ones who are systematically and perhaps deliberately damaging the Swedish economy in order to satisfy the profit interests of their clients."

Then *She* on TV4 made the mistake of asking exactly the question that Blomkvist had hoped for.

"And so you think that the media don't have any responsibility?"

"Oh yes, the media do have an enormous responsibility. For at least twenty years many financial reporters have refrained from scrutinising Hans-Erik Wennerström. On the contrary, they have actually helped to build up his prestige by publishing brainless, idolatrous portraits. If they had been doing their work properly, we would not find ourselves in this situation today."

Blomkvist's appearance marked a turning point. In hindsight, Berger was convinced that it was only when Blomkvist went on TV and calmly defended his claims that the Swedish media, in spite of the fact that *Millennium* had been all over the headlines for a week, recognised that the story really did hold up. His attitude set the course for the story.

After the interview the Wennerström affair imperceptibly slipped from the financial section over to the desks of the crime reporters. In the past, ordinary crime reporters had seldom or never written about financial crime, except if it had to do with the Russian mob or Yugoslav cigarette smugglers. Crime reporters were not expected to investigate intricate dealings on the Stock Exchange. One evening paper even took Blomkvist at his word and filled two spreads with portraits of several of the brokerage houses' most important players, who were in the process of buying up German securities. The paper's headline read SELLING OUT THEIR COUNTRY. All the brokers were invited to comment on the allegations. Every one of them declined. But the trading of shares decreased significantly that day, and some brokers who wanted to look like progressive patriots started going against the stream. Blomkvist burst out laughing.

The pressure got to be so great that sombre men in dark suits put on a concerned expression and broke with the most important rule of the exclusive club that made up the innermost circles of Swedish finance—they commented on a colleague. All of a sudden retired industrial leaders and bank presidents were appearing on TV and answering questions in an attempt at damage control. Everyone realised the seriousness of the situation, and it was a matter of distancing themselves as quickly as possible from the Wennerström Group and shedding any shares they might hold. Wennerström (they concluded almost with one voice) was not, after all, a real industrialist, and he had never been truly accepted into "the club." Some pointed out that he was just a simple working-class boy from Norrland whose success may have gone to his head. Some described his actions as *a personal tragedy*. Others discovered that they had had their doubts about Wennerström for years—he was too boastful and he put on airs.

During the following weeks, as *Millennium*'s documentation was scrutinised, pulled apart, and pieced together again, the Wennerström empire of obscure companies was linked to the heart of the international Mafia, including everything from illegal arms dealing and money laundering for South American drug cartels to prostitution in New York, and even indirectly to the child sex trade in Mexico. One Wennerström company registered in Cyprus caused a dramatic stir when it was revealed that it had attempted to buy enriched uranium on the black market in Ukraine. Wennerström's apparently inexhaustible supply of obscure post-office-box companies seemed to be cropping up everywhere, linked to all manner of shady enterprises.

Berger thought that the book was the best thing Blomkvist had ever written. It was uneven stylistically, and in places the writing was actually rather poor—there had been no time for any fine polishing—but the book was animated by a fury that no reader could help but notice.

By chance Blomkvist ran into his old adversary, the former financial reporter William Borg, in front of Kvarnen when Blomkvist, Berger, and Malm took the evening off to celebrate the Santa Lucia holiday along with the magazine's other employees, going out to drink themselves senseless at the company's expense. Borg's companion was a very drunk girl about Salander's age.

Blomkvist's loathing for Borg was palpable. Berger interrupted the macho posturing by taking Blomkvist by the arm and leading him into the bar.

Blomkvist decided that when the opportunity arose, he would ask Salander to do one of her personal investigations of Borg. Just for form's sake.

. . .

During the whole media storm the main character in the drama, the financier Wennerström, was for the most part invisible. On the day that *Millennium* published its article, the financier was forced to comment on the text at a press conference that had been called for a different purpose. He declared the allegations unfounded and said that the documentation referred to was fabricated. He reminded everyone that the same reporter had been convicted of libel only one year before.

After that only Wennerström's lawyers would answer questions from the media. Two days after Blomkvist's book came out, a persistent rumour began circulating that Wennerström had left Sweden. The evening papers used the word "fled." During the second week, when the securities fraud police tried to contact Wennerström, he was nowhere to be found. In mid-December the police confirmed that Wennerström was formally sought, and on the day before New Year's Eve, an all-points bulletin was sent out via the international police organisations. The very same day one of Wennerström's advisers was seized at Arlanda as he was boarding a plane for London.

Several weeks later a Swedish tourist reported that he had seen Wennerström get into a car in Bridgetown, the capital of Barbados. As proof of his claim, the tourist submitted a photograph, taken from quite a distance away, showing a white man wearing sunglasses, an open white shirt, and light-coloured slacks. He could not be identified with certainty, but the evening papers contacted stringers who tried without success to track down the fugitive billionaire.

After six months the hunt was called off. Then Wennerström was found dead in an apartment in Marbella, Spain, where he had been living under the name of Victor Fleming. He had been shot three times in the head at close range. The Spanish police were working on the theory, their statement said, that he had surprised a burglar.

Wennerström's death came as no surprise to Salander. She suspected, with good reason, that his demise had to do with the fact that he no longer had access to the money in a certain bank in the Cayman Islands, which he may have needed to pay off certain debts in Colombia.

If anyone had asked for Salander's help in tracking Wennerström, she could havc told them almost on a daily basis where he was. Via the Internet she had followed his flight through a dozen countries and remarked a growing desperation in his emails. Not even Blomkvist would have thought that the fugitive ex-billionaire would be stupid enough to take along the computer that had been so thoroughly penetrated.

After six months Salander grew tired of tracking Wennerström. The question that remained to be answered was how far her own involvement should reach. Wennerström was without a doubt an Olympic-class creep, but he was not her personal enemy, and she had no interest in involving herself against him. She could tip off Blomkvist, but he would probably just publish a story. She could tip off the police, but there was quite a chance that Wennerström would be forewarned and again disappear. Besides, on principle, she did not talk to the police.

But there were other debts that had to be paid. She thought about the once-pregnant waitress whose head had been shoved underwater in her own bath.

Four days before Wennerström's body was found, she made up her mind. She switched on her mobile and called a lawyer in Miami, who seemed to be one of the people Wennerström was making a big effort to hide from. She talked to a secretary and asked her to pass on a cryptic message. The name Wennerström and an address in Marbella. That was all.

She turned off the TV news halfway through a dramatic report about Wennerström's demise. She put on some coffee and fixed herself a liver pâté and cucumber sandwich.

Berger and Malm were taking care of the annual Christmas arrangements while Blomkvist sat in Erika's chair, drinking glögg and looking on. All the staff and many of the regular free-lancers would receive a Christmas gift—this year a shoulder bag with the new *Millennium* publishing house logo. After wrapping the presents, they sat down to write and stamp about 200 cards to send to printing companies, photographers, and media colleagues.

Blomkvist tried for the longest time to withstand the temptation but finally he couldn't resist. He picked up the very last card and wrote: *Merry Christmas and Happy New Year. Thanks for your splendid efforts during the past year.*

He signed his name and addressed the card to Janne Dahlman, c/o the editorial offices of *Monopoly Financial Magazine.*

When Blomkvist got home that evening there was a slip notifying him of a postal package. He went to pick it up the next morning, opening it when he got to the office. The package contained a mosquito-repellent stick and a bottle of Reimersholms aquavit. The card read: *If you don't have other plans, I'll be docked at Arholma on Midsummer Eve.* It was signed Robert Lindberg.

Traditionally the *Millennium* offices were closed the week before Christmas and through the New Year's holiday. This year it did not work out that way. The strain on the small staff had been enormous, and journalists were still calling from all over the world on a daily basis. It was the day before Christmas Eve when Blomkvist, almost by chance, happened to read an article in the *Financial Times* summing up the findings of the international banking commission that had been established in all haste to scrutinise the collapse of the Wennerström empire. The article said that the commission was working on the hypothesis that Wennerström had probably been tipped off at the last minute about the impending disclosures.

His account at Bank of Kroenenfeld in the Cayman Islands, containing $260 million—approximately 2.5 billion Swedish kronor—had been emptied the day before *Millennium* published its exposé.

The money had been spread over a number of accounts, and only Wennerström personally could make withdrawals. He did not have to be present at the bank; it was enough for him to present a series of clearing codes in order to transfer the money to any bank in the world. The money had been transferred to Switzerland, where a female associate had converted the funds into anonymous private bonds. All the clearing codes were in order.

Europol had launched a search for the woman who had used a stolen British passport in the name of Monica Sholes and who was said to have lived a life of luxury at one of Zürich's most expensive hotels. A relatively clear picture, considering that it came from a surveillance camera, showed a short woman with a blonde page-boy, wide lips, and prominent breasts wearing fashionable designer clothes and gold jewellery.

Blomkvist studied the picture, giving it first a quick glance and then looking at it with increasing suspicion. After several seconds he rummaged in his desk for a magnifying glass and tried to make out the details of the facial features in the newspaper's screened image.

At last he put down the paper and sat there, speechless, for several minutes. Then he started laughing so hysterically that Malm stuck his head round the door to find out what was going on.

On the morning of Christmas Eve Blomkvist went out to Årsta to see his ex-wife and his daughter, Pernilla, and exchange gifts. Pernilla got the computer she wanted, which Blomkvist and Monica had bought together. Blomkvist got a tie from Monica and a detective novel by Åke Edwardson from his daughter. Unlike the previous Christmas, they were in high spirits because of the media drama that had been playing out around *Millennium*.

They had lunch together. Blomkvist stole a sidelong glance at Pernilla. He had not seen his daughter since she turned up to visit him in Hedestad. He realised that he had failed to discuss her mania for that sect in Skellefteå with her mother. He could not tell them that it was his daughter's obviously profound knowledge of the Bible that had set him on the right track regarding Harriet Vanger's disappearance. He had not talked to his daughter since then.

He was not a good father.

He kissed his daughter goodbye after the lunch and met Salander at Slussen. They went out to Sandhamn. They had not seen much of each other since the *Millennium* bomb exploded. They arrived late on Christmas Eve and stayed for the holidays.

Blomkvist was entertaining company, as always, but Salander had an uneasy feeling that he was looking at her with an especially odd expression when she paid back the loan with a cheque for 120,000 kronor.

They took a walk to Trovill and back (which Salander considered a waste of time), had Christmas dinner at the inn, and went back to the cabin where they lit a fire in the woodstove, put on an Elvis CD, and devoted themselves to some plain old sex. When Salander from time to time came up for air, she tried to analyse her feelings.

She had no problem with Blomkvist as a lover. There was obviously a physical attraction. And he never tried to tutor her.

Her problem was that she could not interpret her own feelings for him. Not since before reaching puberty had she lowered her guard to let another person get so close as she had with him. To be quite honest, he had a trying ability to penetrate her defences and to get her to talk about personal matters and private feelings. Even though she had enough sense to ignore most of his questions, she talked about herself in a way that she would never, even under threat of death, have imagined doing with any other person. It frightened her and made her feel naked and vulnerable to his will.

At the same time—when she looked down at his slumbering form and listened to him snoring—she felt that she had never before in her life had such a trust in another human being. She knew with absolute certainty that Mikael would never use what he knew about her to hurt her. It was not in his nature.

The only thing they never discussed was their relationship to each other. She did not dare, and Blomkvist never broached the subject.

At some point on the morning of the second day she came to a terrifying realisation. She had no idea how it had happened or how she was supposed to cope with it. She was in love for the first time in her life.

That he was almost twice her age did not bother her. Nor did the fact that at the moment he was one of the most newsworthy people in Sweden, and his picture was even on the cover of *Newsweek*—that was all just soap opera. But Blomkvist was no erotic fantasy or daydream. It would have to come to an end. It could not possibly work out. What did he need her for? Maybe she was just a way to pass the time while he waited for someone whose life was not a fucking rat hole.

What she had realised was that love was that moment when your heart was about to burst.

When Blomkvist woke up late that morning, she had made coffee and been out to buy breakfast rolls. He joined her at the table and noticed at once that something in her attitude had changed—she was a bit more reserved. When he asked her if anything was wrong, she gave him a neutral, uncomprehending look.

On the first day between Christmas and New Year's, Blomkvist took the train up to Hedestad. He was wearing his warmest clothes and his proper winter shoes when Frode met him at the station and quietly congratulated him on the media success. It was the first time since August that he had visited Hedestad, and it was almost exactly one year ago since he had visited it for the first time. They chatted politely, but there was also a great deal that had gone unsaid between them, and Blomkvist felt uncomfortable.

Everything had been prepared, and the business with Frode took only a few minutes. Frode offered to deposit the money in a convenient foreign bank account, but Blomkvist insisted that it should be paid like a normal, legitimate fee to his company.

"I can't afford any other type of payment," he said curtly when Frode persisted.

The purpose of his visit was not solely financial. Blomkvist had left clothes, books, and a number of his own things in the cottage when he and Salander had abandoned Hedeby in great haste.

Vanger was still frail after his illness, but he was at home. He was being looked after by a private nurse, who refused to allow him to take long walks, or walk up stairs, or discuss anything that might upset him. During the holidays he had also come down with a slight cold and was ordered to bed.

"Besides which, she's expensive," Vanger complained.

Blomkvist knew that the old man could afford any such expense—considering how many kronor he had written off his taxes all his life. Vanger gave him a sullen look until he started laughing.

"What the hell, you were worth every krona. I knew you would be."

"To tell you the truth, I never thought I'd solve it."

"I have no intention of thanking you," Vanger said.

"I didn't expect you would. I'm just here to tell you that I consider the job done."

Vanger curled his lips. "You haven't finished the job," he said.

"I know that."

"You haven't written the Vanger family chronicle, which was agreed."

"I know that. I'm not going to write it. In fact, I can't write it. I can't write about the Vanger family and leave out the most central event of the past decades. How could I write a chapter about Martin's period as CEO and pretend that I don't know what's in his basement? I also can't write the story without destroying Harriet's life all over again."

"I understand your dilemma, and I'm grateful for the decision that you've made."

"Congratulations. You've managed to corrupt me. I'm going to destroy all my notes and the tape recordings I've made of our conversations."

"I don't think that you've been corrupted," Vanger said.

"That's what it feels like. And I think that's what it is."

"You had to choose between your role as a journalist and your role as a human being. I could never have bought your silence. And I'm quite certain that you would have exposed us if Harriet had turned out in some way to have been implicated, or if you thought I was a cretin."

Blomkvist did not reply.

"We've told Cecilia the whole story. Frode and I will soon be gone, and Harriet is going to need support from someone in the family. Cecilia will play an active role on the board. She and Harriet will be in charge of the firm from now on."

"How did she take it?"

"She was very shaken. She went abroad for a while. I was even afraid she wouldn't come back."

"But she did."

"Martin was one of the few people in our family that Cecilia always got along with. It was very hard for her to find out the truth about him. She also knows now what you did for the family."

Blomkvist shrugged.

"So thank you, Mikael," Vanger said.

"Besides, I couldn't write the story because I've had it up to here with the Vanger family. But tell me, how does it feel to be CEO again?"

"It's only temporary, but . . . I wish I were younger. I'm only working three hours a day. All the meetings are held in this room, and Dirch has stepped in again as my enforcer if anyone acts up."

"The junior executives must be quaking in their boots. It took me a while to realise that Dirch wasn't just an old sweetie of a financial adviser but also someone who solves problems for you."

"Exactly. But all decisions are made with Harriet, and she's the one who's doing the legwork in the office."

"How are things going for her?"

"She inherited both her brother's and her mother's shares. She controls about 33 percent of the corporation."

"Is that enough?"

"I don't know. Birger is trying to trip her up. Alexander has seen that he has a chance to make an impact and has allied himself with Birger. My brother Harald has cancer and won't live much longer. He was the only remaining person with large shareholdings of 7 percent, which his children will inherit. Cecilia and Anita will be on Harriet's side."

"Then together you'll control, what, 45 percent."

"That kind of voting cartel has never existed within the family before. Plenty of shareholders with one and two percent will vote against us. Harriet is going to succeed me as CEO in February."

"That won't make her happy."

"No, but it's necessary. We have to take in some new partners and new blood. We also have the chance to collaborate with her company in Australia. There are possibilities."

"Where's Harriet today?"

"You're out of luck. She's in London. But she would very much like to see you."

"I'll see her at our board meeting in January if she's going to take your place."

"I know."

"I think that she realises that I will never discuss what happened in the sixties with anyone except for Erika Berger, and I don't see why Erika needs to know."

"She does. You're a person with morals, Mikael."

"But also tell her that everything she does from now on

could end up in the magazine. The Vanger Corporation won't have a free pass from scrutiny."

"I'll warn her."

Blomkvist left Vanger when he started to doze off. He packed his belongings into two suitcases. As he closed the door to the cottage for the last time, he paused and then went over to Cecilia's house and knocked. She was not home. He took out his pocket calendar, tore out a page, and wrote: *I wish you all the best. Try to forgive me. Mikael.* He put the note in her letter box. An electric Christmas candle shone in the kitchen window of Martin Vanger's empty house.

He took the last train back to Stockholm.

During the holidays Salander tuned out the rest of the world. She did not answer her telephone and she did not turn on her computer. She spent two days washing laundry, scrubbing, and cleaning up her apartment. Year-old pizza boxes and newspapers were bundled up and carried downstairs. She dragged out a total of six black rubbish bags and twenty paper bags full of newspapers. She felt as if she had decided to start a new life. She thought about buying a new apartment—when she found something suitable—but for now her old place would be more dazzlingly clean than she could ever remember.

Then she sat as if paralysed, thinking. She had never in her life felt such a longing. She wanted Mikael Blomkvist to ring the doorbell and . . . what then? Lift her off the ground, hold her in his arms? Passionately take her into the bedroom and tear off her clothes? No, she really just wanted his company. She wanted to hear him say that he liked her for who she was. That she was someone special in his world and in his life. She wanted him to give her some gesture of love, not just of friendship and companionship. *I'm flipping out,* she thought.

She had no faith in herself. Blomkvist lived in a world populated by people with respectable jobs, people with orderly lives and lots of grown-up points. His friends did things, went on TV, and shaped the headlines. *What do you need me for?* Salander's greatest fear, which was so huge and so black that it was of phobic proportions, was that people would laugh at her feelings. And all of a sudden all her carefully constructed self-confidence seemed to crumble.

That's when she made up her mind. It took her several hours to mobilise the necessary courage, but she had to see him and tell him how she felt.

Anything else would be unbearable.

She needed some excuse to knock on his door. She had not given him any Christmas present, but she knew what she was going to buy. In a junk shop she had seen a number of metal advertising signs from the fifties, with embossed images. One of the signs showed Elvis Presley with a guitar on his hip and a cartoon balloon with the words HEARTBREAK HOTEL. She had no sense for interior design, but even she could tell that the sign would be perfect for the cabin in Sandhamn. It cost 780 kronor, and on principle she haggled and got the price knocked down to 700. She had it wrapped, put it under her arm, and headed over to his place on Bellmansgatan.

At Hornsgatan she happened to glance towards Kaffebar and saw Blomkvist coming out with Berger in tow. He said something, and she laughed, putting her arm around his waist and kissing his cheek. They turned down Brännkyrkagatan in the direction of Bellmansgatan. Their body language left no room for misinterpretations—it was obvious what they had in mind.

The pain was so immediate and so fierce that Lisbeth stopped in mid-stride, incapable of movement. Part of her wanted to rush after them. She wanted to take the metal sign and use the sharp edge to cleave Berger's head in two. She did nothing as thoughts swirled through her mind. *Analysis of consequences.* Finally she calmed down.

"What a pathetic fool you are, Salander," she said out loud.

She turned on her heel and went home to her newly spotless apartment. As she passed Zinkensdamm, it started to snow. She tossed Elvis into a dumpster.

An excerpt from the forthcoming

THE GIRL WHO PLAYED WITH FIRE

by Stieg Larsson

Available from Alfred A. Knopf

PROLOGUE

She lay on her back fastened by leather straps to a narrow bed with a steel frame. The harness was tight across her rib cage. Her hands were manacled to the sides of the bed.

She had long since given up trying to free herself. She was awake, but her eyes were closed. If she opened her eyes she would find herself in darkness; the only light was a faint strip that seeped in above the door. She had a bad taste in her mouth and longed to be able to brush her teeth.

She was listening for the sound of footsteps, which would mean he was coming. She had no idea how late at night it was, but she sensed that it was getting too late for him to visit her. A sudden vibration in the bed made her open her eyes. It was as if a machine of some sort had started up somewhere in the building. After a few seconds she was no longer sure whether she was imagining it.

She marked off another day in her head.

It was the forty-third day of her imprisonment.

Her nose itched and she turned her head so that she could rub it against the pillow. She was sweating. It was airless and hot in the room. She had on a simple nightdress that was bunching up beneath her. If she moved her hips she could just hold the cloth with her first two fingers and pull the nightdress down on one side, an inch or so at a time. She did the same on the other side. But there was still a fold under the small of her back. The mattress was lumpy. Her isolation sharply amplified all the tiny sensations that she would not otherwise have noticed. The harness was loose enough that she could change position and lie on her side, but that was uncomfortable because then she had to keep one hand behind her, which made her arm keep going to sleep.

She was not afraid. But she did feel a great, pent-up rage.

At the same time she was troubled by unpleasant fantasies about what was going to happen to her. She detested this helplessness. No matter how hard she tried to concentrate on something else—to pass the time and to distract her from the situation she was in—the fear came trickling out. It hovered like a cloud of gas around her, threatening to penetrate her pores and poison her. She had discovered that the most effective method of keeping the fear at bay was to fantasize about something that gave her a feeling of strength. She closed her eyes and conjured up the smell of gasoline.

He was sitting in a car with the window rolled down. She ran to the car, poured the gasoline through the window, and lit a match. It took only a moment. The flames blazed up. He writhed in agony and she heard his screams of terror and pain. She could smell burnt flesh and a more acrid stench of plastic and upholstery turning to carbon in the seats.

She must have dozed off, because she did not hear the footsteps, but she was wide awake when the door opened. The light from the doorway blinded her.

He had come, at any rate.

He was tall. She did not know how old he was, but he had reddish-brown, tangled hair and a sparse goatee, and he wore glasses with black frames. He smelled of aftershave.

She hated the smell of him.

He stood at the foot of the bed and observed her for a long time.

She hated his silence.

She could see him only in silhouette from the light in the doorway. Then he spoke to her. He had a dark, clear voice that stressed, pedantically, each word.

She hated his voice.

He told her that it was her birthday and he wanted to wish her Happy Birthday. His tone was not unfriendly or ironical. It was neutral. She thought that he was smiling.

She hated him.

He came closer and went around to the head of the bed. He laid the back of a moist hand on her forehead and ran his fingers along her hairline in a gesture that was probably intended to be friendly. It was his birthday present to her.

She hated his touch.

She saw his mouth move, but she shut out the sound of his voice. She did not want to listen. She did not want to answer. She heard him raise his voice. A hint of irritation at her failure to respond. He talked about mutual trust. After a few minutes he stopped. She ignored his gaze. Then he shrugged and began adjusting her leather straps. He tightened the harness across her chest a bit and leaned over her.

She twisted suddenly to the left, away from him, as abruptly as she could and as far as the straps would allow. She pulled up her knees to her chin and kicked hard at his head. She aimed at his Adam's apple and the tip of her toe hit him somewhere below his jaw, but he was ready for that and turned away so it was only a light blow. She tried to kick again, but he was out of reach.

She let her legs sink back down onto the bed.

The sheet slid down onto the floor. Her nightdress had slid up above her hips.

He stood still for a long time without saying a word. Then he walked around the bed and tightened the foot restraint. She tried to pull her legs up, but he grabbed hold of one ankle, forced her knee down with his other hand, and fastened her foot with a leather strap. He went around the bed and tied down her other foot.

Now she was utterly helpless.

He picked up the sheet from the floor and covered her. He watched her in silence for two minutes. She could sense his excitement in the dark, even though he did not show it. He undoubtedly had an erection. She knew that he would reach out and touch her.

Then he turned and left, closing the door behind him. She heard him bolt it, which was totally unnecessary because she had no way of getting free from the bed.

She lay for several minutes looking at the narrow strip of light over the door. Then she moved and tried to feel how tight the straps were. She could pull her knees up a bit, but the harness and the foot restraints grew taut immediately. She relaxed. She lay still, staring at nothing.

She waited. She thought about a gasoline can and a match.

She saw him drenched with gasoline. She could actually feel the box of matches in her hand. She shook it. It rattled. She opened the box and selected a match. She heard him say something, but she shut her ears, did not listen to the words. She saw the expression on his face as she moved the match towards the striking surface. She heard the scraping sound of sulphur. It sounded like a drawn-out thunderclap. She saw the match burst into flame.

She smiled a hard smile and steeled herself.

It was her thirteenth birthday.

CHAPTER 1

Thursday, December 16–Friday, December 17

Lisbeth Salander pulled her sunglasses down to the tip of her nose and squinted from beneath the brim of her sun hat. She saw the woman from room 32 come out of the hotel side entrance and walk to one of the green-and-white-striped chaises longues beside the pool. Her gaze was fixed on the ground and her progress seemed unsteady.

Salander had seen her only at a distance. She reckoned the woman was around thirty-five, but she looked as though she could be anything from twenty-five to fifty. She had shoulder-length brown hair, an oval face, and a body that was straight out of a mail-order catalogue for lingerie. She had a black bikini, sandals, and purple-tinted sunglasses. She was American and spoke with a southern accent. She dropped a yellow sun hat next to the chaise longue and signalled to the bartender at Ella Carmichael's bar.

Salander put her book down on her lap and sipped her iced coffee before reaching for a pack of cigarettes. Without turning her head she shifted her gaze to the horizon. She could just see the Caribbean through a group of palm trees and the rhododendrons in front of the hotel. A yacht was on its way north towards St. Lucia or Dominica. Further out, she could see the outline of a grey freighter heading south in the direction of Guyana. A breeze made the morning heat bearable, but she felt a drop of sweat trickling into her eyebrow. Salander did not care for sunbathing. She had spent her days as far as possible in shade, and even now was under the awning on the terrace. And yet she was as brown as a nut. She had on khaki shorts and a black top.

She listened to the strange music from steel drums flowing out of the speakers at the bar. She could not tell the difference between Sven-Ingvars and Nick Cave, but steel drums fascinated her. It seemed hardly feasible that anyone could tune an oil barrel, and even less credible that the barrel could make music like nothing else in the world. She thought those sounds were like magic.

She suddenly felt irritated and looked again at the woman, who had just been handed a glass of some orange-coloured drink.

It was not Lisbeth Salander's problem, but she could not comprehend why the woman stayed. For four nights, ever since the couple had arrived, Salander had listened to the muted terror being played out in the room next door to hers. She had heard crying and low, excitable voices, and sometimes the unmistakable sound of slaps. The man responsible for the blows—Salander assumed he was the woman's husband—had straight dark hair parted down the middle in an old-fashioned style, and he seemed to be in Grenada on business. What kind of business, Salander had no idea, but every morning the man appeared with his briefcase, in a jacket and tie, and had coffee in the hotel bar before he went outside to look for a taxi.

He would come back to the hotel in the late afternoon, when he took a swim and sat with his wife by the pool. They had dinner together in what on the surface seemed to be a quiet and loving way. The woman may have had a few too many drinks, but her intoxication was not obnoxious.

Each night the commotion in the next-door room had started just as Salander was going to bed with a book about the mysteries of mathematics. It did not sound like a full-on assault. As far as Salander could tell through the wall, it was one repetitive, tedious argument. The night before, Salander had not been able to contain her curiosity. She had gone out to the balcony to listen through the couple's open balcony door. For more than an hour the man had paced back and forth in the room, declaring that he was a jerk who didn't deserve her. Again and again he said that she must think he was a fraud. No, she would answer, she didn't, and she tried to calm him. He became more intense, and seemed to give her a shake. So at last she gave him the answer he wanted . . . Yes, *you are a fraud*. And he immediately took this as a pretext to berate her. He called her a whore, which was an accusation that Salander would have taken measures to combat if it had been directed at her. It had not been, but nevertheless she thought for a long time about whether she ought to take some sort of action.

Salander had listened in astonishment to this rancorous bickering, which all of a sudden ended with something that sounded like a slap in the face. She had been on the point of going into the hotel corridor to kick in her neighbours' door when silence descended over the room.

Now, as she scrutinised the woman by the pool, she could see a faint bruise on her shoulder and a scrape on her hip, but no other injury.

Some months earlier Salander had read an article in a *Popular Science* that someone had left behind at Leonardo da Vinci Airport in Rome, and she developed a vague fascination with the obscure topic of spherical astronomy. On impulse she had made her way to the university bookshop in Rome to buy some of the key works on the subject. To be able to get a grasp of spherical astronomy, however, she had had to immerse herself in the deeper mysteries of mathematics. In the course of her travels in recent months she had been to other university bookshops to seek out more books.

Her studies had been unsystematic and without any real objective, at least until she wandered into the university bookshop in Miami and came out with *Dimensions in Mathematics*, by Dr. L. C. Parnault (Harvard University Press, 1999). That was just before she went down to the Florida Keys and began island-hopping through the Caribbean.

She had been to Guadeloupe (two nights in a hideous dump), Dominica (fun and relaxed, five nights), Barbados (one night at an American hotel where she felt terribly unwelcome), and St. Lucia (nine nights). She would have considered staying longer had she not made an enemy of a slow-witted young hoodlum who haunted the bar of her backstreet hotel. Finally she lost patience and whacked him on the head with a brick, checked out of the hotel, and took a ferry to St. George's, the capital of Grenada. This was a country she had never heard of before she bought her ticket for the boat.

She had come ashore on Grenada in a tropical rainstorm at 1000 one November morning. From the *Caribbean Traveller* she learned that Grenada was known as Spice Island and was one of the world's leading producers of nutmeg. The island had a population of 120,000, but another 200,000 Grenadians lived in the United States, Canada, or Britain, which gave some indication of the employment market in their homeland. The terrain was mountainous around a dormant volcano, Grand Etang.

Grenada was one of many small, former-British colonies. In 1795, Julian Fedon, a black planter of mixed French ancestry, led an uprising inspired by the French Revolution. Troops were sent to shoot, hang, or maim the rebels. What had shaken the colonial regime was that even poor whites, so-called *petits blancs*, had joined Fedon's rebellion without the least regard for racial boundaries. The uprising was crushed, but Fedon was never captured; he vanished into the mountainous Grand Etang and became a Robin Hood–like legend.

Some two hundred years later, in 1979, a lawyer called Maurice Bishop started a new revolution which the guidebook said was inspired by the Communist dictatorships in Cuba and Nicaragua. But Salander was given a different picture of things when she met Philip Campbell—teacher, librarian, and Baptist preacher. She had taken a room in his guesthouse for the first few days. The gist of the story was that Bishop was a popular folk leader who had deposed an insane dictator, a UFO nutcase who had devoted part of the meagre national budget to chasing flying saucers. Bishop had lobbied for economic democracy and introduced the country's first legislation for sexual equality. And then in 1983 he was assassinated.

There followed a massacre of more than a hundred people, including the foreign minister, the minister for women's affairs, and some senior trade union leaders. Then the United States invaded the country and set up a democracy. As far as Grenada was concerned, this meant that unemployment rose from around 6 percent to almost 50 percent and the cocaine trade once more became the largest single source of income. Campbell shook his head in dismay at the description in Salander's guidebook and gave her some tips on the kinds of people and neighbourhoods she should avoid after dark.

In Salander's case, such advice normally fell on deaf ears. However, she had avoided making the acquaintance of the criminal element on Grenada by falling in love with Grand Anse Beach, just south of St. George's, a sparsely populated beach that went on for miles. There she could walk for hours without having to talk to or even encounter another living soul. She moved to the Keys, one of the few American hotels on Grand Anse, and stayed for seven weeks, doing little more than walking on the beach and eating the local fruit, called chin-ups, which reminded her of sour Swedish gooseberries—she found them delightful.

It was the off-season, and barely a third of the rooms at the Keys Hotel were occupied. The only problem was that both her peace and quiet and her preoccupation with mathematical studies had been disturbed by the subdued terror in the room next door.

The electrifying follow-up to
THE GIRL WITH THE DRAGON TATTOO

Stieg Larsson's

THE GIRL WHO PLAYED WITH FIRE

Available July 2009 in hardcover from Knopf

$25.95 • 528 pages • 978-0-307-26998-0

Please visit www.aaknopf.com